PRAISE FOR RELENTLESS AARON'S SMASH-HIT NOVELS

"[Relentless] is on the forefront of a movement called street-lit."
—*The Hollywood Reporter*

"A smoldering batch of raw erotica and criminality . . . Aaron's [*Extra Marital Affairs*] is a full-throttle tour of a sordid world."
—*Publishers Weekly*

"One of the leaders of a 'hip-hop literature' revolution."
—*The New York Daily News*

Push

"Gripping."

—*The New York Times*

"Fascinating. Relentless has made the best out of a stretch of unpleasant time and adversity…a commendable effort."
—Wayne Gilman, WBLS News Director

"Relentless redefines the art of storytelling…while seamlessly capturing the truth and hard-core reality of Harlem's desperation and struggle."

—Troy Johnson, Founder of
the African American Literature Book Club

The Last
KINGPIN

RELENTLESS AARON

St. Martin's Paperbacks

Relentless Aaron, Relentless Content, and Relentless are trademarks of Relentless Content, Inc. Reginald "Push" Jackson and all related characters are elements of trademarks of Relentless Inc.

THE LAST KINGPIN

Copyright © 2000 by Relentless Aaron.

Cover photo © Karen Black / Getty

ISBN: 0-312-94967-7
EAN: 978-0-312-94967-9

Printed in the United States of America

Relentless Content, Inc. edition published 2000
St. Martin's Paperbacks edition / June 2007

St. Martin's Paperbacks are published by St. Martin's Press, 175 Fifth Avenue, New York, NY 10010.

10 9 8 7 6 5 4 3 2 1

A Word from Your Favorite Author:

Special Dedications: To my friends, both the true believers, the faithful, the fair-weather, and the bandwagon-jumpers . . .

Remember this: I gave up my time, my freedom, my peace, and my sleep for this; and still, you're all welcome to ride with me—to share in and contribute to my success. Thank you for your support, however large or small. I hope that I have proven myself, even if in my heart I know I never had to.

To my friend "Jesse James" and all the Kingpins of the world, as much as this book is about none of you in particular, it is still a tribute to every last one of you, individually. I understand where you've been, where you are now, and where you're trying to go. I'm ridin' with you until you find life to be rewarding.

ELIMINATE THE UNLAWFUL,
THE RACIST, AND ANCIENT
ROCKEFELLER DRUG LAWS, NOW!

To my friend and mentor: Johnny "Jay Dub" Williams: We did it!!! Thank you for keeping me focused during my stretch. You are a true mentor to me.

To Tiny Wood (my close friend and confidant): We're about to even the score, big dog. Get the champagne and cigars ready.

To my friends who are Colombian, Dominican, Puerto Rican, Brazilian, Spanish, Haitian, African, Asian, and others at Allenwood FCI, Otisville FCI, and Fort Dix FCI: Thank you for your support in my personal struggle to be me, to be free, and to be progressive. I hope I represent all you can be.

To Julie and Family, to Emory and Tekia Jones: Thank you all for your faith in me.

To Michael Shapiro, the tax god; to Karen and Eric @ A&B Books; to Nati @ African World Books; to Carla Dean (Editor), Carol and Brenda (C&B Books), Curt Southerland, Sadia, Janet, Darryl, Adianna, DTG, Joanie, Kevin, Lance, Lou, Mechel. To Makeda at Jazzmyne Public Relations, my publicist, banker, diva, and therapist . . . thank you so much.

To Monique, Naiim, Mr. Perkins, Mr. Reeves, Rick, Ruth, Tiffany, Courtney Carreras/YRB Mag (you rock!): Thank you all.

To the many bookstores around the world who carry Relentless Content: Thank you for affording me space on your shelves. I intend to cause a major increase to your bottom line.

Last but certainly not least: to my family and friends. You've helped make my dreams come true. Thank you.

FOREWORD

(By an Anonymous Drug War Veteran)

IN *THE LAST KINGPIN*, the death squads, the gunrunners, and the scoundrels at the bowels of society come tó life, as if you've always known them personally. Relentless has taken the experiences of Freeze (the Kingpin), Rose (the thug gunrunner), Charlucci (the Trafficker), and Roberto Nunez, Jr. (the Colombian drug lord), and he's worked them into what *Scarface* reached for, and what *New Jack City* never quite achieved.

The truth has been fictionalized, as assessed through hundreds of interviews, years of research, and a craftsman's wit, until such reality has been sculpted into an epic tale that spins the mind's eye and captivates the soul and spirit. This is the life and times of the orphan who became a gang member and murderous drug lord; these are the details of the street hustlers who became local icons; the would-be entrepreneurs who were swept into the evils, the malice, and the murder that illicit drug-dealing promotes, as well as the men and women whom they controlled and influenced. This is the story of the sibling orphan who took the opposite road, far and away from the coca leaves that her family farmed and survived by.

There is not another author of this generation, with this degree of talent, real-life experience, and skill for putting life into words, no human being who walks the planet who has control of the unique content such that Relentless Aaron does in this single, mind-blowing tale.

Finally, the game has been played for the last time. The title has been won and the story told.

This is . . . *The Last Kingpin*.

BOOK ONE

CHAPTER ONE

Pam woke into a frenzied, blurry state of semiconsciousness. Her cordless phone was ringing with that chirping sound right by her head. She'd forgotten to replace it in its cradle the night before, and fortunately there was enough power left in the handset to support the incoming call. She rubbed the crust from her face before finally opening her eyes, searching for some clarity at 3 A.M. Even in this foggy, groggy state, Pam could feel something of a hangover; and that was saying something, since she didn't have so much as one drink the night before.

Eventually, she was able to focus on the inch-tall digital images of the alarm clock while wondering: Who the hell is calling at this hour?

And then she thought, Whoever it is, it better be important . . . like an earthquake, a missile strike, or the sky better be falling.

The dream was a good one this time, thank God. She had been sitting under a hair dryer, reading the front page of today's *Washington Post*. The wash and set was a quickie job, something Pam always praised her hairdresser for.

"Congratulations, girlfriend," Jenny was saying to her, already aware of the story in the *Post*. "You're making the street safer for all of us. I just wish I could do more to show you my appreciation." Jenny was always taking simple beauty

shop talk to some other level, making Pam's position with
the Drug Enforcement Agency seem so sensational. And as
usual, Pam would be left at a loss for words. Or on the other
hand, she'd try to find some hidden meaning behind people's
comments—no matter who it was. In this case, Pam wondered if Jenny was making a pass at her.

I just wish I could do more to show you my appreciation . . .

Pam shook the idea from her mind, hating herself for always trying to second-guess people. Always looking for the
lie, or the ulterior motive. Just like a cop, she told herself.

"That's okay, Jen. It's what I get paid for," Pam answered,
hardly looking up from the headline story, an exaggerated
account of the recent DEA sweep in Seattle, Washington.
The story told of . . .

". . . the largest bust in Seattle's history . . . a ring of 57
persons, including some housewives, 6 police officers and
the County Clerk . . . the street value of the cocaine seized
amounted to over $25 million," the paper read.

"Yeah, but . . . it's, like, so dangerous," Jenny exclaimed
in a low, breathy tone.

"Well," said Pam, with her clever eye meeting Jenny's pen-
sive expression, "to tell you the truth . . ." She lowered her
voice, as if to reveal the world's biggest secret. ". . . a lot of
what I do, how I survive? It's dependent on my hair."

Jenny's head and neck cranked back a couple of inches.
Her eyes focused on Pam with a tough-as-nails inquiry, knowing that those words couldn't be true.

But Pam went on lying.

"Yeah, really, because you keep this golden crown of
mine so sharp . . . so fascinating to look at . . . and the bad
guys just lose it. They lose their minds. Really. Then . . . out
of nowhere, bip-bap-boom . . ." Pam's teeth and cheeks produced a sound (as best she could) to simulate the noise that
handcuffs make. At the same time, she took the opportunity
to reach out from under the newspaper. She clasped her fingers around Jenny's wrist, pretending to shackle her.

The moment caught Jenny off guard, and the idea of this

somehow seemed very intense, very real when coupled with Pam's steel gaze.

"Stop playin'," exclaimed Jenny, suddenly getting both nervous and serious as she softly removed Pam's human handcuff.

"Okay, I will. Only if you hurry up and get me out of here."

P am had been thinking up these things while sleeping peacefully, alone, and she was about to take it to another level—an alternate scenario where Jenny actually did have something else in mind . . . that so-called appreciation she'd spoken of was somehow making Pam's dreams warmer, wetter . . . something that was making her sleep an experience as opposed to her body's daily routine.

That's when the damned phone rang. She was still too dazed to know if this was a disappointment or not; still too foggy to wonder how she got to thinking such things in the first place.

B rown, it's Sal. Shake it off, dear. We've got issues."

Issues, Pam considered, as she wiped the remaining residue from her eyes. "Issues" meant DEA business. Besides, it was never personal if Sal Goldridge (Chief Investigator/DEA) called, and especially at this hour.

"Wow. And to think I was gonna put in for that vacation. Maybe try and tan my body a little?" The way Pam said it was as though that was such a foreign idea . . . to relax and feed her body some sun.

"A wha—? Brown, you're dreaming. Wake up, this is serious."

"Okay, okay. I'm up."

"Seattle was good for the Agency, Brown. Real good. But we're on a roll. We don't want to lose momentum now."

"I guess not. So what's up, Chief?"

"About an hour ago FHP pulled over an eighteen-wheeler . . ."

Pam was indeed wide awake now, with her mental motors crankin'. "Florida Highway Patrol," she finally responded.

"That's right. Bell Glade. And Brown?"

"Yes, I'm listening, Chief."

"They think they stopped over five hundred kilos."

"Five . . . hundred . . . kilos?" Pam's staccato response came just as she sat up, her one leg folded in front of her while the other draped over the edge of the bed.

"That's what I said. Found it buried in the front end of a load of corn."

"Dogs?" Pam assumed.

"Well, there were dogs, but it was highway patrol officers who made the stop and search."

"Don't tell me—another illegal search."

"It's possible. It's a long story. But the thing now is, they've got the driver—calls himself Big Slim. Aaanyway, he's being held in their lil' pokey down there. Lord only knows what kinda lawyer's gonna show up or when . . ."

"You don't have to say another word, Chief. I got the picture. I'm already half-dressed . . ." Pam was moving through her bedroom, a brewing storm, with no bra and red satin panties. She threw on a fresh wife-beater that she had laid out for her usual, but now postponed, morning run on the treadmill.

"Is the Gulf on the tarmac?" Pam was speaking of the Gulf Stream jet; the tarmac was a runway at Ronald Reagan Airport.

"It's probably quicker to take a chopper from VA." VA meant Quantico, Virginia, where the community of federal law enforcement agencies called the Pentagon home.

Pam eventually got a chance to exhale before she asked, "What time will they be here?" She was already anticipating her boss and his every move.

"Sometimes I'm scared to think with you around, Agent Brown. It's as if you can read my mind."

"Mmm-hmm . . ." she replied, wondering if he was just buttering her up; that second-guessing sensibility again.

"Ten minutes?"

"Sure," said Pam, already knowing the inevitable. She could even picture the motorcade with two armored SUVs speeding along Pennsylvania Avenue. Silent, spinning lights, that blip of a police siren every now and then at the intersections. "Orders?"

"The usual, Brown. Squeeze him. See if we can't get a lead on the source. This could be big."

"Yeah-yeah, every operation could be big, Chief, as long as Sam tells on Harry, and Harry tells on Frank, and Frank tells on Espinoza . . . and so on and so on."

"Well, you're the best I've got out there in the field, Brown."

Pam lip-synched the Chief's words to herself, since she'd heard those very words so many times before. Then she cut in. "Heard it all before, Chief. Don't you worry, I'll be on the chopper and in Bell Glade before Mister Slim has a chance to scribble graffiti on the jailhouse wall."

"That's m'girl."

When would he ever stop treating her like his daughter? Pam wondered as she pushed and pulled the toothbrush across her teeth, creating her very own visual scenario on the mirror before her. She could see beyond her sharp political facial features; that button nose, dimpled chin, high cheekbones, and otherwise captivating green eyes that folks swore would get her some heavy-duty elected position . . . past her proud, blond crown that (some people claimed) seemed to command a room full of attention. This wasn't the time to ask her mirror the usual questions . . . that whole "mirror, mirror on the wall" bit, wondering why someone as beautiful as she wasn't married off and burdened with a family by the age of thirty-six. If Pam was on her own time, right this moment, she might raise a middle finger at the mirror, cursing that goddamned biological clock.

CHAPTER TWO

It was just past one in the morning when Big Slim popped in one of his old-school tapes. If he wasn't sleepy—yawning every three or four minutes—it would've been a Boney James, Rachelle Ferrell, or John Coltrane CD. Those were his favorite "cruise selections." Some truckers took NōDōz pills. Some chewed gum and kept the windows open. Of course, others took what Slim considered being the soft way out, pulling over into one of the many rest stops or picnic areas for coffee and a nap.

Not Big Slim. He had a wife to bring the bacon home to, and if he felt sleepy he'd simply pop a mix tape into his hi-fi system. Kid Capri, DJ Clue, and Funkmaster Flex were his favorites. And he'd pump up the volume and drive headstrong with that whole ride-or-die attitude. Unless Slim had to stop to piss, most everything else was inside of his fully customized Peterbilt 379—a seventy-inch stand-up sleeper it was called, able to pull any load up to a hundred thousand pounds. A little refrigerator, a CD rack system, a TV, and a microwave oven graced the inside.

The trucker's rule—a nationwide standard—was ten hours on and eight hours off. But Slim was always one to go for it. He trained himself to need less sleep than the average driver. Thus, he'd defy the rule at every opportunity. More hours on the road meant more money in the pocket; fuck what the logbook said. And besides, nobody really enforced the amount of hours a truck driver logged—not if you doctored the record. Slim felt licensed to do that since he was the proprietor of his own business with his own tractor.

Some of Slim's comrades—haters, he called them—joked about his name, but never to his face. They assumed he took the name from an old gangsta novel, even though they themselves never read any, and that he maybe wanted to live that life. But Slim's close buddies (his "road dawgs") knew better than that. They recognized him for his character, that candy-apple personality, how he kept certain diplomacy when it came to opinions or passing judgments. They also respected Slim to the utmost, not because he intimidated them, but because he was a good person. He had scruples and he wasn't a snake. He was hardworking and compassionate toward others; you couldn't ask for more from a person.

Not only that, the man was indeed slim. He had a 6' 5" build, sinewy like a Mandingo warrior. Plus, Slim had that unmistakably dark African complexion. One of a kind. Reason enough for FHP to pull him over.

"Y'r missing a mud flap," said the trooper.

"It's been a long night, Officer. A long night and a long trip. Can you at least tell me how long this'll take?" Slim was making this subtle protest from the backseat of a police cruiser.

"Well, considerin' how you's actin' all belligern't-n-thangs, this could be an all-night endeav'r . . ."

Bo and Satch were brothers on the Florida Highway Patrol. They rolled together this way for twelve years, and they were proud of how many, many, many stops and arrests they had recorded.

At present, Bo was keeping Slim company, paying him little attention through the wire mesh grill that separated the front and rear parts of the police cruiser. From there in the front seat, Bo could more or less oversee the activities outside, the entire search taking place just fifteen or so feet away.

"Now, I'm lookin' here at yer logbook . . . yer itiner'ry seems to me a lil' strange, you droppin' off trash just a half day 'fore ya load up with our good Florida corn."

"Okay. So, gimme a fine. Truckers do it all the time," Slim replied. "Least I cleaned the trailer . . ."

Bo sucked his teeth three times, casting shame over Slim's three-day trip.

"Says here you left New York City's Departm'nt of San'-tation with a load—gotta be garbage—even though yer' log don't spell it all out."

Slim huffed loud enough to be heard, almost thinking out loud: Why is this local yokel, this fat, redneck fuck draggin' this out this long?

"Yes, Officer, I picked up garbage."

"See? Now that wasn't so hard," Bo poked, shifting his eyes smoothly from the clipboard out to the searchlight-illuminated activities in the dead of night, then back to the clipboard. "Momma always told us Bruder bow-ahs that the truth'll set ya free ever' time. Now . . . also says here, you delivered the trash to the Davenport Landfill in Virginia." A couple of the hound dogs were barking just as Bo said this.

Slim rolled his eyes.

"Hey, isn't there a law down here? Don't I have to be ar-rested before you put handcuffs on me? I ain't done nothin' wrong."

"Don't worry, cowboy. Slow yer roll. Only law down these parts is the Bruder bow-ahs law. That comes from good home trainin', and doin' right by the Lord. You do be-lieve in God almighty, don't ya, bow-ah?"

With a huge sigh, Slim vented, "Jeeesus Christ." He chewed the words some so that they weren't yelled.

"See, now you was fine till ya went 'n said the Lord's name in vain like ya did. I'ma make sure we follow procedure to the last nickel tonight, just to teach you a lesson. And, just so ya know? I don't trust you bow-ahs. Neva did. Always some-thin' illegal on those trucks a' yers. Never can be too safe nowadays with you terrorists runnin' 'round. Ya never could know."

Slim stressed, contained within those silvery iron bracelets, wishing he was strong enough to break free, to crash his fist through the wire mesh divider and grab that shotgun that was propped against the dashboard. Or maybe he'd choke this particular "Bruder bow-ah" to death.

"Also says here that ya took some wooden doors from VA to Fort Laudydale . . ."

Now Slim had his eyes closed, forcing himself to imagine another world. Fort Lauderdale struck a chord: The Coochie Coo Go-Go Bar. Yes, a pleasurable thought and an even more pleasurable experience.

Slim had got himself toasted a few months earlier, at a time when financial woes seemed to be closing in on him. Instead of a truck stop, he moseyed into the Coochie, its neon sign soliciting him off of Interstate 95, exit 112, and into that isolated spot outside of Miami. He chose to drink his troubles away. If he was a man who used ten-dollar words, Slim would call Ricky "unscrupulous"; but Slim was reared in south Yonkers, New York, an urban stomping ground that was nothing more and nothing less than any other inner-city neighborhood. So to Slim, Ricky was nothing but a snake. Ricky, with his mangy hygiene, confused upbringing, and weasel ways . . . that fucker caused massive damage to Slim's transmission because of a loose plug—the one that kept the transmission fluid in place.

And to top it off, the visit to Ricky's garage had been more like a favor—because of a friend of a friend. Otherwise, Slim would've taken the tractor to Lee Myles, Devonshire, or anyplace else where professional mechanics knew what the hell they were doing . . . mechanics who wouldn't try and cut corners in order to keep more money in their own pockets.

Do the job, and do it right; there was a respectability in that process.

But, no, Ricky ("Slicky Ricky," Slim decided to call him from now on) had to skip the most important part, securing the cap! Because of that simple oversight, and a missing plug, Slim had to dig into his life savings; he had to pay thousands just to save the truck that provided his bread and butter. And everything was relevant to everything else in his life. Jewel, his wife, wasn't working. She was pregnant with—Slim hoped—their first son. So, the bottom line was that he had to pull the weight for the family.

Orlando Ortiz showed up at The Coochie the evening that Slim was there, mad at the world, cursing any and every-body, and drinking himself to oblivion. This was part of Or-tiz' nightly romp; politicking with the few exotic dancers in this (so-called) house of sin. His primary occupation was to keep his troop of small-time drug dealers in check, making sure that cash and product balanced correctly. Yet, he didn't mind selling cocaine directly to the girls since collecting di-rectly further substantiated his power amongst them. For Orlando, aka Daddy Ortiz, the cocaine business was very lu-crative.

Only now was Slim able to reflect on how this all began: his relationship with Ortiz in Fort Lauderdale, The Coochie, the girls, and meeting some soap opera stud—that was how Slim described him—named Charlucci.

"This is my boss," was how Ortiz introduced Slim to Char-lucci. "He might want to hire you. Or, how should I say . . . acquire your services," Ortiz emphasized with the sly smile. At the time, any business opportunity was mu-sic to Slim's ears, and he was sober enough to hear that these Florida dudes needed to ship produce to North Carolina, to New York; and maybe, if Slim did a good enough job, he could be the one to oversee a whole fleet of rigs, where the same business could be duplicated throughout the country.

From that day on, Slim began to heal financially. He hauled watermelons, bananas, oranges, and corn. Trip after trip, he was paid in cash, able to handle the family burdens.

What Slim didn't know right off was that because of guys like Orlando Ortiz, Charlucci Salazar was the number one cocaine trafficker down in South Beach, the steamy world of bikinis, beaches, hotels, nightlife, endless hedonism, loud colors, thousand-beats-per-minute music, and breasts jig-gling in every direction. South Beach and the sun. South Beach and the tourists. South Beach and its promise of sex-ual fantasies fulfilled.

It was amidst this developing tourist site that Charlucci supplied over twenty mid-level associates; dealers who supplied at least ten times as many drug pushers from the coastline up to as far as the top of the Panhandle. And thanks to naïve workhorses like Big Slim, Charlucci was spreading his virus into the Carolinas and New York. Early on, it was merely jeep-loads of product being moved every day. But it was more cost-effective, and there was less risk to move larger quantities.

Damn! What're they gonna do, empty the whole friggin' truck? I won't get back on the road for hours. I hope they plan on puttin' all those bushels back on the truck like they found them." Slim had a salty threat in his voice, as though he would single-handedly topple FHP. Meanwhile, a few more troopers showed up, joining in on the party where bushel upon bushel of corn was being tossed and stacked haphazardly on the bank of the highway, all of it unrefrigerated in eighty degree weather. At the same time, various insects wildly whipped and spiraled in the dark, just above the produce, while police dogs climbed, sniffed, and barked erratically about the truck.

Bo was still recovering from his laughter at Slim's threat. Then he said, "You just betta hope we don't find anything funny on that truck a' yers."

More barking now. More obvious and dutiful.

"I told ya, man . . . I'm clean," said Slim, trying to play cool, calm, and collected, even if his eye did cut over to see what the commotion with the dogs was about. Somewhere deep in his soul he had a clan name for every one of these rednecks. However, there was no sense playing the "race card" just now; doing so might cause another lynching before sunup.

"So," Bo went on to say, his own eye cutting over toward the barking, "the doors to Fort Laudy, then the corn goes back north. But when does the trailer get cleaned?"

"At the landfill. They bleach it, Pine-Sol . . . all that stuff."

"That so—"

"Hey, Bo!" The distant voice could be heard through the driver's side window and instantly interrupted the conversation.

The search and seizure also came to a halt. Every one of the troopers was soon outside the trailer, or otherwise climbing down. One of them, the one with the loud mouth, was waving at Bo, signaling him over. That's when Slim pursed his lips.

Satch hopped up onto the rig and then reached out to help his brother up into the side door. At once, it was cold and dark, with flashlights directed into the furthest end of the trailer. Bo followed Satch around the thin-wooded bushels of corn, stepping on the floor of crushed ice, inhaling the mixed fumes of bleach, Pine-Sol, and the aroma from an officer's cigar.

"Pay dirt, boys."

"Whaddaya think it is?" Satch asked.

"Well it sure in the fuck ain't corn, that's fer dayum skippy."

"Call the Sergeant, Bo."

"At two in the mornin'? He'll piss a fit at me."

"No, he'll piss a fit at ya if ya don't call. Call 'im, *now*!"

CHAPTER THREE

Pam knew exactly what she wanted before meeting an intended informant. Ultimately, she would use whatever means necessary depending on the man's or woman's level of tolerance; but she would squeeze out some information. Even if her own confrontation with the perp wasn't appropriate, she had a dozen other means. It is with this track record that Pam developed a superior state of mind just prior to a meet. Many times, it's during these very trips, during that trek by land, sea, or air, that she arrives to make these rendezvous eventful. To her, this will be the Super Bowl, the championship playoff, the World Series. And that's just how she prepares, with just as much passion, intensity, and vigor.

The motorcade escort swept Agent Brown from her town house no later than fifteen minutes after her call from DEA Chief Goldridge. From Georgetown's residential area, the vehicles raced out into the early morning over Key Bridge into Virginia and over to Quantico.

"What's the ETA, Steve?" Pam asked from the back of the Suburban, with a light panel and her palm mirror to assist with her lipstick application. On the vehicle's sound system, the blue-eyed soul duo Hall and Oates was performing "She's Gone" at an easy volume.

Everybody's high on consolation,
everybody's trying to tell me what is right for me.

And as usual, Pam took the impromptu song as a message directed specifically toward her. It also served as a relaxer, a theme of sorts to say "she's gone," meaning that Pam was gone once again, off on another mission to rid the nation of drugs and those who sold them.

"Ten more minutes," replied Steve Masters, a DEA agent for eight years—two years less than Pam. Along with Joel Green, Mark Stevens, and Ted Carson, the group was put together by the Chief as the DEA's elite force. He named them MET, for Mobile Enforcement Team. They could be assigned to address any drug-related concern anywhere in the nation at the drop of a dime. On certain occasions, they'd travel abroad if a subject was somehow linked or associated with trafficking in the United States. The missions were covert for the most part, to the point where Goldridge and his boss were the only ones to know the team's goals, whereabouts, and their capabilities. Secrecy was essential, lest any ole agent (one perhaps that was grimy, working both sides) would know about an operation. These days, because the drug trafficking trade was virtually dominated by a handful of invincible drug lords on the international level (as well as kingpins and dealers on the national level), battles were expected. There were spies, bribes, and payoffs. There were murders of agents, law officials, and even judges. With so much money at stake, anyone was a target.

Sergeant Scott on the line," announced Carson, and he handed the active cell phone over his shoulder. "FHP," Carson concluded. Agent Brown reached for the cell, no need for formalities; stick to the procedures, and that was that.

"Good morning, Sergeant Scott. Agent Pam Brown calling to announce our arrival. I believe Chief Goldridge spoke to you earlier?" Pam listened into the phone as she turned a cheek for one last look in the mirror.

"Right. Well, we should be there shortly. What's the situation there? Is the perp talking? Is that so . . . is that so . . .

Hmmm, well . . . I suppose we'll have our work cut out for us . . . Twelfth and Raspberry isn't it? All right, then. See you there."

Like shiny black water bugs, the team of Tahoes and the Suburbans with their distinguishing antennas; their quiet, intimidating influence; and their haunting energy arrived in Quantico, where the agents spilled out onto the tarmac. Within seconds, twelve additional agents surrounded them, everyone's face only slightly recognizable amidst the glare of headlights. More overwhelming were the large, bright letters that stood out on each agent's Windbreaker, hat, and on their various duffle bags. The imposing letters "DEA" cast omnipotence, authority, and raw power over the atmosphere.

There were a few other activities about the heliport as well; perhaps FBI or CIA operations, landing and taking off in their own exclusive efforts of crime fighting. Pam appreciated this support. It was as if the country's own elite force of soldiers, likely thousands of them, were at her beck and call, ready to take on the world's demons. All the while, this wave of energy that she had grown so accustomed to was cast on her—the agent in command—as the others awaited orders.

"Do we have details on the perp?"

"Yes, ma'am," answered an agent, and he immediately approached with an open leather folder. He pulled a DEA memo from its binding and handed it to his superior. There was a professional smile from the agent, and Pam plainly accepted the gesture as just that. Without hesitation, she scanned the paperwork regarding Eric Washington, aka Big Slim.

"Carson," Pam announced and extended the memo to her MET team member. He took it and immediately understood the relevance; the perp was a black man like Carson. Assimilation alone would spark an interest. But again, this was nothing new. MET had taken down more than fifteen thousand dealers, mules, and users since its inception. Between the thirty-plus MET teams across the country, deployed to hundreds of local communities, DEA agents zeroed in on the subtlest and the most ruthless drug organizations. Cocaine, crack, meth-amphetamine, marijuana, and heroin. Ecstasy was big, too, but the budget hadn't been approved as yet for the agency to launch a particular focus on the more exotic drugs. And be-sides, it was a soft concern, not usually carried by the average drug gang, enforced by murders and threats. Nonetheless, each MET team had a "cultural contingent," which was by design sensitive to the practices, the ideologies, and the biases of varying nationalities. The busiest drug gangs were black and Latino, coincidental to the hardships and isolated misery of the inner city.

"Here's the deal. We have a confirmed shipment of five hundred kilos of cocaine in Bell Glade, Florida. It was mov-ing north, so chances are we'll be heading south on this mis-sion . . ." As Pam Brown spoke, dominating—it seemed—the breath of every man in her vicinity, an agent casually stepped through the circle with a clipboard. Hardly looking, Pam signed off for the two Blackhawk choppers, just like that. Over $80 million worth of government machinery was at her disposal. Then she nonchalantly continued with her speech.

"I know you boys haven't had much of a vacation, but our objective remains clear. Penetrate the network and take down the source . . . this could take a few days, it could take a few weeks; you'll hold the course, regardless. The same rules apply; once we board the choppers you will initiate no communication with your families. Stay focused. Agents Masters and Green will handle further instructions. Any questions?" There was no opportunity to blink before she said, "Beautiful. Enjoy the trip, boys."

Pam stepped off and into one of two waiting choppers while Masters and Green instructed other agents on equip-ment, firepower, use of force, and details about the Bell Glade arrest. At 4:30 A.M., agents boarded the Blackhawk choppers, the propellers grinded into a steady rotation, then a more aggressive one, until the birds lifted into the sky with their red and blue lights so Christmas-like against the early morning darkness.

• • •

Ted Carson wasn't an average agent. First, he knew who he was as an individual. He studied his history, stayed abreast of current events, and worked hard to make a valuable contribution. Second, Carson was a native New Yorker who went from social worker to the NYPD to the Tactical Narcotics Team (TNT). It was as a social worker for the welfare department that Carson met the individuals whom society looked down upon as castaways. He came to work at New York's Department of Social Services with the intentions of setting a standard, of being a model.

Wearing a hip cotton sweatshirt, wool trousers, and freshly shined shoes, Carson wanted to appear approachable. He kept an open face, an open attitude. It was a struggle on many mornings to come into work with the same attitude and address the worst-kept individuals as though they were the most important people on earth to him. It was hard to do that when he himself had to get a life, to cope with the ups and downs of being a twenty-something. It was hard to live his dreams despite how wonderful some made it seem. He had to "do him," and then on top of that, he had to come to work and think for others. He had to do all of this without coming across as "plastic"; that phoniness that some of his co-workers wore in the presence of those with hard luck.

Carson took pride in getting to know people, whether it was those (he called them clients) at work, in crowded church basements, or at rent parties in tenement buildings. He spoke out, too, addressing small crowds of piss-poor men and women who were on the streets using every drug available, stealing to eat and sleeping in subway cars or on benches in Central Park. He helped set up housing, work, and drug rehabilitation programs for hundreds of men and women. Having seen people go from living in a cardboard box, and then progress to a private-sector job and an apartment they could pay for showed Carson that a mere helping hand could be of tremendous help to a person. A simple gesture.

Carson had built up such a swell of contributions, helping

so many and absorbing a lot of good feelings along the way, that it was only a matter of time before the balloon was punctured; before some manner of misfortune came along. After all, nothing too good could last forever.

One evening an elderly client of his was slain by police officers. Officers had gone door to door in a gung-ho search for a reported disturbance. It turned out that they were actually disturbing her. When the trio of officers realized that someone was in the apartment, they ordered Mrs. Price to open the door. Mrs. Price was safe at home and made it clear that she didn't want "no parts of no police." One thing led to another and the officers kicked in her door—guns drawn.

"Mrs. Price was executed in cold blood," said her neighbors. "She ain't bother nobody," they reported to the newspapers. There was an Internal Affairs inquiry and the civilian review board did their best to see those officers fry, but political pressure afforded the Long Islanders—officers who didn't even live in the community which they patrolled—the chance to go scot-free, to continue on (even as they were suspended), with their ivy families, in their ivy neighborhoods, with their ivy ways of living.

Since Carson had visited Mrs. Price in that very apartment on that very morning, the news of the tragic confrontation hit him like a landslide of stones. He subsequently decided "enough is enough." He couldn't believe the way those cops decided that Mrs. Price wasn't worthy of living. Just like that, they played judge, they played jury, and they played God.

That year, in the name of "diversifying the force," an advertisement caught Ted's attention and he entered the Police Academy. Qualifying on paper was a cinch. And completing training was like going back to practice for his college track team. In no time, Carson was on foot patrol, interacting with the same people he had counseled. The same people he had helped. Only now, he felt empowered to protect the people he helped to groom. His hard work was his equity. As a New York City police officer, Carson was now attuned to the mainstream. He became a troubleshooter, resolving disputes both commercial and domestic. At one point he even performed midwife duties. On a cold night in January, Carson was patrolling Riverside Drive, close to the end of his nightly tour, when he heard a woman's loud holler. When he sprinted down the bike path almost near the water's edge, he found one woman standing over another. His first instinct was to think the woman standing was an assailant; that she had robbed or beaten the one on the ground.

"She's about to have a baby!" the woman announced. Carson had to shed his coat to keep the woman warm and eventually made 72nd Street's sublevel token booth an instant birthing room. Used newspapers became a floor covering beneath the mother. The baby had no patience. The woman's water broke a few minutes later, ruining Carson's uniform, but all else worked out fine.

Unbelievably, as a rookie, Carson saw very little violence. He remained sharp, visiting the firing range once a week, and winning awards at police sharp shooting competitions. Yet he didn't have to fire his weapon once while on the job, not until the evening of June 15. It was recognized by news broadcasts as the "bloodiest day of the year," and Carson repeatedly relived the events for the two years following such mayhem.

So how long you gonna hold out, Carson?" asked Steve during the chopper ride down to Florida. He saw that his colleague was staring. Again, with that same glassy-eyed stare that always caused Steve to wonder what was on Ted's mind.

"Okay . . ." said Carson, while his gaze lingered out through the chopper's dark glass into the pre-dawn hours. He eventually turned his attention to Steve.

"I give up, Masters. I left my quiz show marbles back at the crib. Could you fill in the blanks for me? Be a little more specific with your question maybe? Hold out on what?" Carson spoke at a volume that was a little louder than the puttering propellers—the soft consistence that penetrated the chopper's soundproof cabin—and at an instance, here and there, the voice and propellers blended.

"Switch your audio on, Carson. Channel four." Both men

had headphones on, both with the wraparound microphone and the capability for one-to-one radio communication.

"What's up?" asked Carson.

"Yeah, exactly. What's up with you? You've been promising me this so-called major moment in your life . . . that ole life-'n-death scenario. Not like I won't get on without the gritty details, but it feels like you've been teasing me." Carson chuckled at Masters' feigned crybaby performance. "No, really dude." He gave a soft punch to Ted's leg just across from him. "You've been staring out into the stars every time we're airborne. If we're on the ground, you're looking through the floor. I can't tell if it's me or if you're just intentionally driving me up a wall."

Steve finally let go of the humor and cast a no-shit expression toward his partner.

"So, basically, even though we've been working together for, like what, three years? You still wanna know if your co-worker is some psycho cop who's ready to explode when the wind shifts."

"Well, that did cross my mind. I won't lie to you. Shit, if you decide to go postal, I'm gonna be the first to go down." Masters made the sound effects of gunshots, with his upper body jerking, pretending to endure the impact of bullets.

"Not funny."

"Okay, so why isn't it funny? You can trust me. Maybe I can even help or something."

"Too late. You had to be there. It was a bunch of coincidences, really. While I was on the force—it was the fifteenth of June—I'm up on 96th chattin' with John, the owner of Birdland nightclub. I'm off duty that day, standing outside. Nice night, ya know? We're just kickin' it, talkin' about that chick . . ." Carson snapped his fingers, an attempt to trigger the memory. "Diana Ross' daughter . . . it might be Rhonda. Yeah, I think that's it. Anyway, she's inside the club performing to a standing room only crowd. I'll never forget it. The two of us stepped outside for a few minutes. Just for some air. Next thing I know, shots are fired and my body is burning. Next time I had my eyes open was in intensive care.

Of course I lived, and I'm still here to tell about it, but it was close, Steve. Too close."

"Phew, man, how long they have you in ICU?"

"Almost six days, man. Six fuckin' days. Sheryl's hair was falling out because she was pulling at it. Keisha was too young to know what was going on." Masters' eyes turned to the floor. Ted was looking out into the morning again. "Kindra wasn't born yet. Bottom line is my wife had to go through that shit. Fuck what I was feeling . . . fuck the pain, or all that therapy. It's the family, man. The family. The bullet is still somewhere in my head, and all I can think about is the wife and kids."

"They catch the guy?"

"They tried to. Turned out that a few thugs were racing up Broadway taking potshots at whatever they saw. I was only one out of thirty-one people shot. Twelve were seriously injured, not counting me, and four died."

"It wasn't your time to go."

"Hmmph, that's what the psych said."

"Punks."

"Hmmph, that's what my preacher said."

"But did they catch them?"

"Get this. They led police on a wild-goose chase through Midtown. Even civilians helped with the chase, a bread truck, a taxicab . . . the perps had to be doin' sixty, seventy, eighty miles per hour on New York City streets."

"Isn't that the speed limit over there?"

"Is that Jersey hatin' on New York again?" Masters smirked at Carson's sharp wit. "Anyway, television news helicopters picked up the chase and even broke into other programming to carry it live. The close-ups were even clear enough to catch the knuckleheads smokin', drinkin', and laughing as they outwitted officers. Eventually, police were able to drop a spike strip on the FDR Drive, puncturing the tires."

"All this was on TV."

"Recorded for infamy. I got to watch it later when I recovered. Sheryl recorded it."

"Imagine that."

"When the car rolled to a stop, they got out on the parkway like friggin' cowboys. All three had at least two guns. Automatic weapons. Extra clips. They started walking down the center lanes like they expected a fair duel."

"You know what? I remember this. I saw the footage on that show, *World's Most Daring Standoffs*. The police had them surrounded, traffic was at a standstill."

"Mmm-hmm . . . and they climbed over the median where cars were still, parking lot style, and they shot some more folks right behind their steering wheels. Then the snipers picked them off from the air from a nearby overpass. It was bloody, man. Bloody."

"And don't tell me . . . the man who shot them got all the publicity."

Carson shrugged, a way of saying so what.

"Shit, Carson. If I'd been in your shoes, I'd be in the twilight zone, too."

"Anybody can catch the hot one, man. Anybody."

"It's crazy. Like a few guys get a hard-on for death and just start shootin' . . . target practice. Changin' people's lives. Like 9/11 or somethin'."

Steve fed into the momentary silence before asking, "So where does this leave you?"

"Sometimes I don't know, Masters. Sometimes I just don't know. I really haven't been the same since. I use to be this superman for humanity. I really cared a lot about the little guy. I still do, I guess. But so many of them want the easy way out, the easy way up. If it's not easy, then it's that 'by any means necessary' attitude. Like life owes them something. They don't wanna pay rent on earth; they just wanna take, take, and take."

"So how'd you get to be DEA?"

"The brass at NYPD knew about my scores on the firing range. I won a few trophies 'n stuff. They were putting together a force called the Tactical Narcotics Team and wanted the best men on the force for the operation. I was recruited. Violence quickly became an everyday thing. Raids left and right, as much as five in one day. I can't tell you how many bodegas, drug dens, apartments, and private homes we crashed. We were like guerillas in paramilitary uniforms."

"Something like we're doing now."

"Well, really, the DEA is more civilized about it. Snitches, confidential informants, dime droppers, they make life so much easier. And these dealers today, they don't even know what hit them by the time we show up."

"Some of 'em."

"Yeah, thank God for bulletproof vests."

"And headgear, too."

Those big, effortless, mechanical black birds, lowered the MET team into Cape Canaveral, where two mobile units were waiting. Speeding down the coastline in identical SUVs was dream-like, as if the agents never left the vehicles in Virginia; as if they'd been towed along somehow attached to the Blackhawks. A new day was beginning throughout the sky as the convoy came to a stop outside of the Bell Glades police station. Agents stepped out of the vehicles, some remaining on post outside, and others joining Pam Brown as she led the way, somewhat marching into the small station. No sense in having all fifteen crowd things inside.

There were just three officers to administer things at the station. Satch was on the phone giving his girlfriend the usual excuse—"police business"—for not being there by her side. He was sitting on a desk farthest from the front entrance, yet he was the first to recognize that the Feds had arrived.

"Gotta go," he told the third girlfriend in as many months.

In the meantime, brother Bo was dozing off in a leather swivel chair, feet up, head back, and mouth half opened with an annoying snore. There was also Sergeant Scott, who was into yesterday's paper.

"Sarge," Satch announced. "They're here."

Scott looked up and just as soon swung the handful of newspapers at Bo's feet. "Get up, Bo. Bo!" The second and third agents had already come in as primaries, as they would on a drug raid, before Pam stepped ahead of them.

"Sergeant Scott? Pam Brown, DEA."

"Alrighty, ma'am, Bell Glades' finest at your service."

"Agents Masters and Carson," she indicated with a sales-person's flair. And then it was business as usual. "Can you show us to the perp?"

"Sure can. Satch—the keys." The entourage followed the hometown boys through what could've been the stage for a spaghetti western, a main room followed by a corridor and a half dozen open-bar jail cells. Big Slim was kept in the last cell. A prostitute made a kissing sound as the strangers passed.

"Mind yer manners, Mike, else we'll put a muzzle on ya."

"Oh, Mr. Sheriff, would you please, oh please, do that for me. I'm just so into bondage."

"Goddamned freak," Sergeant Scott mumbled as he fid-dled with the keys.

"What happened to him?" asked Carson the instant he saw Big Slim.

"Oh, a little accident on the way to the station. He tried to get away."

With hands in her jacket pockets, Pam took in a deep, frustrated breath and nudged Masters. He took directions from her and sprang back toward the front room. Pam then told Carson, "Help him up off of the bench to that couch in the front."

"But, this is our prisoner, miss—"

"I'll tell you what, Sergeant Scott . . . the best thing for you to do now is step back out of my way. If any of your men interfere, I'll have you locked up in your own jail cells for in-terference with a federal investigation plus a half dozen civil rights charges."

Scott, with his hands on his hips, was appalled at the idea of some woman talking to him like that. In the meantime, two agents carefully helped Slim from the bench. His face had been bludgeoned and his clothing ripped here and there. Scornful gazes were passed between the locals and the agents. The DEA was now in charge.

CHAPTER FOUR

"Can you hear me?" Pam crouched down into a squat and placed a compassionate hand on Slim's knee. The way he was seated in that bucket crouch, his legs appeared to be the major burdens in life. To have to carry, drag, lift, and manage with these extensions couldn't be a luxury. But then again, Pam considered, the guy would never need a ladder to change a lightbulb.

Slim's eyes must've been all cried out the way they lay there under swollen lids. Pam could only cringe at the sight of him, turning her head away, squeezing her eyes shut, and cursing the locals. Already she could see that they'd screwed up this bust from A to Z. If only she could salvage what was left of this guy's common sense.

"Listen, I can see that you're not exactly in a speaking mood, but perhaps you and I can help one another." She gave a soft squeeze to his kneecap for emphasis.

Good, she thought. At least he's trying to establish eye contact.

"This must be a nightmare for you, Mr. Washington, or would you rather I call you by your handle?" Pam knew damn well that the man's nickname bespoke his reputation. She was also familiar with the fancy letters painted on his P-379. A name (or "handle") like that would undoubtedly win the trucker fame over CB airwaves. Pam counted on that being sweet music to his ears. "Big Slim?" There was eye contact again. Beautiful. "Let me share a few things that I know about you, Slim . . ." Pam could feel a bit of tension in her thighs and thought about her boss waking her up this morning; no chance to hit the StairMaster. She managed to keep her balance as she partially stood up and then sat next to Slim. He didn't show concern.

"You were born on April twelfth," she began, "as an only son. Your sisters are Shaniqua and Dawn. You have a half brother named Eddie. You went to Yonkers High School where you played basketball and ran track and field . . . oh, congratulations on your medals, Slim. All-County. Penn Relays and the State Championship in the long jump. Mostly first and second place, you must've been a catch." Pam lifted her foot to cross the opposite knee now as casual as could be in her DEA Windbreaker, the wife beater underneath, the cap, stonewashed jeans, and boots that could get her up any hillside, or if necessary, through muddy water.

"I was surprised that you didn't take the offer to the University of Maryland. That's got to be kicking your ass when you think about it, but my guess is you've reconciled; you're content with following in the footsteps of your stepfather, a vet who served in Nam. The rest is fodder, something my twelve-year-old niece could've found out: how you graduated from high school and then took the dive into the Army. Basic training at Ft. Leonardwood, Missouri . . ." Slim finally turned his head to face Pam. But she was still rambling, impressed with herself. "Your MOS was an eighty-eight Mic, and you were stationed in Missouri and then West Point where you were honorably discharged. The highest rank you earned was Spec four, or corporal—same difference." If Slim's jaw could've dropped to the floor it would've, but it was too busted up to do much of anything.

"What I don't know is what made you decide to get into trucking?"

At this point, Slim figured this white woman to be his guardian angel. After all, she did get him out of that cell and rebuke the local cowboys, or else she'd been following him for all of his natural life. He felt comfortable enough to talk to her, or to at least try.

"I just—ouch!" Slim raised his hand to his cheek.

"Somebody get me a cold soda, a towel, and some water. Do it," ordered Pam. And while two agents scurried to the task, she re-addressed the prisoner. "You take it easy, Slim. Don't feel pressured to speak if you don't want to." Pam didn't mean that, but it felt like the right thing to say.

"No, it's okay," said Slim.

Bingo.

Slim continued. "I love the trucking business; I'm driving and I feel free on the road. I sing my"—Slim winced—"songs. I dream my dreams. I can do me."

"What do you dream about, Slim?"

Slim considered the question, searching his mental think tank.

"One day, I wanna have a big fleet. Like a hundred trucks. Thank you." Slim took the cold can of Coke while Pam dabbed his face with a warm, damp towel. A nurse couldn't have done better.

"Wow, a hundred, huh?" Pam considered the numbers. *One hundred trucks, two skids of cocaine on each, that's . . . damn . . . one hundred twenty thousand tons.* "Big dreamer, Slim. And what might I ask would these trucks be carrying? Corn?"

"Hey, listen, Miss . . ."

"Call me Miss P."

"Okay, Miss P. I don't know nothin' about no drugs. Nothin'. Never used them. I was never interested. I'm too afraid to even try a joint. My eyes water when I'm around the stuff."

"So, Slim . . ." Pam put her elbow to her knee and her cheek in her hand, giving close scrutiny to Slim, his demeanor and his words. She was a walking, talking lie detector. "How can you explain the two skids on your truck? There's something like five hundred kilos back there, man. The stuff didn't just appear out of the clear blue." Slim wagged his head. She pressed on. "Okay, walk me through this." Pam put her hand out for a clipboard and Carson passed it to her. She flipped a page or two before finally letting it go. "You took trash from New York City to the landfill in VA. Then you had the truck cleaned."

"Right there at the landfill," said Slim.

"Okay, did you check the trailer before you left?" Slim nodded. "Then you picked up doors in VA. Did you watch them as they were loaded?" Again, Slim nodded, and then took another sip of Coke. "So the doors went to Ft. Lauderdale?"

"Yup," Slim answered after an audible swallow.

"To the Home Depot."

"Exactly."

"Then it's off to the farmer's market in Tampa. Was the trailer empty from the Home Depot to the market?"

"There is no trailer, only the tractor."

"All right. Now we're at the market. Paint the picture for me. You pull in. They load. Where were you when this took place?"

"Actually, I didn't see anything loaded. The trailer was already done when I got there. I just checked in, signed some papers, and hooked up the rig."

"Hmmm. And you've been driving ever since?"

"Ever since."

"Okay, Slim, I want you to be honest with me, because this answer will decide your fate. You're an independent contractor. You deal directly with the buyer and the seller. I have an idea that your buyer and your seller of the corn are unsavory fellas. Not your average farmer. Not your average grocer. I want to know what was going through your mind when you met these people. Where did you meet them? How much they offer you? And, if the amount of money was also unusual, didn't you get suspicious? Why did you go along with this . . . this shipment? Was it the money?"

"Listen, Miss P. I'm a truck driver. If you need something

delivered—anything but a baby—I'll deliver it for you. Yes, I'm guilty."

Pam changed her expression to *"oh really?"*

"I hauled garbage right before I hauled produce, but I ain't crazy. I wouldn't carry no drugs on my truck. And, if I knew about it, I . . . well . . . ain't no way for me to know, simple as that. But, as far as money . . . ain't enough money in the world to keep me from my wife Jewel and our little Slim Junior. No money!"

Pam let some silence pass between them as she continued to look into Slim's eyes. If he looked away, if he digressed, she'd turn him back over to the dogs and leave him there to handle his own problem. Instead, she'd go check on the corn hustlers. A Fed case wouldn't stick on Slim on account of the illegal search. The pretrial motion would find the case tossed out the door before opening arguments, even before a jury was selected. A waste of time and taxpayers' money. But, on the other hand, if Slim kept his poise, if he could maintain eye contact and that sincere expression with no fidgeting and unnecessary sips from that empty soda can, then Pam knew he was telling the truth. She would wield her raw power to have Slim set free. She'd be his godsend, his relief from a long night. But then, of course, she'd need his help with one minor task.

"Tell you what, Slim. I want you to give me the details of your contacts on this shipment. Show me how your manifesto corresponds with your hours logged, and how your bills of lading match with your contacts. I want every detail down to the mustard seed. I'm gonna see that you walk out of here within the hour on my magic carpet."

"What about my tractor?"

"You can have everything but the . . ." Pam looked at Carson. Carson looked at Masters. Masters looked back at Pam. "Hey, Slim, I have an idea. Are you still in shape to drive?"

"Sure am. I might need another one of those Coca-Colas but I think I can manage."

"Great," Pam replied with a note of conspiracy in her voice that the other agents immediately understood.

• • •

Before leaving Bell Glade that morning, Pam threatened the locals, informing them of certain legal repercussions for the illegal search and the subsequent assault. Furthermore, there'd be a publicity nightmare relating to racism, a backward police procedure, and the questions about so much coke along with speculation about other such shipments. Pam only cared to keep the incident a secret so that she could catch herself a whale.

CHAPTER FIVE

Brian Carter don't exist no more, you just remember that. And tell all ya little hoochie friends the same thing. My name is Freeze. Always been Freeze, always gonna be Freeze. Got that? I don't give a fuck if we did know each other in high school. And for real . . . I got hos finer 'n you that shine my alligator boots. So, you can't even step to me 'less you pay yo' respects, bitch!" Freeze's head had a light bob as he spoke. He was gritting on Stacy, the party promoter standing before him at the bar. A couple of his goons (Butch and his right-hand man Squirrel) were within bitch-slapping distance of Stacy, who was otherwise a dimepiece with her flirt-worthy eyes and a party girl outfit that promised all types of possibilities. Stacy's locks made her look a bit regal tonight, secured high on the back of her head and hanging down in a slight tail. For a second, all those good looks seemed about ready to succumb to tears; Freeze was making a scene in front of a club full of partygoers.

Stacy had her hand on her hip now, giving Freeze that look—No you didn't just call me a bitch!—and she sucked her teeth before making that around-the-way-girl spin, with that fine ass all in their faces as she strutted away.

"Imagine that ho's nerve, askin' me for my address like I need to be on some mailing list. Psssh . . . what she think, just 'cause she promotin' some comedy night here that she can just step to a nigga? That bottom-bitch needs to get a job."

Squirrel chuckled at the thought, but Butch wasn't about all this chat. He kept an eye on Stacy; kept a stone face until he was sure that she let it go. Nothing worse than a woman scorned. And everybody knew how hard Stacy and Lisa worked to get Manhattan Proper poppin' on Tuesday nights. He didn't wanna have to be the one to have to tie that girl up in a Dumpster later.

"She do got a job, Freeze. Honey works at the electric company. A nine to five."

"See what I mean? She ain't even makin' no money here. Why else would she still be on the nine-to-five tip?" Freeze lifted the mouth of the Dom Perignon to his lips and swigged before he said, "Remind me to have that bitch fix my electric bill. It's good to have people in place when you need them."

Squirrel was wondering how Stacy could ever be "in place" for Freeze, especially after that lil' interaction. Naturally, Squirrel realized his boss was just blowin' hot air, as usual. Then his attention shot across the crowd to the stage.

"And I love my heavy womens, but I gots to talk about 'cha . . . especially you heavy ones. I mean you step to a dude all sultry . . . you know, the sexy voice and all. Only thing you missin' is a good man—no really! Y'all say 'all I want is a good man,' when the truth is, all you need is someone to break you off a little sump'm, sump'm. Word up! You want somebody that ain't afraid to tap all . . . that . . . ass you got. I mean, I don't blame you. That's a lotta ass to be satisfied! Word! And y'all don't be checkin' the heavy fellas either. Nah! Y'all want us skinny dudes. Y'all swear we gonna do that shit right. But for real, you get a skinny dude like me around a big girl wit' a whole lotta ass. Shit. I'll get caught up in that crack like some dental floss! Nah, seriously." The comedian, Talent, had the crowd hollerin', lurching back and forth in their seats.

"For real! I had a heavy girl take me home one night, she said, 'Talent . . . rub my body down with some lotion.'" The way Talent dragged out some of his words, impersonating a naïve girl (with the ghetto drawl and the shallow state of mind), had the audience in stitches. This was one of his signature affects; that, and how he made the hearty CLUCK! sound with his gums and tongue. He continued with his impersonation:

" 'Talent, kiss my body with your sexy lips', so I rub her body. I kiss her body. I'm all excited 'n shit. Then she goes, 'Talent go order me some Domino's Pizza.' " The audience exploded with loud and raucous laughter.

"I think an orgasm for a heavy woman is different from the one I know. Word up. See, I want my juices flyin' all over her. She wants juice, too, but the juice from those sausages and those pepperonis! I'm trying to get all hot and sweaty. She wants somethin' oven-baked with steam comin' off it . . . I'm trying to get so excited that I'll blow the fuck up at any minute. But a heavy woman? As long as you got food for her, she's excited. Oh yeah. And you keep on feedin' her . . . she gonna blow up all right, 'specially if you light a match near her. 'Cause when that ass lets off one of those monster farts? BOOM!" Talent made sound effects that caused the audience to scream, cry, and stomp. The heavy people included.

"But, don't you take it personal ladies, 'cuz remember it's just co-medy!"

"That's a funny nigga up there, Squirrel. But I'd hate to see a big woman get mad at him."

"Nah, he aiight. Ain't nobody really taking that comedian stuff too hard. They just tellin' it like it is."

"Yeah, but when that nigga come knockin' at our door for some protection, don't say I didn't tell you so." Freeze took another pull at the champagne, maintaining his low profile/high profile image, not really laughing at the comedian like the others were, but enjoying the show deep down. This was his life. The only time he really (sort of) socialized. He wasn't there amongst a community of well-dressed black folk to network, to chitchat with the local hos, or to dance. No. Freeze was there to be acknowledged, but not bothered.

Respect this gangsta, but don't look at me for too long. Check out this full-length smoke fox fur coat . . . this 25-karat diamond on my pinkie . . . my gold-framed Gucci glasses. Check out these ma'fuckin' alligator boots. Probably cost more than everything you got on, nigga. And yeah, check out my lieutenant holdin' the keys to my Bentley Continental T double-parked outside with the turbo 420, the sheepskin carpet and platinum rims. That's right, nigga . . . three hundred grand sittin' out there with the doors unlocked . . . dare you to take it . . . dare you to even brush up against it. That'll be your last day on earth, bitch-ass nigga. Probably still livin' off yo' momma.

Brian "Freeze" Carter. He was extravagant, no doubt there; part pimp and part hustler. Part Funkadelic, part James Brown, and part Snoop Dogg, with black wavy hair that curled down to about shoulder length and sideburns curving down along his lower cheek into a well-groomed goatee. From a rear view, Freeze might pass for Jimi Hendrix, James Brown, or Prince.

Even in his own mind, Freeze wasn't sure what he represented. He spoke and dressed like a pimp. He carried himself like a celebrity. He was addicted to cash money, hustling—all that. And most of all, he didn't care who he victimized to get what he wanted. Still, when you faced him you had to respect his conviction that this was Freeze: take it or leave it. And, despite all else, there was nothing fake, phony, or fraudulent about the potential violence he kept with him. The Tec-9 he kept under the front seat, the .45 in the glove compartment, and the pump-action Maverick, that pistol-gripped shotgun he liked so much, was kept in the Lincoln Navigator back at the crib. And these weapons were merely his personal stash.

Squirrel always carried a Mac-11 fully automatic with thirty-round clips at the ready. It was strapped in a nylon casing, usually concealed under the fashionable black leather coats he wore. Sure, Squirrel was a small man (though proportionately shaped for 5' 4"), but he had that big dangerous amount of firepower with him. Butch, on the other hand, was big enough to take most any man with his brute strength. But ever since he became the hard body, a bodyguard that Freeze relied upon, Butch needed something substantial to back up Big Dog's gangsta ways—the drugs, the money, the grimy character. Even at the local hangouts it was necessary to be packin'. Whether it was comedy or even if Freeze and company had to stop by a deli for a quart of milk, Butch always had to be right there, ready for war. You never knew what might go down. If the cops attempted to stop them, if they even thought about making a mountain out of a molehill, the trio had enough firepower to turn a busy city block into any instant cemetery (no witnesses). There weren't any dead cops to speak of. Not yet. But the potential was still there. The possibilities were endless.

For now, the crew was grouped-up in the crowded, festive Manhattan Proper, a spot that Tony Cooper maintained for over a quarter century; here, even a visitor could have plenty of good times, laughs among friends, drinks, and parties, parties, parties. The kind of place you wanted to call your second home.

Freeze's cell phone was vibrating.

"It's too noisy in here, hold on." Freeze pushed the hold button on his phone and made a head-jerking motion for Squirrel to come along. Butch automatically knew he'd need to lead the way for an easy, yet affirmative, parting through the sea of patrons. Outside, there were the parked cars, double-parked cars, and two lanes of traffic making the attempt to snake along the one narrow lane that was left to pass through. A late-night crowd was scattered along the facade of the club and outside of the all-night pizza shop across the street. Somehow, it seemed that Mr. Cooper's consistence with "The Proper" was lost amongst all of this; how decades of hard work was all being taken for granted.

"I'm back. What was that again?" Freeze was back on the cell phone looking up and down Linden Boulevard for no particular reason. Butch and Squirrel posted at arm's reach.

"Get the fuck outta here . . . get the fuck outta here. Is that right . . . oh yeah? Shit!"

Freeze pulled the phone away from his face to visibly check the display. The phone seemed to be working fine, still with the "on" light showing.

"Must've got cut off."

"What happened?"

"That was Big Slim, the dude that brings the shit up here from Florida. Says he blew a tire and almost hit somebody on the road. Says that he'll be almost eight hours behind schedule. Then we got cut off. But my cell is good. Problem gotta be on his side." Freeze looked to the sky for an answer.

"That changes things a little. It puts the delivery time at high noon," he said.

"No good," Squirrel said, reading Freeze's mind.

"This is a big one. Plus, we got mad commitments on that shit. We gotta take delivery. No ifs, ands, or buts about it."

"I hope this shit's just a fluke," said Squirrel.

Freeze wagged his head before saying, "The way the man got this set up is sick. I don't really call Slim direct. That's the deal. He's not supposed to call me direct either, unless there's an emergency."

"A late delivery is an emergency?" Squirrel asked.

"That's what I'm sayin'. So somethin' gotta be wrong." Freeze raised the cell phone and hit #42. It was the speed dial to Ortiz, Charlucci's main man in South Beach.

"It's Freeze. Yo, can you talk?" Again with the north and south search down Linden. "Yo, man, Slim just hit me . . . hell yeah it was him, who else named Slim gonna call me?" There was another pause. Then Freeze said, "Says he had a blowout and will be late, 'bout noon—eight hours late. Yeah, I know this is a problem. First, ain't no contact 'posed to go down, regardless a' what. Second, a flat tire ain't no fuckin' emergency. Oh, and we set up delivery for four in the morning, not noon when the sun is out." There was another pause. Freeze listened, and then said, "Cool. I'll be waiting."

Pam informed Chief Goldridge of her progress and gave her opinion on Slim as well as her suggestion on which direction to take the investigation. He agreed with her call and approved the order for a support team of twenty additional agents, air and Coast Guard units to be on call in New York. It was 10:00 A.M. when agents arrived at the

Bronx Terminal Market, a few blocks away from Yankee Stadium, with a ramp in, a ramp out, and a service road that ran along the back behind the parallel rows of warehouses where boats once docked along the East River.

Most of that back there, the yard, the broken-down trailers, and the varying degrees of scrap metal were the result of some major distributors of produce who switched delivery to the west side of Manhattan more than ten miles away. A sign of the times. Today, the yard and the docking area behind the warehouse were deserted (almost a junkyard), rarely used, and home to a brood of stray dogs. Even for the homeless souls in the area, this was akin to a backyard; put up a cardboard box, and this was a bedroom with a view of the polluted East River.

The DEA had other plans for the area today.

Agents Brown and Evers drove a Santini garbage truck down the in-ramp. There were a couple of vehicles behind them and then there were Agents Simpson and Billings in a U.S. Mail truck. Most of the terminal's business took place between 5 A.M. and noon. So, any movement along the old cobblestone drive would be easily recognizable, which made this plan all the more difficult.

Agent Stein got a kick out of doing the disguise bit, coming up in an upper-class family and all. He was amused that a Harvard degree could get him so far in life. Today, he was filthy looking, and thanks to the nasty wool coat that his dog used as a cushion, he also stank like the mangy mutt.

Agent Denver was more or less Stein's partner, or at least that's how she felt with him teaching her the tricks of the DEA trade. When she wasn't a rookie, Denver was a wife and mother of two. Today, she was just another bag lady in a torn, forest-green raincoat that had greasy yellow daisy designs. She was looking for empty soda cans and bottles, pushing a carriage down the catwalk that ran along the loading dock in front of the eastern row of warehouses.

Many of the steel gates were closed after a long morning of business, but for a few notable outlets: Jay Walsh Produce, Fortune Foods, and Bay Rite Kosher. On the west side of the cobblestone road, Finer Meats & Produce, City Orchard, and Best Deli Supply were still doing business as well. On both sides, the catwalks and loading docks were littered with cardboard boxes and bits and pieces of vegetables that fell from the morning's purchases.

A lot of the small mom-and-pop delis from Harlem, the Bronx, and Westchester made the Bronx Terminal Market their source for wholesale fresh foods, fruits, and vegetables by the bushels and baskets; and chicken, ribs, and pork by the pound, plus all of the fixings. Many of these warehouses, especially those open now, catered to the general public, as well. In a way, this place was a smart mom's best secret, where she'd buy chicken wings, sausages, and bacon in bulk. She'd save money by storing this food in a freezer back home, the envy of her impulse-buying neighbors.

The gate to Corn on the Cob was down, but the padlock was not there, how it was supposed to be, according to Slim, the CI (confidential informant). As a CI, Slim was expected to play both sides of the field, to act and perform on behalf of the agency. This also meant that for all intents and purposes, Slim was to be protected from harm.

"Radio check, radio check. Okay, first my set-ups . . . Brown and Evers?"

"Gotcha loud and clear. You think we can get extra pay for getting our hands dirty? I thought we were enforcement, not removal."

"Easy does it, boys. Stay focused. Garbage removal, law enforcement—same thing. What about you, Simpson? How's the mail delivery going?"

"Billings is at the gate to All City Fruits. They're closed, so his next plan is to get a neighbor to accept delivery. All's well."

"Very good. Stein?"

"In place." Stein sneezed as he responded. Then he said, "I have a view of the whole east side rear entrance. Very little activity. Nothing happening with the target."

"And you, Denver?"

"The west side is the best side. Business as usual." Denver

was rubbing her nose as she spoke into the mic under her sleeve. And like the others, she had an earpiece concealed by a flopping rain hat. The way she was loaded up with the fake belly/breast combination strapped under her oversize clothing, no one would see her as anything more than an overweight, hunchbacked vagabond, picking and hunting for scraps of food for the evening's meal.

"Good money. Seager, what's your twenty?"

"I'm in the UPS garage on 138th. The troops are ready and waiting. It's gonna be your call, Masters."

"Hold tight. Our man is taking the ramp off of the Cross Bronx Expressway as we speak. He's heading south and should be at the market within ten minutes." Agent Carson was in the passenger seat of the van. Masters was in the rear, while Agent Cane drove.

"Carson to Brown, come in."

"Brown, go." The reply was audible over the receiver in an unmarked dirty white van.

"Do you have us? We're getting pretty close."

"You guys look like roaches from this high up, but I gotcha. How's Slim holding up?"

"So far so good. He's singing now. A bad singer he is, too."

"At least his wire is working. This should be business as usual guys. As soon as somebody gets a make on the contact, when the first skid hits the platform, we go in. Lock, stock, and barrel."

"At the ready, boss."

Pam Brown pulled the mic aside from her headset as she leaned forward to tell the pilot, "Push ahead of the East River. I want to get a visual on our boys in the water. And stay at two thousand feet." The chopper's propellers puck-puck-pucked along with Pam's voice.

"You got it, ma'am."

For ten years, Agent Brown had been part of these undercover operations; three of them as a supervisor. And she realized that this was to be the moment of truth; one of those dangerous moments that separated the men from the boys.

On her mental chalkboard, she could see the six backup units and a total field force of fifty men (including two women) who secured the perimeter of the market's four-block stretch. She had no doubt in her mind that in mere moments the raiding force would sweep in and arrest everyone involved. The charges would be levied as "conspiracy to traffic, distribute, and sell five hundred kilos of cocaine." Next would come the long and arduous process of feeling out the perps for information, the false promises, the bullshit, the deals with the U.S. Attorney, and so on. What else was new? All in a day's work.

CHAPTER SIX

Worm was the husky one; and Shorty was, well . . . shorter 'n shit on a curb. At first sight, you couldn't imagine what the two had in common. But, between them, as gunmen for Freeze (they called Freeze "Big Dog") the two had accumulated seventeen notches on their respective belts. A notch symbolized a dead body (whether by war or execution), and Worm had ten of 'em at last count. To mark the occasions, he tattooed a teardrop on his inner wrist for every deceased person. Shorty had an ongoing argument with Worm, saying that he actually, and in fact, did have ten bodies—not seven.

"Just 'cuz they ain't heard from them three should be enough to tell you the real," explained Shorty. He couldn't come up with any tangible evidence—no photos or testimonies. "So, you need to take my word on that there."

His was a unique method; he didn't much care to hang around even for a minute after the deed was done. He did a few "stop and drops" (he called them), where he'd walk right up to a target in broad daylight, or dead of night, and shoot him at point-blank range. But one of the three unresolved issues (as far as Worm was concerned) was a drive-by on East Tremont. All Shorty could say was blood was everywhere and that there was an obituary. Yet, both shooters knew damned well blood didn't mean deceased, and that an obituary could be made up by anyone who knew how to place a classified ad in the *Daily News*.

"Yeah, but that Puerto Rican dude was a done deal, yo. I stabbed that mothafucka till he looked like a water filter," argued Shorty.

To which Worm responded, "Show me the body, man. That's all I'm sayin'. Wasn't no funeral for the dude. We ain't actually stepped in Gilmore's Funeral Home to see that job. So, that shit ain't legit."

"Man, you just jealous 'cause you ain't the only thorough mothafucka on the planet."

"Could be. But if I'm not, at least I'm in first place."

"You ain't in no—"

A car rolled up.

"Yo, wassup, Squirrel?"

"Peace. Y'all ready?"

"Shee-it . . . is you ready, nigga? I was born ready," replied Shorty.

"Yeah, man, we ready," added Worm.

"Okay. They got it set up down there. DEA agents got the drop spot cased out. But we got a lead on 'em hours ago. They got about forty, maybe fifty agents on the ground, and they probably got a helicopter." Squirrel had that jerking motion, something of a habit, where he turned his head immediately, establishing eye contact, but with no one in particular. Now he shifted the eyes and head to Worm. And there was this big smile, like this was really getting to the good part.

"Did you here that?" said Shorty, excited.

"They're all gonna be waiting for a delivery—one of those eighteen-wheelers. There's a big yellow corn on the cob on the trailer, can't miss it. Pigs'll be focusing on that. But what Big Dog wants is to make an example out of a couple of agents. To let 'em know can't nobody fuck up his money. You feel me?"

"Huh. Oh, I feel you all right," answered Worm, who was mounted on his Mongoose alongside Shorty. Shorty had a Yamaha SRAD. But individually, both killers had that powerful 250cc-plus engine strapped between their legs. The bikes were red and blue, respectively, and both men had black riding suits on with black gloves and helmets. The contract today was for $2,500 per body, double the usual money Freeze paid.

"So, we should keep it movin'," added Worm. "Ain't this goin' down in the next half hour?"

Squirrel nodded once, his dark glasses reflecting the bright midday sunlight that watched over New York. It was obvious that Shorty was through talkin'. He pulled his two 9mm Beretta semiautomatics from inside of his leather outfit. At the same time, he affixed his horizontal tie-down shoulder holster, pulling and adjusting it so that it seemed fitted to his body. His entire outfit now (the leather jumpsuit, the holster, and the bulletproof vest underneath) added that bulky armor to his upper body. Shorty then took up the pistols from his lap one at a time and ejected each magazine to be sure all thirteen rounds were in place. He smacked the clips back into the handles and stuck each into their sleeves.

While part one of the deadly duo secured the Velcro straps under his arms, Worm was already slinging a belt around his neck and shoulder, attaching the close-end hooks to the back and front loops welded to his street sweeper (the pet name for Uzis nowadays). Shorty let out a sigh, rolling his eyes as he did; it was his way of acknowledging that his partner, Worm, had "a chair or two missing from under his table."

In the meantime, Squirrel was amused at the two and how they playfully hated on each other, even as they surgically prepared to take human lives.

"Not for nothin', Squirrel, but who was the rat on this shipment? I want that job."

"We don't know yet. It could be the driver. We're not sure."

"Well, you let me know when you do find out. I'll do that job for free, on the house—no bullshit." Shorty mashed the kick-start with his heel and the motorcycle's engine roared. Worm did the same and the two zipped out from the overpass, leaving Squirrel behind in his black Jetta.

"Freeze," Squirrel spoke into his cell phone, "the milk-men are on the move."

With so much else going on, Freeze was a few miles away in Harlem, just leaving Sylvia's restaurant with an order of his favorite combination: barbecue chicken, collards, and yellow rice. With a wireless cell phone mic plugged to his ear, he got the play-by-play from Squirrel. All the while, Butch was his shadow in and out of the popular soul food spot.

"Well, I guess somebody's gonna be in for a surprise lunch. I just wish I was there to see the fireworks," said Freeze.

"Hey, stupid question. Is the man gonna make up for the delivery?" asked Squirrel.

"Already covered that. He's takin' the loss, says I'm one of his biggest customas, says I was worth the hit. I told 'im what we had in store for the pigs that are tryin' to set us up. That's my personal gift to the man."

"Damn. He's takin' a bite on five hunned keys? That's like eight mil."

"True that. But that don't mean shit to those boys down the way. Besides, some things you just don't question."

"So when do we take the next delivery?"

"It's already on its way. Tonight. Midnight. Queens."

"You's a bad ma'fucka, Freeze."

"Okay, I accept. Now for my next bad mothafucka move. What do we do when a bust goes down?"

"I know—phones, beepers, stash houses—all of it changed or tossed."

"See? I wish I had more dudes on the ball like you. That's the only way to stay ahead of the pigs."

Squirrel couldn't tell if Freeze was being patronizing or serious.

Freeze quickly resumed focus to say, "I need that done by five P.M."

"Done. We'll watch the evening news together. A toast to the D, to the E, and to the mothafuckin' A!"

"Yeah," said Freeze with a chuckle. Then he cut the call and climbed into the passenger's seat of the Navigator. Butch circled around to drive. The phone chirped again.

"Yeah. You're late, man. Tell me something I don't know." Freeze immediately slapped the phone shut and tossed it in the narrow space on the dashboard. "Goddamn police, tryin' to earn they money," Freeze chuckled again. "Them ma'-fuckas got balls, checkin' in an hour early and a day late. Why the fuck do I pay these pigs?"

S lim had dual emotions brewing in his mind. He was both relieved and worried to death. Relieved, because that DEA lady believed him. He was off the hook. She rescued him from those hokey cops down in Bell Glades. But, then again, Slim was worried sick about what was about to go down. He didn't have any choice but to deliver to the market, and there was no way of escaping all of these agents following him, watching him, listening even.

And then there were the drug dealers to worry about. He wondered if there was already a hit out on him for being late. No. He hadn't given the DEA lady Ortiz's name or Charlucci's name. He made up some names. Same with the contact in the Bronx. Ain't no way Slim would snitch, regardless what kind of time he'd be facing. His wife and child would just have to handle fate. If he had to do twenty or thirty years in prison, at least he could do so as a man and not a punk or a rat. And for all he knew, if he went in as a rat, he might very well be converted to a punk. He knew the stories well enough to keep his mouth shut and he watched enough of the crime dramas on TV to know how to trick that DEA lady.

But what about the New York drop? What was gonna happen now? Now . . . with the bogus telephone call to the contact . . . with the excuses . . . Is this gonna work?

Slim had an idea. A way of informing the New York boys that a setup was in place. Maybe this way he could save his life a second time. Slim began to croon. He began doing the a-cappella thing, knowing damn well that he'd be heard loud and clear by all the agents—a small audience, but an important one nonetheless.

> There I go, there I go, there I go . . .
> there I go . . .
> pretty, you are the soul
> that snaps my control.

Slim could sing the song on key, but he chose to be a nuisance. He wanted his small audience to be annoyed quickly. In the meantime, he wiggled his boot off, reached down into the hidden slit under his seat, and pulled out his cell phone. He dialed New York with his toe just in case these Feds were spying from the buildings he passed as the eighteen-wheeler lumbered off the Major Deegan thruway.

He knew he was getting closer to ground zero, and he was paranoid (to say the least), thinking that there were agents up in those windows, on street corners, and elsewhere. Anybody who wore sunglasses or baseball caps was suspect. He just knew that there was a helicopter up there somewhere with binoculars focused on him, maybe even one of those satellite surveillance whatchamacallits.

It was close now; he'd have to cross over 155th Street and head on down the road that cascaded onto the strip where the Bronx Terminal Market was located. There was no time to waste. The drop wasn't three minutes away. Slim slipped in one of his mix tapes and began rapping with whoever came over the truck's sound system. Slim turned his rig into a one-man party.

"Go Slim! It's your birthday . . . Gonna party like it's your birthday!" he chanted. "Hey, I hope I ain't lost you DEA guys. Hope I'm not driving too fast. And I hope you get these dope boys. I hope you lock 'em up and throw away the key. Those punks. The nerve of 'em sellin' drugs in New York. That stuff could even be in my children's school. Go DEA! Go DEA! It's your birthday!"

Slim was a riot, hoping that whatever he said would sink in. He was sure he poked in the right number on the cell phone and that the green "connect" signal was on. If the New York contact didn't get the message . . . if they didn't realize he was warning them, then they were mental blocks. Retards. Slim used his toe again to depress the "end" button and he reached down to slip the phone back in its hiding space. Now he was as knee-deep into this ambush as he'd ever get.

He squeezed his eyes closed and said a prayer as the truck eased down the dock in front of the establishment. He had to perform the labors of love now, swinging the tractor out into a wide angle where the front end sort of swerved into a half moon. Then Slim would cut the wheel to the furthest extent so that he could back the trailer up against the dock. The truck would still be at an angle, but that was how all deliveries were made.

Slim looked out to the left and right through the portholes, those windows that made a trucker appear to be cramped up in that cabin. He could see folks scattered, busy as usual, but he was unsure who was watching him and who could care less. In a way, it was as if everyone was watching. In his rearview mirror, he could see a postman carrying a package. He was next door to the drop, knocking at the gate. Slim ignored it and got to climbing down from his high-in-the-sky seat that made a road dog feel as though he was on top of the world. It was that feeling he had to shed now, only to be the mere mortal who was suddenly scared shitless, suddenly awakened by reality that he was being used. Big Slim, the possum.

Way down the stretch of fresh food outlets, Worm was doing what others might consider a motorcycle trick, climbing the steps that led to the five-foot-high walkway. He was moving at a speed that was beyond slow and less than top speed. It was fast enough still to frighten the few folks who jumped out of his way. Sure, he had that weapon under his armpit; but for now, the motorcycle was an even deadlier weapon.

Worm picked up speed once he recognized the big yellow

stalk of corn that designed the broadside of the eighteen-wheeler. There was no sensational plan here, nothing strategic to be followed to the tee. Just that Worm was psyched up and hyper. He was expecting agents to be hunched down, hiding behind this and that, not expecting to be hit from the back. For all he cared, anybody who wasn't busy carrying purchases was gonna catch a hot one today; and that meant $2,500 per body.

"Holla at 'cha boy!!!" Worm shouted under his helmet, zooming in on two sets of DEA boys, thinking how fucking stupid these guys had to be wearing those big-ass letters on their backs—nothing but targets. There was a big white U.S. postal truck on the side of the block where Worm was, and the other vehicle, a dark blue sedan, was across the cobblestone road parked catty-corner to where the delivery was to take place.

Worm thought there should be more police, perhaps many more, somewhere out there. But that didn't matter now. Four targets would be good enough for him: $10,000. Ka-ching! But of course, if others should come out of the woodwork with those padded-up paramilitary outfits they liked to wear, they'd better lay that ass down, 'cause Worm was ready to lay 'em down if they didn't. For good.

This took balance, to ride his Mongoose with no hands while he took hold of the sweeper. In that instant, Worm realized there were even more agents up on the roof adjacent to the platform on which he was speeding. Already, he was calculating how his ammo would be used. There were thirty-round magazines taped back-to-back, snug in the weapon's housing. He knew from past drive-bys that sixty rounds could spit within less than a minute. His concern was focus and aim.

"Be the bullet," he told himself, knowing that where his eyes could see was where the lead would be sent. He was close enough now; close enough to see the agents on the roof with AK-47s. Worm was shooting at them now, taking aim at the group in front of him, then across the street, then up on top above those targets. He didn't care at this point who was hit or how. He didn't care about their backs being turned or that they were caught off guard. All he knew was he had to keep it movin'. He had to keep the pressure, he had to keep his finger depressed on the trigger, and he had to keep those metal casings flying until there were immediate casualties.

Shit! We're under attack!" shouted Agent Case. Only minutes ago he'd checked his weapon, readied the bullhorn, and hopped out of the driver's seat. Case was aware of the primaries, the six men in full raid gear who were waiting in the rear of the U.S. postal truck. But where were they now?

Carson was the first to realize what the hell was happening. He wasted no time in lunging toward Masters by his side, both of them toppling down onto the grimy area below the loading dock, with a morning's worth of debris, oil spillage, and tire residue soiling their everyday casuals. "Case! Case!" Masters saw the agent a few feet away, barely moving.

Even from a distance, Agents Bowers and Evers could hear Case's warning, although the gunfire was a distant second to the loud motor of the garbage truck. The two were at the back of the truck now, on the opposite side of the eighteen-wheeler and the menacing, violent gunfire, operating the lift that pulled those heavy metal trash containers up by chains and hooks.

The container was tipping now, with its contents emptying into the back of the garbage truck. An operator was to rattle the container at this point and then pull the lever for the container to be lowered again. But Evers and Bowers bolted for the front of the truck, reached inside for their firearms, and split up to answer the need for assistance.

Simpson heard it, too, and immediately shifted his attention to the rapid gunfire. Things seemed to be happening so fast out there, outside of the safety of the postal truck, that it was hard to get a hold on where the attack was coming from or how many were doing the shooting. All he could think of was Billings out there without a gun in hand, knockin' on gates for some bogus package delivery.

"Yo! Billings! Take cover!" Simpson yelled out from the driver's side window. But now bullets were hitting the postal truck. Popping sounds riddled the exterior like metal raindrops. Simpson made a quick dive through to the back of the truck. The team back there, all in body armor, with automatic weapons, looking like black Mutant Ninja Turtles in their paratrooper suits, were already shouting.

CHAPTER SEVEN

"Go! go! go!"

In assault formation, agents were crashing through and springing out of the truck's rear doors.

"What the fuck is happening down there? Who gave the command to move in? Hey! Is anyone hearing me?"

"Brown, this is Carson. We're under fire down here! Case is down . . ."

"Down? Down!???"

"He's hit, ma'am—bleeding heavily from the collarbone."

"Who initiated?"

"I can't say. I believe we're being pinned down by automatic weapons. Sounds like Uzis. I saw a man on a motorcycle. Shit! OH GOD—we need a medic over here. Fast! Hold on, Case. Hold on!"

Pam Brown's earpiece was busy with varying messages. Carson was speaking to her, and then he wasn't—somehow captive in the emergency at hand. Pam felt helpless with her boys down there in an unexpected battle. And now one of them was hit. Critical. Time to call in the reinforcement. Shit.

"Seagar! Come in, Seagar!"

"Seagar here."

"Move in, Seagar. Move in. We've been made . . . we're

under attack!" Pam was squeezing the armrest and her left foot was tapping the floor of the chopper in a nervous repetition. How could they know we were coming? She considered the variables, then growling at the pilot, she said, "Take me down."

This crisscross drive-by attack was Shorty's idea. It worked once before when the two hit the Puerto Ricans in a battle over some petty bullshit turf war. One of those dudes had the audacity to blame Big Dog for a heist. Heists were taking place in every borough, and still they wanted to pick Freeze. They slandered the wrong mothafucka.

The drive-by followed and both Worm and Shorty were happy with how it worked. First, they had the element of surprise going for them. And second, just when the targets thought they knew where the attack was coming from, just when they (maybe) pointed and fired in that very direction, another attack was launched a moment later, once again blessing the occasion with an element of surprise.

It was no different now at the Bronx Terminal Market, as Shorty shot up the steps and across the platform opposite of Worm. He could even see Worm in the distance, attracting all the attention, fire spitting from the weapon in his hand. Split-second timing was essential right now. If Shorty didn't maintain the impact of the offensive strike, the enemy would get a chance to think; an opportunity to aim and possibly hit his partner. He acted fast, already waving two guns as he maintained balance of the motorcycle with his hips and thighs alone.

With the Rugers firing, Shorty was gunning for the dark blue suits, with those big yellow letters being all the targets he needed. Shorty was certain those vests and padding would prevent any serious damage. That's why he aimed for the heads and lower bodies. And within seconds, he emptied half of the thirteen-round clips from each pistol. He didn't bother counting casualties, but there were fallen agents. Of that he was sure.

◆ ◆ ◆

The whole purpose of an undercover disguise is to go unnoticed. But that theory was so far from the truth right now.

Stein, with the homeless alias and the Glock 40, was on the east side around back. When the ambush went down, he was deep into his act, being nosy—near as he could to the back of the cocaine drop. But as soon as Pam Brown put the fire in his ass, he shed his mangy wool coat and prepared for war. He slid the Glock from that Velcro-adjustable, pancake-style holster on his hip and sprinted around to assist.

When Agent Denver emerged from the west side of the markets, she came face-to-face with her fate. She managed to get off three rounds, hitting the larger gunman and his motorcycle as he descended jumping down off the platform. But he was coming too fast and too erratically for her to escape his fall. All of it, the heavy mass of metal with an injured gunman operating it, slammed into Agent Denver, leaving machine and flesh in a smoking, bloody, mangled heap.

The tactical team from the postal truck was ineffective considering the element of surprise and the speed at which Shorty was moving. They were all lying flat in the middle of the road in effort to lessen his visible targets, aiming their various weapons at the speeding gunman from less than a hundred feet and expanding. The shotguns weren't appropriate for long-distance shooting, and those with the AKs simply missed their target. Shorty was already airborne off of the edge of the platform.

Reinforcement teams were alerted about the ambush, and they began forming a barricade with their vehicles near the entrance and exit to the area where the markets were located.

In the meantime, Pam Brown ordered the chopper to land in the yard where all of the debris was—the disabled vehicles, discarded truckers' tires, and stray animals scurrying about on the east side in the rear of the strip of markets. It was difficult

to get an aerial view of the melee in front because the platforms were hooded and the overpass of the thruway was so
close. She just decided that this would be the time when
she'd get her hands dirty—show her mettle. If it's on, it's on,
she determined.

Just as the chopper was hovering down to nearly forty
feet off of the ground, Pam spotted one of the gunmen racing along the back, kicking up a smoke screen of dirt in his
wake. He was doing a wheelie now, and she could see he was
a short son-of-a-bitch, maybe even shorter than a jockey.
And now what was he doing? Standing up on the seat? Doing tricks??

"Follow him—right there!" Pam had a tough voice; affirmative, but not too excited or overanxious. "Can we get
lower? Maybe I can get a shot at him."

"I can try. It looks like he's boxed in, though."

Pam considered this while she was panning the area. Her
agents were closing in behind. Three sedans were in pursuit
while others were on foot, apparently having cut through
from the loading docks out front. There was a parking
garage in the distance closed off by a concrete barricade
weathered by years of neglect and erosion. Weeds had
pushed through the asphalt and vines climbed along the pil-
lars. Pam figured the gunman was headed there, maybe his
way out of his dead end. Where else would he go?

To the immediate right of the abandoned garage was a
massive wall, big and tall enough to be a dam. The wall was
graffiti-ridden, with three competing designs painted on its
surface—the faces of hip-hop's greatest personalities: Big,
Pac, and Pun, with names that seemed to explode in bright
colors on the wall right above the legendary images. In an instant, Pam could see that this was the wall that was recognizable from the thruway, an artistic expression that she'd seen
maybe once or twice before. Creative if she did say so herself.

But where's he goin'? "Oh shit! He's not going for the
garage." Pam took an emotional, audible breath that seemed
to inflate her eyes in their sockets. "Oh . . . my . . . God."
Pam dragged the words as she watched in horror.

◆ ◆ ◆

Shorty may have been playfully hatin' on Worm, but Worm was his partner for life. And they had a pact. They would never allow the other to be arrested or taken to jail. They'd never bitch up when it came to covering one another under fire. And finally, if one man took a bullet, then the other would feel the wound as well. A lot of others may have claimed that ride-or-die attitude, but Shorty meant it. He lived it. He walked the walk. The last things Shorty saw after Worm was shot down was a lot of smoke, twisted metal, a shitload of cops, and his speedometer reading 110 mph. There was also the matter of the three hip-hop legends on the great wall before him; his heroes next to Worm. Now that Worm was gone, Shorty assumed that "fuck it" attitude.

While the motorcycle bolted straight for the wall of rap legends, he performed his last stunt, climbing up on his seat until he was standing tall and facing his enemies. He emptied any rounds that he had left, spraying live lead at the army of vehicles chasing him. He also aimed for the chopper overhead. Seconds later, there was a fourth painting on that very wall: the blood and guts of that crazy-ass killer, Shorty.

CHAPTER EIGHT

ey! I was hoping to see you. Can you tell these dudes that I'm one of the good guys—to take these cuffs offa me?" Slim was subtle and confident about what he wanted. He also had a twisted grin across his lips, directed at the agents who were in the vicinity, in front of the police cruiser and outside behind the DEA lady. He was going above their heads.

"Oh—geee, Slim. Sorry about that. Say, Slim . . ." Pam was standing before the open door, mere feet from where Slim looked up at her, listening. "Do you know what this is?" If silence had a sound, it would grind and screech and burn rubber right about now. Pam was holding a cell phone that looked to be Slim's own. The one which he kept hidden (he called it his grimy line) in the driver's seat of his tractor.

To fill the moment, Slim played it off, resuming his acting routine. "Uh . . . that's my phone," Slim exclaimed, wearing that great discovery on his face. "I lost that thing. Where'd you find it?"

"Slim, this isn't your phone," said Pam in a cold tone of voice. "It's the one we switched with yours back in Bell Glade. It's the one we have linked up with our communications network, as if we were your personal operator eavesdropping on your little . . ."

Pam suddenly flipped. She was yelling at the top of her lungs and she also threw the cell phone hard at Slim's chest.

Now, she lunged at him. Screaming, "You son-of-a-bitch! You asshole! I believed you! It's because of *you* that six of my agents were shot and killed today!"

In the meantime, while Pam's hands were clenching Slim's shirt, nearly ripping it from his torso, EMS personnel were carrying the bodies, rolling them on gurneys, and filling their ambulance vehicles. The true story was that three of six who were shot were in critical condition. One by one, the trucks raced off to the nearest emergency room. There was a coroner's wagon as well for the two dead agents.

Pam slapped Slim and was steadily pounding on his chest in a fit of rage that others had never seen before. She was red-eyed and crazed; and now her subordinates were prying her off of Slim, trying to get her out of the car and back to her senses. Slim appeared to be paralyzed with his eyes fully dilated, looking like he had just shit his pants.

"I promise you," Pam finally managed to say, wiping a bit of spittle from her mouth with her wrist, "I'm gonna have you prosecuted to the fullest—every single charge that the law will allow—" Her words were barked, with that fiery determination powering them. "—And once you're convicted, I'm gonna see to it that you're buried so deep in the earth, so far under the jail, that they'll be able to see your slimy ass on the opposite side of the planet."

Masters was the closest of all the agents surrounding their supervisor, helping to console her as best he could without crossing the line of professional ethics, that thin line between man and woman. For most of the agents on the scene, this had been a tumultuous experience, being pinned down under those heavy showers of hot lead. For a couple others, it was point-blank tragic. But, bigger than all of that, this string of events was only the beginning.

No shit . . . no shit . . . ain't that a . . . you sure you ain't pullin' my leg . . . damn, it was like that? As long as you okay, that's all that matters, right? Good. Listen, keep in touch with me. Lemme know of any further developments. Dig it?" Freeze laid down the cell on the table, close to where the collective of diner table items (sugar, salt, pepper, and ketchup) were situated under the window. He could see passing traffic out on Merrick Boulevard. And of course, even though his mind wasn't with her at present, Tonya was sitting across from him in the booth inside the USA Diner, wondering if she had his attention.

"Sorry, baby. Usual politics," Freeze explained, even though he didn't necessarily have to. His girl was looking especially fine this evening, with her lips like shimmering raspberries in that sexy pout.

"You think I can get a word or two in before that goddamned phone rings again?" Tonya was becoming irate. And all the attitude in the world was tied up in her expression.

"Whateva," said Freeze, cavalier as he could be. Yet his eyes shifted behind those Gucci shades of his, checking to see if Tonya's volume attracted attention. So far, it didn't.

"Okay, so good for you. I got a point to make here, so could you put your business on hold for a couple?"

"Business is always first, baby. But go 'head and say your piece."

"You know, Freeze, you 'n I been doin' this thing for like two years now and I ain't sayin' I don't appreciate us or nothin'. It's just I need a little goddamned attention now and then. Our love life is so fuckin' simple it makes me sick."

Freeze was listening, but not really hearing Tonya. His mind was on the phone call. *Damn. Both of his shooters dead. They went down blazin' 'n all, but damn. Shorty. Why'd he have to go out like that?*

"Nightclubs, diners, shopping, fucking—that's all the fuck we do, Freeze. And then, you bless me with a leather coat or a fur and you think it's all good? Well, it ain't all good . . ."

I hope Squirrel took care of the phones and pagers. We need them shits quick, no tellin' how close the Feds are to us. At least we got some of them Feds. That'll show 'em not to fuck wit' us. Gotta get a message to Florida. Tell 'em 'bout our little payback.

". . . can't we go on a vacation once in a while? Maybe to

Vegas or Hollywood or the Bahamas? Can't we even go to the beach or on a picnic? And anotha thing . . ."

"May I take your order?" the waitress asked, showing up out of nowhere in her apron and innocence.

"I ain't eatin'. I'm sick of diners." Tonya directed her venom across the table.

Freeze ignored her and said, "She'll take a turkey club sandwich, hold the bacon, and I'll—"

"I said, I ain't hungry."

"I'll have the biggest steak you got in the house. Throw in some baked potatoes and corn. We'll have a bottle of champagne, too. Your best."

"Will that be all?"

"I am not—"

"Yes, that's all." Freeze cut Tonya off again and with his eyes alone willed the waitress to go on about her business. Tonya was about to speak again, but Freeze took his forefinger to his lips and said, "Shhhh." In the same motion, his other hand reached under his jacket and pulled out a thin jewelry box. He laid it flat on the table. Tonya's eyes followed it as Freeze slid it in front of her. She would've put her hands on her hips if she were standing.

Instead, she said, "See what I mean? You think you can just buy my way to happiness, and that ain't gonna work, Freeze." Freeze opened the box as Tonya stuttered, looking down at a sparkling diamond necklace. On it was a pendant, also embedded with diamonds. Cash this baby in and you'd have enough for a down payment on a car.

"Fr-eeee-ze." Tonya sighed, and maybe his name oozed out from her delicious lips on its own. Freeze lifted the necklace from the box and encouraged Tonya to lean forward so he could drape it around her neck. She melted like butter in his hands, taking his palm to her check. "Oh Freeze . . . it's . . . it's beautiful. I swear you make me feel so special sometimes. But I'm such an ungrateful bitch." Freeze was thinking the same thing about her: the part about being an ungrateful bitch. "It's just . . . I'm miserable without you, man. If I'm not with you, I don't have no social life. But even when I am with you, I can't say I have a social life. Your guards be around us like shadows; sometimes I think I know Squirrel better than I know you."

Freeze had his elbows on the table, his hands together and his fingers in a steeple. When Tonya brought up his boy's name (it was the way she said it), it almost sounded as if there was more to read between the lines . . . as if she'd considered fucking Squirrel. In the next split second, Freeze slapped the shit out of Tonya. He didn't even wind up, just put it out there like a flash, one time across the whole of her cheek. She was leaned over toward the window now with her hands covering her face as though to protect herself from a second attack.

"One thing you ain't gonna do, woman, is disrespect me. The fuck I look like, a rubber plant you can just bounce shit off of?" Freeze looked at his palm now (the weapon), maybe to see if he was injured. He rubbed his hands together, though without lotion, and eventually they came together as if holding a softball under his chin. He looked at Tonya, remembering that two years earlier the bitch was working at a fast food joint making chump change. She didn't even know how to dress. Now he was lacing her in Dolce & Gabbana, Versace, and a wardrobe of that Baby Phat gear. He changed her from a bum bitch into a hundred-thousand-dollar bitch . . . and she wanna make a scene at the goddamned USA Diner?

"You can stop all that shit, girl. Stop actin' like a scared animal. Take your sorry ass in the bathroom and clean up. Go on."

Tonya gradually straightened herself and got up to head for the ladies' room. She maintained one rule while she was with Freeze or out in public: she wouldn't cry.

"Whassup, Tonya." Squirrel spoke as he passed her, strolling to the seat she just rose from. Tonya didn't answer Squirrel, just diverted eye contact. It was one of the few times he'd seen her pretty eyes in a state of agony. It made him ask, "Whassup with her, Big Dog?" Squirrel sat across from Freeze now.

"Ain't shit. She just needed to fix her erection."

"Huh? I ain't even gonna ask."

"Good idea. You got the shit?"

"Mmm-hmm. Here's your personal phone, and here's your hot phone. The contact numbers are on the backs. Oh, and a couple of two-way joints. When our people find your old numbers disconnected they'll probably get at me and I'll give 'em the new numbers."

"Or, you can handle the shit yourself. I tell ya, Squirrel, sometimes I get tired of the same ole mess. It gets to the point where I'm sick. Here I am doing like five hundred keys a month and I still gotta deal with stupid mothafuckas. The bum-ass cops callin' me an hour 'n a half after I done already heard shit through the grapevine. Plus, I got pushers on the street, ma'fuckin' hoods who think they dealers, street thugs who think they entrepreneurs. Everybody wants to be Big Dog. They get a little money and get stupid. Ma'-fuckas don't wanna play they position. And when they get stupid, they gotta get dead."

"I dig it," said Squirrel. "Chips was one a' them. Dumb as a bag a' rocks. Asshole blew his first piece of change on a goddamn platinum Cadillac jeep. Then he drove the shit all through the hood like he's the Pope coming to town or some shit."

"Mmm-hmm, and we told that fool to take it slow, that he'd draw too much attention."

"You ain't gotta tell me, Big Dog. We did the right thing. Fo' sure, like four other people took over his customers. I even got a trick who's fitty-five. Fitty-five fuckin' years old. Livin' in the suburbs, up in Rockland County. She's running a fuckin' casino in her house, got all kinds a' housewives coming over to gamble and do blow. Plus, she got these young Chippendale dudes who come over and bang them mommies daily."

"How much she in for?" Freeze asked, his eyes cutting over to the ladies' room in the distance.

"Eight keys a week. I know it's small, but shit adds up. Then, I got Pops over in Atlantic City. That ma'fucka is doin' it big. He takes down like ten keys in a week. Plus, he wanna go higher. I'm like, 'Slow down, Pops 'fo you overdo it.' Ma'fucka think he's thirty years old again, carryin' two guns 'n everything."

Freeze uttered a slight inward chuckle, finding the idea humorous. An "old head" pushing coke like that. Like he was a cowboy from the Wild West.

"So then, we got all five hunned spoken for?"

"If you count De Jesus, them bodegas, them North Carolina dudes and Tuck. Tuck is the biggest fish. He's waitin' on a hunned keys, just as much as all the bodegas put together. Up on Fordham and Two-four-one, too. He even got mad customers up in the hospital, Fordham University, plus that whole shopping strip from Boston Road to Jerome."

"Make sure we get on that later. I definitely want a piece of him. Now 'bout tonight. Queens."

"I just got off the phone with Will, the dude who works at the funeral home. He's ready for the drop."

"Good. This is real quiet. Charlucci sent the load on a fish truck, even got lobster and crab legs on that motha."

Squirrel made a face when he heard "crab legs."

Then Freeze said, "Man, you ain't had shit if you ain't had a plate of crab legs. Lemme find out you ain't into seafood like that."

"Only when it comes to the freaks, Big Dog. I'm a deep sea diver when it comes to that." Squirrel stopped himself from licking his lips. Just the thought . . .

"What else we got?"

"That's it, really. We gonna spring for the funerals, right?"

"Sometimes I think we should buy stock in that funeral home as much business as we givin' 'em. Yeah, do that shit right. Them boys represented. I still can't believe Shorty went out like that."

"Dude said some of Shorty's bones is stuck on the wall with all his blood," said Squirrel.

Freeze wagged his head. He said, "Yeah, do that shit right. I don't care what it costs." *Where's that bitch at*, Freeze wondered as he looked over to the restrooms again.

"Your food, sir," the waitress offered. Squirrel got up.

"I'm out, Big Dog. I'm checkin' on this dude Roscoe for our new . . . to ahh . . . replace them two."

"I gotcha," Freeze said, wanting to avoid further conversation. "Handle ya business."

CHAPTER NINE

By far, Gilmore's Funeral Home was a booming business. The headquarters (a two-story, redbrick, Colonial-style building, complete with ivory-white columns and windowpanes) sits smack-dab in the heart of Linden Boulevard. And Linden Boulevard being one of the busiest arteries in Queens, Gilmore's seems like the calm amidst the storm. Manicured lawns, colorful flower beds, and a simple picket sign has been the Gilmore appearance for decades. To the left of the building, on the same large property, there was a row of one-story garages, eight of them in all, and a two-hundred-car parking lot. Disneyland entertains tourists, Toyota makes cars, and Gilmore's buries folks.

Will Chambers came to work at Gilmore's by no coincidence. When his uncle on his mother's side died, Will's mother suggested that her son try and work there.

"Try and do something useful . . . something of value with your life," she had said to him. Never did Will imagine that he'd come to work in the vicinity of dead people; however, once he got comfortable, once he showed care and respect for those to whom he tended, Reverend Gilmore took him in, trusting him as a full-time employee. Once Will had full access, it wasn't long before he was corrupted by the promises of great wealth. He was at the point in life where he was impressionable: to be locked into a job where there was certainty and security; to feel like the mule doing the same played-out thing every day; to realize what the ceiling would be for someone like him (on the one hand) and then to see the bling-blingin' (the fancy cars and fly lifestyles) in the street, in magazines, and on television ("Those damned videos!" his mother used to exclaim) was a reality that he chose not to comprehend. It was an imbalance, which he chose not to pick apart to find out how or why. It all just put two sides of the street in his face, the bling-bling or the job thing. One or the other, and the choice was obvious to him. Yet, without a viable plan to obtain wealth in a righteous way, Will was easily swayed by that age-old rumor, the wherewithal to acquire something for nothing.

Freeze was the CEO of the something for nothing industry, the buying and selling of drugs; Squirrel was his general manager. And Will was working for two separate missions. Squirrel had no choice himself but to make frequent visits to Gilmore's, since operating and managing such an organization called for supporting one another during childbirths, weddings, graduations, hospitalizations, and finally, funerals. If someone served well during their time with the organization, it was only right to reciprocate. So, Freeze made trips to the wakes for his most productive pushers and associates.

There was Disco, the mothafucka who sold weed just as much as he danced. There was Sherry (President's woman). President was one of the main reasons why Freeze excelled early in the game, leaving the weed and the pills alone to get to the big white rock or the great white powder. So, when his baby's momma got caught up in an eight-car pileup during the winter, Freeze came through. He paid for the arrangements and attended the funeral. There was even his man Rashid. Rashid carried a big piece of Church Avenue up until he was stabbed to death. Freeze couldn't figure out what the man was doing outside at the subway station—after all, Rashid kept more than a dozen rides that cost him $50,000 or better.

Oh well . . . easy come, easy go, Freeze determined. And after he arranged for King Ike to replace Rashid, he paid for the arrangements and attended the funeral. Naturally, progress took its course and Freeze became less accessible to the dealers he serviced. And when larger amounts of cocaine came into the picture, the casualties of the so-called drug war added up. If there weren't slayings over who sold what to whom, or who owed what to whom, then there were all of the dudes (fallen soldiers, Freeze called them) who fell prey to the justice system. Freeze could remember all of their names at one point. Akbar. Jimmy Dean. Matthews. Peter, and on and on.

But eventually, brothers in the game who ended up on lockdown with twenty-five years or better were too many to remember. Eventually, to Freeze, those cats were thought of as the sacrificial lambs. And Freeze told himself time and time again that he'd die first before taking that same fall.

These days, Freeze had others to keep up with all the business management. He'd just send Squirrel in to represent. And then Squirrel began to delegate. How many times he'd gone to Gilmore's, sitting beside family members in mourning as they lined up for a "consultation" with the reverend, he couldn't count. People were dying every day, Squirrel figured. And one way or another, they had to be taken care of when their time was up. Go Gilmore.

Once Squirrel found that these consultations were but lengthy sales pitches coupled with prayer, he demanded to cut to the chase.

"You handle it," he told Will. And Will had done so dozens of times since they'd originally met. Death certificates, viewings of the bodies, casket selections, and in some instances, even deciding what would be marked on the tombstone.

This particular visit to the funeral home (the follow-up delivery) was real sensitive, so Squirrel was there to see the shipment through from A to Z. He was able to get with Roscoe earlier to take him and his Mo' Money Brothas on as additional support. And now, as the rig weaved its way through the open gate, Squirrel could see a number of the MMBs in their specific positions. The Queens Public Library was just across the street; Rasta-Terhane was standing in the dark doorway. Squirrel presumed the dreadlocked gunman to be cocked and loaded with that oowop—the machine pistol that had a two-hundred-yard reach and sprayed on command.

There was also Tec-9; and that wasn't merely a name for that notorious semiautomatic, it was also the nickname for the Mo' Money Brotha who was sitting on the stoop outside of the tax preparation office, also across the street. Where he sat was mighty dark, but anyone who knew Tec-9 also knew he kept the "heat" closer than a hand in glove. Then there was Roscoe, standing closest to Squirrel.

"Who's the fourth man?" asked Squirrel.

"He goes by the name Rook. Like the rook on a chessboard," said Roscoe.

"How come I ain't meet him?"

"He's like that, like a rook. Laying back in the cut, inconspicuous-like, holding down the line. But just 'cause you can't see him don't mean nothin'. He'll come out blazin' if anything pops off. Believe it."

"Yeah, well, I don't like dealin' with ma'fuckas I can't meet in person."

"You gonna have to take my word, Squirrel." And then Roscoe changed the subject, saying, "By the way, this is a helluva idea for a drop. Who would guess?"

"Mmm-hmmm," Squirrel said, with an all-aware expression that still hung on to the idea of trust. He still wanted to get a look at Rook, but there were more pressing concerns right now.

As the truck pulled in to park, its engine made the asphalt vibrate below both men, knocking, squeaking, and finally hissing its exhaust fumes. Will was signaled now, and he emerged from inside the funeral home to open the garages and ready the hearses.

Wearing his signature green Kangol hat, Roscoe looked on from a short distance with his hand on the 9mm. He considered the events that brought him to this funeral home in the middle of Queens, working for one of New York's most powerful underground figures. If it wasn't for the money aspect, the $2,000 cash for securing the late-night transaction, Roscoe would be back in Brooklyn now. He'd be doing his own thing. Running his own game. And, now that he thought about it, how notorious could this Freeze cat be if he needed MMB to do his security?

Roscoe recalled something about the two shooters that met their Maker earlier that day. And maybe that's why Roscoe accepted the challenge. To show these guys how the job is really done, how to really secure a high-risk mission. Eventually, word would get around and it would add to the MMB equity. "Roscoe did big things with Freeze," they'd say. But shit, Roscoe thought. Why isn't it the other way around? How difficult could it be to do what Freeze does? Buying large and reselling to a network.

Then Roscoe did the damnedest thing. He considered what other thorough dope boys around the way—the hardest gangstas—would think if he took Freeze out. After all, those Italian boys took out their own man—that Castellano dude. Tiger Woods took out Jack Nicklaus. And someday, Roscoe figured, a young buck's gonna flatten Michael Jordan's record. Everybody gets outdone one way or another. That was life.

Roscoe and MMB did their part until the transaction was done with. Squirrel stood by the whole time while a few of his helping hands removed the load of fish and cocaine. They carried all of it into those garages where the hearse limos were parked. Then the eighteen-wheeler eased out of the lot with four black Cadillac hearse limousines trailing behind. A half hour later, the parties disappeared, scattering in different directions. That meant a street-value of twenty million in cocaine was now making its way into the boroughs of New York.

Slim had been processed by law enforcement in the past— a ticket here and there—usually in some small town where the highway patrol was working to meet their quota of collars. But this was a first. The Feds. Everything in here seemed such a big deal. He was initially transported to Federal Plaza, a downtown conglomerate of granite and limestone buildings that embodied all the various law enforcement agencies (departments of this and that). It was a machine meant to keep crime and punishment in check. The police station; the courthouse; the jail.

There were two vehicles, both sedans, which took Slim on that ominous trip to the Metropolitan Correction Center. They moved through traffic at high speed, along the expressway and along a few city streets, as if Slim were some foreign spy and this was a top-priority mission to lock him up. Four agents escorted him in handcuffs and shackles. They were silent for most of the "perp walk," now and again consulting one another about the processing of their prisoner— looking at one another with that stupid look whenever Slim had a question.

It was dark out as the motorcade came to a halt at the driveway entrance to MCC-NY, yet Slim could see how everything was concrete and galvanized steel, made to contain human beings of any size no matter how violent or dangerous. A massive steel door lifted mechanically and the vehicles crawled into a garage. Two agents remained in the garage and two proceeded with the processing.

NO FIREARMS INSIDE, a sign read. And Slim observed the DEA agents as they placed their weapons in a wall cavity. Then a heavy iron door opened and the agents helped Slim into the foyer. There was enough glass for Slim to see into the control room, with its video monitors, switches, buttons, phones, and indicator lights. The gatekeepers could also see Slim through that same glass, but somehow they didn't seem as intimidating as all of the architecture and mechanical systems that they controlled. Inside, there was an instant climate of subordination. Constant locking and unlocking of doors. Constant coordination of all movement. Penny-perfect efficiency. A man in surgical gloves told the agents, "Okay, he's ours now." And the agents removed the cuffs and shackles. Slim was fingerprinted, brought to another room, and directed to strip. Once his street clothes were placed in a brown grocery bag, he was given a series of commands. Butt naked in front of a total stranger, Slim submitted to every request, wondering all the while if the guy had to see naked bodies like this all day or night—*how can he sleep at night? Maybe he gets off on looking at assholes and balls?*

Following orders, Slim lifted his arms and showed the palms and backs of his hands. He lifted his testicles and then turned around to bend over and spread his ass cheeks.

"Okay, put these on," the guard said as he handed Slim used underwear, undershirt, socks, and pants that stretched to fit the waist but not his body. Minutes later, a woman came in and asked Slim a series of questions. *No*, he didn't plan on killing himself, nor was he having doubts about his future. *Yes*, he had family at home who cared about him and whom he one day expected to return to. *No*, he had no allergies and he never testified against anyone before. The woman extracted a tube of blood from Slim and he was put in a jail cell, the "bullpen" they called it, where there were benches and a sink/toilet combination. Slim could only curl up and recount all the shit he'd been through in the past twenty-four hours. It was enough to make him doze off, to make him want to wish it all away. Or, at least, try to.

At the bar inside of the midtown Sheraton Hotel, Pam Brown sat staring. Her hands were cupped around a six-ounce glass of rum and Coke. A traveler saw that she was alone and took a shot at striking up a conversation. Pam could virtually read the guy's thoughts: *What the hell. It's one in the morning. She's alone. I'm alone . . .*

And then, to qualify Pam's thoughts, the guy said, "I noticed you were alone. You mind?" He indicated the stool next to her.

"I'm not alone," said Pam. "I'm with fifteen others—all men. And yes, I *do* mind."

"Oooh, real affirmative type, aren't you? I like affirmative women. They know what they want, and—"

"Listen, it's been a long, long, long day. And I really don't have any patience for a lonesome traveler who's looking to plug up somebody's hole." Pam was facing him now, with those no-nonsense eyes, one of them with the brow raised in a dare. The traveler had grabbed a pretzel. And now, thanks to Pam's quick wit, he was nearly choking on it. There was sudden coughing, then the guy lurched over the bar, catching Pam off guard. She became immediately concerned, not wanting to touch the guy, but feeling behooved to assist.

"Bartender! Water! Please, he's choking."

The bartender, cute enough to be a runway model, hurried over and poured, all in the same swift movement. The choking man took the glass with both hands like a feeble nincompoop. Pam didn't see the man's eyes or how he avoided meeting hers. She didn't even realize that her hand was on his shoulder.

"Are you all right?"

"Sure. Sure. Why don't you stab me next time?"

"Or shoot you. How about that?" Pam countered once she realized he was okay. "Good night," she said, and took Mr. and Mrs. Two Feet across the carpet toward the hotel elevators. Any other time she may have considered a fling. She might have fed into the traveler's little performance and played the submissive role just so she could get her rocks off. But there was too much going on. Too much to think about. She had Slim; that much was clear. But to get behind Slim's eyes, in his head, that was the key now. And time was of the essence. Because come daylight there'd be a public defender at Slim's side telling him all about the fact that the DEA had nothing on him, that there had been an illegal search down in Bell Glade, and that the abrasions on his face would help him get bail at the arraignment. The magistrate would have pity and Slim'd be set free. Pam had to get information from Slim, and she had to do it at once. Two hours' sleep was all she'd need. Then she'd be off to MCC in lower Manhattan.

• • •

For Steve Masters to wake his supervisor, he had to ring her room a half dozen times. Finally, they stopped for a coffee as a jump-start before heading over to MCC. The staff at the detention center invited the agents in, and before long they were walking the hallway, that inner labyrinth of the jail. A guard showed them to an empty room that was used for attorneys to meet with their clients or, in this case, for law enforcement to bargain with prisoners.

"I can't even count the number of meetings I've had like this, where I've had to negotiate with these . . . these miscreants. And every time, it's like I'm sitting at one more poker game." Pam took in a lungfull of air and blew it out exhaustively.

"You'll win this time. I know you will. This is just another mule. He's got no stake in the big numbers; not even a slice of the cake. It's not like he's experienced with these types of situations. Not like you are."

Pam widened her eyes at Steve's confidence in her.

Then Carson said, "We may have a card up our sleeves, Boss. You ran through every detail about Slim except one." Carson was looking into a thin file for Eric Washington, aka Big Slim. Pam took the folder from the agent and looked over Slim's last bank statement. That's when they heard Slim's muffled protests outside in the hallway.

"Naw, fuck that!!! I ain't going near that lady. I don't care!!! I ain't going in there. Get me a lawyer! I need a phone call!"

Even behind the glass the racket was loud and passionate enough for the agents to realize what was happening. They stood up to take a look at how Slim was struggling against the two guards who escorted him toward the attorney/client room. Apparently, since he stood tall enough to get a glimpse through the picture windows, Slim had noticed the agents first. Pam rose from her seat and approached the door to the room. When she opened it, Slim froze. The two guards seemed about ready to call for backup.

"No, it's okay. Please." Pam addressed the guards, indicating that she could handle it from here; that she'd be able to restore sense in this erratic prisoner. She went on to say, "Slim. Slim, I got a little out of hand earlier. I'm sorry, really sorry. Please forgive me. And trust me, I didn't come here to hurt or attack you."

Slim was going through it right now, the images and flashback sensations from Bell Glade and from the scene at the Bronx Terminal Market. Sure, he was in deeper than he let on (with the drug trafficking and all), and he probably deserved an ass whipping when it came down to weighing and measuring things. But clearly, he didn't easily feed in to being a victim. Let nature and universal law pay him back. Let God balance things out, not this DEA lady.

"Will you forgive me, Slim? Will you give me a second chance? I really need you right now. Really."

Why did this lady penetrate Slim's mind so easily? There was something so affectionate about how she came across to him, so promising. On the other hand, Slim knew that never in this lifetime would he be friends with this woman. She was from a much different world than he was. And yet, they were a part of the same game.

"Come on." Pam was forward about it, taking Slim's arm and helping him up. Just her touch was enough to soothe his senses, to cross the wall between the worlds.

Back in the attorney-client room it was quiet enough to hear the central air systems hum. Slim could sense the guards out in the hallway, looking in and wishing he'd make one false move.

"There are a couple of things I want to talk about, Slim. Let me start here, and bear with me, some of these photos are gruesome. This was Karen; she was a college student and wanted to be a doctor. She wanted to help people. Now here's Karen after she jumped off the Chesapeake Bay Bridge in Maryland."

Slim looked at the second and third photos of this Karen girl. He had to wince at how pale and clammy the girl's skin looked. Slim had a different flashback now, to his friend Kendall (another road dawg) who was cut off by a driver on the Tappan Zee Bridge. Kendall tried to avoid hitting her, but in doing so, he crashed right through the guardrail, truck and all, falling a few hundred feet to his death. Slim had to identify the body later, and came to realize that Kendall didn't look too much different than this girl here.

"Now, check these folks out, Slim. There are just seven people on the sheet. Housewives. A few students. Two blue-collar workers. You know what they all have in common? They all take the bus, Slim. Well . . . one day a driver lost control of his car; he jumped the curb and plowed into a crowd of twenty-five people at high speed. Now, here's the photo of the tragedy. The seven people I'm showing you here are the ones who died. Oh, there's one other person I didn't show you. An elderly woman. This is she. The driver slammed into her first." Pam lowered her head. Slim squeezed his eyes closed. Remorse.

"Now there's one more set of photos, Slim. See this team photo? It's a football team, nothing special, college-bound high school hunks with so-so grades and good families. Now, this is Brittany, Slim. Brittany was a fourteen-year-old mentally disabled girl. She was riding her bike near the field where these boys had been hanging out. Their practice was cancelled I think. Um . . . to make a long story short, Slim, these boys, ages sixteen to eighteen, lured her off her bike and behind the bleachers at the school they attended. They persuaded her, Slim, a helpless teenage girl. Slim, are you ready for this? They raped her for hours. Hours, Slim! Can you imagine that?" Pam's voice trembled. Her eyes watered. And she withdrew from speaking further, sitting back in her chair with her hand gripping her own face as if to squeeze away the agony.

"Let me be frank with you, Slim. Or as they say, lemme keep it real with you. There is a link between all of these people that I've showed you. They're all victims of drug abuse. Not—" Pam swallowed and a tear welled up in her eye. "Not only that, Slim, the college student, Karen? She's my sister's daughter. My niece. The elderly woman at the bus stop? She was my mother." And now the tears did run. "And the fourteen-year-old, Slim . . ." Pam's voice withered. Her body shook. "The mentally disabled girl that those boys gang-raped? That was . . . this is Brittany. She's my daughter, Slim." Pam lost her composure. She stood up and headed for the door. "Excuse me, please excuse me," Pam said through her sobs. She stepped out and away, leaving Slim with Carson and Masters.

Damn," Slim gasped, reflecting on it all. Carson wagged his head, conveying to Slim that this might be the first he'd ever heard of that story.

"Damn is right, Slim. Drugs are destroying her family . . . our communities. Now do you see why we need your help?" Carson pulled his chair up to sit closer to the prisoner.

"Let's deal, Slim. Here and now. I can get you out of here. I can get you out of here within an hour."

Slim nearly inflated at the sound of the agent's words. He had to adjust himself in the seat to offer his undivided attention. His eyes seemed to grow as well. "H-how?" He barely got the word out.

"I need a name, Slim. A real name. Not something made up. No fiction. I need the people you picked up from. I need the people it was going to. I know you can help us, Slim."

"I. . . . I ain't no snitch, man. I just can't do it."

"Slim, you've gotta look past all these little schoolyard ethics—these little bullshit games about tattletales and pity pat. This is the destruction of people's lives we're talking about here. Those tragedies you just heard about are only her stories. What about mine . . . his? What about yours, Slim? Just do the research and you'll find that there are some kind of drug-related tragedies somehow, someway, somewhere in the circle of people you know."

Slim looked away from Carson, looking for a ghost on the wall to his left.

Carson couldn't tell how far along the man was, deliberating or fighting his conscience. "Tell you what," Carson said. "I'll do you one better. I don't know how you're doing financially. I'm sure these big-time dealers are paying you well, but . . . I think I can get you a few dollars for your troubles."

The idea sparked Slim's interest, but not so much as to shift his weight from one side to the next.

"How 'bout twenty thousand dollars? And your rig back."

Slim blinked, shook his head and took a look deep into Carson's eyes, maybe to find truth. "Now you're talkin'. Whadda I gotta do?"

It didn't take an hour. Slim agreed to turn on his Florida contacts, since they were farthest from his concerns back home and because he figured he'd never see them again. But not those in New York; that was too close. Too much like suicide. Slim told the truth about Ortiz, the front man for Charlucci. He told of how they met and where the DEA could find him. He detailed the Coochie Coo and how Ortiz had equity there.

After a while, Agent Masters stepped out to make some preliminary phone calls. Yes, there was actually a bar named the Coochie Coo. When he called there and asked for Ortiz, the person on the other end of the line answered, "Who should I say is calling?" Masters hung up. It was all he needed to hear. He stepped into a staff lounge where guards would lunch, where they'd get away from the realities of their job, and found Pam reading the *New York Times*. There wasn't a peep about the Bell Glade bust. But in the Metro section, the front page gave hasty details about the failed DEA sting in the Bronx:

DEA STANDOFF NETS 3 AGENTS,
2 GUNMEN DEAD.

It was messy, and Pam was glued to every word. She digressed for an instant, wondering what her hairdresser, Jenny, would say. Would she still praise Pam? Or would she be critical? And why all of a sudden did that matter?

"Hey, you okay?"

"Sure. How's it going in there?"

"We closed him. I checked out a name he gave us; sounds like a Class One. Maybe even an eight-forty-eight. I can only assume at this point. But, if we put two and two together—the five hundred keys, the setup in the Bronx—I'd say we're onto something big."

"Did you make the offer?"

"You bet. Only, I saved us five grand. He went for twenty. We couldn't have done better with cheese and a mousetrap. Of course, he doesn't get a cent until we get convicts. But, I think he's ecstatic about being a free man. As soon as you sign here, they're ready to process him. He's ready to go home."

Pam took the clipboard and scratched her signature four times. Slim was but a UPS package to be signed for.

"Done deal. Oh . . . by the way, that was a superb performance in there. I'm gonna make sure to nominate you."

"Huh?" Pam said with a peculiar smile.

"For an Oscar," said Masters, evoking Pam's proud smile.

CHAPTER TEN

Freeze was winning. He never had to touch or see the cocaine he was dealing and distributing. So there was rare exposure. He had supervisors, like Squirrel, who kept tabs on all of the mid-level people. He had enforcement, which was now handled by Roscoe and his Mo' Money Brothas. And that was all he needed to clear a 150 percent profit, not inclusive of the twenty thousand he paid per kilo.

The past few years had been spent building his rep, his business, and his organization. Then there were the shipments from Florida. They started with mere trips back and forth by car. Five, ten, and even fifty kilos at one point. When the cars became too small, Freeze rented a couple of commercial couriers with vans to transport 100, 150, and 250 kilos. There were just two large shipments by eighteen-wheeler. Two months before the Bell Glade bust, there was a 500-kilo shipment. It took only days to distribute.

Because of Freeze's track record and client base, the drugs mainly served individuals who found it necessary to sell in order to finance their personal usage. There was a trick that Freeze learned, pertaining to how to mix the powder base cocaine with methamphetamine, a chemical that stimulates the brain's reward center and its choices of fight or flight.

"There's a switch in our heads," a local pharmacist had explained to Freeze. "Something like a pleasure center. This stuff jams open the door to that place in our minds, forcing an addiction. It's really paranoia," the pharmacist told Freeze. "If there is no fulfillment of that need, there is initial irritation and inevitable rage."

Freeze even considered the sale of meth itself. But it wasn't a ghetto fabulous drug like cocaine. In the hood, cocaine was made popular by movies like *Scarface*, *New Jack City*, and *GoodFellas*. Those movies glamorized the product on a worldwide scale. They made it a standard. So, instead, Freeze stuck with what he knew worked; only he spent a measly $80 a gram for the meth made available by his pharmacist friend and had it mixed in with what he sold.

With hundreds of customers already seeking a mere high, the new "freeze"—"Lemme get some freeze," they'd say—was introduced unbeknownst to users. They sprinkled the powder into basic tobacco and smoked it. They snorted it by the line with a rolled-up dollar bill as a straw. They shot it into their veins by soaking it in boiling water and then extracting the fluid into a hypodermic needle. This "trick" with the meth pushed sales through the roof because the same customers were returning for more three and four times a week. That first 500-kilo shipment was Slim's work. It also made Freeze a multimillionaire within a two-month period.

There were close to forty associates on Freeze's payroll. The streetwise cats who drummed up business, served as lookouts (or "hooks"), and watched over his various "stash houses." This was a good feeling, to be the pimp, to have everybody working for him. Never the other way around.

With the money, Freeze indulged in luxury, yet he wasn't "out there" being stupid on some major shopping spree. Sure, there was still that love-hate relationship he had with the need for attention. But for the most part, his was a steady growth. He dressed in all the fashionable designer names and loved those full-length furs, the minks and the foxes. In his safe, he kept a small tray of diamond rings and 24-karat-gold chains, medallions, and watches. In Co-op City where he lived, Freeze purchased an entire floor—twelve of those two- and three-bedroom apartments in his building. The small city was going through its own sign of the times, with the apartments being sold off as condominiums.

Once Freeze bought up the entire twenty-third floor, he contracted an architect and construction company to convert the twelve dwellings—knocking out walls, building others—into a single residence, complete with a game room, a heaven-sent home theater, a dining hall, and eight spacious bedrooms. The elevator was fixed so that it would only stop or open at the twenty-third floor if accessed with a key. Besides the super, Freeze had the only key. And Freeze even had *that* changed.

In the parking garage where most residents parked their cars, an area was cordoned off so that Freeze could keep his fourteen luxury vehicles and six fully loaded trucks. He also contracted a private firm for around-the-clock security. All told, this kingpin made all the necessary adjustments to stay in the hood and to be comfortable in the meantime.

After those expenditures, Freeze still had $500,000 in savings. Cash that he kept stored under a marble floor. Once the second shipment of 500 kilos made it to New York, Freeze could already count the easy two million he'd make. It would only be a matter of time, after the returns came in from the various consignments, that he'd have cash in hand. He'd be able to physically count, spend, or even absorb himself in the paper if he wished. And this would be considered a "good problem." However, Freeze never considered what he'd do with or where he'd stash so much money.

Selling the second load was also a lot easier than the first. The network was now in place. The users either grew smart enough to sell more than they snorted or they became throwaways; useless. Drug rehab, jail, or dead. But in the network, there were some pretty thorough mid-level people; men and women whom he could count on less than ten fingers. De Jesus was a fixture in and around the New York club scene, with his curly hair, pinewood complexion, gold medallions, and his face on the back of his custom-made leather jacket. He worked Roseland, the Ritz, Roxy's and Bentley's as a regular.

He only frequented other clubs like Club New York, Club USA, the Pussy Cat, and the China Club. He stayed away from the Palladium because everyone knew that they had an in-house racket that was not to be crossed. Still, De Jesus had ties to the classy spots, the jazz clubs like the Blue Note, Iridium, and the Five Spot. It was simply a matter of persuading a waitress here and a busboy there. Surely, their subordinate finances could stand the boost. Finally, De Jesus put together a group of girls, twenty-somethings, who served up the dope in swanky places like the Rainbow Room, the Waldorf Lounge, and the Carlyle Club, which overlooked Central Park. It seemed as if there wasn't a hot spot in New York that De Jesus couldn't touch. He consigned twenty-five kilos to supply this circuit and the need was growing now with the help of the methamphetamine additive.

The network also served sixty bodegas in remote corners of every borough. But these weren't necessarily bodegas— inner-city delicatessens. Lucky just used that term as a label for the delis, video stores, candy corners, fast-food joints, and even two shops where they fixed tires. Lucky was the runner who made the pickups and the drops to and from the various spots. Sixty locations in the Bronx, Brooklyn, Queens, Long Island, and Manhattan kept him busy every day of the week for nearly fourteen hours a day. Lucky was responsible for 100 kilos.

Both De Jesus and Lucky reported to Squirrel as their supervisor, but they worked for Freeze. If they aspired to do anything on their own, it was kept quiet. They were afraid of Freeze. They all knew about his track record; what he had done to that dude Chips and that other traitor named Juice. Word was that Freeze beat Chips to death with a wooden bat, and then left him at the bottom of the Hudson River with his souped-up Maxima shackled to his ankle. Rumor has it that the guy was down there to this day.

There were "employees" and then there were independents. Pops was an "independent"—or mid-level associate. A. C. was the nickname Pops used for most of his life. A. C. was the acronym for Atlantic City, New Jersey. Yes, there were others who claimed the nickname, but the more substantial your game was, the more you owned the name. Pops had set aside his rambunctious, fearless lifestyle a long time ago, when he hit age forty-nine. At fifty, when he had the big anniversary party, all the big New Jersey, Philly, and Delaware players and hustlers came out to represent at Bally's Hotel and Casino. That was the event during which he announced the end of "A. C." and the new beginning for "Pops."

"All you playas and ballers, you mothafuckas who I've known for most of my natural life, it's time to change the game. Now I may be the old head of the group, but in Africa, they'd call me king. The Italians would call me a don. You slick-ass mothafuckas gon' call me Pops from now on!" There was a cheer and a wave of laughter, everyone accustomed to A. C.'s wild ways, his wild mouth. But ultimately, every single person in that hotel ballroom owed A. C. something. He had some important impact on each and every one, even the wives. So for the majority, this outrageous, obnoxious attitude was acceptable. It was also at this stage of his life that he decided to turn up the volume on his bread and butter.

"I need to push it up to fifty, maybe sixty kilos, Squirrel. Y'all gotta stop keepin' me down."

"It ain't like that, Pops. We just need to be sure all our shit is spoken for. We're not like Macy's with the seven-day return policy. If we commit, it's set in stone. And we expect to be paid."

"So? Ain't I come through for everything I ordered before?"

"Yeah, but . . . okay, I'mma keep it real, Pops. You're gettin' to be that age when you should be slowin' down. But here you are wanting to go hard, like you still in your thirties."

"So? Age is nothin' but a number, young buck. And I do feel like I'm thirty. And I don't use that Viagra shit either."

"I don't know, Pops."

Squirrel had come out to the event a little amazed by all of the brotherly support, but unsure of why these old heads all dressed in '70's pimp gear, why they were treating Pops like a rock star.

"Are these all your people? Do they work for you?"

"'Course not, young buck. But they're some hellified resources when I need 'em."

Resources. Squirrel wondered what that meant in dollars and cents. "Well, I'll tell you what, Pops, I'll run it by Big Dog. I'll let you know. For now, let's get on with the business at hand." On that evening in the parking lot of Bally's, Squirrel took a green duffel bag from the trunk of his Jetta and passed it to Pops. Pops in turn passed three duffel bags of cash to Squirrel, the balance for the last drop.

"What's the breakdown?"

"We're even up till this drop. There's one-fifty here. The usual: twenties, tens and fives."

"Don't you dudes take C-notes out here?" Squirrel asked. "It'd make shit a whole lot easier. A hundred and fifty grand should fit in one bag."

"Ever since I been hustlin' I've taken nothin' but small change. The hundred can get shaky. I seen some real good counterfeit shit. Real good! So, instead of questioning it or walking around with a dagg'n currency whatchamacallit to verify every big bill, I just take the small stuff."

Squirrel made a face and said, "Whatever. See you next week."

"Yeah, and work on sixty keys for me."

Squirrel didn't mind stretching the consignment for his associates, so long as they came through when they were supposed to. In the meantime, he'd walk them along and add on as he did. There was no room for excuses. Damn sure not from employees and especially not from independent contractors like Pops.

Miss Sharon was another story altogether. Squirrel could see that she was getting up in her years as well. But he also witnessed firsthand Miss Sharon's lil' at-home enterprise. He could see for himself where and how her money was coming in. Pops might've been winin' and dinin' the ballers, gamblers, and tourists, persuading them that he was the source out in A. C., but Miss Sharon was accommodating a full house, day and night, where suburban housewives came to be entertained and to get high at the same time.

She had the best of the middle and upper class there in her home; like the senator's wife whose life purpose seemed to be two lines of cocaine and frequent liaisons with the Chippendales-type studs Miss Sharon invited over. Once when Squirrel was over the house, he had to suppress his laughter when he caught a glimpse of the senator's wife. She was in a daze, coming out of a walk-in closet. He could see the twenty-something stud behind her even in the low light, zipping his pants up. Meanwhile, he got a close enough look to notice that she still had some white powder on the tip of her nose and semen there on the edge of her lower lip. The woman had to be all of forty-eight years old and didn't show a hint of guilt. This was the "environment" that Miss Sharon created.

"Come in," Miss Sharon said, greeting Squirrel with his leather jacket and the matching satchel over his shoulder. "Don't be shy for goodness' sakes." Miss Sharon was taking Squirrel's fascination as a weakness. "This way."

Squirrel stepped past the woman in an apron who'd opened the front door for him, swaggering across the wood floor to follow Miss Sharon. Right there in the first room, the living room, three ladies were busy leaning over a coffee table with straws up their noses. Lines of white powder disappeared before Squirrel passed through the room. He'd never forget that woman's face, the one to the left, who looked so much like his Auntie Glenda with her cocoa butter skin, auburn-tinted hair, and dazzling eyes. Not too skinny and not too fat, the sight of this woman made Squirrel wonder if his aunt wasn't doing this very same thing somewhere else. A muscle-bound hairless cat was crossing Squirrel's path, tray in hand, in a Speedo.

"That's Randy. He's one of my houseboys," Miss Sharon explained as she took Squirrel's arm and crossed the threshold into the dining area. The distant music that Squirrel couldn't make out came in a bit clearer now. It was outside, beyond the sliding glass doors, on the back patio. It was one of those 120-beats-per-minute techno compositions that he knew from the dance clubs. Only now, the music seemed to set the pace out there. Smiles. Sultry eye contact. Dancing and touching. It was all constant movement amongst maybe four dozen people.

The women were up in their years. The men were young and barely dressed. Nobody was swimming out there either; perhaps too consumed with the attention they were getting or giving. There was a whole Tarzan-meets-Jane atmosphere outside. Clusters of women in dresses or knee-length skirts stood around and beside the half-naked studs, touching and caressing their arms and chests. The sliding door suddenly opened and a couple scurried in, giggling as though they had a secret. Without a word, they moved along toward the front of the house where the entrance hall and stairway were. Squirrel couldn't help but to follow that brief energy with his eyes.

"Lust, baby. That's all I sell here is lust. And you should know something before we take one more step . . ." Miss Sharon had Squirrel's arm in hers like the couple that had just passed, and caressed his biceps affectionately. "A few of my lady friends have asked about you."

"Me?" Squirrel nearly jerked his shoulder out of its socket, he was so surprised.

"Yes, sir, you. They know a good time when they see one."

"I ain't for sale, Miss Sharon. I'm here on business. Business only."

"Mmm-hmm. But trust me, baby, everybody has a price."

"Uh-ungh." And he wasn't joking either.

"Okay," said Miss Sharon, taking that deep breath that lacks belief. Then she said, "Let's take care of business."

There were double doors there to the left of them. Miss Sharon's approach was enough for the no-neck dude standing there (probably the only dressed man in the house) to open the doors for her. A swoosh of noise and movement hit Squirrel all at once as he followed the homeowner across the carpet and through an obstacle course of game tables where black-jack, poker, and baccarat activities were on going. Every table was busy with groups of older women (none too leather-faced or feeble) in their regal hairstyles and concentrated eyes.

"Place your bets," called out a dealer with his inflated chest and bowtie. It was amusing how all of the men in the room looked so much alike, with their bare chests and black bowties. Despite the differences in race and skin tone, the dealers appeared to be cast from the same mold, with their dashing smiles and alluring attitudes. Some of the women were fawning even while they were losing money. Still other Tarzan-types strolled through the room with trays of refreshments for the guests. Squirrel recognized the farthest part of the room, just past the roulette wheel, where he'd been with Miss Sharon before.

On the way, Miss Sharon received a series of "hello"s and "how are you?"s, until she was confronted by two women who jointly asked, "Is that him and how long you keepin' him?" They asked these questions in a way that was not to be so forward, but to be overheard at the same time.

"Mrs. Ewing, Mrs. Jeffreys, meet Mr., uh, Squirrel," Miss Sharon said with that raspy cigarette-deep voice of hers.

"Well, hello there, young man. Would you like to give a mature woman a bit of company?" Mrs. Ewing was right up-front about it, stepping out in front of Miss Sharon to take hold of Squirrel's elbow. She was in semi-possession now.

"Uh." Squirrel had a dumb face on, not wanting to disrespect the woman who tried hard to be the temptress.

"Oh, come, come. You young men have so much time and energy on your hands. Why not?"

Now the other woman, Mrs. Jeffreys, stepped in. "Yes, you certainly do look to have a certain energy about you. You must be twenty-one? Maybe twenty-two?"

"He surely can't be more than twenty-five, darling. Now give the young man some room, won't you?"

Miss Sharon had to suppress a smile herself as she looked on from a few steps away.

"Ladies, ladies, please." Squirrel would no longer be

sandwiched by these two, old enough to be his aunt and mother with streaks of silver in their hair, arched brows that were drawn too high over their cat eyes, and the mild wrinkles that formed as a result of spiritless cheeks. He politely wrestled himself out of their vice grip, saying, "I'm really not one of Miss Sharon's boys. I'm just here for business. Nothing more, nothing less."

"Oh, don't be silly," Mrs. Ewing said, working her way back to him with a condescending gaze as if he were a son disobeying his mom. "You young ones need a good woman to take care of you, to help you out with some of that . . . energy . . ." Then she got close enough to whisper, "To tuck you in at night."

Squirrel gritted his teeth and looked away at the same time. Then he decided what to do. Mrs. Ewing was engulfing Squirrel with her abundance of Liz Claiborne perfume, close enough for him to make his move.

"Oooh!" Mrs. Ewing jumped like a bunny. Squirrel had grabbed her behind in such a way that his fingertips wedged up into the fold of her ass, almost intimate enough to take her temperature. While the woman stood there trying to catch her breath, Squirrel took the opportunity to slip away, almost pushing Miss Sharon through the intended door.

"I told you." Miss Sharon was melodic with her words.

"Yeah, but you didn't help things any." Squirrel was firm in his reply. "Now, can we please get on with this? And when we're done, I'm taking the back way out." Miss Sharon was still smiling as she went to the wall safe of her lavish home office. Squirrel could hear the commotion behind the door in the homemade casino, where Mrs. Ewing and Mrs. Jeffreys were knocking.

"What is up with those women?" Squirrel asked while he took in the surroundings. He'd been here in Miss Sharon's office once before and thought these surrounding to be peculiar possessions for a woman up in her years. But now, upon further examination, she didn't seem so out of place. Contemporary furnishings. Shag carpet. Exotic wall hangings. Erotic paintings and sculptures. Miss Sharon, the freak.

"Just clients, babe, looking for a good time." Miss Sharon handled the stacks of cash, placing them from safe to desk, as she elaborated. "Mrs. Jeffreys is a new client, really. Tired of all that Jehovah Witness nonsense she was tied up in, going door-to-door every day like a good missionary. It was Mrs. Ewing that pulled her in the house one day, instead of brushing her off like we usually do, and introduced her to the game."

"The game? You mean them ladies be sellin' dope?"

"You're kidding, right? Baby, those two ladies bring me more clients than you'd see on a busy subway platform. Plus, they use the stuff occasionally. Mrs. Ewing does, anyhow. I can't say I've seen Phyllis, her friend, using. Not yet. But as tough as those two run together, taking turns with my houseboys 'n stuff, I wouldn't put it past her."

"Damn. I guess anybody can be down," Squirrel mentioned as he recounted the money she stacked. All the while, he wondered about the older women that were in his life. His mother. His aunt. Damn, I don't know what I'd do if I found out my mother was doin' coke. Damn, come to think of it I really need to give my moms a call, drop her some money. That check she gets can't stretch too far without shit bein' miserable.

This was one of those moments for Squirrel, that flash of thoughts and ideas that he couldn't help or prevent. Usually, these would be bad dreams to be had in his sleep. Never during times like this when money was being counted, when he was expected to be sharp and alert.

"Did you hear me? Hey, you okay, baby?"

"Oh yeah. Just thinking . . . something on my mind, that's all. Cool. Uh, this makes seventy-five. Next week, I can pick up the balance." The balance was fifty thousand.

"Baby, I'm gonna need you to come back at the end of this weekend. I don't like having so much money in the house. And I have a big party goin' on this weekend. All of my clients will be here. Ain't enough room in my safe. That's why I asked you to bring up eight this time instead of the usual six. You did bring eight, right?"

"Got it right here, Miss Sharon." Squirrel opened the satchel and pulled out eight tightly wrapped bricks of cocaine. Then he stuffed the cash into his bag by the handfuls. "If I can't make it up here, is it all right if I send someone?"

"Who?"

"Maybe Butch. He's tight with us. Real tight."

"I don't think so, baby. I only deal with you. That's the way it's always been. Ain't no sense in rockin' the boat. If you can't make it, I'll have to make do. I'll find somewhere else to put the cash, but at least try to get here."

"I will, Miss Sharon. Uh, the back way out of this place. Please?" Miss Sharon smiled as she finished putting the drugs in the safe. The last images Squirrel recalled that day at Miss Sharon's home was her shutting the safe as well as a framed painting of a nude woman. Some ugly piece of art, though: a woman sitting back on a couch, relaxed, as she looked out through a window toward the horizon. Squirrel almost froze when he realized who that was—the nude woman in the painting. Miss Sharon? A freak??

CHAPTER ELEVEN

If Squirrel knew, if he really knew about Roscoe and the MMB, about their little extracurricular activities outside of selling the meager two kilos of cocaine that was sold to them, there was no way he'd have trusted Roscoe to oversee Freeze's drop shipment. Sure, the deal went smoothly, and Squirrel even threw in two kilos on top of the two grand he promised. But the idea of exposing such sensitive details, the how and where of the transaction, should have been considered more carefully.

Roscoe first met with Squirrel on a night when both crews happened to cross paths at Manhattan Proper. Queens was out of the way for both groups just to be entertained, which spoke more to the lure and magnetism of the event than anything else. But unbeknownst to Freeze and his boys, Roscoe was on a mission. He, the Rasta mon Terhane, Tec-9, and Rook were out as usual, scouting the nightclub circuit for drug dealers. It didn't matter if the dealers were known or unknown, knee-deep in attitude or surrounded by their legion of dope boys, runners, and enforcers. None of that mattered to Roscoe and his Mo' Money Brothas. In fact, those red flags were good news to the MMB. It meant that they had found another target.

The decision to start jackin' was triggered by a simple conversation while the crew was parked in Tec-9's new

Camry. All four of them were fucked up; high on the stub of weed they passed to one another.

"It's nice," Roscoe had commented.

"Yeah, I know. That's why you takin yo' time passin it back this way."

"Nah, man. I'm talking about the ride, man. The ride is smooth. Some shit I'd even take my girl out in and fuck her brains out on the hood."

"Better than them fuckin' Maximas. Five-o be clocking them rides 'cuz they know only dope boys drive them."

Terhane jumped in and said, "Watch it, boti-bwoy. Me sista drive one a' dem tings, ya-know. And she ain't no drug deela, eeda."

"Well, you know what I mean," Tec-9 replied with a furrowed brow.

"Yo, this shit is nice," Terhane said after taking a pull from the weed. "Sometin' on dis here?"

"Ain't shit," Roscoe said. "Just hurry and pass that 'round."

"Easy, mon." Terhane took another pull before passing it to Rook. He had been quiet all this time and wasn't expected to speak unless he had some real deep shit to share.

"You hear that shit, man?"

"Hear what? Ain't shit but Jill Scott takin' some walk on the radio."

"Naw, man. That crackling sound like Rice Krispies."

"Yo, Rook be trippin'. Ain't no cracklin' goin' on."

"That wasn't Rook talking! That was me, dog." Terhane corrected Roscoe, who was sitting in the backseat beside Rook. "I'm sayin' there's some cracklin' goin' on. Y'all don't hear it?"

"Oh, yeah. Now I hear it," Roscoe leaned over and whispered to Rook. "That's what they mean when they say 'this is your brain on drugs.'"

All of a sudden, Terhane let out a frightened holler. He jumped up in his seat, squirmed around as if to dodge and duck something. "Shit. They firin', man. Get down!"

The other three swung their attention to the left and right, looking out the vehicle's windows with utmost worry. In the meantime, the Rasta pulled out the oowop from his crouched position in the passenger's seat (almost balled up like a scared child) and began firing at the front windshield.

The report from the fusillade was deafening inside the small cabin and it reinforced the notion that, indeed, there was a war going on. Roscoe and Rook bolted out of their respective side doors, while Tec-9 did the same, escaping from behind the steering wheel and the pieces of glass that splattered as a result of the spray of the bullets. While the three were outside of the vehicle, guns drawn and looking every which way for the origin of the attack, Terhane was in that same spot, emptying the machine gun through the opening that had been the front windshield of the Camry.

Standing outside in the night, unconcerned with where they were—on the side of the Grand Central Parkway, a rest spot that wasn't fifty feet away from passing traffic—Roscoe, Tec-9, and Rook eased out of the stupor that had them play along with Terhane's own freak imagination.

The next day, it was Roscoe, the leader of the MMBs, who stepped to Terhane and apologized. "Yo man, I'm really, really sorry about that last night. Really sorry, man."

"For what? Stop that shit, mon."

"I'm talkin' about the smoke. Man, I will never, ever hit you with that shit again."

"Whatchu mean?"

"There was coke sprinkled on that shit we was smokin'."

"That shit done sent you out yo' mind, bwoy. Takin' your dick out, trying to piss on us? Man, I swear I was gonna shoot yo' nasty ass."

Roscoe sucked his teeth and said, "You buggin', man. I ain't do no shit like that. That was *you* trippin'. *You* tryin' to kill all of us. You! And you wasn't the only one. Ma'fuckin' Tec tried to run out into traffic to catch a goddamned cab. Traffic is doin' like sixty miles an hour and this nigga want a taxi in the middle of the thruway!"

"Looks like we all betta lay offa dat shit, mon. I know I can't remember shit, but I also know that I was feelin' good as a mothafucka. Where you get dat?"

"That's the shit Freeze and his boys be sellin'. They makin' big money sellin' that shit, too. Good money."

"How good? Betta den we doin' wit' weed?"

"What? Nigga, where you been hidin' out? Yo' head in the sand or somethin'? That cocaine is wassup. For one key, they buy for fifteen, sixteen, even twenty grand; you can turn around and sell it for almost double and triple what you got it for. You can sell that shit and become rich with one deal."

"So why we been doin' only weed?"

"'Cuz a mothafucka get caught up wit' dis' much—I mean dis' fuckin' much—you can kiss Christmas good-bye for the rest of yo' natural life." Roscoe held his thumb held against his pinkie to display how little an amount was necessary to catch a big prison sentence. "But with weed? We ain't lookin' at nothin' but small time . . . time you can do standin' on yo' head."

"Shit. Y'all loud as a motha," Rook said, straggling out of another room, his hand holding the top of his head. "Head is killin' me."

"'Sup, Rook. You all right?"

"Pssh, what the fuck was we doing last night? I remember some wild shit on the Grand Central. You cats is off the chain."

"We was just kickin' dat dere . . . talkin' 'bout some coke shit."

"That's what we was smoking? Gaaah-damn! That stuff had me spinning. I don't think I can stand that no more. I might end up killing somebody."

"Yo, but check it, Rook. Ros been kicking science 'bout dem bwoys be selling dat shit," said Terhane.

"They making cash hand over fist. That's what I'm saying."

"But, the risk is crazy, man. They got a lotta balls to do some shit like that."

"Nah, it ain't that. What it is is they got a little dough now and think they invincible. Think they can't get got."

"Plus," Rook added, "them dudes probably never been hit hard; so, what they don't know won't hurt them."

"Not until they catch it. But a ma'fucka catch a twenny-year bid . . . a life bid, then they basically stepping out of one game and into the next. They don't know what hit 'em. And the cats that are still on the street don't really learn shit from that nigga. He gone. He fucked up. That's all they know. A couple of dudes might get the message, but the majority of ma'fuckas still wanna be Nino Brown or Tony Montana."

" 'Who built this me! Who put this thing togetha? Me! Fuckin' cockroach!' " Tec was up now, sitting up on the couch where he crashed the night before. He caught a piece of the ongoing conversation and jumped in to do his best Scarface impression.

"But, lemme ask you something." Rook was directing his words toward Roscoe. "What makes these dudes wanna risk all that? I mean, we talking hardcore ma'fuckas that just don't give a fuck?"

"Fuck naw. I know a preppy, white college boy been selling that shit for a couple years. Put himself through school and got a house and cars. Then you got straight ignorant dudes who just think they big dogs 'cause they got a gun and some money. I told you. They think they invincible."

"Okay, so . . ." Rook's mind was cooking now. "If a dude is gettin' dough, say two or three thousand a week . . ."

"Huh? You betta try twenny or thirty thousand a week at least."

"Okay, so say that. He's getting, what, a hundred Gs a month?"

"Maybe more."

"So where you think he's keeping all that cash? He can't be keeping it in a bank."

"Or in his socks."

"Where would you keep a hundred grand if you were in that game?"

"Shit!" Rosco exclaimed. "I don't let twelve dollars out of my sight, much less a thousand. I'd probably sleep on that."

"Exactly. Okay, another dumb question. Let's say, just for example, that you jacked a cocaine boy," Rook said.

"Uh-huh."

"And let's say you got caught by the police. How much time you think you'd get?"

"Maybe a year. Depends. Armed robbery will get you five, eight, even ten years."

"Yeah, if—big if—you get caught."

"So?"

"So?? Man, feel me on this. If a ma'fucka taking down twenty or thirty Gs a week, a hundred a month, and we can jack 'em without getting caught? Then really, they takin' all the risk for us. Let them do the sales. Let them make the transactions."

"Damn, you keeping it gulley ain't you, bwoy?"

"So you wanna rob ma'fuckas now?"

"Why not? It ain't like we gonna kill nobody. Just make a withdrawal." Rook made one of those phony grins that showed he was serious.

"Rook got a point, Roscoe. I been seein' these dudes myself, all done up in diamonds'n shit, like they ma'fuckin' Bill Gates of the hood. The ones that flash they shit? Them 'noxious ones? Those are the worst. I already know a few I wanna put a cap in."

That discussion, those events are what preceeded the Mo' Money Brothas' newfound trade as bandits; or pirates, if you asked them. Sure, there are the crooks in the hood. But now there were the crooked crooks. Shit was about to get dirty.

Freeze was that next target for the MMB on the night the boys met up at Manhattan Proper. They saw Freeze in his ghetto fabulousness—with his diamonds, his fur, and his boys (probably packing) next to him. They assumed that to be his Bentley Continental T double-parked outside. All the signals were there.

The quartet was becoming good at this, spotting a big fish, following him, figuring out his routine. Then they'd whet his appetite and make a small buy. A cookie. An eight ball. Maybe even a bird. Then they'd step it up to two birds. All it took was one, in most cases, before the MMB was ready to move in. They kicked in doors; they'd ambush cats at a traffic light. Sometimes they'd pull up on a dude right out in a club parking lot, or at the diner, after a long night out. Once, outside of the Red Coach Diner up near Gun Hill Road, Roscoe and company were finished with a night of club-canvassing when a group of six in a silver Navigator pulled into a parking space. The women with them might as well have been invisible, considering how the bandits were fiending after their marks.

There was the dressy one with his mink, his fedora, and his Rolex glistening in the moonlight. There was the lanky dude squeezing on his china-doll cutie, and there was another, a kiss-ass who had been driving. The flashy one took hold of the other two women, and they started off through the parking lot, laughing and whatnot as they approached the entrance to the Red Coach. With only scarves to disguise their faces, the MMB emerged from between some vehicles on opposite sides of the party. The kiss-ass was the first to realize a jack was going down. He was also the first to catch it, as Rook swept the butt of his sawed-off shotgun into the guy's belly. Then Rook punished him with an over-the-shoulder strike to the back of the head. Before the others realized what hit them, before the kiss-ass even let out a cry, Tec gave the order.

"Lay it down, bwoy."

"On the ground. Now!" Roscoe affirmed. The women let out sharp cries but were encouraged to hold their tongues as the gunmen pressed the noses of their automatic weapons to their necks or skulls. Pockets were pilfered, body parts were groped, and handbags were stripped away all within minutes. Without planning or knowing more about their victims, the MMB pulled this off, one of their first few jacks.

Yet, by the time they'd purchased two kilos from Squirrel, more than a dozen jacks had gone down successfully. The group became efficient, with duct tape, plastic cuffs, bulletproof vests, and fearless, experienced objectives. By the time they figured Squirrel and Freeze to be their next hit, they'd already gone to neighboring states like Connecticut and Jersey, and also to Philly. They understood that to go into virgin territory would be less risky, where folks wouldn't be hip to the series of jackings MMB had executed.

Now, these drug dealers with their $30,000, $50,000, and $100,000 stashes of cash, their jewelry, and their furs—regardless of their security—all of it was taken by force. And all of it was making the MMB as rich as ten dealers put together. With only one or two hits a week, and with four of them to divide the cake, they always had money, but at the same time, they were always hot for more.

"Besides," Rook had said, "who're these cats gonna call? The police?" The boys all laughed at the idea at the time. But the shit stopped being funny after Tec had to wet a guy up (somebody trying to play hero) during a jack. They weren't even sure if the man lived or died. There wasn't any mention in the newspapers because it all happened too damn fast. Ever since, the MMB planned every moment of each "job" as seriously as they would a bank robbery. No time for jokes. No time for funny business. This was a job. And to leave a person alive after a robbery was a plus. It meant there'd be no homicide charges hanging over their heads. It meant a good night's sleep. It meant one less family in mourning.

It was a good thing (for somebody) that Squirrel called MMB to situate some backup to secure the exchange at the funeral home. Otherwise, Roscoe and his boys had planned to hit Freeze. The call merely threw a wrench into the plan; suspended the jack for a minute. However, this close-up involvement with Freeze's people also showed Roscoe that there was a lot more promise in this particular jack then expected. It showed just how vulnerable this crew was.

They were initially prepared to kidnap Squirrel. They would make him lead the MMB to the stash where money was kept. Roscoe didn't care about the drugs; there was too much jail time involved for possession alone. If he wanted to, he could've laid 'em out at Gilmore's Funeral Home and took their shit. How convenient it would've been to have those dead bodies right there, ready for the draining of their body fluids. But now, knowing that they had the big fish's confidence, there'd be no jack, no kidnapping; not until some other research and preparation was done. If the MMB was gonna hit Freeze, they'd be sure that it would pay off and pay off big. Every detail would be looked at with surgical attention.

BOOK TWO

BOOK TWO

CHAPTER TWELVE

The objective of a salesperson, regardless of what he or she sells, is to get a person happily involved with a product. The faster, the better. A speedy transaction could only be completed, however, if there is a willing and able buyer. The larger the quantity, the more sensitive the relationship. The relationship between Freeze and Tucker Wilson was just that type of association. Tucker was Tonya's brother. And he only met Freeze by accident.

At the time, Freeze and Tonya had gone out for a drive. Freeze had the Ferrari 550 Maranello out for the occasion. It was an all-black model and glistened just like Tonya's lips, like his diamond medallion around her neck, and even like her eyes, all glossy and wet, as they were when she lay underneath Freeze, the cocaine king. But this was how Freeze saw his possessions: as spectacles. He couldn't decide if he was out driving to show off his car that cost him $225,000 (fresh off the showroom floor) or if he was showing off Tonya, who might one day cost him just as much.

They cruised up the West Side Highway, along the Cross Bronx Expressway, and back down the FDR Drive alongside the East River.

On a whim, Freeze took the Manhattan Bridge down near Canal Street and parked outside of Junior's, a bakery and restaurant in Brooklyn where all the "in" people went.

By coincidence, Tucker was there at the same time, dining

with some of his stockbroker buddies. Not that Tucker was a stockbroker himself; he was but a bank teller down on Water Street. Yet, he worked where they worked and hustled like they hustled. The novelty of a black man working in the financial district was fading these days. There was finally inclusion in an industry that for so long "blocked the blessing." The bottom line now was that a guy like Tucker associated with this crowd simply because his interests were similar.

The brother and sister made eye contact, and Tucker could read Tonya's silently worded warning loud and clear: "You better not dare." Tucker kept the peace, and did not approach them. But it was the next day that he stopped by the house to address Tonya about her secret boyfriend.

"Who's Mr Bling-Bling?" Tucker asked.

"What you need to do is stay outta mine," Tonya shot back. "I didn't see you with no date!"

"Yeah, well, if I knew we were gonna have a showdown, I'da got me a crackhead bitch for your boy to serve up. Then we woulda had a reason to meet."

"Oh, so you came home to rank on yo' little sister, huh? Think you all high-and-mighty on Wall Street wit' 'cho boojie, wanna-be-white buddies. Mothafuckers that think like you, like they betta than everybody else."

"Girl, you better have some respect for your elders."

"Elders? Lemme tell you something, you Oreo cookie in a suit. You ain't been around me long enough to be my elder. You ain't never had time for me my whole childhood, so don't even come back from your sweet-ass penthouse preaching shit about I'm your this or that. You ain't shit as far as I'm concerned. Not even good enough to sniff my shitty drawers. Now step!!" Tonya had one hand on her hip, the other simultaneously curled in the air, directing him to keep it moving. It was clear to Tucker that his sister had a whole lot of pent-up rage in her heart just beckoning to fire at him, ready to explode. He could almost imagine the things she'd say.

That was then. A year ago. These days, however, one would never guess that Tucker Wilson was once anti–bling-bling or antidrug. When the third tech-stock/dot.com fallout hit Wall Street, there were more than just the tragedies: that broker who jumped from the American Express building; the other one who shot his wife, kids, and himself; even more than the tough luck that caused companies to drop off the planet. Hundreds of financial district employees were demoted. Laid off. Fired. Tucker was one of them.

That was when the ironies of life and fate set in. Attempt after attempt led to plenty of possibilities, but no job. There was the unemployment office, where he had to stand in line and rub elbows with those he might've frowned upon in his leaner moments. There was the repossession of his Mercedes, and when he couldn't retrieve that, there was more rubbing elbows on the subway. Eventually, Tonya let out a great big "I'll be goddamned" when Tucker had to move out of his independent world and back home with Mom and Pop, not to mention the sister who he'd crossed one too many times.

Although Tonya was certainly bitter when it came to her brother, the fire had lowered some to the point where (at least) the two could coexist in the same house. Tonya wasn't a homebody anymore. She was young and wild enough to shake her thang, old enough to make her own decisions, and street-smart enough to know the difference. And Tucker might've had his reservations about her way of dressing like a nymph, about her bouncing in and out of the house at all hours, and about the different expensive vehicles that would pick her up and drop her off so often.

But what could he say? His bank account was closer to "E" than he'd ever feared. And here was his sister wearing more value in clothes and jewelry than he had money to his name. Already miserable and jobless, now Tucker could only adjust his perception from jealousy to envy.

"Goin' out with the pharmacist again?" Tucker mentioned, noticing Tonya rushing around the house. He was watching TV. Tucker, the couch potato.

"Tuck, you're not gonna take it there again, are you? 'Cuz if you are . . ."

"No. Don't trip. I was just gonna say have a good time. That's all."

Tonya's grimace slowly transformed; more of a question than a genuine smile.

"Mmm-hmm. Ahh . . . thank you, brother dear." And just like that, the past was put away in the far-off place that could be considered a burial ground for pain and hurtful memories. "He's really not that bad, Tuck. And he treats me better than anybody I been with." Tonya shared these thoughts later as the siblings got to talking.

Tucker wondered, Who have you been with, lil' sister? Who have you met that could measure up to your dope-dealing friend? Is it all the money—not the man—that's treating you so good?

"Well, as long as you're happy, sis," was all that Tucker could really say.

"Is that Tuck speaking? My brother? The hater? What's got into you?"

"I had to get off my high horse. Come back down to earth."

"Well, welcome back, bro."

From hating to tolerating, Tucker inevitably needed money. The unemployment checks had stopped coming and desperation was setting in. Tucker realized shit was definitely desperate when he had to begin borrowing money from Tonya.

Then it was one of his Wall Street buddies, someone who put two and two together to conclude that Tucker's sister was rolling with a supplier. "The goddamned black Scarface," he called him. "He's a fucking dealer, dog. Of course he ain't gonna turn this down. Besides, what harm could it do to ask? You never know." Tucker's peer had explored the possibilities of a new trade—selling cocaine to their associates downtown—and it threw him. It stifled all manner of common sense and pulled at every fiber of ethics left in Tucker's conscience. At least he was now curious. Even if he didn't have the heart to jump out there and cross the line, the line he knew as the demarcation between right and wrong. And still, Tucker had not made a firm decision to go with it, to get his hands dirty. Not until Rose showed up at the house.

When the doorbell rang, Tonya was the first to greet Rose with one of those hugs that was personal but not sexual; right at the borderline for two cousins. However, Tonya liked Rose, even if his was just a nickname for that "thug lifestyle." Rose reminded her so much of Tupac, the icon that she'd just missed meeting when she was younger. The hip-hop legend had just left the Sneaker Circus where her uncle (Rose's father) was taking her for a birthday present.

"Pick two pairs, any two pairs," her uncle had exclaimed. And now, here was the cousin who reminded Tonya of that day—of her unruly, whimsical emotions for a celebrity rapper.

Rose showed up in his classic b-boy gear. The backward baseball cap, even though he wasn't a baseball fan. The recent shape-up that left a thin layer of hair on his head, even if the do-rag always covered it. His signature jersey with the double zero team number covering most of his torso. The cargo baggies and the combat boots.

Tucker was behind Tonya and guessed that Rose might not be interested in greeting him as heartily as he had Tonya, thanks to Tucker's little high-and-mighty profile of the past. But Rose wouldn't know all that Tucker had been through. He hadn't walked in his shoes. Tucker made no excuses. He just stepped forward in an apologetic, open approach and greeted Rose as though this was a well-deserved reunion. It had Rose wondering, not exactly sure what this was about. That was expected. So, Tucker just kept it real. He explained the difference between the old him and the new him and that he never intended for his cousin to be a victim of Tucker's own ignorant ideologies and prejudices.

"It's just how I grew up," Tucker later explained to Rose. "I was always doing things, always involved in something. It made me a well-rounded person, able to exist amidst prosperity as well as poverty. I learned to speak well and read a lot. I became more aware. But all that I was able to experience showed me a more desirable side of life, to me at least. And I decided to keep on moving in that direction. Decided I wanted to mingle with money people instead of don't-have-money people. And—don't get me wrong—it's not necessarily a better lifestyle, just different, with its own set of problems."

Tucker explained his financial fall and how he wanted to be as down-to-earth as possible. He even talked to Rose about the recent proposal that had come his way.

He didn't say, but Rose showed up to his cousins' house more out of necessity than anything else. He needed to get away from his old ties, the gang he ran with back in Brooklyn. There was a war going on out there, to the point that every day was a battle.

Rose wasn't one to back away from a fight. It was just that the ignorant challenges seemed endless. The streets were pregnant with hustlers and possibilities and their own measures of joy and fascination. But the problem with opportunity was that while everybody wanted it, everybody was not willing to work hard for it. And in many cases, the lawless would take what they wanted. Rose recognized the need for the average Joes to protect themselves against the lawless, and for the lawless to push on with their own goals, whatever they were. So he capitalized on servicing both needs. Rose, that tight-bodied street thug with the heart of dynamite, who was always wearing red hats or jerseys or jackets. Rose, who was born and bred in Brooklyn and whose father was a take-no-shit thug now doing thirty-to-life in Lewisburg for murder. Rose, who became the one to visit if you happened to be in Brooklyn and needed a gun.

"I can't say I know too much about the drug game, Tuck. But I deal to all kinds of dudes that sell it. They need guns to protect their business. I provide them. Supply and demand. Really, if you think about it, it's the same thing." Rose then told Tucker, "If you do decide to get in the game, I got your back."

• • •

T ucker's mom was an editor at *Reader's Digest*. Fifteen years at the same company; five years away from retirement. His father worked at IBM. He was a general manager now, with a ways to go until he reached the level that was equal to the Mrs. Nonetheless, he was proud of his position, his job.

With the parents in their busy lives—the high-level jobs, the bowling team (for her), and the lodge (for him)—Tucker and his young sister Tonya were left to explore life on their own. While Tucker might be considered a momma's boy, living at home at the age of twenty-two, Tonya was considered a grown-ass woman at nineteen, able to move about on her own. She was one of those young women that (so far) hadn't given her parents any reason to toss her out of the house.

Circumstances in the Wilson home being what they were, Rose wouldn't ruffle any feathers to move in and sleep in the guest room. It was almost as though the parents didn't notice.

"Just don't keep no guns in the house, Rose. Please. At least respect the house enough to do that."

"Ain't no problem, Tuck. You got it. I ain't staying too long anyhow. Just enough to set up in Harlem. Business'll be booming before you can blink an eye."

In time, having Rose around felt like somewhat of a resource. Tucker couldn't put all the pieces together just yet, but (in the back of his mind) it had something to do with that proposal from his Wall Street buddy. Yes. Business will surely be booming, in more than one way, thought Tucker.

T ucker and his sister had a few more conversations before he realized that he didn't even have to communicate with Freeze. Squirrel was the one to meet with Tucker. Squirrel was the one to set down the simple rules, the bit about a phone call, and a location for a quick transfer of product. Short and sweet. No strings attached.

Within weeks, the relationship grew. Tucker went from

an eighth of an ounce, to a fifth of an ounce, to an ounce, and then to a kilo. He learned the lingo, the terminology for those amounts. The "cookie," the "eight-ball," or the "onion" was slang for an ounce; and the "bird" was another name for a kilo.

By his second month of dealing, Tucker wanted to kick himself in the ass for not doing this a lot sooner. He realized that he should've known that these Wall Street types, these stressed-out, burnt-out tight asses (exactly what he once was) would need their artificial lift to help make it through the day, to help them stay awake to reach the expected quota for the week. He should've known that these cats had the money to pay him, and that they'd pay him premium prices for the product he guaranteed.

Before long, Tucker was rolling in dough. Smiling at Tonya like she was God's gift to Freeze. Now, when he said, "Have a nice night out," he really meant, "Baby, you just keep serving that man's ass until I can call him my blood relative." Only when Tucker was relaxed would he feel a bit guilty about his thoughts concerning Tonya and her man. But then, he'd recall, she knew him before Tucker got in the game. And then he, too, would say (adopting the saying from Tonya and she from Freeze), "It is what it is."

By Tucker's eighth month in the drug game, all he dealt were kilos. He was getting them on consignment by the dozens and more or less subcontracting his territory (the financial district) to other subordinates who sold the drugs to individuals. The growth was inevitable, something Squirrel never doubted. Tucker was becoming a mid-level associate, an independent contractor who was dependable. Tucker, the kingpin.

"Are you sure you can handle it?" Squirrel asked when Tucker ordered 100 kilos.

"Is the sky blue? Man, this shit is getting so big I'm gonna have to duplicate myself just to spend the money I'm bringing in. You doubting my word?"

"Not at all, Tuck. I just need to make sure. Your biggest

order so far was seventy. If I set you at a hundred, the Big Dog wanna make damn sure he gets paid. This is like, two million. And you know we don't take checks."

"So what? Listen. I got people waiting. I need the stuff. Can you do it or not?"

"Yo, dude, slow your roll wit' that. I ain't no punk."

Tucker changed his tone. "Okay. I can dig it."

"So, what's it gonna be then?" There was a pause.

"How 'bout I give you some cash on delivery?"

"How much?"

"Say . . . one fourth. Five hundred."

"Cash?"

"Cold cash."

"Now I know we can deal."

Squirrel guaranteed the delivery, and Tucker expected a phone call by noon. But when no phone call came, when Squirrel wasn't able to be reached, Tucker assumed something went wrong. His concerns, coupled with his waiting customers, grouped with his own anxieties about keeping his word and forced him to take other measures. The first idea that immediately came to mind was Rose. Didn't he say he dealt with others who sold it? Didn't they have their own contacts? Surely Freeze and his boys weren't selling to all of New York.

"We can try the Dominicans," Rose told him. "I know a dude named Sosa. He got a spot in up in the Bronx. Deals big, too. I sold 'im some guns a few months ago."

"Can we get to him? I mean today?"

"I can do one better. Let's take a ride."

Tucker and Tonya's home was buried on the extreme east side of the Bronx; a two-story house settled on a block of similar dwellings. Riverdale was probably as suburban as the Bronx got, offering easy access to the parkway and splendid views of the Hudson River and New York City just minutes away.

That day, both Tucker and Rose jumped into a metallic blue Lexus GS 500, a sports luxury vehicle that drug and gun money purchased, and they zipped off to the nearest pay phone. Rose got out and punched in a pager number. Then he hung up and waited with his hand still on the receiver, waiting for Sosa to return his page. The phone rang a moment or so later and Rose did most of the small talk.

Tucker wondered what slang and code words Rose was using on the line as he sat still, deep in thought. The driver's side door shut with Rose back behind the steering wheel and it shook Tucker from his brief spell. Rose also wore a smile.

"They're waiting for us," he told his cousin. Then the two glided north on Broadway further into the North Bronx. Before they reached 218th Street, where the meet was to go down, Rose pulled the car over to the curb. They were next to a bus stop with a glass pavilion. There was only one commuter waiting there, but the two in the car were certain that their activities were hidden behind the tinted windows of the Lex.

"Here," Rose said, even before he pulled the gym bag from under his seat. He unzipped it in a single fluid motion. "You should have one of these, just in case." Rose held out a 9mm automatic, urging Tucker on. "Go 'head."

Tucker hesitated, suddenly stuck in time. That gun could've been a candy bar. A deck of cards. Even a pack of cigarettes. That's how casual Rose was with the weapon, like it was just another something. Tucker finally took the gun.

Rose took another weapon out of the bag that looked to be a shotgun, smaller than a rifle and a little larger than a pistol.

"Damn," Tucker exclaimed. And he didn't have to say what he was wondering.

"Nothing to get crazy about. It's a submachine pistol made in Japan."

"Yo, listen, man. I'm a nonviolent kinda dude. But we gettin' ready for war up in here."

"Reality check, bubba. Always outsmart the other guy. Always be prepared, and never underestimate."

"But I thought you did business with these guys."

"I did. And I still do. And don't get me wrong, the Dominicans are cool as shit. But anything can go down at anytime. They say you can walk out of the safety of your home and get hit by a bus. Well, if I can, I'd like to have a warning to have a fighting chance in hell. This"—Rose held up the pistol like 007 would, gazing at it with pride, before going on—"is my fighting chance."

When the Lexus came to a stop again, it was on 218th Street and Broadway. They were double-parked adjacent to a flower shop. "Now we wait."

"For flowers?"

"No." Rose looked around. "For him."

Tucker cocked back his head, all sorts of gross ideas floating through his head about guns, drugs, and . . .

"A kid?" Tucker said it like he couldn't believe it. "A kid?" he asked again, this time to himself.

"Just watch. Listen. Learn." Rose said this just before the subway train rumbled overhead. Meanwhile, the brown-skinned boy—couldn't have been older than ten or eleven years old—approached the driver's side window.

"Qué pasa?"

"Talo bien," was about all the Spanish that Rose knew. That and *"sí."*

"Y el tigere, quien es?" the youngster asked in that broken slang that Dominicans used in the street.

"I'm the man," Rose replied, as usual. What he was supposed to say.

"Bien, bien. Uno momento," the kid said and he disappeared across the street. Rose knew this routine by heart, the way Sosa did business. The way he stayed unexposed. Safe.

"Now what? And what the hell was y'all talking about?" Tucker said.

"We wait, number one. And number two, we were using the code."

"You and a kid, using the code, while I'm trying to do a million-dollar drug buy?"

"Easy, cousin. Just sit tight and let it happen."

Gen-U-Shine Car Wash was situated on the corner across from where the Lexus was parked, where the codes were exchanged. The sole proprietorship and enterprise owned by Sosa and family consumed nearly an entire block. Its entrance was along the side street, on 218th, and vehicles rolled through, assisted by conveyor belts and mechanical devices, toward the exit on Broadway. The order had already been placed over the phone—Rose saying, "I need fifty of them things"—so the pickup was but a 1-2-3 transaction. The deposit for the dope was there in the trunk, in two Nordstrom shopping bags. Rose drove halfway down 218th and into Gen-U-Shine's entrance, unconcerned with today's special: Full Wash and Wax Coat—$9.99

He followed a Dodge Caravan and agreed to take the special—part of the act, in the event that five-o was watching. Five-o could be the florist, jealous of the car wash getting all that business. It could be the dude operating the mini–hot dog stand, even if he was making good money from all that traffic Sosa generated. It could even be the dude driving the white Dodge Caravan in front of him. Who knows?

Rose told himself these things as the Lexus was directed through the car wash. Halfway through, during the sudsing, everything suddenly stopped. Those big felt flaps that smacked the vehicle's exterior fell lifeless as dripping mop heads. The suds oozed down the tinted windows like some murky wet dream. Before visibility was possible, Rose could make out three shadows, Sosa and his boys, and unconsciously he rubbed the gunmetal concealed under his red jersey.

Some men wiped perspiration from their brows, others (when there was risk in the air) would fidget or scratch or clear their throat. But not Rose. He was reserved and relaxed, caressing his trusty weapon, ever alert and aware.

"That's one ugly dude. The heavyset one, is that Sosa?" Tucker asked.

"Mmm-hmm. But the one to watch is the beast to his left. If that nigga ain't carrying two toasters under his jacket, then the sun is black and blue."

Tucker considered this, but couldn't help thinking how Sosa looked like one of those gorillas from *The Planet of the Apes* movie—the one with the voice like an outboard motor.

"Sosa! My man. How you doing, my friend?" Rose said with the trying-to-be-Latin speech effects.

"Rose, *mi amigo*," Sosa responded with the cheesy smile, like he saw thousand-dollar bills stretched across their chests. His English was retarded, too.

"You come-a for the good white powder, aye? No more guns?" Sosa left the *R*'s and *T*'s out of his vocabulary, and his attempt seemed as phony as bottled tap water. Rose knew to play along with Sosa's plastic personality, familiar and clear about what Sosa was most interested in. Money.

"No, no, *mi amigo*. Me just help-a my cousin here. His name Tuck."

"Tuck? Me no deal with Tuck. Me deal with Rose. Rose good business for long time."

"Me understand, Sosa. Me want more money . . . me have guns and cocaine."

"Oh! You want de cocaine. You make-a de money. Me *comprende*. No problemo. You wanna fifty? Me give-a you fifty. But me no deal with a new customa. Me no know you cousin."

"*No problemo*, Sosa. You and me. Now let's deal." Rose wanted to get past the small talk, past the feeling-out process that the Dominican was putting him through. He had Tucker retrieve the two shopping bags from the trunk of the Lexus and one of Sosa's men, the dangerous one with the no-shit stare and the scar across his cheek, was fast behind him. There was a bench to the side of the car wash trail and Sosa had his subordinate check the money there. As the scarred man did the counting, Sosa made a head-shifting gesture to a man in a white Gen-U-Shine jumpsuit. He subsequently returned with another uniformed man, both carrying duffle bags filled with the bricks of cocaine.

Now, Sosa's man nodded. The money was all there. Sosa made a gesture in response, and just like that the deal was done. One hundred kilos of cocaine, most of it on consignment, handed over without any verification of the product or its purity. There was no need, so far as Rose was concerned. He'd sold Sosa a couple hundred thousand dollars' worth of guns in the past years. Colts, Glocks, Uzis, and Ingrams. It was a realization by both men; a knowing that one or the other had enough firepower to put an army to sleep for good.

"Why do I feel so relieved? Like I just got away with murder?"

"You should feel like that so you don't take these types of transactions for granted. You just pulled off a deal as large as an airline buying a new jet."

"Yeah, I never thought about it that way. A goddamned corporate merger. Shit!"

"Only difference," said Rose, "is these are street deals. Them corporate cats can't come into our game and do what we do, with codes and ethics and shit."

"And the average street thug can't come into the corporate arena, either. Nine out of ten times the corporate game has codes, signs, and gestures, too. Shit the average nigga can't understand, and really, if a corporate cat even sees a dude who don't belong around his game, he'll call five-o in."

"'Cuz that's that shit where force rules. Five-o be the ones that secure the corporate deals. Corporate-gangsta deals; the type of deals that get people out of houses so malls can be developed. Or the deals that abuse pension plans."

"Whoa. That's that science, dog. For real. 'Cuz their game is supposed to be the legit one. The respectable one."

"Well, believe me when I tell you," Rose explained as he wheeled the Lexus down Broadway, "a mothafucka gonna respect this here just as much." Rose pulled the submachine pistol from his waist and slipped it down under his seat. "More than just as much."

Despite the failed shipment, Tucker was able to fill his orders and keep his own clientele happy. He'd also do the consignment thing with his own runners. He sold a little of it himself as well, and he would take from Peter to pay Paul just so he could build capital. Becoming wealthy wasn't as easy as it seemed.

• • •

Squirrel was pissed. No word from Tucker and (he eventually learned from Freeze) Tonya had left the USA Diner alone that day when Freeze smacked her. Probably in her feelings about the incident. But also, Tonya hadn't been seen since. Squirrel wondered if that did have something to do with Tucker's lack of communication. Tonya and Tucker, brother and sister, both of them missing. This didn't sound too good.

CHAPTER THIRTEEN

Even as Tucker was selling product to his Wall Street crowd, building his empire, Rose was building his own little game (or rebuilding it) as well. The clients in the Bronx, in Harlem, and even up in Westchester County (clients which he'd been servicing while he lived in Brooklyn) were more of a priority now. Before, Bed-Stuy, Brownsville, and Canarsy were once his stomping grounds; hanging out on Flatbush, hitting off the crews and gangs in the Red Hook and Marcy housing projects, stretching his client base to the Italians in Brighton Beach and Coney Island.

Now, Rose had parts east and west of Harlem. He was servicing dozens of 9mms to the gangs on the Lower East Side, in the South Bronx, up in Soundview; and he had a ruthless group of thugs up in Mt. Vernon known as the Young Bloods. Rose always kept a personal stash of sixty guns such as 9mms and Glocks. His personal favorites varied, depending on what he was doing. If he was on the block, or shopping with his mom or sister's children, Rose carried a .357 Magnum. Tucker was curious about Rose and his personal stash, especially after the meeting with Sosa.

"Number one, the .357 is strong and it has a longer distance. So, if someone is trying to get at me and, well, let's say they try to get away, and the fool-asses left me alive . . . Well, at least I have something that'll reach 'em. They won't be goin' far. Number two, with that much power, I'll be able to keep people up off me."

"You mean if they happen to see the gun?"

"No. Hell, I ain't trying to scare nobody. I'm trying to put holes in 'em. And three, the revolver is more reliable than an automatic. Sometimes they jam up, like the Tech."

"So, what if you're just hanging out with the boys, like at the park or a party?"

"Well, I do very little hangin' out. Mainly, I'm workin', tryin' to get paid. But if I do go out, I'm keepin' a 9mm on me. Like a Ruger with a forty-five clip. I usually carry three forty-five clips with me. Now if there's beef, like, if I find out somebody's coming to see me, I'm keeping two guns on me. Chances are, a Mac ten and a four-five in my pocket. I'm also gonna have two dudes backing me up. There's gonna be AKs and Tech-nines all over the place."

"Damn, Rose, sounds like you know your stuff about them guns."

"Got to. Selling guns is a dangerous business. Nine out of ten times when a gun deal goes down somebody gets shot. Yeah, don't get that fucked up."

"I didn't hear you say anything about the Japanese joint, the one on the Sosa meet."

"Oh, I was just trying that out for the first time. Tell you the truth, I didn't like it."

"Trying it out? Dude, you talk like you wanted to test the damn thing." Tucker chuckled with his words. But down deep this wasn't funny. All the talk of guns led him to wonder if Rose was keeping his word about no guns in the house.

"Once, I went with this West Indian dude . . . Winston. He had a few customers who wanted nines. They were dope boys from 149th Street, uptown."

Rose explained the whole story. How he went up into the apartment, a building set up like a maze, where the dudes (three of them) were waiting, smoking and talking shit.

The tough-talker had a baby face; everything seemed enhanced, with his lips, ears, and forehead appearing too big. Too big for his body. He looked like he belonged in a cartoon chasing Bugs Bunny. Another guy appeared to be a gopher, a peon. Rose got the idea that he was a white boy who grew up in the hood but who just never fit in. The last guy was a yes-man. He had a patch of hair that was white like a skunk. They were immediately unhappy with the guns Rose brought.

"Man, those nines ain't shit. Made in China. I had one that fucking exploded on me," said Tuffy.

Winston panicked, wanting so bad to make a deal, to make his bullshit commission. "Hey Rose, why don't you show 'em your own heat?"

Rose was spellbound, he couldn't believe that this two-bit middleman opened his mouth about that. Rose figured, what the fuck. He'd just go buy another one. He took the personal 9mm from under his jersey, unloaded the tech clip he kept in it, and laid the nine on the table beside the three cheap pieces. Rose stood by and watched as the leader of the trio raised the nine and looked it over.

"What're you doing?" Rose asked loud enough for his voice to carry. The baby-faced man didn't answer. He had just popped in his own clip, arming the gun to mean business.

"Tell you what, Mr. Rose, you wanted, what, five hundred for each of these? And how much for this one? 'Cause you're gonna lose it anyway."

"Lose it? Lemme tell you something, buddy. I ain't never been robbed before and I don't plan on ever gettin' robbed."

The dope boy already had Rose's piece stuck in his belt. "Well, what we'll do is give you a thousand for all four guns. Take it or leave it."

"Take it or leave it?" Rose had a careful eye on everyone in the room. At the same time, he observed the scene, the chipped paint, the leaking faucet, the smell of a cat somewhere. Rose swore to himself that if this dude dared to reach for the nine . . .

He reached into his rear pocket for his backup. Now Rose had the upper hand.

"Yo! Easy man, we ain't mean nothing."

"You musta thought I was a punk or something—but now who's the punk? Huh? Huh? Huh? Don't even try it, pretty boy! This might look like it's a joke, but size ain't everything. I got five shots up in this, one for each of you and the extras for you."

Rose pressed the business end of the Firestar .45 up to the temple of the leader. "Get on the floor! Now!" When they did, Rose frisked all three dudes. He told the West Indian to stay his ass put in case he was a part of this all along. "Okay, where's the stuff?"

"What stuff?" answered the tough guy. Rose pulled the trigger, popping a bloody wound in the leader's leg. He yelled like a hyena.

"Now we'll try this again." Rose pressed his foot on the man's leg to stop him from tossing around on the floor. "Where is the stuff?"

"In the stove! The stove!!!"

Rose could tell the truth had come out by the expressions on the others' faces, like they'd just been raped. He wagged the gun at the West Indian, and obediently the guy went to the stove and opened the front. From where Rose stood, he could see the contents. Drugs. Money.

"Bring it. All of it," he said. "So, you were gonna rob me, huh? Big man with a gun, huh? Gonna give me a thousand dollars, huh? Take it or leave it, huh? Well, I'll tell you what . . . I'm gonna take five hundred for *each* of the ugly guns. I'm gonna take eight hundred for *my* gun . . ." Rose was peeling money off the bundles of cash. "Plus, I'm gonna double that amount, no, how about triple, say . . . four . . . five . . . how about eight Gs? Yeah, that's it. I'm gonna take eight grand, plus all your coke." Rose wasn't done. He had the skunk, the peon, and their injured leader take off their clothes and then locked them in the bathroom.

Through the door, Rose told them, "Now you all know where the West Indian lives, and he knows where I live. If you got beef about this, you come and see me. I'll be sure to show you my other work, let you test the bullets, too!"

Rose followed the middleman down the steps, listening to him apologize most of the way. He figured the guy to be naïve, not part of a conspiracy—he was too dumb to do something like that. "Hey!" he said to the dude as they reached the lobby of the building. When Winston turned, Rose swung, back-handing him square across the grill. "Stupid mothafucka."

After hearing Rose's story about the cats up on 149th Street, Tucker knew for sure he didn't want to ask about his cousin's personal stash, or if he'd been keeping any of that at the house. He just kept his mouth shut. But Rose must've been reading his mind.

"You're wondering if I'm selling guns out of your house, aren't you?"

"The thought did cross my mind."

"Let's take a ride."

"Again?" Tucker asked. It hadn't been more than a few hours since that trip to Sosa's car wash, and now those activities in his body started again; the spinning thoughts, the queasy stomach, and the racing heartbeat. It was clear now that any ride with his cousin could be his last. Hearing about and seeing some or all of those different kinds of guns had Tucker edgy, worried, and even a little afraid.

It was something like being with a superhero during a killer storm—the storm wouldn't be a threat to the super-hero, but for anyone else, for anyone without such super-powers (that would be Tucker), the best bet would be to find protection under the hero's cape.

Tucker shrugged his consent and soon found himself gliding down the West Side Highway into Harlem.

"They call this street Striver's Row. I can't tell you why because mostly I see nine-to-five workers filing out of their homes like cattle every morning. If you call that striving, well . . ."

Tucker listened as Rose had the car crawling down a block full of brownstones and town houses. He assumed that Rose had a friend who lived here, until he pulled out a set of keys and led Tucker up four narrow flights of steps. Tucker immediately figured that there was no way in hell anyone could get a refrigerator, dishwasher, or any other substantial appliance up these steps; nothing larger than four feet, anyhow. The stairwell was also dimly lit, like a doghouse might be, with the meager light that might be cast through the opening. Actually, with such a dingy, discolored carpet covering the stairs, the interior wasn't far off from what a dog would find comfortable.

At a loss for breath Tucker said, "D-damn, Rose! A dude could spend all his"—he swallowed some air—"energy getting up here. By the time he gets to the top, he could die and the EMS people might even die coming to rescue him." Tucker got out a full sentence, but he was trying to catch his breath as well.

"Believe it or not, there's a science to this."

"Yeah, learn to fly. Or else, keep your ass downstairs."

"No, I mean since I've climbed them so many times I've got it right. You just reserve your air. And then, of course, there are those that should keep their asses downstairs for their own safety. That's why I chose this spot. I don't want many visitors."

"You? Whatcha mean, you don't want many visitors? This is your spot, cuz?"

"There's a rule I have," Rose said as he opened the door, key in lock. "I don't do business where I sleep. But, for now, I'm sleeping at your house. So now I do business from here."

The confines of the fifth-floor apartment immediately closed in on Tucker's senses. The front door couldn't even open all the way, forcing the two to squeeze inside.

"This a studio?"

"It's small like a studio, but I have two bedrooms, a little kitchenette, and a bathroom. Works for me."

"So, this is where you come every day when you leave the house?"

"Basically. Come on through. Lemme show you around."

Tucker figured this would be short and sweet. On a wall along the way there was a black velvet poster of an African Queen who was naked from the waist on up. Her hair was braided like a crown of sorts, glistening with all of its twists curving all around her head in a spiral design. There was a second black velvet poster, it could've been the very same woman, with the pretty eyes, cheeks, and lips. Instead, this nude had her hair blown out in an Afro that could outdo any of the Commodores.

The hallway reached into a large room with tall ceilings and little furniture. Earth tones saturated the room with large throw pillows, wheat-brown carpet, kente cloth curtains, and candles that were situated here and there. A scent of plant life and some kind of spice hung in the air.

"I just can't believe you've been keeping this little spot from me all this time."

"Hey, weren't you the one to say no guns in the house? Besides, this is how I operate. I did it this way in Brooklyn, too. You ready?"

"Huh?"

Rose was opening another door; this one had a padlock.

"Tuck, my main man, my big dog cousin, let me introduce you to . . ." Rose paused for effect. Then once he swung the door open he said, "Wolf."

A muscled pit bull emerged from the dark room. He looked to be yawning as he swaggered out into the open. Tuck was still as stone. Trying to keep from climbing the wall or pissing his pants. He made the mistake of establishing eye contact with Wolf and the dog snarled.

"He's waiting for you to smile, so go 'head and smile before he attacks you." Tucker manufactured a smile. "Don't worry. He ain't in the mood to eat you or nothin'. He's trained real good—the quiet, lethal type. He do like me . . . wait patiently and strike without notice." Tucker took a second look at Wolf and realized there were scars.

"What's up with the scars?"

"That's how I found him. His owner use to use him in dog fights. He probably won a thousand joints; but the last one didn't go too well. That nigga was ready to dump Wolf in a trash compactor, until I stopped him."

"And you keep him locked in there all day and night?"

"Only while I'm gone. It's not like punishment or anything. That's his job—to guard my stash."

Tucker was thinking cocaine when Rose said "stash" because he too had stash spots. More curious about the room now, Tucker still couldn't help being concerned about Wolf.

"Easy, boy. Easy. That's it. This is cousin Tuck. Come on Tuck, give a smile, dammit. Pet him so he won't be a problem."

Tucker eased further into the room and stroked the top of Wolf's head. This was a sho' 'nuff leap of faith, causing him to want to pee.

"Okay, boy." Rose went and opened a window where there was a fire escape. Wolf meandered over to the window like it was routine, climbed up and out, then went up the fire escape steps.

"Smart dog."

"Yeah, he'll be up on the roof. That's where he lounges and takes in some sun. Thinks it's a resort up there. You should see him." Rose turned back toward the room and finally flipped the light switch.

"Ohhhh, shit," Tucker said in an exhale.

"I call this my war room, as in ready for war. These are the pistols over on this side; .45s, Saturday night specials, .38s, Magnums, M-ones, Glocks, Rugers, Berettas, and them Chinese 9mms I told you about . . . over here I got twelve-gauge joints with pistol grips, tactical slings, and barrel mounts for extra ammo. This is the Remington five hundred, the six hundred, and the eight-seventy. Here's your Winchester twelve hundred and thirteen hundred, the Massenberg five hundred, six hundred. These are different scopes for them . . ."

Tucker's eyes were following along and his ears hearing, but his mind was elsewhere, trapped in a blurry state of disbelief. He was suddenly lost. Ask him his name and he'd probably make a stupid face in response.

"These are my automatic assault weapons; extremely sensitive stuff here. M-16s. AR-15s with the red dot sight features; the machine guns; the oowop, which is basically a baby Uzi. Here's your AK-47, the Tec-9s, and next to the heavy stuff I got your ammo. Hollow points, buckshot, banana clips, all of it—maybe a couple thousand rounds. Finally, here's your Kevlar vests, masks, holsters, all that commando shit. The hunting knives, switchblades, and daggers complete my store." Rose sounded like a regular salesperson in a department store.

"Rose, who—who buys all this . . . .all these guns? You supplyin' the Marine Corps?"

"You writin' a report?" asked Rose. He gave the question (and Tucker) a second thought before going on to say, "You'd be surprised who I sell to. I get the local thugs, gangs, and drug dealers. I get working-class people who don't wanna go through all the licensing bullshit. They bring their friends and so on and so on. I also get private detectives, believe it or not; usually the ones who fucked up their license. One or two mercenaries come to me for the high-end shit, and I still have my Mafioso clients out in Brooklyn. It's a big business."

"I see that. You're stocked up like a damned department store. How long you keep this stuff?"

"I get a nice turnaround. These'll be gone soon, then I'll restock."

"Selling drugs is much less complicated, compared to this. People know what they want, and they just go."

"It's the same here. People know what they want. And what they don't know, I help 'em."

"What's the profit margin?"

"Profit *what*?"

"Margin . . . I mean, what do you spend and what do you make?"

"Okay, take this high-point assault rifle. If I buy a case, they're like one-ninety each. But I sell 'em for six hundred apiece. I can get seven, maybe more, if the buyer is desperate. The Tec-9 is dirt-cheap—two-fifty. I sell 'em for fifteen hundred. Some of the pistols, the Davis, the Lawson, I buy for sixty or seventy-five. I sell 'em for three, maybe four hundred."

"So, you're doing two or three hundred, even a thousand percent."

"I don't know about all that. I just know I'm gettin' paid."

"Sheesh, I never imagined you, my cousin, the god-damned gun specialist."

"It's a living."

Up until that afternoon when Rose showed Tucker how intense his profession was, how he was gettin' his hustle on, Tucker merely accepted his cousin saying "I got your back" as a figure of speech. He had no idea just how important or how thorough a resource that was. He had no idea how necessary that support might be at this time in his life.

It was a Friday, business as usual for Tucker, when he'd make his rounds down on Wall Street, Water Street, and parts of World Trade Center. In his neck of the woods, he didn't have to carry product or guns. He didn't even need to announce his arrival at the reception desks of the locations he visited. In a dapper three-piece suit, and with a name tag (usually provided by his associates), Tucker would stroll past any such formalities as doormen, security guards, and secretaries; he'd meet "his people" in staff lounges, cafeterias, and even in stairwells.

All of this constant activity to maintain his growing empire, taking orders in person—a kilo here, a kilo there—in an effort to bypass those damned electronic devices. Didn't these other drug pushers get the point by now? Didn't they know that cell phones, pagers and even e-mails weren't secure? That the Feds were hip to this convenience and made it their routine to listen in? On the evening news there were features that showed drug gangs in this and that city and how they were being taken down one by one. But was anyone watching these reports?

Tucker's strategy was a simple one: know your customer, know his capabilities, and always be able to supply the demand. He didn't spend his postgrad years in the financial industry without learning these things. Service. Supply and demand. Networking and organization. And yet, none of that business sense could help him with his latest problem.

It was following his busy day downtown when Tucker was confronted by his sister.

"He smacked me, Tucker! And hard, too." Tonya ran to her brother in tears.

He embraced her and seethed at the same time. Sure, he and Tonya had it out on occasion, cursing and all. And he had plenty of "I told you so" in his throat. However, the seeds that Mom and Pop instilled had taken root and grown strong despite these two siblings sprouting off in their different directions like wild weeds.

"No one put their hands on me, Tucker, not even Daddy." Tonya sobbed in and out of her words and this infuriated Tucker.

The first thing he could think of was driving up on Freeze—Tonya told him where they sometimes hung out—and blasting a hole right in his chest. He'd seen enough guns now to feed the urge. But having the balls to actually do something like that was another story. He had to admit to himself that he didn't have the heart that Rose had. It didn't seem to come with Tucker's state of being. What Tucker did have the wherewithal to do was cut Freeze (and his boy Squirrel) off as suppliers. Maybe his decision wouldn't have as big an impact as a hollow-point bullet in his chest, but it might hurt a little. And so Tucker had ignored Squirrel's attempts to reach him. He was doing business with Sosa and the Dominicans now.

CHAPTER FOURTEEN

Rose became more than just a cousin to Tucker. More than just a teacher. The two were becoming brothers. Tucker was coming over to his cousin's Striver's Row stash spot more and more frequently. He was even keeping his own product and cash there, figuring this place to be more secure than a bank. Even the pit bull Wolf accepted Tucker like a part of the family, play-fighting with him from time to time.

The cocaine that Rose took from the three dope boys on 149th amounted to four kilos. Because he got the dope for free, he could make maybe $160,000 if he sold it to individuals who used. He'd only make half as much if he cosigned it to dealers who already serviced users. But Rose was busy with the guns, so selling was out of the question. And besides, he had a bad taste in his mouth for drugs.

He eventually made a deal with a girl named Misa Stewart. She was about eighteen years old with a college girl's wit, a gang member's street savvy, and a businesswoman's attitude. It was only because she was a friend of a friend that Rose agreed to deal with her in the first place. And even then, he had to meet her at a public place. The Apollo Theater, they decided.

"There's an old-school show I'm going to, Ice Cube, Snoop Dogg, and them," Rose told her when returning her page.

"Oh, yeah. I heard about that. But don't they have metal detectors at the rap shows?"

"Yeah, but that's at the entrance, when you come in. They don't have 'em where I'll be coming in, through the back door."

"Oh," Misa said, but thought, Excuse me.

"I'll just make sure to leave a ticket for you at the front. Just bring ID to prove you are who you say you are."

"Not a problem," said Misa.

"And don't forget the five hundred. Cash."

"Oh, don't worry. I'll have your money. You just make sure you have what I need."

Rose quickly realized that Misa was not to be pimped. And already he liked her attitude. He hung up the phone and went to his arsenal. He thought about Misa, her situation and what kind of equipment would best suit her. He didn't know too much about her, just that she needed something reliable for a possible beef.

THE CONCERT

This wasn't just any "old school" concert at the Apollo. It was a hip-hop legends concert where the old-school groups, icons, and has-beens came together for a one-night-only event. The show was also broadcasted on pay-per-view cable and MTV as well. New York City radio personalities hosted the event. There'd be a tribute where some of the current chart-toppers would perform Tupac, Biggie, Easy-E, and Big Punisher compositions. Although the hip-hop nation had dozens of other fallen or slain personalities to whom respect was due, these four were the ones who stood out by far. The comedian/actor Chris Rock cohosted the event with the radio personalities. He caused a wave of spontaneous laughter to shake the auditorium and its sold-out audience of two thousand with his opening monologue.

"Dayum—hip-hop! What up, hip-hop?!! Is everybody up in this mothafucka or what? Shit, all the major people are here . . . all the rappers, all the producers, the rappers who became producers. The producers who think they can rap. The ones who hire rappers and producers because they don't have talent. We got all that under one roof. Gaaah-damn! Then of course we got the hip-hop mogul up in here. Give it up for Russell Simmons.

"See, Russell is to us what Shakespeare is to the white man. Yeah! They got Abraham Lincoln . . . said he freeeed the slaves. Well, we got a man who liberated us, and freeed our voices. That's right! Russell Simmons. They got Columbus . . . said he discovered America. Well, we got the man who discovered Def Jam . . . we got Russell Simmons. Oh yeah! That's right. They got their Calvin Klein and their brothers named Brooks. Well, we got a man who brought us Phat Farm . . . we got Russell Simmons. They got Rockefeller, Lee Iaccoca, Thomas Edison. They got Trump, Gates, and Greenspan. They got the Pope! And who do we have? Oh yeah! Russell Simmons! Fuck! What happens if Russell dies? I'm already starting to make plans for my retirement, just to synchronize them with Russell's biological clock—no shit! 'Cause when Russell kicks the bucket? I'm thinkin', hmmm . . . a whole *lot* of mothafuckas gonna be callin' in sick . . . traffic jams from Hollis to Manhattan . . . florists, tailors, and chauffeurs busy as a army of ants . . ." The audience seemed to be looking for the punch line in the joke, wondering what Chris Rock was leading up to.

"But me? Naahhh . . . I'mma be smart wit' mine. I'mma make sure I lock down my tickets to the after-party! And you *know* there's gonna be an after-party for Russell!"

Chris went on for a few more minutes of heart-wrenching comedy before he introduced a couple of his cohosts.

"Here they are . . . you all have heard of the song 'Me and Mrs. Jones' . . . well, give a big Apollo applause to the Hater and Miss J." Chris waited there onstage for the hot radio morning show hosts to appear, but nobody was coming from backstage. Then there were voices that could be heard loud and clear over the sound system. The comedian looked every which way wondering where the voices were coming from.

From Rose's point of view, sitting in a box seat in the upper reaches of the auditorium, this was obviously an act. But he found it amusing nonetheless.

"Listen, I'm gonna tell you again. I want an extra five hundred or I'm not goin out on stage. I already hate half of these assholes. These fake thugs, these half-homo storytellers who think their shit don't stink. So, for me, it serves no purpose to go out there."

"Is this blackmail? Extortion?" asked a desperate, distinguished voice. "Are you holding me up for more money at the last moment?"

"Hell no, not me. Miss J here, my associate in crime, is calling the shots. Miss J? Give 'em a piece of your mind."

"It's like this, Mr. Promoter . . . it's real, real simple . . . pay us off or we're going home now! I could be home gettin' my toes sucked, getting my ass . . . well, you know. Just say I could be having a lot of fun. Pay up!"

The audience was listening in to all of this, laughing and hollering, fluctuating back and forth between various emotions. There was the sound of paper flipping, ruffling; that desperate, distinguished voice again; only now it was counting the bills.

"One . . . two . . . three . . ."

When he was done, Miss J said, "Now, for me!"

"Well, I never!"

"And you never will, either, if you don't pay up, you half a homo!"

"One . . . two . . . three . . ."

Then a man took aggressive strides out to Chris Rock, standing amused out on stage. The man with his meek presence whispered something to Rock.

"O-kay! Once again . . . they are the hosts of New York's blazin' morning show, the Hater . . . and Miss J!"

There was a rumble of activity including everything from foot stomping to whistles. It was a love-hate relationship that kept these radio hosts so successful. The two emerged from backstage, the Hater swaggering with disinterest and Miss J bouncing with the energy of a live wire.

"Come on, Hater! Let's do this, so we can hurry up and be out of here!" Miss J could be heard even though she hadn't quite reached the microphone.

"All right, all right," he answered. And once he finally got up close to the mic, an exhaustive breath escaped his lips and he said, "Enough already with the applause. Please. I ain't no entertainer or rapper. I don't tell jokes and frankly, I don't even like my job. I'm just here. Got it? So don't expect me to do backflips onstage or dance or sing. Don't expect me—"

Miss J tapped the Hater on the shoulder, an interruption before she whispered in his ear.

"Okay . . . before I start spitting my venom all over you—because that's just what I do—please give a round of applause to Snoop Dogg for coming out, giving you that incredible opening performance."

As the audience applauded, a man with wild hair was causing a scene at the rear of the auditorium. From a distance, the disturbance could be heard to some degree.

"Get offa me!" the guy was yelling while trying to pry loose from the two Apollo ushers. "Lemme go! I'm tellin' you, I'm gonna git you fired!" Somehow the guy broke free halfway down the aisle.

"Ah, excuse me . . . ah, excuse me, usher?" Up onstage, the Hater was speaking into the mic but trying to conduct a one-on-one conversation. The entire auditorium was tuned in to the discussion.

"Ah yes, you. Uh . . . I don't know how to tell you this, but that guy you're after? He, uh, works with us. That's Rowdy. He's one of tonight's hosts."

The ushers, ever uncomfortable with all the sudden attention, released the man. They adjusted their uniforms and even helped their quarry off of the floor. With apologetic expressions they backed away as Rowdy strolled down the aisle with renewed pride.

"Ladies and Gentlemen . . ." the Hater said this with apprehension. "Please give a round of applause to Rowdy, my, uh, partner in crime." There was a minor argument once

Rowdy got to the stage regarding his being late and causing a disturbance. Miss J, once again, reminded the Hater that there was a show going on. "Oh—excuse me. On to bigger things. For our next performer . . ."

Those guys are too funny."

"Oh. Hey there. I didn't think you'd make it."

"Just running late. Sorry," Misa replied and sat next to Rose. The two were amongst the four others who had box seats.

"Ever been to the Apollo before?"

"Once. Saw the Sounds of Blackness and Mint Condition. My mother took me, but we sat down there—tenth row, orchestra seats. I think these are better, though."

Rose nodded, then directed his attention back to the stage.

"That it?" Misa asked. Rose was still focused on the stage. He nodded just the same. Misa's expression perked at the revelation. She glanced at the gift-wrapped box, with pink wrapping and a sky-blue bow, between Rose's feet.

"Let's get out of here," Rose said, already determined to get the business out of the way.

"I was looking forward to seeing the show," Misa said as she rushed to keep up with him.

"What if I suggested we meet in a movie theater or at a baseball game?"

"Now that you mention it, I kinda hate baseball."

"Me, too. I'll use that spot next time," Rose answered.

Misa thought, Next time? She followed Rose through the hallways, down two flights of steps, and into the lower lobby in the basement of the Apollo. Misa could tell that they were underneath where all of those hip-hop fans sat because of all the rumbling overhead. Applause. Foot stomping. Whistles. Some of the audience noise filtered through the vents in the basement. And then Misa realized that there were speakers down where they were, sending a low-volume sound through the halls and lobbies.

Rose pushed a door open that had a sign—STAFF ONLY— and Misa found herself in low-lit corridor similar to what she'd seen on television when basketball players leave the court. They'd stroll down these type passages to reach the locker rooms.

"I guess this'll do." Rose pulled the bow off the box and then the lid. He held it out for Misa to see. "Go 'head. Take it out. See how it feels."

As low and intimate as Rose's voice was, Misa had to shake the idea that he was speaking sexually. She looked left and right; the coast was clear. Then she took the pocket-size 9mm pistol from the box and the pillow of tissue therein.

"So, if you don't mind me asking, what's a chick like you need a piece for? You ain't gonna rob nobody, are you?"

Misa wanted to address the "chick" in Rose's vocabulary but—and this felt like a first—she kind of liked how he said it; it might imply somehow that she was a subordinate to this friend of a friend.

Some laugher seeped through the vents again; probably them radio hosts, Rose figured as Misa flipped the automatic weapon side to side.

"Just . . . protection."

"Protection," Rose repeated. A hint of doubt. Misa put the gun back in the box and Rose covered it, still waiting for answer.

"Yeah, you want your money now?" Misa was already going into her handbag. It was some designer name that Rose never heard of. Some funny name.

"Whatever. Can I walk you out to, did you drive?"

"No. That's all right. I'm cabbing it tonight."

"Listen." Rose touched Misa for the first time and she took offense, burning a hole in the back of his hand with her eyes. Rose withdrew his hand, then said, "If you don't mind me saying, I think you're full of shit. I don't think you've ever used a gun before and maybe, just maybe, you're scared of somebody, to the point that if you don't know how to use this, if you don't use this right, you could get yourself killed"—he snapped his fingers—"just like that."

"If you don't mind, Mr., uh Rose, can we get this done with? Here's your money. I'd like to leave."

Rose took the folded bills and counted them slower than he might otherwise. Then he opened the box once more, grabbed the gun from inside, and handed Misa the empty box. She took the box, not quick enough to realize what just happened.

"Hey, come back here! Hey!" Rose left out of the same door and Misa was fast behind him. "See, now you gonna make me get stupid up in here," she said. Rose didn't slow. Misa sucked her teeth and said a few "mothafuckas" under her breath as she chased him. The two breezed past the constellation of late arrivals, drawing a look here and there before they reached the sidewalk just under the marquee. Rose saw what he wanted and started off again, leaning toward the closest taxi. Misa had "I'll be damned" written all over her face, but she didn't let up. She didn't want to scream or make too much of a scene so as to alert police. In the back of her mind she asked herself what they (the police) would do if she let her emotions run wild and shouted, *"Hey! He got my gun! Stop him! He's got the five hundred I paid for a nine!"* It would be suicide.

Rose was in the backseat now, but instead of closing the door he left it wide open. Misa had to stop herself, to get control. She couldn't understand what this guy was putting her through; how he had her lose her bearings so quickly. She had to take a breather—she felt as though she'd just done the fifty-yard dash in a speed walker's record time. Eventually, she got in beside Rose.

The taxi ride took an hour to get from the Apollo (on 125th Street) to 138th Street. Rose had the driver take "the long way," which included snaking through Central Park and then back up to 138th. By the time the cab reached Rose's crib, Misa was dreamy-eyed and tenderhearted. The little lipstick that she had on was smudged and the lips themselves were swollen from the friction that only passion, lust, and pleasure could produce. Rose's lips were a little swollen as well—and the driver's face was reddened from so much eaves dropping. Rose, the kisser.

What took place thereafter wasn't the usual for Rose. Usually this might be another of those one-night stands. But that's not what went down. He showed Misa his crib, then introduced her to Wolf and his personal stash of weapons. Usually, Rose might be twisting this hottie's back out, showing her his other personal stash. But it didn't work out that way with Misa. He just couldn't take her there; to that state of worthless, impulsive fast-food sex. She was bigger than that. Instead of the here today, gone tomorrow scenario, Rose took Misa to the roof that night. He taught her how to shoot the 9mm. Taught her how to load and unload it. How to wear it so that it was readily available. Such activities were not uncommon up in Harlem.

As the evening grew into morning, the two sat up there on the roof and talked until the moon was in another place altogether, relocated from far east to far west above their heads. Misa told Rose about her crew. The Hot Girls, she called them. She told him about Charmaine, the rough (but not necessarily sharp) girl who always wore her diamond bracelet (whether during fight or flight) and the skullcap tight over her shoulder-length hair. "Sometimes, I think her skullcap is too tight on her head," Misa joked.

Misa told Rose about Trina, the sexy one, who loved furs, skimpy outfits, and women, probably as much as she loved men. Chanté was the darkest of the Hot Girls, and she always kept that primitive straight-from-the-jungle look with wild dreads sprouting in every which way (like short, limp asparagus stalks); she wore all kinds of fashionable camouflage outfits as well to accent her attitude.

Finally, Misa talked about Iris and Liza Fuentez, the two Latina sisters who had recently overcome some hardships in their own worlds. Both girls were nineteen years old and pretty enough to be actresses, songbirds, dancers, or fashion models. But they grew up in a suppressive environment. They grew up in Spanish Harlem, on a block where buildings were just as crammed together as the families living in them. It wasn't just brother or sister, or mother or father in the apartment. There might be in-laws, cousins, and best friends living there, too. That meant additional trash, odors, the noise of loud salsa music and kids playing out in the hallways.

For Iris and Liza, growing up was never an easy process. There was always drama that they'd witness and sometimes become a party to. Misa knew the sisters ever since she went to P.S. 104 with them. She couldn't help observing them as friends do, learning about their ways, their practices, and a little of that lickity-split Español, too.

It was sometimes peculiar and sometimes ironic to see how a lot of young girls from the inner city lived alike, with the fascination for hair color, jewelry, and all things fashion. The frivolity of it all was constant throughout the hood; the fanatic embrace of the teen idols and pop stars, their love and pride for those who "represented" them throughout the decades—Rita Moreno, Gloria Estefan, Lisa Lisa, Salina, and Jennifer "J.Lo" Lopez.

Misa spoke in depth about the realities of Iris and Liza's family, explaining how their situations (no matter the issue) were simple, copied over and over. Day after day, it was always something. Fights. Domestic disputes. All of it taking place so often that police presence was constant, with the locals recognizing officers on a first-name basis.

Fortunately for Iris and Liza, who were not quite twins, they were able to sidestep the various hood dilemmas without scars; visible ones, anyhow. Perhaps it was because they were pretty and had so many friends that they made it through. Whatever the case, these two survived that never-ending itch cycle where the boys chased the girls, and the girls fought and clawed and cut each other over boys. There was that whole self-perpetuating black hole of wasted energy, of experience, of whim, love, and hate; all of that was the reality of the hood.

When it came time to shed the family shell, to start doing what big girls do, Iris and Liza fell in line with club-hopping, partying, smoking cigarettes (sometimes weed), and many of the activities the other teenage girls did. They'd need to target a man, preferably with the fly ride and the respect of his peers.

Misa explained, "Iris felt some jealousy because Liza found a man first. All the jealousy made her a little stuck-up bitch. Iris still ain't got no man. But check this out; Liza ended up getting with one of the Nietas you know, them Latin gang dudes. He was dealing 'n stuff, making mad cash. But then there was some argument, some shit, and they came and killed him, execution-like."

"Okay, so what's this got to do with you buyin' the gun? What's it got to do with you, period?" Rose asked, trying to push Misa to make her point.

"Iris and Liza, Chanté, Charmaine and Trina; they all my girls, to the death. People know us as the Hot Girls. When one has beef, we all have beef."

"So you run a gang."

"We run together, that's all. We ride."

"Ride?"

"Everybody got bikes. GSXR 1100s. We bought 'em a few years ago; ready to get the new shit, too."

"You mean all you girls are a damn motorcycle gang?"

"Not like the Hells Angels or anything."

"No hairy armpits and beards?"

Misa chuckled. "No . . . and no Harleys, either. Those are so ugly."

"Where y'all ride?"

"We do the strips over on Rockaway, the Conduit. We do Eastern Parkway, Linden and Atlantic. Wherever shit is poppin'."

"Ain't those racing strips?"

"What, women can't race?" Misa made a face.

"Well . . ."

Misa sucked her teeth and said, "Nigga, my girl Chanté won three Gs once. One race. Cash money. Trina be poppin' wheelies with her thong showin', and the rest of us can get down, too. Don't get it twisted."

"I gotta see this," Rose said doubtfully. "But, get to the part about the gun."

"I think it's jealousy, really. You know, the way other peeps look at us. Hatin' and shit. I just think we gotta be ready for Freddy, you feel me? Life is dangerous on the streets."

Rose eventually did feel her. He even invited Misa to bring her friends to Striver's Row so he could teach them all correctly how to shoot, to load, and to carry. Funny thing was, as they were introduced Rose felt as though he already knew each girl. And the group of them hit it off like old friends. He even took a financial bite when he gave the Hot Girls two additional 9mms. Not the cheap ones, either.

As their relationship grew, Rose found out much more than he would've guessed. It never crossed his mind to ask Misa early on just what it was that her Hot Girls did for money. How did they survive? How did they eat? Charmaine, it turned out, didn't purchase the diamonds she wore. She was "gifted" in the check and credit card fraud game. The high-priced jewelry and leather she wore was "acquired" through her criminal know-how. What she didn't wear, she sold to fences.

Trina, the girl who wore the expensive furs and skimpy undergarments, had a good trick game. She was a pro at targeting money and those who had it. By night, her "office" was T&A, in the South Bronx, which became the new "tittie spot" when The Goat was shut down. The club owner was running a shabby operation and he let just about anything go. Trina used that opportunity to turn tricks. If the customer was from out of town, she would seduce him to a motel room and, without so much as a kiss, she'd take him for every dollar he had. In all, she had nearly a dozen triple-A clients who each knew her by different names. Lady T. T-Baby. Tee-Tee. Tina. Trina could come up with a million of 'em. It was her way of keeping her pussy exclusive, or so she'd make it seem. On a bad night, Trina was bringing home $1,500.

"Okay, so now I feel like I know you chicks personally: Trina at the T&A, Charmaine with the check game, Iris lives with Liza ever since Liza's man was murdered—and it sounds like the guy was handling his business, too. What did he leave, like a quarter of a million before he bit the bullet?"

"Basically."

"I bet y'all been livin' lovely off a' that dough."

"Mostly, we argue over it. But yeah, we livin'."

"And then, I can't forget about Chanté, who races for prize money. That leaves you," Rose said while they all sat in a group, smoking weed and talking shit on the roof. "How you eatin', Misa?"

"Hmmmph . . ." Misa made that sound through her nostrils alone, then said, "A little of this, a little of that."

Rose asked, "What's that mean? Trina does a little of this and a little of that, too."

"Nigga, don't even try it. Remember you the one who taught me how to use a piece," said Misa, with a no-nonsense look in her eye, as she issued the mild, playful threat. Even Trina looked at Misa for an explanation.

"So? What you sayin' then?" Rose asked.

"I don't have nothing against Trina and what she does, 'cuz I know she does that shit good. Ain't no bad blood 'tween me and my girls." Trina had a saucy smile concealed.

"Stop beating around the bush." Rose changed his tone to one she'd remember from the taxi ride, amidst those soft kisses.

"I . . . I sell a little shit. Just to get by, nothing major. A few regulars keep me eatin', ya know?" Misa had some guilt about her. Rose read it as humble pie. And that's when he finally figured out what to do with the cocaine he had stripped from those 149th Street dope boys.

Misa didn't stop coming around. Rose passed her those four kilos and expected nothing in return. However, Misa was honorable. She brought back $40,000 in a gift-wrapped box; a pink-and-blue bit like Rose had done with the 9mm at the Apollo the night they met. It was symbolic and romantic at once, and Rose was thrown off by the idea of Misa's devotions and sense of duty.

It was also at that moment that Rose allowed himself to go all the way. The kissing a few weeks earlier and on subsequent occasions was but a warm-up. Maybe it was the money, the idea of Misa being such an aggressive woman—whatever. Rose was hot with passion. And he took Misa's love. It was selfish, intense, and all-consuming. When it was over, in the morning, instead of guilt, Rose felt liberated and attached. He was glad for his decision to wait; happy that Misa was more than just a one-night stand.

After only six months since relocating from Brooklyn, Rose had a little family going in Harlem. Misa and her Hot Girls were constant visitors (maybe twice a week), creating a small party every time they were over. The others knew Misa and Rose were an item, but nobody dwelled on it. For the most part, it was something about Rose that these six women admired and respected. He filled a void for them and they embraced it heartily.

The family was complete. Resources were too numerous to realize. Rose with the arms, Tucker with the drugs. Misa with her Hot Girls. All told, the eight of them created a helluva cash flow together.

CHAPTER FIFTEEN

Y o, this is the part, man. Damn! Straight drama. The music is even making my nerves bubble. It's like . . . I want him to turn around and get that snitch, but then again I don't . . ."

Tucker was cheerleading while watching the movie *Heat*.

"I want him to get away. He got the money, he got the girl, and he got his freedom. But if he goes back, he risks it all . . . just to clear the account . . . just to make the story politically correct. Damn! That fucking rat is gonna catch it!"

"Like the man said, don't mess with anything that you can't leave in less than thirty seconds," said Rose.

"Yeah. Dig it. But the girl he got is so damn fine. It's a pity—hey, what's the station out here? I think we're losing WOW 103."

"Try K-nine-seven," said Rose as he looked over at Tucker in the passenger's seat. "You can't make up your mind, huh. The DVD player. The radio. The DVD player."

"Call it my fascination with electronics. There's something about images and sounds that I just gotta have."

"Ever since you started making big green, you been changin' man."

"Changin'?"

"Yeah. Changin'. You and the gadgets. You and the designer labels. You and the crackhead women."

"Come on, Rose. I keep a beeper, a cell phone, and sometimes this DVD player. Sometimes. As far as the clothes, the only designer name I'm wearing now is my Rocawear joints."

"Yeah. And that's just your shirt and pants. You probably got Calvin drawers on and what about them Prada gators I seen you with?"

"So, sue me."

"I am gonna sue you if you let them crackhead bitches of yours in my crib again."

"Ain't shit, Rose. They just clients."

"Yeah, client crackheads . . . I can understand the young one, Tuck. She's your age. I'd even do her on a bad day; but did you have to bring her mother into it, too?"

"Whoa, whoa, whoa, dog. I didn't plan that shit. Yeah, they both came to the crib to buy a couple ounces they said, but the daughter was the one to suggest the quickie. I'm not turning that down, dog. That's Dawn Struthers! A god-damned fashion model! I showed you her spread in the *Essence* mag."

"Yup. And I still don't believe my eyes."

"Anyway, I let her and her moms in to pick up the shit. Next thing I know, they want to do a couple of lines on the kitchen table. They say they can't wait till they get home. Dawn gives me the eyes, that lil' wink they do, and next thing you know I'm hitting it doggie-style in the bedroom . . ."

Rose was cruising at 50 mph on Interstate 95 headed for North Carolina. He was making good time, having reached the outskirts of Richmond within five and a half hours. The two were expecting to hit Durham within two hours and in the meantime were tolerating the beat-up brown Dodge Dart they were using in an effort to curtail any idea that they were cash rich and up to no good.

"So, I'm hitting that ass, man; I'm telling you there ain't nothin' in this world like some good, wet, supermodel pussy."

"Yeah, but she was on crack, dude. You don't get no points for that shit. You coulda just as well got a blow-up doll."

"I don't sell them crack, just powder."

"But you put the meth in the powder."

"Well . . ."

"Yeah, you do . . . and when you do that it turns up the high like five times. The bitch is gonna come running to you every day, like you her oxygen. Then she's gonna treat you like God 'cause she thinks you are God."

Tucker sucked his teeth. "It's all mental."

"You're telling me it is."

"Okay, so I'm guilty. But I know one thing; if the shit I'm serving them is gonna make a bitch and her moms do me . . . at the same time? Just call me guilty, guilty, guilty."

Rose wagged his head, telling himself um-mmm-mmm. He couldn't imagine the arrangement.

Tucker told him, "Don't knock it till you try it, dog. And like I said, it wasn't my idea."

It was a long drive and Rose was in the mood to be amused. He eventually asked, "So while you're banging the *Essence* chick, Moms just creeps up on you?"

"I swear to God she did. Before I realized what was happening, moms got my shit spread open with her tongue making lizard sounds in my ass!"

Rose, with a head wag, said, "That's that crackhead shit I'm talking 'bout. Ain't no woman in her right mind gonna come up from behind and lick your ass while you bangin' her daughter. She's gotta be ten cents short of a dime upstairs."

Tucker shrugged and went back to concentrating on *Heat*, which was playing on the device in his lap. "This is the part. Psssh . . . smooth mothafucka. Got the hotel cleared and getting ready to blow a hole in dude's chest. That's what I'm talkin' 'bout. That's the heart. That De Niro–type shit."

Rose listened to his cousin but he also thought hard about the monster Tuck was becoming. He knew where the blame would lie. The guns, the drugs, and the money. It was all going to Tucker's head. He never cursed this much. Never got so involved with the females. Rose only hoped Tucker wasn't violating one of the ten crack commandments: "Don't get high on your own supply."

CHAPTER SIXTEEN

In Fayetteville, Rose had business to take care of. He'd exhausted a lot of his automatic weapons, the stuff that he knew as his "bread and butter." The stuff that paid for his cars, for some of the expensive dinners he indulged in, and for that one-way trip to Africa he'd take one day. It had been a minute since the last time he'd come down this way for a purchase. But the agenda was pretty much routine. There were a few gun fairs to go to. Two of them in North Carolina alone. A third was in South Carolina near the Marine Corps boot camp on Parris Island. There was also that ex-Marine down there, a friend who sold stuff he'd stolen off of the base. They were dirt cheap, but the best weapons in the business. Rose was looking forward to picking up a couple of those phased-out NATO flash grenades—those with the rounder bodies, before they went to the narrow design. Just something to have, Rose figured.

When he came down this way, Rose always stayed at his Aunt Julia's place. She had moved from The Grove, a cluster of housing developments that most recognized as "the projects," and into a one-family house over on Ridgeway, a three-minute walk.

Rose would only be down for a three-day stay, long enough to meet his contacts and fill the Dodge's hidden compartments with guns. In the meantime, Tucker planned to check out the area, and maybe he'd confirm some things that were said about the product down here. That it was inferior, cut way too much to compete with what he pushed up in New York.

Tucker strolled along Merchants Road, one of the main arteries in town, with its shops, boutiques, and eateries. He thought it was strange how similar this looked to 125th Street. Except for the darker asphalt road, the excessive telephone wires and wooden poles . . . except for all the young trees that lined the strip, this was as urban an area as in New York's Harlem, as in Cincinnati's French Quarter, or as on Newark, New Jersey's Broad Street. Very ethnic. Very busy.

Tucker knew he was out of pocket and far away from anyone who knew him. And it was a fact that tourists got jacked for cars, jewelry, and money. So he kept a low profile behind shaded glasses, in humdrum clothes and a blue-and-white Tarheels cap. With all this bustle he'd go unnoticed for sure.

It was outside Church's Fried Chicken that a young kid—he couldn't have been older than twelve—solicited Tucker.

"Smoke? Blow?" The kid didn't even keep it a secret. He was a walking, talking billboard.

"Whatchu got?" Tucker asked.

"Whatchu want?" the kid shot back, replete in a Panthers football jersey, baggy jeans, and fresh Nike kicks.

"A lil' somethin small. I ain't tryin' for nothing big. Maybe a onion."

"Yo! Really? Yo, follow me. I gotta—hey!" The kid was breaking up. A bit disoriented and overanxious. "See that video store?"

Tucker looked across the street toward a shop that was less attractive than other businesses on the block. Then he nodded.

"So, when you go, ask for nineteen eighty-four."

"Nineteen eighty-four?"

"Yeah," the kid squealed. "Nineteen eighty-four."

"Then what?"

"Just push forty in the tray—get yo' shit 'n go."

"Just like that."

"Mmm-hmm."

"Bet." Tucker made the buy. Then he took his phony video rental—a plain cardboard box with the ounce, a Saran-wrapped packet of cocaine, inside—and he returned to Aunt Julia's house.

"The video store, huh?" Aunt Julia caught Tucker by surprise. Not because she appeared from out of nowhere but because of the way she said that. Like she knew he had drugs in the bag.

Tucker was caught somewhere between what to say and what to not say. "I . . ."

"You're wondering how I know?" Aunt Julia had her hands on those baby-making hips. Julia had that wide hourglass effect goin' on—the one that a lot of thirty-somethings are packing after a few children and many more soured dreams.

Tucker was speechless.

"I done seen hundreds of them setups, youngun. Ain't nothing new if you lived where I done lived. I may come from the old school but that sho' is dem drugs they sells at the video store. Ain't no sense in bein' shy. Do whatchu gotta, baby."

"Aunt Julia, I don't use no dope."

"Sure baby. You can tell Auntie Julia anything."

"Really."

"So whatcha doin'? Sellin'?"

"Maybe. You know any users around here?" Tucker figured he'd ask since the cat was already out of the bag. And Aunt Julia seemed extremely open for an old-school broad.

"Where I used to live. The Grove projects got two ladies, they use to be my neighbors when I lived there. They black and white and they sniff so much a' that there stuff that I'm fittin' to go into business myself. 'Cept 'n that ain't really possible on account of Junebug. Ain't nobody sellin' around here unless his name on it."

"Oh, yeah?"

"Sho' 'nuff. Whatchu want wit' a user? Since you just bought you some down the way?"

"The truth? I'm lookin' to give this to them."

"Give?"

"Yup, for free. Nothin'."

"Huh? Oh, I get it. You lookin' for a trick."

"Nope."

"I give up."

"Just put me on with them ladies." Tucker felt himself picking up Aunt Julia's slang. Her accent, too, just to assimilate.

Aunt Julia made one phone call and set it up. She had to tell the women twice what Tucker wanted to do, how he wanted to give them some free blow. At the same time, the women didn't want to wait for him to come over.

"He might get lost, bein' new around these parts 'n all," it was suggested. So they hurried over to Julia's place.

"I wanted to see your new place anyways, Julia."

"Wow. You really made ya mark, woman. Cain't be nothin' but proud a' you."

The taller woman was nicknamed "High Yellow" behind her back. The other woman, shorter and less of an Amazon than her friend, had a head of hair that towered over her face. Tucker pictured her as a shorter version of Tina Turner only her legs were gross, with those ugly blue veins swelling under the skin. Ugly Legs was quiet, docile even, while the taller woman did all the discovery.

"So whatchu usin' us like they do dem ginney pigs? This some bad dope?"

"Not at all, boo. I was just lookin' for users from around this way. I think my stuff is ten times better than the stuff y'all got."

"Ten times, huh? Good as Junebug's?"

"Maybe better than that."

The two women looked at each other, then back toward Tucker. He felt that familiar pattern about them, that first impulse that users followed, with the idea of that ultimate high speeding around somewhere up in those empty heads of theirs. Some kind of rush that comes from all things dangerous. It was as if Tucker had suggested, "You can be *really* alive if you try this!" That's how High Yellow and Ugly Legs were acting.

Tucker gave them the package from the video store, the stuff they were most accustomed to. Then he gave them two of his own gram bags. He overheard the tall one say, "It's party time," as the couple took the samples into Aunt Julia's bathroom. There was a slight argument behind that bathroom door, something about being able to try Tucker's stuff first—then silence.

Twenty minutes later, the two had still not emerged from the bathroom.

Aunt Julia said, "I hope they didn't leave my bathroom a mess," and then she left to pick up groceries on Merchants Road. In the meantime, Rose returned from a run. He had a nylon tennis bag which Tucker knew for certain had guns in it, not tennis rackets.

"What's cookin'?" Rose asked, lowering the bag on the couch with the sounds of gunmetal hitting and scraping each other.

"We have company. A couple of your aunt's friends are in the bathroom."

"Oh." Rose didn't think much of Tucker's statement until it suddenly hit him. "Did you say a *couple* of her friends?"

Tucker nodded. He was sitting back in an easy chair, watching *Wheel of Fortune* on TV for the images alone. The sound in the living room was care of Boogie D playing the latest jams on the radio.

"What're they, fixin' somethin' for her?"

"Yeah, they're fixin' somethin' all right."

Rose shrugged, yawned, and said, "I'm gonna lay it down. Long trip, long day, and it's back to the rock pile tomorrow."

"Anything I can help with?"

"Naw. Thanks, but this is a one-man job. Pops always said if it ain't broke . . ."

"I know . . . don't fix it," Tucker said with a smile. But he knew damned well that there was no advice of Rose's dad he'd ever take heed to. To even think about the old head in cuffs, shackles, and behind bars was a tough image to shake.

Tucker also knew that Rose was bigger than that. He had much greater potential than to wind up in prison. But even that was a confusing thought. Wasn't Rose doing the type of dangerous shit that might put him away for life?

On the second day in North Carolina, while Rose was off at the Empire Gun Fair in nearby Charlotte, Tucker found himself serving cocaine soup kitchen–style. At first he was apprehensive when Aunt Julia's friends returned to the house at 7:30 in the morning (for God's sakes) for some more of Tucker's product. They didn't expect it for free, either. They had cash in hand.

"Listen, I'd better meet you somewhere else and do this. This is Auntie's house—she wouldn't want—"

Aunt Julia overheard this and stepped up to the screen door where the three conversed. "Just what is it Auntie Julia wouldn't want? Whatchall talkin' 'bout over here? Ain't you girls come over here yesterday and mess up my bathroom? Whatchu want now?"

Tucker was relieved when he saw her smile as she said this. At least she wasn't really upset, he thought. But Aunt Julia went beyond that and invited the two in again.

"This house looks better every day, Julia. You sho' doin' yo' thing. Need a maid?"

"See, you know I was gonna ask her that."

"Ya slow, ya blow, bitch," the Amazon said. Tucker was pulling the screen door closed behind the ladies when he noticed someone else. A real skinny woman whose eyes seemed too big for their sockets. She was out there on the walkway with her hands on her hips.

"You got a friend out there? Some skinny girl?"

"Oh, m'bad. I forgot. Julia, you think we could bring Brickhouse in for the party? I mean . . . for a minute?" Julia swore she heard the big-haired woman say party, but the sentence kind of drifted off at the tail end.

"Who's Brickhouse? She from The Grove?"

"Nah. She from 'cross the way. The Chestnut Ridge Projects."

"Oh." Julia looked out of the living room window and asked, "Why they call her Brickhouse?"

The other lady held in a chuckle, knowing damned well Skinny sold her house to buy a brick of cocaine. Signed over the deed to a dealer over there named Preacher who now rented the same house back to her. And, because of that, people started calling her Brickhouse. The response to Julia's question was, "Sho' can't be on account of her body 'cause the bitch thin as nails."

Tucker let out a short laugh, having never heard the metaphor before. He was also amused at how these women, up in their years, would talk so candidly, so straight from the hip about one another.

"Why not? Bring her in. You responsible for anything missing from in here," said Julia. The warning caused Tucker to look a second time, considering what his challenge might be now having to play cop and all.

Once all three women were in the house, the air seemed to change. There was desperation, hunger, and a bit of fright in their eyes. One woman was shaking a leg nervously. Tucker wanted to ask her to stop. Instead, he offered her a seat. Thin-as-nails (aka Brickhouse) kept looking at the ceiling, and then the floor, and then she picked up in her nose and couldn't figure where to wipe it off. Tucker turned away.

"So wassup?" the Amazon asked.

"You tell me," Tucker replied.

"Can we get down again?"

"Whatchu lookin' to spend?"

"Whatever!" Brickhouse finally broke her silence. Tucker was relieved like the others to see Skinny's hands stuffed in her back pockets. They worked out the money end and the women made a powder room out of Aunt Julia's leisure area. And just like that, a brood of Fayetteville locals, in groups and separately, snorted up Tucker's drugs. The various reactions occurred; from the head jerking to the sudden loud outbursts, to the shaking limbs. For as long as they could stand it, Aunt Julia and Tucker sat and watched the three with no shame. It was like watching a movie; tragic, yet comical all at once.

Charlie "Junebug" Johnson had been a defiant one ever since he was an adolescent the height of a fire hydrant. In preschool he was squeezin' girls' asses. In grade school, he was lighting up and tossing stink bombs down the hallways while classes were in session. Junebug never saw junior high school or high school like other boys his age. He instead joined up with them Trent Boys. And by age twelve things got out of hand.

School was nothing but a cover-up for a group of boys who folks around the way knew as "them Trent Boys." They spent their days stealing. They stole bicycles from neighborhood children, clothes and sneakers from the local mall, and there was always a house to break in to when the owners were working. By evening, them Trent Boys were on the street corners smoking weed, drinking beer, and trying to act grown.

Although Junebug and the others weren't gun-toting thugs (yet), a few of them toyed with BB guns and pellet guns. They busted out windows and streetlights. They shot at stray dogs. When those targets became boring, the Trent Boys began holding people up. They started on elderly pedestrians until they became experienced enough to go for local merchants. The pellet gun was heavy like a Glock, and very believable when waved in front of a shop owner. But the proprietor of Jay Jay's Grocery saw through the charade. When he pulled out a sawed-off shotgun in response, Junebug and company were trapped.

One of the fake gunmen had nerve enough to shoot his pellet gun at the proprietor and ended up with his arm shot clean off at the elbow. The three others froze in horror at the sight of Stretch and his missing forearm.

The following week, Junebug was a resident of Stonewall Jackson Training School for Boys. All the troublemakers were sent here, stripped of their liberty, their families, and their rights until they earned "twenty one fifty." It took the average young buck six to seven months to earn enough points to be freed: 2,150. Any infraction or incidents in this community of the knuckleheads, the misguided, would result in points lost.

But no matter how many problems a boy had inside of Stonewall, Dobbs, or Summer Cam training schools, the law said that at age eighteen—despite the points lost or earned—a boy was considered an adult and therefore had to be freed with his preadult activities stricken from the record.

But even after Junebug left Stonewall Jackson at age eighteen, he still couldn't stay out of trouble. Fights. Stealing. Acting up in class. To him, life was a blank canvas painted with the hopeless colors of high risk, violence, and a what's-yours-is-mine attitude. His very plan when he left Stonewall was to 1) get hold of a 9mm automatic; 2) visit Jay Jay's Grocery as a wiser, leaner threat, more so than that man would ever imagine; and 3) one day become a kingpin.

Danny "Preacher" Williams had a different North Carolina upbringing than Junebug. He was raised down the way in the Chestnut Ridge Projects. These housing developments were located on the other end of Fayetteville and made of redbrick, visibly different from those cinder-block dwellings that made The Grove look so cold and lifeless.

And while Preacher could've easily become part of the local gangs as a boy, he sidestepped those realities through his parents' planning. They had their own point system that ruled Preacher's childhood. If he did good, he'd receive a silver star. If he did great, he'd get a gold star. In a household of six brothers and sisters where he could've easily been overlooked, young Danny stood out as the star achiever. On weeks where he'd receive the most gold stars, Danny would be blessed with a gift of his choice. He earned a bike. He earned a home video game. There was that remote-controlled airplane, too.

During the summer and on school breaks, Danny was sent to the farm that his uncle owned. It was a shift from first gear to fifth, to shed his hip street clothes for a pair of dungaree overalls similar to what his Uncle Jimmy wore. Year after year, season in and season out, Danny would labor in his Uncle Jimmy's tobacco fields, sitting up there on that big harvester rig, racking the tobacco leaves that the pickers accumulated.

As Danny got older, he became experienced, with arms long enough for him to now reach over and pick the ripe, yellow leaves. And every week the tractor would crawl down those same dirt paths until each level of ripened leaf was striped from the tobacco stalks. Danny not only picked and racked tobacco, he also learned the "curing" process, where inside of one of the barns, heat blowers were concentrated under the picked tobacco leaves until they were eventually dried, bagged, and brought to market.

When work was through, the tools and tractors were returned to one of the few barns. Then it was off to the main house for showers, food, and sleep. This was the routine day after day and week after week. And there was really no choice in the matter. That's just the way it was. A youngun just had to put in his work to help the family. It was the price to pay to breathe, to exist.

Danny did graduate high school, after which he began attending Durham Central College. But by his eighteenth birthday, the young man hit a wall. Those role models that he came to admire from around the way were more enticing than his Uncle Jimmy. These characters broadened his perspectives on life in a whole different way. Furthermore, those videos on BET every minute, both programmed and in commercials, sent messages to him that were intoxicating. He liked women even though he had not yet experienced true love. There were a couple of girls in school with whom he had sex but in comparison to the things he was watching, something was missing. Why weren't these girls wearing the thongs and the G-string outfits? Why weren't they loose, shaking their asses like in the videos? And what college parties he did attend paled next to the party life that the rest of the world seemed to be living.

One night changed Danny's life; that night that he decided Preacher would be his moniker. Omar, a fellow student from Central, suggested they get away from the usual. They'd never been to this club, The Hideaway, before so they took the plunge. Just over the threshold of the hole in the wall, these were obviously Fayetteville natives mulling about, making it a crowded venue. In T-shirts and shorts, in skirts and tanks, the college crowd was becoming livelier as the two wandered deeper into the mix.

The music that penetrated the atmosphere was thick with beats created by a couple banging congas somewhere in the club. There was little light provided by lanterns on the walls, and the windows were grated and mostly black. The tables against the wall were all busy with foursomes and six-somes squeezing in, cramming where there was already very little room. Candles and ashtrays sat atop the tables. Every bar stool was occupied, so Preacher and Omar made the best of it, leaning against a wall. Preacher observed all of the dark effects in the place and was reminded of a blacksmith's shop he'd been to.

After a while, the drinks warmed them. The music and beats seemed to speed up. Some of the girls in the club began standing on those same tables, dancing around the candles and teasing the men in the crowd, licking their lips and lifting their T-shirts to just below the nipples. The blond woman behind the bar was flirtatious too, kissing most of the men she served.

There was a point that Preacher struck up a conversation with a woman. She spoke about college, about being away from home, and about hard times. Then he realized that the funny feeling below his waist wasn't an urge to pee. The girl was fondling him. At first it was slight. But when she saw he liked it, she became more aggressive. Preacher excused himself to visit the bathroom. A woman was leaving as he stepped in. There couldn't have been room for more than three people in the space. Alone now, Preacher stepped up to the urinal and whipped out the magic wand. He envisioned Ms. Hands-On while he worked to reach some kind of release. He closed his eyes. His breathing turned heavy. Sure enough, the college girl came in the bathroom behind him and seduced her way into a reach-around, helping her new friend with her body pressed up against his back. All Preacher could say was, "Oh shit!" as he visited that most bizarre climax.

Omar and Preacher left that club, that oasis, with separate agendas. They never saw each other again. Preacher left school that next week, deciding to live the life he dreamed. He processed his Afro into a slick, wavy mane like the hairstyle those characters had in the old blaxsploitation films. He tossed the casual, scholastic attire and cashed in his textbooks at the school bookstore. He reinvested that and his savings into duds: the hip-hop gear like those party types wore at The Hideaway. It didn't take much. Finally, he made that venue his home away from home. He studied it. He networked. And he milked the environment of its resources until he was in a position to hustle everything these partiers craved. He saw that weed was a staple, so he dealt it. He dealt it like he once picked and racked tobacco. Only now, he was making the money. He was taking the product to market. In time, Preacher had folks coming to The Hideaway just to pick up weed. To pick up packages that they'd break down and resell to others.

Hey baby . . . they say you the man in here. Maybe you could help me."

"Oh yeah?" Preacher had that extra-slick look goin' these days. The burgundy two-piece suit replaced the hip gear. He had a goatee now and a razor-sharp mustache. There was that sparkling diamond ring on his pinkie. His whole image was different; never would he pick or rack or cure on a farm again, to labor like a slave. To look at him now, everybody calling him "the man" and all, you'd never guess that he spent many long hours in dungaree overalls.

"Maybe. Depend on what you want." Preacher didn't look to see who he was talking to at first, too busy scanning the crowd of fifty-plus. Always scouting for the money.

Now Preacher was looking at her from head to toe, in that slow, chauvinistic way that had his nose wide open, his head tilted just so, and his eye searching for flaws. "Ohhh . . . man. Look at you! You ain't from 'round these parts are you?"

"Nope. I'm from New York, originally."

"And now, lemme guess. You're going to North Carolina University."

"Well, almost. See, I started school there but then something happened with the money. Then I . . ."

The girl was a fuckin' menagerie. Had to be. Preacher stood there looking at her, looking through her. She was going on about switching schools and attending Durham Central, about living with her grandmother. But Preacher was more into the tight, midriff football-jersey on her. The number 50, big as all glory, stretched over her incredibly healthy breasts. Her hair was a couple of shades darker than her coffee-brown skin, frizzed out and reaching her shoulders. The shorts she wore started just below the navel and ended where her thighs began. She had to be package-wrapped for him. Especially for him. Preacher had to snap out of his stupor just to respond to the girl.

"Did you say a job?"

"Yeah. I need to get money, and quick. My situation ain't pretty."

"What can you do?" That was Preacher's usual line, but in this case, he meant it. He didn't want to come on too strong to this chick. She was just too fine, with her brows all arched and her lips glossing like candy. He'd already decided that he wanted her in a few compromising positions, indeed. But there was something about the girl. Did she say her name was Peaches? Something told Preacher to slow his roll. He couldn't see himself taking advantage of her like a local, like a one-night stand or a pushover.

"I . . . I can waitress. I can . . ." Peaches looked over at the bar, not wanting to lie. "Well, I can learn to do that."

"Bartend?"

"Um-hmm."

"It takes a special talent to do that, sweetheart. Stick to what you know. You waitress before?"

Peaches took a discouraging breath, not wanting to be limited. "That's a cinch. Take orders. Pick up dirty dishes. I—"

"You too fine to be a con artist, baby. I asked you a question. How 'bout a straight answer."

Now Peaches took a deep breath. Her voice became unsure. "Okay, see, I was an assistant for this producer-guy back in New York. He was holding these talent shows at a restaurant called Wells . . ."

Preacher rolled his eyes and folded his arms. The package before him was losing its wrapping. And she obviously read his mind since she changed her tune.

"No, wait, hear me out—please. See, I was doing a lot of the guy's footwork. Organizing stuff, seating patrons at tables and sometimes I would help the waitresses when the crowd was really busy."

"So you really didn't work for the restaurant, you worked for this . . . producer guy."

"Uh . . . yeah. Yeah, you right."

"So why you couldn't come right out and say that? Maybe I'm looking for an assistant. Maybe I'm looking for a girl to organize my shit." Preacher injected profanity in his words. He talked down to Peaches just to establish dominance. He could go that route, now. Funny how he gave this chick more credit than otherwise—before she even opened her mouth, she was a queen. About to be treated like a queen, up until the point she opened her mouth. But now . . .

Preacher smirked when Peaches apologized. Now he moved closer to her, close enough for her to smell his musk fragrance. "You know, I just might be able to work a chick like you." Preacher could sense the girl's anticipation fading in to where the remorse had been. "I like your look. You may be able to make me some money." One could see that Peaches didn't know what he meant specifically and that she didn't care. "Whatchu need money for so bad?" Preacher was still up real close on her now. She had to back up against the bar. He spoke intimately in her ear. "You one of them crackheads with a habit to fix?"

"N-no . . ." Peaches said, her voice trembling, her brow wrinkled. She couldn't even see Preacher's face now, just the side of his head, that shiny black hair just an inch or so from her cheek. Preacher was still in her ear, making her feel like a defendant. Peaches perspired. He had her shook.

"You one a' them AIDS bitches tryin' to pass around the bug? Or your daddy raped you and threw you out the house? Whatchu really 'bout, huh?"

Peaches was so caught up in Preacher's bold words that she was speechless, stuttering, breathless. "I can't believe you asking me this. I—" Like a hurricane, Peaches pushed past Preacher's womanizing and spun out through and between The Hideaway's busy crowd. When she reached the front door and then the sidewalk, she slowed to catch her breath. It was drizzling outside in seventy-five-degree weather but Peaches felt free, leaning there against the exterior window of the club.

Distress and stirred nerves seemed to blend well with the rain, and how it began to mat down her hair. And to think she got all pretty to meet "the man." Just as Peaches regained control, an olive green Range Rover shot out from an alley beside the club and pulled up to a stop at the curb in front of Peaches. It was Preacher.

"Get in!"

"No!" Peaches said, but didn't move.

Preacher wasn't new to the game. He'd touched and tested the best of them up till now. Peaches, he assumed, was nothing but another pretty face cut from the same cloth as any of them other chickenheads he'd hit and quit. Just a little of that up North attitude with her. But Preacher was determined. He knew how to walk it and how to talk it.

"Listen. If you're waiting for me to apologize, forget it. I said what I meant to say. But, one thing fo' sure and two things for certain, standing out in the rain like that ain't gonna make you no money. So get in before you get too wet for my leather seats. I'll take you somewhere to eat."

Peaches had already made the angry fa[...]
the stage of outrage. She tempered it dow[...]
and eventually took that apprehensive, sl[...]
the sidewalk and into the waiting luxury [...]

Preacher got to know Peaches better that night. I[...]
with the drive-thru window at Shoney's Big Boy. They ordered a load of fried shrimp, some fish-and-cheese sandwiches, and shakes. Peaches satisfied her hunger, the first
good meal she'd had in months, and was talkative enough to
paint a clear picture for Preacher. Something was amiss at
her home up north, of that he was sure. Probably her parents' marriage broke up, trickling down to hurt her college
financing. Peaches was a busy schoolgirl, too. A cheerleader.
Studying communications. Pursuing a broadcasting career.
But she barely completed one year in college, just the liberal
arts part of the curriculum.

Although Preacher sympathized with her, he didn't let on
about his own failed attempt at the very same school. From
the Big Boy parking lot, Preacher took Peaches to his crib, a
house he was renting over on Bainbridge Road, not too far
from the Chestnut Ridge Projects where he grew up.

"It's already one in the morning," Preacher said to
Peaches as he cut on the lamp closest to the entrance of his
crib. "No sense in you going home tonight."

"Do I have a choice in the matter?" Not exactly arguing
her concern.

"No." Preacher wasn't smiling, but she could take it to
mean whatever she wanted, it didn't matter to him at this
point. "Now let me say something I've been looking forward
to saying all night." Preacher slumped down on a couch.

"What's that?"

"Show me your breasts."

CHAPTER SEVENTEEN

No street thug or drug dealer could really understand what this is like. They couldn't. If they could, then they're evil."

"You think they give shit, Ted? This whole game turned up ten notches the day Reagan declared the war on drugs. It's crazy how much power words have. He was probably on some publicity trip, a campaign move in case the nation decided two terms wasn't enough for the presidency."

"Don't hate on Reagan, Steve. He's responsible for all the money that was poured into this thing."

"What's this don't hate shit? Is that a black thing?"

"Real funny, man. I'm being serious. We know the drugs are a problem. The babies. The addicts. There's crime and violence just to maintain the addiction. We can't just let it go on like it is. We can't let people just kill themselves."

"Hey, you don't have to preach it to me, Ted. I'm on the right side. Remember? I don't like drug dealers. And frankly, after these latest casualties, it's my life's mission to get rid of these . . . these . . . miscreants."

"*She* uses that word a lot. Miscreants. You think she's feeling anything? She looks so hard and callous."

Agents Masters and Carson were sitting idle in a cruiser, the third in a procession of marked and unmarked vehicles that had now come to a halt along a blacktop path on the grounds of Washington Cemetery in White Plains, New York.

This would be a long morning; it usually was for full funerals. The uniformed officers organizing their force. The agents from the various federal law enforcement agencies falling into place. The tending to the mourning families and the sensitive details of the coffins, the flags, and the service. There'd be a twenty-one-gun salute, with the bagpipes, the uniforms, and all the brass in attendance. And this was only one of the funerals to be held. Pam had just emerged from the second vehicle in the procession just behind the immediate family's hearse with the two escorts on their motorcycles.

She stood there now, leaning back against a black limousine, bespectacled in dark shades and suited in all-black: blazer, turtleneck, slacks. She had no idea of the conversation that was about her.

"Hard to tell what she's feeling. This is the way she usually is. I can't say I've ever seen her cry."

"Maybe she's a robot underneath that hard body."

"It's possible. In this day and age, anything's possible."

A cemetery caretaker was discussing things with some handlers now, addressing issues regarding the coffin. And then the coffin was removed from the hearse.

"You ever think about lying in one of those?"

"We all gotta go someday, Ted. Some sooner than others."

"I guess."

"You scared?"

"I can't say I am. I'm more concerned with Sheryl, Kindra, and Keisha. They could be the ones standing over there like those families."

"Well, if it's any consolation, Ted, you know I'd look out if . . ."

"If what? If I bite the bullet? If I become the next casualty? The next hero?"

"You're not going anywhere my friend." Steve put a hand on Ted's shoulder. "Not if I have anything to do with it."

• • •

P am stood beside Agents Masters and Carson throughout the funeral ceremony. There were jitters in the air and many sad, expressionless faces, but only the immediate family cried. It was almost as if the agents had to uphold a certain integrity. As if they weren't able to show emotion. When it was over, after the flag was taken from the coffin, after the coffin made its descent, and after the show of compassion to the family, Pam and her subordinates held their own ceremony back in Manhattan at the hotel bar.

"Here's a toast to the fallen soldiers."

"To the fallen soldiers."

Pam didn't say anything, just lifted her glass in unison and emptied the drink in one long swallow.

"I don't know how to ask you this except to come right out and ask, Boss. Are you all right?" Masters and Carson shared a mutual acknowledgement.

"You know, even though Agent Denver wasn't part of Mobile Enforcement, I can still feel the pain left behind. Two children"—Pam gestured to the bartender for a refill.

—"two children, now motherless. I know this may sound crude, but I'm glad I'm childless. I couldn't bear working, operating, knowing I had kids at home."

Carson considered her words, about to ask what that was supposed to imply for agents like him who did have families.

"But perhaps," said Pam, "I should keep my thoughts to myself."

"Either way," Master interjected, "those guys are going to hell. We're headed to Florida, aren't we?"

"Tomorrow morning. I'm taking the same unit. Total of fifteen agents. By the close of business today, I want Dade County alerted, not the police department or our DEA people either. You need to reach the Chief U.S. Attorney, get clearance for the operation."

"No enforcement?"

"Not a one. Not even a police dog. The only way we are likely to succeed with Operation Snowfall is the takedown has gotta be a surprise. That's the key."

CHAPTER EIGHTEEN

Bianca George hadn't even opened her eyes, yet she was living out the forthcoming morning in her dreams. It was the usual long night for her, ending at one A.M., when she finished touring the club circuit. She dropped off to sleep like a two-ton boulder, taking with her all those images, those faces and fashions, those sounds of the gabbing, gossip, no-holds-barred yakety-yak, the music of this DJ and that. From her club-hopping thoughts, she meshed in thoughts of Jason, her five-year-old son. She'd fix a bowl of Cheerios and strawberries for him, feed off of some of that early morning TV hype, and drop him off at preschool. There'd be some errands to run: a pedicure, the First Miami Bank to deposit a few checks, and she'd look at a newer cell phone while her Volkswagen Bug was being washed and waxed. Back home for phone calls. Once Bianca reviewed her day, she thought hard about Charlucci.

Her heart began to quicken at the picture of him and the controversial relationship that they had. That's when she adjusted herself in bed, cozying up with her silk sheets and pillows as if determined to give these thoughts extensive attention. Here it was, a year after they made the commitment; he'd be hers and she'd be his. Sure, neither would really "own" nor control the other, no master-slave relationship here but it was what a couple did. They'd give of themselves wholly and freely, unconditionally. At least, that's what Bianca did with Charlucci. She gave him things she kept as special. Things she'd given no other man. Things she never even imagined giving at all. Jason even took to Charlucci as the father he never had. That was Bianca's biggest issue. Yes, she loved that man. Yes, the sex was good. Sometimes it was explosive. And yes, Charlucci was a man who (at least) came close to that of her dreams. But the negative for her was his profession.

Everybody knew Charlucci was "the man" down in South Beach. He was "the man" in North Beach. Damn, he may well have all of Miami locked up in his cocaine network. Sometimes Bianca thought about things from a different perspective; she considered that maybe she was a straphanger, part of Charlucci's hunger for fast cars, fast cash, and . . . But she didn't consider herself fast. Sure, she was morphing in the flash and glam of South Beach. The "it" girl who was twenty-one but who could pass for eighteen if she didn't wear her lengthy hair up most of the time. And then there was the mascara for her eyes and the lip gloss that gave her both depth and lure. But that didn't necessarily count as "fast," did it?

Bianca had indeed made a name for herself in South Beach. That easy, open, career-minded attitude; the humility, compassion, and all that helped Bianca move up in life from her cheerleading popularity at Miami Beach High to organizing and hosting parties at Liquid, at Touch, and at Level. She promoted belly dancer/fire thrower events at Nikki Beach Club, coed mud wrestling at Fuel, and—if you had to ask you didn't belong—tasty brassiere parties at Crowbar.

And she was always well put together for her outings and engagements, whether it was a top-shelf occasion at Miami's Art Museum or Boheme, where she'd "rough it" wearing jeans and a skinny tube top under a rustic leather jacket. If it was hot, she didn't mind the ripped T-shirt with the holes cut strategically for that peek-a-boo effect. Maybe that was what made Charlucci think she was fast. But this was South Beach. Bianca's life. She knew virtually everyone. All the "in" people. All the "in" places. There was nothing fast about that.

If the United States has three legs, then along with New York and L.A., Miami is one of them. South Beach might be considered Miami's big toe, where tourists come and go. Here, just like the other hot spots, you can run into Will Smith or get robbed. The only big differences are the landscape, the room to breathe, and there's a great big inground pool called the Atlantic Ocean.

You get the idea that the type of people who live here or who travel thousands of miles to be here live loosely, they don't count tomorrow till it comes, and, maybe, they couldn't make it anywhere else. Collins Avenue is to South Beach what Broadway is to New York. It's what Hollywood Boulevard is to L.A. or what Michigan Avenue is to Chi-Town. If there isn't a motel, a strip mall, or a restaurant to your left or right, then you strolled too far off of the coastline and you're probably drowning.

Rumor has it that South Beach is very '80's when it came to gangsters seeking refuge. But, of course, that's what the gangsters themselves are saying. They say that the place is more for fishing (for women) or more for celebrities and those who live off of being a certain celebrity's friend. Sometimes, however, the most obvious place to hide is exactly the place to hide.

Now that the DEA's Mobile Enforcement Team was on to Charlucci, there was a wager going that he had a framed picture shaking Puff Daddy's hand. Cheezin' like a buffoon.

"Thanks for coming down. I heard about your work in Chicago, San Diego, and the one just recently up in Seattle. We're honored, Agent Brown."

"Thanks for the welcome. Can we talk somewhere?"

"Sure. Follow me." Peter Van Dyke, the Chief U.S. Attorney for the Southern District of Florida, led Agents Brown, Masters, and Carson down a carpeted corridor where flags for the nation, the Department of Justice, and the State of

Florida stood between wall hangings of the current administration: the president, vice president, and secretary of defense. On the opposite wall were portraits of the eight Supreme Court justices. There were half a dozen offices between the lobby and Van Dyke's office. A couple of energetic young women were moving here and there. Law books or papers in hand.

"Yes . . . well, we're quite familiar with Mr. Charlucci. A big dealer down in these parts. We're guessing that his operation is doing large numbers, probably moving hundreds of kilos on the streets . . ."

Hundreds? What is this guy, a moron? He obviously wasn't aware of the stop in Bell Glade or that it might somehow be related to Charlucci.

". . . but we can't seem to make anything stick. Not only that; whenever we impanel a grand jury, an indictment is never handed down. For some reason this guy has got good fortune on his side." Van Dyke handed Agent Brown a folder.

"This? This is his file, sir? That's all?" Pam asked, but her mind was calculating, thinking about that quite familiar comment the U.S. Attorney just mentioned.

"I'm afraid so. Some surveillance reports on a few addresses. Photos of some street deals. A number of arrests, his subordinates."

"Where's . . . I don't see any photos of him."

"That's been the problem, too. Nothing. Not even a high school photo of this guy."

Pam was reminded of the bet the others made on the flight down. "Who's the girl?"

"That's the closest individual we could come up with, his girlfriend as best we could tell. Dominican, I think. And that one—with the beret—that's the front man for Charlucci's deals. At least, that's what we believe."

"What's with the kids?"

"There are eighteen there on that page, but we believe there are dozens more. Those are the hooks; they man street corners, they hang out in shopping malls, movie theaters, and, of course, schools. The few that we've been able to catch have kept their lips sealed. That, or they really don't know who the boss is."

"You've arrested these kids?"

"There are three of them that we've sent to family court. Juvenile division. The others we questioned and let go."

Pam inquired, "They didn't have anything on them?"

"They made the solicitation. Of that we're sure. But on many occasions they led our undercovers on wild-goose chases. We dragged them in just to shake 'em up with some questions, some threats, but we got nothing. It's almost as if he trained these kids to undergo interrogation."

Listening to this, Pam knew that wasn't as far-fetched as the U.S. Attorney made it sound. It was the Virginia Mobile Enforcement Team that infiltrated and shut down an operation in which a father taught his three teenage kids to gather up buyers from the local shopping district. The file read the start date of the investigation, listed the local police and drug enforcement officers who worked the case, and it showed a record of arrests relating to the "Charlie File." Pam wanted to wag her head at the naiveté with which this investigation was being handled.

"I was about to call your local DEA fold down to join us until your people said . . ."

"They told you right, Mr. Van Dyke. Nobody but nobody is to know about our operation. I can promise you, with your total cooperation we'll flush this guy out and you'll have yourself a handful of convictions."

"Sounds good to me. What do you need?"

Pam walked over to a map of Collins Avenue and the South Beach district where Charlucci was reputed to be operating. She traced her finger along the map, close to where the most red pushpins indicated arrests.

"Is there a place somewhere, say, in this area where we can set up our headquarters? I'm gonna need rooms for my agents and myself, plus one unit for our satellite office."

"Hmmm. There's mostly condos and motels in this area. Let me see." Van Dyke had a sharp nose that protruded over his mustache and goatee; it seemed to wiggle when he spoke. Now, his beady eyes shot up toward the fluorescent lighting and the ceiling. Thinking. "As a matter of fact, yes. The World Class Motel on Collins. It's right here. About a half-mile from the Fontainebleau Hotel."

"What makes the World Class so special?"

"The owner and sole proprietor, Monte Rivera—let's just say he owes me a favor."

"Fine by me so long as he can accommodate us and not get in the way. Think he'll have enough room for my agents?"

"I'm almost sure of it."

The following day, a bus pulled into the oval drive out in front of The World Class Motel. There was a huge decal dressing the side panel that read: THE SUNSHINE EXPRESS, indicating that it was some type of tour bus. Maybe even another one of those shams that flood the Miami Beach tourist industry with the free dinners and one-night stays, come-ons that serve to lure wayward travelers to overstay their welcome, to spend some of that $3 billion a year that comes into the Sunshine State.

A troop of men and women stepped off of the bus with shoulder bags and carry-ons, flowered shirts, shorts, sandals, and shades under those wide-brim straw hats and caps. Once inside the lobby, the group was escorted past reception and up to the second floor (the top floor), where their rooms were reserved.

Minutes later, one of those suites, Room 216, turned into a satellite office for the Mobile Enforcement Team. Computers were set up along with their dedicated remote access lines to Washington and the DEA's central intelligence. From this moment, any name that was entered into the terminals would be run through a thorough Interpol check, complete with access to classified personal and financial histories. A small arsenal of weapons was set aside in one area, a supplement to what each agent already had as his or her own personal issue.

There was a small table that was used for ammo. In

another area, communication devices such as Motorola two-way radios, wiretaps, and cell phones were set charging their DC power packs where necessary. On the floor against a wall were suitcases that contained a supply of binoculars, telescopes, night vision devices, and cameras.

All of these law enforcement amenities were being situated by field agents, while Pam was a few doors down in her own suite. For her, the launch of a street operation began with a refueling of mental tools. Back to the basics, a trip down memory lane. Her training in Fort Bragg in North Carolina. It had been many years since she first went there, and there had been a few refresher courses since.

But underneath the traditional training, what impacted Pam's life most was her acceptance by the agency to undergo training for so-called hostile measures. This was exclusive training and detailed information that prepared Pam for unconventional warfare. Things like torture and interrogation. To stay abreast of particulars, she had her "Recipe Book." Or so it was titled. Yet behind the paisley decoration on the outside cover of the book (too obvious a diversion in Pam's opinion) was an extensive manual that was the "meat and potatoes" of what tactics were used to get intelligence out of people. These methods were, by far, frowned upon by the U.S. government and every human rights organization. In some cases, there were methods that were downright unheard of; illegal, even.

Also, Pam knew that if certain politicians ever got wind of such tactics, if they even knew she had such a manual (one she and a training mate "appropriated" during their engagement at Fort Bragg), there would be an investigation that would rock the Justice Department. So, for all intents and purposes, and as far as the government knew, the activities that she and her agents were aware of included the "conventional training." Learning how to jump from a plane, how to survive in jungle warfare. However, Pam, as well as others who passed the course, called that kids' stuff.

This booklet she had, on the other hand, was the unconventional activity. It was knowledge that made the difference between mice and men—training for the purpose of torturing human beings; techniques to challenge those guerilla forces in the jungles of Colombia, of Brazil, and of Peru, where the drugs originated. Techniques that would challenge the drug lords and their armies who raped and killed and dragged people from their homes and shot them just to empower the organization. Sure, these things happened frequently on foreign soil. But nowadays, such lawlessness was an everyday occurrence in the United States. Occurrences that compelled Pam to keep her own game tight.

"Agents may cause the arrest or detention of perpetrator by recruiting informants, use of counterintelligence (hiring CIs from within the criminal organization), fear, payment of bounties for delivery of perps (dead or alive), extortion, beatings, false imprisonment and if necessary, execution.

"Agents may cause the arrest or detention of the perpetrator's parents, immediate family, relatives, or friends.

"Agents should not make threats unless they can be carried out and the perp should realize that such threat can and will be carried out.

"Agents may suspect and proactively spy on and neutralize possible subversives who disguise themselves as politicians or law enforcement, for they are in a position which poses lethal dangers to agents."

Pam knew the word *neutralize* to be a euphemism for murder. These teachings of army combat skills, coupled with the CIA's covert methods of surveillance, interrogation, and sabotage, were sometimes essential to combat various drug trafficking organizations. Actually, reading the manual made those images resurface. The images from those videos she watched. The Vietnam interrogations and torture, how to detect bombs and the aftermaths of bombs that have been detonated. Oklahoma City. New York City's World Trade Center. 9/11 and TWA's Flight 800. Those images played back, and then other memories were warmed into existence. The crack babies. The dope fiends. The drug-related murders and executions. Bodies left for dead in alleys, in parks and schoolyards. Again, Pam was reminded that this was war. And the army, her army—Mobile Enforcement—was in place now; ready to drop the curtain on Charlucci and his South Beach enterprise. Operation Snowfall was in full swing, whatever the cost.

CHAPTER NINETEEN

Nightfly had mixed feelings about this meeting. Half of him, probably the lower half, wanted to run. The Caribbean. Hawaii. Japan. Whatever. The other half, where his brain was stirring, wanted to carry on. Stay the course. Go ahead and meet with Charlucci. Get this over with and come face-to-face with fate. It could mean certain death, or it could mean another chance. Nightfly wouldn't have to look over his shoulder for the rest of his life. He could go on keeping his organization, his friends, and his family.

That was a big concern of his, to be able to keep his cushy lifestyle, his crib, and his toys. To give all of that up would defeat his whole purpose of getting down with this drug game.

Nightfly finally arrived at the loop that led to the rendezvous, Charlucci's beach house just outside of South Beach's busy Ocean Drive. Already he could see where the muscle car—a 1970 Oldsmobile Rallye 350 with a blinding yellow exterior, black racing stripes, rear-end spoiler, wide tires, and that fearsome big block V8 engine under the hood—was parked amidst a team of street bikes. He could imagine all of them, the fast car and the motorcycles, transporting him somewhere along a riverbank; perhaps rolling over his dead body a few times for good measure. Charlucci's boys were waiting, smoking and (Nightfly thought) maybe discussing how they'd finish off a deadbeat.

Nightfly was driving a blueberry-colored Hummer, probably the only strength left to claim. And it was now, as he disembarked from the vehicle, that he wondered why he ever drove this truck down instead of a softer ride. He didn't want to give any impression that he was ballsy or tough. Not now. Right now, Nightfly didn't mind being a punk, harmless and weak.

Ortiz stepped up and frisked Nightfly. "He's waiting," Ortiz said in a way that was more fateful than friendly. Nothing like the man Nightfly had been meeting with during the past year to pick up product. To drop off money.

Nightfly descended a short case of steps and followed a long path that snaked among potted plants, grass, and stone statues. Every footstep Nightfly took accompanied a memory considering the amount of business he'd done with Charlucci; more than 400 kilos in the eleven months he'd been dealing with "the man" and the few conversations they'd had since.

It wasn't as though they knew each other well enough that they "hung out" or buddied up for a day at the horse races. This relationship was strictly business. Charlucci supplied and Nightfly was, more or less, one of his salesmen.

Nightfly pulled open the screen door and immediately suffered that blindness one experiences when crossing from a bright, sunny day to the inside of a much darker dwelling. The beach house wasn't too much darker, not so that Nightfly couldn't adjust within a few seconds. He'd never been here before. And he absentmindedly thought the beach house to be some small shack; windowless, with a straw roof by the water's edge. But indeed, Charlucci's place was large enough for a couple to live in permanently.

"Come in. Have a seat." Charlucci was a bold, dark figure to the rear of the main room, standing with his back to Nightfly and looking through a wall-size window out at the beachfront. Rippling waters, seagulls, and a perfect horizon were alive behind the man who was now developing, no less than a Polaroid pic, right before Nightfly's eyes.

There was barely breathing room before Charlucci turned

and strolled toward the couch opposite the one where Nightfly sat.

"So, we have a little problem," Charlucci began while he
set his tumbler on the coffee table between them. No "hi" or
"how are ya." Not in the least.

"Yes, we do." Nightfly was relieved to hear the man say
"we." It might help with his intentions. "And I need your
help."

"My help? You kiddin' me? For what?"

"I wanna find these guys. Teach 'em a lesson if I can."

Charlucci nestled back against the soft leather, extending
his arm across the top. The definition of his biceps showed
beyond the short-sleeved crewneck he wore. Nightfly
couldn't make out Charlucci's expression, wondering if he
was questioning his nerve or if he was really considering his
request. As usual, Nightfly was imagining things.

"I'm not interested in what you want. And I don't care
about any beef you got with whomever. What I'm interested
in is, number one, where's my money. Our deal is eight
days. Not ten days. Not two weeks. Eight days."

"I know. I—"

"Number two," Charlucci cut Nightfly off, not to be interrupted, "I wanna know the details of why my money is late.
I was told about the little heist. My guy told me about a
stickup . . . et cetera, et cetera. But I been doin' this too long
to be the fool. I want details. And if I find out you're lyin' . . .
that this is all an act?" Charlucci did that gesture where one
puts one's fingertips together then kisses them audibly. "You
can kiss your ass good-bye."

"But, Charlucci . . . we were stuck up. It went down just
like I told Ortiz. As far as the money, you know I can work
that out. I've been regular with my payments up till now."
Nightfly rambled with his explanations. "You must have a
dozen, maybe two, like me. You sayin' you can't lay back a
minute on my debt till I can get things right? I just need you
to front me again. Even if you could do half, I'll make good
in no time."

"Listen, you imbecile. You listen, and listen good. Yes,

you been movin' shit for a while now. But that only means
you should have plenty money put away to take care of this.
And, I'm talkin' cash money. You owe me two point two."

"Well, I got my titles, my condo on Ocean Drive, my cars
and jewelry. What do you want?"

"Fuck your little titles, trinkets, and toys and shit. I ain't
interested in nothin' but cash."

"But I'm tapped out, Charlucci. For real. They wiped us
out. Took the coke. The cars. The money. They shut down
our damn stash house, plus killed one of my best men. That
ain't no small loss. It ain't . . ."

Nightfly went on to explain how four gunmen kicked in
the door. A neighbor saw that much. They tied up the lookout, even nailing his hands to a wooden two-by-four. They
cut his throat and stabbed him in the chest.

Charlucci was not really listening 100 percent to Nightfly's alibi. He was more tuned in to the body, the gestures and
his expressions. Meanwhile, other things were going through
Charlucci's mind. No. Nightfly wasn't the only associate to
help move the 2,000 kilos of cocaine that Charlucci received
each month. There was the Baltimore-Washington group.
There were the boys in Atlanta. The group up in Philly, Jersey, and Delaware. Of course, Freeze was moving 500 kilos a
month in New York.

And Charlucci had his group of teenagers who helped
run his local organization. Sure, they were only pushing ten
kilos a month, but it was ten kilos with which Charlucci
made almost three times his cost. Where the product was
costing him sixteen grand per kilo, he'd have Ortiz delegate
the breakdown of the product into small amounts. Twenty-,
fifty-, and hundred-dollar bags. Like worker bees, the
teenagers would hustle the malls, schools, and the beaches
up the coastline. There'd be a headache here and there, an
arrest or problems with the money. But overall, it was a substantial cash flow that Charlucci could count on.

It was unfortunate, he thought, that Miami Beach didn't
consume as much coke as he had access to. If they did, he
wouldn't have to be concerned with issues like Nightfly,

who worked the nightclub scene, or the traffic stop by the locals in Bell Glade. He would be able to cut out all these middlemen and oversee everything himself, keep all the profit. Yet and still, Charlucci didn't mind how things were set up now. There was very little exposure and, for the most part, the associates were coming through with their financial obligations. On time.

No. Nightfly's situation wasn't as big as Charlucci was making it to be. But this was more than a money issue. This was about respecting the game and not being the sucker. Not being played like a pushover. Lose that integrity, that image of power and diligence, and there goes the game. Game over. Everyone would follow Nightfly, treating Charlucci any ole way. Trying to get over where they could.

"Tell you what. I'm gonna front you fifteen keys."

"Fifteen? I can off that in ten minutes. You wouldn't even get a chance to blink your eyes before I had the money. Can't you do like fifty? Makin' up for a hundred keys is a lot of work at fifteen."

"I don't care. Fifteen. And if you don't take that, then . . ."

"Okay. Okay. Fifteen. I'll move it, come back with the money, and then I'll take another fifteen, right?"

"Yeah. Right. But that don't mean I forget about this holdup. Now, what did these gunmen look like? What'd they wear?"

"Average thugs, I guess. Black and Latino. I ain't got no names, Charlucci."

"Not necessary. I'll have my boys look into it."

"Well, if you find out—"

"When I find out. You better believe I'm gonna find out who did this."

"Well, when you find them, could you help me take care of 'em?"

"Your beef. Not mine."

"Yeah, but they slowed up the money. Your money."

"Your responsibility. But I may be able to hook you up with a guy I know. He takes care of things for me. You'll have to pay 'im."

"Damn, I can't win for losing."

"We're done here." Charlucci was already up from his seat. He picked up his tumbler just to keep his hand occupied, not interested in shaking hands with this visitor such as business associates would do.

Once Nightfly crossed the threshold and proceeded up the path, Ortiz approached.

"You ready?"

"Huh?" Nightfly was confused.

"The boss made you a deal, right?"

"Yeah."

"Well, I got the stuff. Let's go."

"You mean you're coming with me?"

"You got it. We might as well be lovers 'cuz if you gotta shit I'm gonna be there. I ain't letting you outta my sight till the note is paid in full."

Nightfly didn't think about this until he and Ortiz were on the road, but the man obviously had things laid out in advance. He already knew he'd give up fifteen keys and that Ortiz would be Nightfly's buddy for a while. The idea made Nightfly draw in enough air for a deep, frustrated breath. He had to give Charlucci more credit for a white boy.

As soon as business was done, Tara emerged from the bedroom. She was an actress whom Charlucci met through a friend. Twenty-one years old and dazzling with her hazel eyes and illuminating blond hair, Tara was in a bathrobe now. Her gaze was sultry. Wanting.

"You done?"

"For now, yeah."

"Can I get crazy with you? Is the coast clear?"

"Uh, sure. Why not?"

And at Charlucci's cue, Tara pranced across to the wall unit that housed a stack of stereo components inside its glass enclosure. That familiar retro sound, reminiscent of Afros and bell-bottoms, began to filter through the speakers.

"Oooo love to love you baby . . . oooo love to . . ."

Donna Summer's voice provoked Tara's silky movements

as she swerved and slithered there before Charlucci. She played with her terry-cloth robe, making a progressive triple X offering to her audience, with the full-body nudity and the bend-over back shot that would be as alluring as his favorite juicy steak; all up in his face and whatnot, calling for satisfaction. This was all happening to him, for him.

But his mind wandered. He thought about Bianca. He thought about business. He wondered how long things could remain this good. Bianca wanted him as her soul mate, as her husband, but she was asking too much to want him to leave the business for good. So what if her father was one of the old head smugglers who got slumped? That would be a deterrent for anyone in and around the game, especially the daughter. But that's the chances you take, Charlucci considered. You made your choice in life, and failed or prospered because of it.

Besides, Bianca's goods were to die for. Much more exotic and saucy than this blonde bombshell putting on a show for him. Tara was all the way down on hands and knees now, doing that feline crawl and coming closer. Charlucci just sat there, lit a cigar, and anticipated what Tara might do for him now. Would it be the usual? A slow blow? A wheelbarrow maneuver with her hands on the floor, like last time? Or would she go for his toes again? There was little to imagine with Tara. Most intriguing was that he could see her on the big screen at one point, as the envy of millions around the world (people she'd never know), virtually popping her video in their video players on a whim; while on the other hand, he was getting the best of her in a whole other way. One that the others could only dream of.

There were other things for Charlucci to consider. The loss of 500 kilos going to New York was no small hit. And now, coupled with the 100-kilo robbery from Nightfly, there'd be a lull in cash flow for at least the next thirty days. Nunez would certainly ignore a request for additional time on the forthcoming payment. So this was a killjoy, to have Tara's mouth on him, pulling at him like some cow and loving it, while knowing that within the next few hours he'd have to get to his crib to access a couple of safes. He'd have to wipe them out in order to follow through with the routine drops. Nunez's orders: drop off the cash to Liberty Bank Services, the satellite office for the offshore banks which held Nunez's accounts.

Ordinarily, the cash would be accumulated, counted, and wrapped at the Island Place, his waterfront condo on Bay Harbor. For sure, activities at the cash spot would be slow this week. So, since Charlucci already had his savings wrapped and counted at home, that would be his next step.

After the performance, the sex, and the orgasm with Tara, Charlucci had Michael, big enough to be a wrestler, escort him back into town. Utopia was a posh seaside community with three high-rise buildings. Charlucci owned the penthouse in the tallest of the three where mostly two- and three-bedroom residences enjoyed the ocean view. Inside this gated section of South Beach were landscaped gardens and the privacy that Charlucci felt each time he returned home. He didn't have too much time to make the best of all available amenities like the tennis courts, the sauna rooms, hot tubs, or the clubhouse. But when Bianca visited, when she stayed over, it didn't take much to persuade him to join her up on the roof for some cuddling at poolside.

"Have the crew at Bay Harbor help out at the Collins Avenue safe house this week. Leave just two hands at the cash spot. That'll be enough to count this week's draw."

"Everything cool?"

"Yeah. Your salary is still intact, Michael."

"Aw, Boss, you ain't gotta be so blunt. I meant it. Can I do anything?"

"Nope. Not at this—actually, yes." Charlucci almost forgot, already giving in to Nightfly's explanations. "There was a hit on that guy I just met with."

"Yeah, Boss. I heard . . . yesterday, right?"

"Mmm . . . over two hundred thousand in cash and all the coke. A hundred keys." Charlucci wheeled the muscle car off of Ocean and up to the gate. All he had to do was wave (and he didn't have to do that) as he passed the guard who controlled incoming traffic at Utopia. In the meantime, he directed Michael to look into Nightfly's story.

Michael waited in the car, parking in the underground garage, while Charlucci took the private elevator straight up. As soon as he got in his front door he could hear Bianca's voice recording on his machine. There was once a day when he would run and catch a call like that, before a girl hung up. But this was another life he was living. Cavalier. Rich. Sometimes heartless and unfeeling. Charlucci wasn't as absorbed in all of his surroundings these days: 2,800 square feet of fine Italian furnishings, glass walls, a spiral staircase, chic wall hangings, potted trees, two French limestone–tiled Jacuzzis, and broad terraces and balconies. At one time he'd stand in the center of it all and immerse himself in pride and sensations that his possessions encouraged. Now, as he went for a remote he kept hidden in the fold of a La-Z-Boy recliner, this was all something to shrug at. Like riding a bike for the four hundredth time. Nothing special.

Finding the remote, Charlucci pointed it at the bearskin rug on the floor. As if magically, the area underneath the rug began to rise, forming a square impression in the off-white floor covering. He stepped over and snatched the rug from the portion of the hydraulically controlled floor. There was a safe there, as though it was set on the floor itself. Charlucci spun the knob, entering the combination. With the safe open, he removed stacks of prewrapped cash and set it all on the floor. He went to get a tennis bag and filled it. Then he went to the master bedroom where there was a full bath, again with the remote. This time, the large bathtub lifted from its base, also controlled by hydraulics. From the safe therein, Charlucci took out the balance of three million, all due to be delivered to Liberty's office by the close of business.

With the safes, the bearskin rug, and the tub back in place, Charlucci started off for the elevator but was slowed by his conscience. He turned to a table over which a panel was built into the wall. He pressed a code into a keypad and turned a volume knob. Bianca's message filled the room.

"Charles, it's me. Jason is with the sitter this afternoon. I was wondering if we could have a bite to eat. Maybe at Tutti's. Page me, huh? You know I hate talkin' to your machine. And by the way, this is not an apology for our discussion. I still . . . I still feel the same. Nothing's changed. 'Bye!!!" Bianca practically sang the last word and it so reminded Charlucci of how they first met.

It was at the Paramount Grill at the Adventura Mall. Second floor. He was looking for a Christmas present, a farewell gift for his soon-to-be ex, Darlene; she was shopping at Flash for lingerie.

Bianca was with Bess, her friend since high school, shopping for herself after a weeklong hunt to satisfy her extensive list of friends. Charlucci was alone at the bar ordering the southern-fried quail. Bianca and Bess went for the blue cheese mashed potatoes and collard greens. From that coincidence, to the phone calls, to the run-ins at Liquid and Level and at the Living Room, Charlucci finally got Bianca into bed with him. She was tipsy and probably gave in against her better judgment; however (so he later heard), Bianca never stopped bragging about how he gave it to her so good that she got "hooked." Even now, he realized it was difficult for her to just ignore the physical benefits in order to keep with her conscience.

Enough with the emotions. Charlucci couldn't be held up any longer. There was money to deliver and commitments to keep. He took to the elevator for the nonstop trip to the underground garage. Michael was right there to take the bags and toss them in the trunk. From there they headed for Liberty Bank Services with an hour to spare.

A way from the lush lifestyles, the scattering of all things commercialized, the cosmo surroundings with Internet and all that, the Montalbos owned a cottage on Delray Beach, not twenty miles north of the epicenter of Charlucci's South Beach empire. The Montalbos were in their seventies now. Paul Sr. would be eighty before the year was out, but Lu Anne kept him feeling like he'd only recently brought in the white hair; as if he wouldn't need Viagra, or a shelf full of medication, or (one day soon) managed health care. The cottage was Lu Anne's sanctuary while it was Paul's getaway.

For thirteen years, he'd been here and only here, ducking an old arrest warrant for skipping bail just as many years ago. He figured this was how he'd go out: elderly, happy, and a free man living off of the money he earned as a smuggler.

If Paul did leave the cottage or the beach area, which was very isolated, it had to be top priority. There was no way he'd risk arrest by some hot-dog cop who was looking for stripes and spend his remaining years in jail. So far, Paul had gotten out three times in over a decade. There was the opening for *Smuggle*, the movie that had so much of his lifestyle in it he felt it calling him. There was a visit to a private clinic for his heart condition. And lastly, there was his partner Bobby's funeral. He'd only die once, so Paul took the risk.

Lu Anne was Paul's wife of thirty years. Ever since he jumped bail, she submitted to this way of life, far from their friends up in Jacksonville. Far from the people they once were. These days, besides watching surfers, young lovers making out, and the tides washing ashore, Paul satisfied his hunger to remain a player by helping Charlucci. He'd known the young dealer for most of his fifteen years in the business and could trust him enough to lend his hideaway as a safe house, the first stop in Charlucci's process.

Deliveries came to the cottage by one of two means. The larger amounts arrived in the secretly welded compartments of six black Jeeps Cherokees. Charlucci had an attached garage built with an indoor passage to the cottage just for this purpose. The vehicles would arrive, the motorized garage door would swivel open and closed, and one by one the loads would be removed behind closed doors. The product was then carried and stored down in the basement, after which the drivers sat together to enjoy one of Lu Anne's home-cooked meals. Like clockwork, they left immediately thereafter, looking forward to the next trip to and from Miami Harbor—the next delivery of cocaine.

There were other deliveries that were more frequent and

began to involve heroin in addition to cocaine. Twice a week taxicabs would pull up to the curb of the foliage-rich, picket-fenced outskirts of the Montalbos' home. Women in their twenties, professionally dressed with an overnight bag in tow, would step out and strut across the walkway and up to the open porch of the cottage. Most of these visitors were non–English speaking strangers, and in some instances, they'd be back a second time, now with a little more English in their vocabulary.

Inside the cottage with its outback atmosphere of pine walls and floors, indoor plants and other such rural reminders, the women were accommodated as if this were a hotel stay. A bed-and-breakfast. They were shown to one of four bedrooms where they'd sleep for two or three nights at most. Mrs. Lu Anne (as the women learned to call her) would prepare the finest meals of local seafood, beef, lamb, and poultry cuisines. For dessert, the women looked forward to her homemade ice cream and maybe a white chocolate mango crème brûlée. With the meals there was always plenty of bottled water and a few sizable laxative tablets to induce bowel movements.

These accommodations were not any free-for-all offerings to just any professional woman. They were by design. The vacationer's view of the Florida Keys sunset, the healthy meals, and the relaxed atmosphere were all conveniences so that during their stay, the women (the "travelers") would each excrete twenty balloon-wrapped "fingers."

How things were set up on the Colombian side of the association was not Charlucci's concern. However, this much he did know: Nunez would send the women on a thousand-dollar, five-hour ticket from Bogata Eldorado Airport, complete with passport and visa and specific directions to follow. They didn't just fly into Miami. That was too typical a red flag for the airport's customs agents. Instead, the travelers would fly into Washington, D.C., where they'd tour the Colombian Embassy for a half hour. Then it was off to Miami. This routine would suggest political involvement in Washington before business in Florida. It helped to paint a more substantial portrait for those passing through the customs routine.

Once in Miami, Charlucci had assurances in place; a certain taxi and its driver watching for the prescribed outfit. One traveler might be a woman in a canary yellow business suit and cherry red pumps. Her carryall bag might be red as well, with yellow flower imprints. The driver would take the travelers to the doorstep of the Montalbos' place in Delray.

Up till now, this routine was unstoppable. The Nunez-Charlucci association was successful because the travelers were smart. They did what they were paid $3,000 per trip to do. To act. To perform. And after that healthy meal and some relaxation, the toilet would stay busy until the balloons reappeared. Sometimes an experienced traveler could carry up to thirty or even forty balloons at seven and a half to nine grams of product in each. In the end, these amounted to a quarter kilo or more per traveler. It was a slow trafficking in comparison to the amounts that came in through Miami Harbor. However, in the eyes of the principals, any amount of product that got past U.S. enforcement and controls, so long as it was cost-effective, was a worthwhile endeavor.

CHAPTER TWENTY

This is our man. Black beet. Earring loop. Sideburns with the mustache and goatee. Ortiz."

"Who's the one with the dreads? Looks like a bush on his head." Masters asked this and then turned his eyes back into the binoculars. The two agents, Carson and Masters, were in a taxicab now. The "on duty" signal up on the roof wasn't lit, but that didn't stop folks from approaching the car.

"That's a good question right now. Van Dyke is supposed to set us up with a local snitch, a guy who the U.S. Attorney's office has used before. Apparently, his information is top shelf," Carson said.

"I've heard that before. Uh-oh, here's another one."

The pedestrian was a mop-topped man in a trench coat. He tried the handle on a rear door just behind where Agent Carson was at the wheel. Now came the abrupt knocking at the window.

"You think this is the informant?"

"Nope. Supposed to have blond hair; looks like a punk rocker or something," Carson said, relaying the specifics. "Out of service," he added through the window, raising his voice to be heard. He waved the guy off at the same time. The man cursed Carson and walked off.

"This ain't good, man. These people are looking for a ride and about to blow our cover."

"Cover? We're in a goddamned orange-checkered cab. A friggin' billboard advertisement."

"Now that I think about it, there's gotta be a dozen cabs out here trying to pick up the late-night crowd. This is maybe the best way to be undercover except for these . . . see, here comes another one."

"Hold up. That could be our informant."

The agents braced themselves waiting for the man to approach. He grabbed the back handle unsuccessfully. Then he turned to the driver's side window. The voice was muffled, but Carson could make out the words. Carson touched a switch on his door and the locks popped. The lanky, blonde kid couldn't have been more than twenty-three. His eyes were beady marbles stuck in the sockets. They were dilated, too, as though frozen with surprise.

"Hey, dude. What's up, dude? Killer crowd, huh?"

"Who're you?"

"Name's Joey. Joey DeAngelo. Friends call me Pickle. Joey Pickle."

"What's that about?"

"I used to do some porno. Still do, actually. And, well, my pecker looks like a pickle."

Carson didn't return the disbelieving glance that Masters sent his way. He just sort of concentrated on the informant. How edgy and nervous he looked. Shifty eyes. Stuttering and uncertain. Babbling and repeating things. Talking about unimportant shit.

"So, y'all trying to put the hook on Charlucci, huh? Is that right? Huh?"

"Just tell us what you've got for us, Mr. Pickle." Now Carson did look at his partner, humored by the "Mr. Pickle" moniker.

"Whaddaya need? I know it all. I got loads of data." Joey snapped his fingers on both hands. "I got shit the man himself don't know."

"Oh, really?"

"Really. I mean, I might be the man you're lookin' for. The one who makes your case stick. I even got eyes out there checkin' shit for me, like, I got my own investigation goin' on, for real-for real. Say, you got a cigarette?"

"Why don't you start with Charlucci? How does he move his product? Where? With who?"

"Okay, see he's got these girls, right . . . like real professional chicks. They drive up the coast like every day. But he's payin' 'em like fifteen hundred a trip, right, so I know it's funny, like, they gotta be carrying shit 'r somethin'."

"How do you know the professional-type chicks?"

"Well, my boy is a salesman at Juki Boutiques on Palm Beach. They sell gowns and shoes 'n shit. I mean, real topshelf shit, for real-for real. So, Diane is the manager there and my boy Jimmy Z, he's got a band 'n shit called Da Bomb. Well, he works for the broad. And one day Jimmy Z goes for a ride with Diane. She drives a Benz usually, but for this trip he tells me she took a cab to some parking garage. She goes up to a Honda Civic, takes a key from under the car, like from one of the magnet-type boxes, and they drive up to Fort Lauderdale. She leaves the car in a parking garage up there, takes Jimmy Z shopping, and she gets back in another car coming back to Miami."

"Really." Carson had a pen and pad, taking notes.

"For real-for real. But that's not the end of it. My boy Jimmy Z ends up bangin' the boutique manager."

"Diane?"

"For real-for real. So, she tells him the real. She's getting fifteen hundred just to drive up the coast and she switches cars each time."

"Really?"

"Yeah. Now, Jimmy Z lives with the broad. Like a boy toy 'n shit. She tells him what to do and he does it. She pays him good, too, like a male prostitute."

"Really."

"For real-for real. He's licking her shoe heels, her ass, all that. But then she takes out some blow, she wets his joint and covers it with coke. Then she sucks it clean."

"Your boy do drugs, too?" Masters asked with skepticism.

"Every fuckin' day. Both of 'em. He sniffs it out of the broad's navel. She sniffs it from the crack of his ass."

"Really?" Carson asked with a hint of enthusiasm.

"For real-for real. She turned my boy out 'cause he was never this freaky. Never."

"You said women, as in more than one."

"Oh yeah. Jimmy Z tells me this Diane broad is only one out of a dozen. See, I figger the cars gotta be loaded. I figger she's a mule for the man."

"And you're sure this Diane works for the man."

"Word to my motha!" That statement made Masters recall the failed rapper Vanilla Ice. And, suddenly it was eerie how much Joey Pickle resembled Vanilla Ice, Eminem, and every other white rapper who walked and talked with a street lingo. It told Masters how much the cultures crossed. How what appeared to be one thing, like a young white kid, might not necessarily be that stereotypical puritan.

The agents didn't need any more specifics about Diane, the manager at Juki's, or Jimmy Z, her boy toy, but they asked Joey anyway. Just to keep him talking. Already, they knew a team would be investigating the boutique by morning.

"What else do you know about Charlucci?"

"I know he's seein' this chick that promotes the clubs. Bianca? Somethin' like that. She's got a young son and he does that TV commercial for Tommy Gear. I seen a segment on that *Entertainment Tonight* show where they had up-and-coming child stars. But I think the man got somethin' happenin' with that Tara chick, too. You know, the hottie from the *Scream* movie and the *Smuggle* flick?"

"The actress with the million-dollar body?"

"Yo! That chick is da bomb, man. I think Charlucci's bangin' her, too."

"And pray tell, how do you know this?"

"I seen her in that *Ocean Drive* magazine. And he was next to her—I mean, he had his back turned, but I know it was him."

"And from that you think he was bangin' her."

"I'm telling ya, man, I'm never wrong."

"Right. What else."

Carson and Masters took turns, tossing the leading questions back and forth.

"Well, you know he lives in Utopia, right?"

"Really?"

"Oh yeah. All the players live there. I'm talking the jet-setters. The millionaires. Even the Versace broad lives there."

"Hmmm . . ." The agents played along as if this was the first they'd heard about Utopia. "You think he operates from there?"

"Who knows? Maybe. The guy's like a ghost for real-for real. I do know he has a lieutenant who does all his dirty work. Goes by the name of Ortiz."

"Is that so."

"Yeah. He's like his main man. Does a lotta deals 'n stuff. Big shit."

"How big?"

"Well, I know this guy who deals in Baltimore."

"Baltimore?" Carson was about to say what he knew: Joey Pickle, you never stepped a foot outside of Florida. But he didn't speak on it.

"Sure. I told ya, I know people. For real-for real."

"So, how did you meet this Baltimore guy? What's his name?"

"Stan or somethin'. I can't remember. We were locked up one night down here in Dade County. I got into a fight with some fag at the Forge, Little Louie Vega was the DJ that night, too. Bad mothafucker, dude, for real-for real. I get locked up and there's this guy, Stan, he's bugging out, talkin' about a bum rap. A setup. Some shit. Said he's from B-More and come down to party."

"Really."

"I got to askin' him who he knew down here. He said Ortiz. Bingo. I knew what he was down here for. And he goes, you know him? I go, yeah, kinda! Then he goes, you think he set me up? I go, no, and the B-More dude tells me they were about to deal at Liquid. They were gonna set up a thing where a chick drives up to B-More, the whole parking garage bit. And I'm thinkin', bingo!"

"So you think Charlucci's doin' the same deal like with Diane going to Fort Lauderdale?"

"Bingo. I'm thinkin' he might be sendin' broads out left and right. I'm wishin' I was one a' them broads—fifteen hundred a pop ain't no joke. Just for a drive."

Carson and Masters fed each other a knowing gaze, both of them calculating the ideas . . . the women drivers . . . the cars and the parking garages. How many women? How many trips? How much product? Better yet, how many truck drivers like Big Slim?

"Hey, there's Ortiz right there."

"You don't say. What a coincidence." Carson, the actor. "Who do you suppose that is with him?"

"Oh, that's Nightfly. He's always in the clubs. My friend bought an ounce offa his people once."

"His people?"

"Yeah. Nightfly deals in the clubs, man. Hey! I thought you were the feebies—the DEA—the big dogs. Ain't you supposed to know this shit?"

"Where's Nightfly work out of?"

"All the clubs. Crowbar, Nikki's, and Fuel. He's the man."

"I thought Charlucci was 'the man.' "

"Of course, Charlucci is the man, for real-for real. But, Nightfly is the club connect, know what I'm sayin'? He's a friend of that Ingrid chick, Madonna's friend. Connected. I'm talkin' con-nect-ted."

Carson and Masters made eye contact. Madonna's name was a big red flag.

"You think she's part of this?"

"Who, Ingrid?"

"Ingrid. Madonna. Any of them," asked Carson, fishing for more.

"Who knows? Maybe. He's always in the photos with her. Almost like they're partners, for real-for real." There was a pause, and the agents could thank God who ruled over motormouths that Joey Pickle shut up for a spell. In the meantime, they watched as Ortiz and Nightfly boarded the Humvee and lurched from the parking space out in front of Krave.

"Here we go."

"Hey!" Joey Pickle was thrown back against the seat.

"Sit back and enjoy the ride, Mr. Pickle. It's gonna be a long night."

Earlier that day, Carson had been doing a solo surveillance until he met up with Masters outside of Krave. He began his day at The Coochie Coo, the little topless bar just off of Interstate 95 where Slim first met Ortiz. Carson wore trucker's duds and a cap going in there, and he spent a hundred bucks tipping the girls until Ortiz showed up.

He followed Ortiz to a motorcycle shop on Washington Avenue, where Ortiz joined up with a group of bikers. From there, they made their way to the beach house off of Ocean Drive. From a distance, Carson noted the plates on the bikes as well as on a 1970 Oldsmobile Rallye. He took photos with the help of the 400-zoom lens Minolta and he'd done the same when Ortiz and Nightfly drove off on a daylong tour of various businesses. And, when it got dark, various nightclubs. All the while, Carson reported to the satellite office at the World Class Motel on Collins. According to Pam, this might just be the beginning of something huge. She had Masters meet up with Carson, and now they were on the biggest tail of the case.

While they tailed, the Pickle talked.

"They had the nerve to call this club Crack House?"

"It's actually a gallery," said Pickle, correcting the agent. "There are big murals on the walls now . . . women's faces; their expressions while they're reaching orgasm."

"You're shittin' me, Pickle."

"I'm dead serious! For real-for real. I was on a shoot once; the flick was called *Back Door Thrills*."

"Don't tell me. It was an anal sex porn."

"Hey! You seen it?" Joey Pickle lit up.

"Uh, no. Just a good guess," Carson replied and then looked at Masters with that expression: you better not say a word.

"Well, on the shoot I'm bangin' this black chick real good. Reeeal good. She's squealing 'n shit like she's beggin' for her life. I really can't tell if she's actin' or if I'm really killin' the bitch. But I don't care, see, 'cause that's the game. That's what they paid us the thousand bucks for. Anyways, while I'm in her back door, there's the regular camera guy with the video hookup. Then there's the director, the fluff girl . . ."

"What's a fluff girl?"

"She's really a porn chick too, but not for this flick. She sucks my prick right before we shoot. Gets me nice and hard for when the director yells action. Also, if we have to cut and start again, she gets me back up to speed."

"Okay, so . . . go on." Masters with the adjustment in the passenger's seat.

"Well, there's this other dude with a flash camera. I'm talkin' still photos. So, like every other minute this camera dude is takin' close-ups. I'm talkin' reeeal close. He's all up in the chick's face, snapping away."

"Okay, and you say that to say?"

"Those are the flicks they blow up into murals. I seen some of them myself. In there. A chick I banged on my last shoot. The mural is up on one a' them walls."

Both agents turned back toward Crack House. There were throngs of patrons in line. A bouncer with a tight T-shirt and dark glasses played God at the velvet rope permitting those that he wanted to step through. Some women had hot pants, rock star shirts, and mirrored sunglasses. Hats and bags with studs, rhinestones, and sequins. This was the thrill-seeking crowd. The walking, talking fabulousness. Stylish beatniks, in fashion, in rogue, cool cats. The Jesus sandals and shiny belts. A Paris Hilton type of crowd.

The agents were curious (at least) to go in and see what the excitement was all about. The Pickle must've read their minds.

"Want me to get you in?" Both agents knew that was a joke because they were empowered enough to gain access even to a bank on Christmas morning during a citywide evacuation, if they so wished. But they also knew that a bold entry wouldn't be appropriate. Plus it would defeat their purpose.

"Uh, why not? Can you do it quietly? Without the staff knowing who we are?"

"Of course! You're about to see the Pickle at work!"

Carson fretted the imagery, him at work. Meanwhile, he moved the taxicab from the no-loading zone and into a regular parking space.

At the front of the gallery-turned-nightclub, the trio worked their way through the glitter, the pomp, and the hip. The Pickle went ahead while the agents stood back and wondered how out of place they felt.

"I feel like I've just been dropped in the middle of a wet dream, surrounded by living, breathing free love fantasies," Masters said. The agents laughed enough to loosen up. And now, the Pickle was standing near the muscled doorman waving the two on.

"That looks like us."

"I'll be damned. The punk has got a little juice after all."

Inside, the venue was elegant, with a new modern feel to it. The entryway was a rotunda with a mosaic floor design that featured a floral combination of blue bahia, yanos, osprey, and green marble. There was a blue bahia tabletop set in the center. At various intervals, bay windows were set into the rounded perimeter of the rotunda. Inside the glass windows were video displays, flashing teaser snapshots of what could be expected farther in the gallery itself. Potted palms and plants were situated here and there. A brilliant chandelier was suspended from a skylight above the mass of heads in the lobby. Meanwhile, excitement was brewing, upbeat music streamed throughout, and conversations fueled a constant murmur.

"Shit. They must've spent a fortune in here."

"At least."

"And this is just the start. Wait'll you see inside." Joey Pickle excused himself, leaving the agents alone, while he went to shake hands with a friend. They wondered about Ortiz and Nightfly.

"I'm dyin' to see the face of the girl. The one Pickle was supposed to be bonin'."

"I know. Me, too. I just can't imagine him, this twerp, with anything more than a hunchback from one-eye island."

"Even she might be too good for him."

"Hey, Dorian, Tommy . . . this is Jimmy Z, a buddy of mine. Jimmy, this here's Dorian, an art critic from up north. And this is Tommy, his partner."

The agents started to question what was going on here with the phony names and all. But the name "Jimmy Z" threw them right in check.

"The Jimmy Z? Nice to meet you, buddy. How's it goin'?" As hip as Masters could muster.

Jimmy was too aloof at the moment to realize that his name rang a bell. His curly black hair seemed to be oiled up and his pale skin complexion was almost as shiny as his hair.

"Cool, dude. Real cool. You partyin'? I ain't seen you before."

Carson, at least, figured "partying" meant doing drugs.

"We're from outta town. Here for the thrill, the entertainment. We're just trying to taste it all." Carson let his eyes wander until they froze on a girl strolling past. She had on a hot pink and yellow minidress with a black and white splatter-paint tube top. Her purse had a long chain draped across her shoulder and chest.

"Punked out, ain't she?" Jimmy Z with the description.

Carson was stuck for an answer, feeling ever awkward with his casual attire. "Uh, yeah. Right."

"We'll catch y'all later. I'm gonna check out the scene inside."

Instinct almost set in, the agents both ready to grab up Jimmy Z and interrogate him. But why mess up things now that Pickle had just saved them the time and effort of penetrating the Juki Boutique and the alleged conspiracy that included its manager.

"Don't worry. We'll catch up with him later. He'll be here all night. Trust me."

Masters shrugged his shoulders on behalf of the DEA

and the agents followed their informant (big mouth and tour guide) down the promenade, mood-lit and foggy from the smoke machine back in the main hall where all the activity was waiting. The music was louder and reflections from laser lights danced against the walls of the darkened corridor.

"Sheesh, this is like one big orgasm," Carson spoke up. Masters was silent, with his eyeballs panning throughout the venue. It was dark in here, except for the images on a dozen giant screens and half as many JumboTrons.

Smaller monitors were perched in stacks, like trees, and pin lights were fixed to some flexible rods that somehow earned an effect of leaning branches over the heads of partiers. Indeed, the screens were all illuminated with images of women in climax. There were various nationalities, all casting the ugliest, most awkward, agony-filled expressions. Mouths opened wide. Eyes wild and hair seamy and disheveled. Nothing but nudity. No visibility of the partner, whether it might be a male or female, and plenty of perspiration. Many of the monitors presented slide shows. Others were slow-motion features that melted from one ingénue to the next. There was never a dull moment. The music was jazzy and synthesized, yet heavy with bass and drums. The sights complimented the sounds and vice versa.

"Just standing here is sucking the life out of me, Teddy, to the point of exhaustion."

"I hear you. I can feel my breathing. Heavy."

"Hey, can you guys drink? Or is this considered on the job?"

"We're on the job. But we better get a soda or something in our hands. Make it look believable, ya know?"

"Yup," Masters answered both Carson and Joey. The three of then approached a bar in the center of the room. "This is a first, champ. I've never seen so many obviously sexual images, but at the same time, it's really not rated-X movies or the magazines."

"You're right. These guys, whoever is operating this place, are brilliant. They took the highest moment out of the world's most universal activity, something everybody does, and they put it right out there in an amazing presentation."

"On one hand, you know it's sex. But on the other, it really isn't. They left out the sex."

"Mmm-hmm, I guess. But then, why do I feel like I'm getting a hard-on?"

The female bartenders were wearing pumpkin silk see-thru tops, tan ostrich hot pants with the zipper slightly pulled; they also had on matching bracelets, and cute bows in their hair. Moving from person to person, group to group, was a woman who appeared to be the hostess. She had personality and energy in her smile and eyes, a lemon silk charmeuse halter-top and mint green wide-leg drawstring pants. There were other waitresses who meandered where tables were situated on varying platforms and balconies. There was a mezzanine where some stood looking down, leaning over the railing with their drinks in hand.

"I wouldn't mind moving in here. Living here."

"Don't get crazy on me, Carson. Remember . . . crack babies and triple homicides. Stay focused. There's Ortiz."

"Right. Right. What am I sayin'?"

Then they went home. Ortiz lives in a small house in lower South Beach. House can't be larger than some toolsheds I've seen in Jersey."

"And Nightfly, I checked him out. His name is Robert Jones." The field agents were back at the World Class Motel describing the day's events, the late evening events, and the subsequent Interpol checks made on Nightfly and Jimmy Z, whose name Masters found to be Jimmy Fears, son of Carole and Mark Fears, a couple of high society types who chaired various organizations in the Miami region. Interpol told it all.

"He's in a luxury apartment on Arthur Godfrey Road, here in Miami. He lives good. Operates the club circuit, supplies a group of college types, seven guys and fourteen women as far as I could find out. But there's something else. The grapevine has it that one of Nightfly's guys was murdered just days ago in a robbery," Carson with the secondhand details.

"And did you . . ."

"I already checked. Joshua Dillow. Dropped out of college in his sophomore semester. Ran out of money. Started in the gigolo business. A male escort. Did good. They say he had a client list of some of Miami's cream. Get this: Laura Alverado, producer at Fox; Sophia Marks, owner of Sophia's Restaurant on Collins; Marcela Goldman, operator of Paul Mitchell Salon on Lincoln Road. Oh, and Laetitia Lowe, real estate investor for Power Luxury Properties."

"Okay. So we've got a male prostitute that bangs the big-money ladies. What do you make the connection out to be?"

"I'm not sure yet, Boss. I've got to do some more digging. But here's what I think is strange. This Charlucci organization is super-large. And Jones, aka Nightfly, is rollin' pretty large himself. Humvee, a luxury apartment, stylish clothes, the whole nine."

"Okay."

"Now, this Joshua Dillow? Two slugs in the head at close range. Supposedly, he was working a stash house that belonged to Nightfly. It's not clear how much product, money, or weapons were taken but there were four men in ski masks. That much is on the record. It just doesn't add up."

"What doesn't? The women? The robbery? What?"

"I ran Dillow's name through the Interpol as well. A nice bank account. Connections in high places. Drove a Cadillac Deville, over fifty grand for that alone."

"So? Get to the point, Masters." Pam was still sleepy.

"The point is Joshua Dillow doesn't sound like a low-level type. He's too out-and-about to sit and man a stash house."

"Go on."

"All the low-level functionaries, the runners, the hooks, and especially the stash lookouts we ever knew are lacking self-esteem. They're nobodies, a lot of them lowlifes. So, if Dillow was seeing all of these society women, getting paid to turn tricks for long enough to have two hundred thirty thousand dollars in his savings account, why would he risk that life to make a stash lookout's measly wages?"

Pam considered this for a moment. "It sounds like more a question for Miami Homicide than a MET issue."

"Perhaps, perhaps not," Carson intervened. "But, now if the murder, homicide, whatever, if it took place inside the stash house and if the stash house was Nightfly's and if Nightfly is getting product from Charlucci and if Charlucci is doing better than five hundred kilos of coke as principal administrator, organizer, and lender, five or more persons, et cetera, et cetera, then we could be talking eight-forty-eight."

Masters added, "With the death penalty."

"Exactly." Carson with his two cents.

"All right, all right. Put the puzzle together. Get me some solid evidence on that, and cross your *T*s and dot your *I*s. Make it stick. In the meantime, we've got all the locations that Ortiz and Nightfly went to. We've got Nightfly's college types that you say deal in the clubs. There's your Jimmy Z and the boutique manager. I'm really interested in that. If what you tell me is so, if Joey Pickle's information is on point and Charlucci is sending women out all over the place in this car-switching scheme, then my friend, Operation Snowfall is more like a blizzard. I may need to increase my staff."

"I'm thinking about bringing in Coco Love from Philly. I'd like to put her on the Nightfly."

"Good idea. Call Central and have a ticket waiting for her. Make sure she's down here tomorrow by noon. If she gives you flack, tell her it might help her boyfriend. Tell her what you have to. We need her."

"I don't think we even have to go that far. Really. Coco is making such good money with these operations, infiltrating the organizations and such. I think she's starting to like it, as in the risk. It all gets her excited. She's been calling us for work."

Pam smirked. "Good, get some sleep. I'll see you both to-morrow."

CHAPTER TWENTY-ONE

People meeting people. That's what South Beach is really about. Naturally, there's the lure of attractive, rich, hip individuals from all over the world. Those to whom money is no object. But, for the average person, the local or the tourist, these movers and shakers were an illusion of sorts. Unapproachable. Part of Florida's latest hyperbole. The shameless luxuries, the living in paradise, the famed nightlife—it was all just bait to lure the masses.

"Come to South Beach, there's no place in the world like South Beach."

The bottom line was the friendships, the associations, the business deals, and the networking. People meeting people. Nightfly practically lived inside the nightclub circuit. Jimmy Z was there for the thrills, a local musician who hungered to be a part of the fast lane, music or no music. Joshua Dillow made it his business to see who, what, and where. Who's who, what really mattered most, and where did it all transpire? It was a resource of his trade, his livelihood. The male hooker.

Nightfly befriended all of these thrill seekers. These young, wayward locals who chased the dreams and fantasies of others and who snorted the sensations along the way. It was essentially Nightfly's resource and trade to know these characters, his "customers." They paid his bills, bought his luxuries, and turned him on to other customers. Sometimes, such associations led to bigger things, good and bad.

Jimmy Z made the biggest mistake inviting Joshua Dillow to his family's Thanksgiving dinner. It was even Jimmy's suggestion since he'd known Dillow for about six months; knew how Dillow loved his music. Dillow was compatible for what Jimmy felt were all the right reasons. The two liked good-looking women. They critiqued them all the time. Who's a ten, who's an eleven, who's finer than that download chick?

The big shock for Jimmy, after the double dates and the dozen or so engagements where Jimmy's band rocked, after Dillow met Jimmy's family after the holiday meal, was that Thanksgiving night. Da Bomb's drummer was a no-show for a gig at Café Nostalgia. Jimmy Z was bummed out about it and instead of staying at the Café, instead of drinking away his miseries, he stopped by Level to see Nightfly for some blow. He bought an eight ball and drove up Collins Avenue for a place—any dive would do—where he could settle in a booth, somewhere in a dark corner, and get his high on. Eventually, Jimmy Z found Club Tantra tucked away on an unassuming corner of Pennsylvania Avenue and Espanola Way. The place had a grass carpet floor and the atmosphere was moody enough for all to see the large screens where the *Kama Sutra* movie played over and over again. Jimmy Z ordered a Tantric Kiss (just a martini, really) and sat far away from the others, rolling his twenty into a short straw and snorting up his white powder that formed thin lines aside of a turquoise glow stick. In the distance, Jimmy Z saw a constant whirl of activity. The lighting of cigarettes, the bartenders shaking shakers and making small talk; the dancers and their merriment, the chic posers, the educated, the silly, the sophisticated, and the funny-looking.

Some guy in a black T-shirt with a pearl necklace print stood out. A checkered handkerchief was tied around his neck and his hair was moussed up into a slick Mohawk. His biceps were sinewy and his facial features were sharp as a Ken doll. The woman with him was wearing a striped Gucci dress that seemed to be torn about the shoulder and where the slit was showing a lot of her thigh. She also had the strap of her bra showing, falling off her arm to where the dress started. Black stilettos and black fishnet stockings finished her outfit. Her brunette hair was wrapped like a punk rock singer's, with swatches of it falling over her eyes.

There was something about this couple; the fun they were having, the touching, the kissing and intimate whispers. It was almost as if Jimmy Z was watching a movie, zoning out. The guy was all smug, young. The woman was all over him, older. The scene would fade in and out as the drugs traveled Jimmy's system, tingling in his veins, washing his mind with fresh, artificial energy.

Jimmy Z felt wild, yet satisfied. He was looking at the couple again. The failed gig was a distant memory now. It was just the couple, the effect of the drug and now, the martini. Jimmy Z took the drink in one gulp. He felt the rush and held his breath. He let out an exhaustive gasp. The heat in his mouth stabbed at his senses. He trembled. To the ghosts sitting with him, Jimmy Z said out of nowhere, "That's my mother!" He gritted his teeth, made a few contorted faces; his mind raced from unsung image to unsung image. He lowered his head and upper body to where he was slumped over the table; his hand reaching over his shoulder into his T-shirt and scratching at his back. He did this as he cut his eyes, as he thought. He closed his eyes and opened them again. Hoping this was a dream. Bad drugs, he hoped. Now, his head was lying on his arm, still allowing one eye to absorb the reality. His mother happily married for decades. Mrs. Carole Fears, chairwoman of the Foundation for a Better Miami. Chair to the Committee to Restore the Everglades. Friend to the Versaces and the mayor, and coordinator of the Community AIDS Partnership.

That massive bubble of security was now exploding in Jimmy Z's face; shattering into bits and pieces that were his childhood, his former life. He recalled the Thanksgiving dinner now. How Dillow kissed the back of his mother's hand. And didn't she receive flowers in the weeks to follow?

Yes. That was Dillow over there, with his mother hanging on to him like some older, drugged-up hoochie.

Jimmy Z followed his mother's Mercedes that night. The two stopped at Level. Jimmy Z didn't even bother going in. He waited, as did his mother behind the wheel of the Mercedes. He so wanted to storm up to her. To bang on her window with a crowbar or a hammer. To scare the shit out of her: Mom! What are you doing with my friend?

But Jimmy stayed put, still trembling. Dillow emerged from the nightclub within ten minutes and the Mercedes headed down Washington and then over to Hammon Avenue, where they parked across from the Colony Hotel. Like two teenagers, they trotted across the street and into the lobby. Before Jimmy could think of what to do, after he squeezed some of the life out of his face, Dillow and Jimmy's mom backtracked to the Mercedes. Jimmy figured the restaurant in the hotel was closed. Either that or the hotel rooms were all taken.

Fuming now, he expected them to maybe search elsewhere for a bite to eat and for a hotel room. But it was nearing two in the morning. Businesses were closing. Many restaurants announced last call at midnight. Jimmy fretted the Mercedes' movement, its cruise up to Bar Harbor, the turn onto Hollywood Boulevard and up into Pembroke Pines, till it pulled in the driveway. The Fears home. The house was dark. The outdoor lights and a lamp inside were on autopilot, that much Jimmy knew. If the lamp was off it meant someone was home, a family tradition and a security measure that lasted for years.

Jimmy concluded that his father was away. A business trip, as usual. The couple quickly moved from the Mercedes into the side door, disappearing inside the house. Both curious and enraged, Jimmy used his own key to quietly enter the house around the back. There was giggling and rough-housing further into the house. Then it was quiet. The silence turned to passionate sighs and moans. Jimmy stopped in his tracks the instant he reached the doorway of his father's study. He could see little more than shadows, and that's all he needed to see. The Gucci dress was there on the floor by the threshold.

Four months ago, when Jimmy stumbled upon that encounter—his mother with Joshua Dillow—he immediately knew what he wanted done. But he had neither the heart nor the money to do it. So he turned to Nightfly. The next thing he knew, the newspapers, the six o'clock news, and everybody else was reporting the drug-related murder of Joshua Dillow. And running into his friend on the club scene was inevitable.

"You know, soon I'm gonna have to charge you my regular rate if you keep this up. You're taking advantage of a good thing here, abusing the privilege."

"So, what's your regular rate, ole buddy ole pal?" Jimmy was being sarcastic in response to Nightfly's threat. A Latino man with sideburns and a goatee, with an earring and a beret, stood a few feet away from Nightfly. Ortiz had a serious look on his face.

"I gotta start charging you a hundred a bag instead of fifty. Things are . . . tight lately."

"Lately."

"Yeah, lately." Nightfly was hoping that Jimmy Z would get the message. Did he have to bring it all out in the open, and didn't Jimmy see Nightfly wasn't alone? Jesus! Nightfly turned away and Ortiz joined him, his shadow.

"He's a friend of mine. I think he's hooked," Nightfly explained.

"Why don't he go to one of your people and pay the regular rate? Why you pamperin' him?"

"It's a little complicated. He runs a local rock alternative band and we sorta got close."

"None a' that homo shit, I hope. I mean, I don't care if that's what you're into, that's your business."

"It's not like that, Ortiz. The guy's just a friend is all."

"Yeah, a dependent friend." Ortiz made some sense out of Nightfly's so-called associations, the types of people he dealt with, did business with, all of his connections. There wasn't a face that he didn't plant in his memory. Not a conversation that he didn't ear hustle in on and record in his mind's playback. As the night progressed, just before Night-fly was finished meeting with his various subordinates, Jimmy Z approached him again. This time, Ortiz was at the bar kicking it with the happy face bartender.

"Damn, Jimmy, you're jammin' me up, dude."

"What gives with the hoodlum at the bar? He's lookin' at you like a goddamned secret service agent."

"Just some shit goin' down, bubba. Shit you don't need to know about."

"You see the papers? The thing with Dillow?"

"Did I see the papers? What? Are you mental? I made that story. Isn't that what you wanted? His body on a slab, right? Well, now you got it."

"Damn, Fly. I sorta forgot all about that shit."

"You forgot? The dude got your moms strung out on coke. He's bangin' her three ways from Thursday behind your father's back, turnin' her out . . . and you forgot? You need to lay off the drugs, dog."

Jimmy Z said nothing. Just found himself breathless and at a loss for words.

"Forget the newspapers, Jimmy. Forget Dillow and try to forget what he did with your moms. See if you can get her into rehab, 'cause she should be strung out looking for a new supplier about now."

"Yeah, I never thought about that."

"And I also need a favor from you."

"Anything, Fly."

"I'm in some deep shit because of you."

"Me?"

"The bit the other night? Dillow?"

"Uh-huh."

"I had to tie it into a drug robbery. I had to hire some hit men to do the job—promised them I'd keep it between us, that they'd be able to keep all they found."

"Yeah?"

"Yeah, but the big man, you know, Charlucci, he's got this guy on me hard. It's gonna be this way till I pay off all the money."

"How much?"

"You don't wanna know."

"I do wanna know."

"I'm out for over a mil."

"Oh shit!"

"Oh shit, is right. But I got an idea of how to get 'im off my back."

"What? Just tell me what I gotta do."

"Even if you have to lose a friend?"

"What kind of friend?"

"A close, intimate friend."

Coco Love had been deep in her sleep. It was another bad dream where she was at a restaurant having shrimp scampi with her man, Mustafa. He was on his cell phone again, but she didn't care. The man was bringin' so much money home, slingin' Ecstasy pills to Philadelphia's high rollers, buying her and her baby girl every imaginable luxury, so much so that almost nothing mattered. She felt secure, pampered, a queen. She could breathe like none of her friends could imagine. As long as she could provide for her baby girl, as long as she had a roof over her head, a decent wardrobe, and a night on the town every once in a while. As long as Mustafa was hittin' it right, it didn't matter that he was part of the game.

Since the very beginning when they'd have dinners at Zanzibar Blue, Coco submitted to Mustafa's every sexual need, anything he asked. She was revisiting one of those occasions now in her sleep. And just as she was about to climax, there was a loud noise, an implosion. There was smoke everywhere. Tear gas. Men in dark, bulky outfits like the Mutant Ninja Turtles she took her daughter Asia to see. Weapons and red dot lasers pointing all over. She could never finish that dream like she wanted to, where the sex was complete and where she would cuddle within her man's arms. The dream just ended abruptly.

This time there was a legit interruption. The phone was ringing and Coco reached for it without thinking; without waking. She couldn't even mutter hello before the recording sounded in her ear: "This call is from a federal prison. This is a collect call. The cost of this call is . . ."

The recorded voice was not unusual to Coco. She sometimes looked forward to it. At other times, she dreaded the recording. Now was one of those times. Coco pressed 5 on her phone to cut the recorded voice short. To accept the call.

"Hey baby," Mustafa said in a tone too chipper for 6 A.M.

"Mmmm . . ." Coco responded, more as a reflex response than anything else.

"Oooh . . . I like hearing you moan so early in the morning. It reminds me of how I use to wake up with you naked in my arms."

"Mmm-hmm." She hated how good that idea sounded.

"Everything good?"

"Mmm-hmm."

"Asia okay?"

"Mmm-hmm, she's fine."

"Sorry to wake you, baby. I just wanted to hear your voice."

"Okay. So . . . now that you've heard it, what?"

"What's new? The job treatin' you okay?"

Coco thought to herself that Mustafa asked her these same fuckin' questions only a day and a half ago. Nothing like another of these predictable prison phone calls.

"Mustafa. Nothing's new. The job is good. Asia's good. I'm good. We're all good, you're there, I'm here, and no there's nobody here in bed with me. Did I answer all your questions?"

"Dag, baby. Wassup witchu? You have a bad night? It won't be much longer, baby. As soon as they answer my appeal, I'll be back in court for re-sentencing and home before you can say 'do me daddy.' "

"Mmm." Coco had been hearing this same story for a month of Sundays now. Mustafa had been sentenced to twenty-two and a half years eighteen months ago. And Coco had grown accustomed to this stale routine. They weren't growing together as much as they were growing apart.

"You gotta have faith, babe. All the answers lie in faith. Just believe."

Coco wagged her head. She wanted to hang up.

"Listen, remember the day I visited? The time you told me I could see other men while you were away?"

"Okay."

"Remember when you told me to handle my business? You said, 'Do you.' Remember?"

"Yeah, okay. So?"

"Well I'm giving you some of your own advice, daddy. Do you. You call here like every other day with the same ole spit."

"Hey, watch your mouth, Coco."

"What? You callin' my house, on my mothafuckin' dime, tellin' me to watch my mouth?" Coco was becoming more confident with every passing second; every word out of his mouth was fueling her anger.

"Take it easy, baby."

"No. You take it easy. Lay it down, Mustafa. Isn't that what you said you do at Allenwood? Lay it down? Well, do you and lay it down. I'm about tired of the bullshit. I'm tired. I'm tired. I'm tired!" Coco put the phone down. She silenced the ringer and wiped away a tear. Asia was awake and crying now. More frustration.

Coco got up out of the bed and picked up the baby from the crib. She rocked her back and forth in her arms.

"Shhh, baby. I'm sorry. Mommy's sorry to wake her little flower. Shhh." Coco's tears were falling onto the baby's face. At first, Coco managed to wipe her own away, to wipe them from Asia's face. Then she abandoned the fix-it attitude and held Asia against her, crying with her. Tears everywhere. Coco rocked her child repeatedly, aching for a way out, an escape from this madness. This trap.

It was after a cup of tea, after the baby's bath and the preparation of Asia's breakfast that Coco realized her pager was vibrating on the nightstand. The pager and its messages were always a good thing. Nothing but people who wanted her. None of Mustafa's friends or business associates. The pager was all about Coco and Asia. Coco checked the digital display and saw a familiar code 222 at the end of a 305 area code and phone number. She immediately picked up the phone and started dialing.

"Coco Love, calling collect," she noted for the operator.

"Thank you. Please hold the line."

Coco was putting the morning's dishes on the counter near the sink. She'd wash them after the call, after she dropped Asia off at her sister's apartment up on the fifth floor, before she'd have to head out to work.

"Coco, it's Agent Carson. How are you?"

"I'm good. Is there work?"

"Sure is. A lot of it, too. We're gonna need you down here in Miami by noon today."

"Noon?"

"Yes. Noon. The ticket's already waiting for you at our Philadelphia office, 6th and Market." There was silence between them.

"God . . . I . . ."

"Is there a problem? Can we expect you down at the office within the hour?"

"I . . . I . . ." Coco looked over at Asia, playing with a LEGO set on the living room floor.

"Coco, I need an answer now, or else I'll call someone else for the job."

"I'll be there."

"Good. Your flight leaves from Philadelphia International Airport at 9:30 this morning. US Air. It'll drop you at Miami International by 11:15, 11:30—about that. We'll have a car waiting for you there. Same procedure as always, Coco."

Coco took a deep breath then said, "Okay, Carson. How long this time?"

"Hard to say. You'd better prepare for a while. And kiss the baby for me. Give give your sister my regards, too."

"Sure." Coco hung up recalling how Carson helped to smooth things out with Tracy, her sister, during the Seattle operation. The job kept her away from Asia for three weeks.

There were days when she couldn't even phone home. At least she got paid well, almost $13,000 for that one job. And the work was simple. Meeting all kinds of people; getting to know them good. Some of them real good. One or two times she didn't mind the intimacy. In the end, MET snatched her out of the mix and shipped her home with some pocket change. A week later, the check arrived in the mail care of the U.S. Treasury.

When Coco first met with the DEA it was under entirely different circumstances. They threatened her with imprisonment. They threatened to tie her in to Mustafa's trafficking conspiracy and told her she'd give birth to her child while she was behind bars. The mere idea frightened her to death. She went along with what they asked. Answered their questions. Who did Mustafa spend the most time with? Where did he hang out? Where did he keep his money and drugs? Who leased cars for him? Coco was able to answer most of these questions without letting on to Mustafa or his associates that she was cooperating. Coco's information led to the arrest of twelve others, including Mustafa's father.

Agent Carson took a special interest in Coco; one, because his supervisor had him to do so, and two, because he could understand the humble conditions, the practices and constitutions of the inner city that she called home. He understood desperation, hard times, and the habits which poverty consciousness encouraged. Carson also came from a childhood of sugar water and choke sandwiches. It was the conversation Coco had with Agent Carson over coffee and muffins—not really a date, just a coffee break during the Mustafa investigation—that helped to change Coco's point of view from someone who was a part of the "other side" (even if indirectly supported by the enterprise) to someone who could assist with subsequent investigations. Sure, Carson knew the inner city customs, and so did many other agents for that matter. But to have a person who wasn't jaded by the agency's truths, to have a person who knew the slang, who was street-smart and who wasn't a stranger to the game, to have all of those resources, all of that knowledge in a woman, an attractive woman, was an asset to the agency. Besides, she didn't smell like a cop. She didn't look like one, either.

BOOK THREE

BOOK THREE

CHAPTER TWENTY-TWO

In Africa, there are many millions of poverty-stricken individuals—the homeless, the hungry, the dying—even though Africa is the earth's wealthiest nation when it comes to natural resources. In the United States, there are also many millions who are poverty stricken. It's a slower, more subtle death—even if only psychological—but it's death nonetheless.

Still, the United States is wealthy beyond compare when it comes to housing, food, and other such resources. So whether it's diamonds, gold, or oil in Africa, or if it's shelter, corn, or cold cash in the States, these abundant resources are always useless unless they are traded off in return for the equal balance of what living requires. Just as a person cannot eat gold or diamonds, one cannot be sheltered by corn or actual paper money. These resources must be traded. In order to be traded, they must have a market.

In Colombia, where agriculture dominates, poverty still cries out loud despite the country's wealth of natural resources. This instability among the people spills over into politics, and is closely tied to the unequal distribution of such resources.

The Colombian economy is heavily dependent on the production of coffee, but this is mere ethical theory and also highly sensitive to fluctuations in the world market. Set aside the theories and the traditions, and you will find that their most profitable natural resource—except for the millions of people who live there—is the cocaine that is produced there.

So, as Africans need to bring their gold and diamonds to market, and as Americans must fill empty apartments and attach burden and need to their concept of money, Colombian farmers, in their quest to compete in a universe of what's really important and what truly matters, must turn a profit from their richest crops. Accordingly, Colombians must turn their cocaine into gold, housing, and other resources which they don't have and which they need.

The latest details of Colombia's contribution to the States' consumption of cocaine were printed in black and white, documented in the DEA's Drug War Report. The document was originally the result of a recent congressional investigation into drug production, trafficking, consumption, and enforcement.

However, State Department officials, federal law enforcement agencies, and the White House have created a commission to represent the joint effort to update the Drug War Report in light of the dramatic changes that have taken place in the past decade. "The Drug War" itemized the particulars so that any uninformed person—government employee or not—would be up to snuff after having read the report. It marked the foundations, including maps and diagrams showing villages and settlements where many crop workers lived; waterways and shorelines where cocaine was said to be transported; fields, valleys, lowlands, and hills where hundreds of crops were located; and rain forests and jungles where processing was camouflaged in huts and makeshift labs. The report detailed the people, their dialects, their problems, their living conditions, and even their average intelligence. Finally, there were specifics about the government, the political system, and the history of drugs in Colombia.

It said that much of the illegal trade in Colombian marijuana and cocaine—especially with the United Sates—became a major source of income by thé 1970's and 1980's, even rivaling the value of legal exports. Then, the established government was marred by extremes of violence that tested Colombia's long-term commitment to democracy. Terrorists kidnapped and held captive a number of foreign ambassadors; and in 1984, elements believed to be linked to the most powerful drug lords assassinated the Minister of Justice.

In 1985, guerrillas entered the Palace of Justice in Bogotá and held a number of captives. The outcome of the siege was a massacre that left more than one hundred dead, including a number of Supreme Court judges. There was a bottom line here: the most powerful drug lord, the man who grew to be more powerful than even Colombia's authorities, the man who the United States attempted to extradite for what the government considered international crimes—Pablo Escobar was telling the world by his actions that he wasn't going anywhere. Nobody—not federal, not political, and not military—was coming to take Escobar from his homeland.

These events pointed to an ominous growth in the strength of drug traffickers who had their own armies, their own fortresses, and their self-installed sovereignty.

Frustrations continued in both Colombia and the United States, including corrupted officials, law enforcement, and ongoing antigovernment guerrilla activities. In fact, the drug trade dominated the 1990 presidential campaign, where three candidates and hundreds of other people were killed by drug traffickers in a backlash against tougher drug trade policies.

After what had to be his seventeenth reading, Steve Masters put down the 250-page report and turned to his supervisor with a question. Agents Carson, Stevens, and Green were also present in the South Beach satellite office.

"So, be honest, or as honest as you can," said Majors. "Did we kill Escobar? I mean, is it like they say about the hanging of his associates, of his family, and of his associates' families? Torture and the whole nine?"

Pam looked at her subordinate with a second or two of concern, and then she averted her eyes.

"I'm not sure what you mean. Do you mean 'we' as in the DEA? I couldn't tell ya. I wasn't there."

Masters inhaled impatience and exhaled a sigh of disbelief. "Come on, Boss . . . you? You're Washington's golden girl. Anytime they come up with a major operation where they need to fish out a subject, no matter how complicated, they call you."

"Correction, they call on me, but I head the MET. So, in actuality, they're calling on us."

"Okay, us. But you can't say that you don't get that privileged information . . . the juice underneath all the rumors and opinions."

"Maybe."

"So? What gives? If we're supposed to study the so-called drug war, and if we're supposed to learn all of the details about who, what, and where, don't you think that it might be to our advantage to know the truth, even if it hurts?"

Pam got up and approached Masters. He was still seated by the hotel window with the report in hand. She put a hand on his shoulder. "Sometimes, what we don't know won't hurt us." With that said, Pam turned and left the room.

Agent Masters sat spellbound, and eventually, broke the silence by saying, "It must pay to be someone important in this game."

The others, saying nothing, looked at each other and then went back to their part in Operation Snowfall.

CHAPTER TWENTY-THREE

That environment of one ultimate drug lord is now considered ancient history. But the effects of his reign are felt today. While Pablo Escobar appeared to be the last person anyone would want to cross, Roberto Nunez did just that, more than twenty-five years ago.

Buried in the forests of Bogotá were hundreds of hidden huts that processed cocoa leaves into 100 percent pure cocaine. These huts—some made with corrugated tin and others with mere branches and rocks—were set outside of the farms and facilitated the simple steps of creating the cocaine. It was in these huts that the white crystalline liquid, the juice of the cocoa plants, was extracted and then converted into the hydrochloric salt of cocaine—that fine white powder that found its way to the streets of New York, North Carolina, Miami, and most every other town in the land of Britney Spears.

Roberto Nunez graduated from simple farming, to overseeing leaf pickers, to managing a hut for Escobar. Soon, the greed set in. He decided that his contribution to the cartel was worth more than the $2,000 he received per crop. The bundles that filled almost three quarters of the open-air hut became more than the by-product of a farmer's labor. These tightly packaged squares were more than a consequence of three or four crops that were harvested during the course of a year.

He never considered that stealing would be ten times easier than selling it. He never considered that whomever he did
sell it to might be setting him up for a fall. All Roberto knew
was that in other countries, such as Europe and especially
the United States, these same bundles of white powder were
worth millions. He realized that the hut he managed was
filled with what was called "the white man's high," and that
it was only a matter of finding a middleman to connect him
to his riches.

Most everybody feared Escobar. The poor farmers, villagers, the police, and even government officials were
afraid for their lives. But it was Roberto Nunez who played
along as the honorable manager of a hut, while at the same
time setting aside a stash, an accumulation which was big
enough to earn him financial freedom, yet small enough that
nobody would notice it missing. Besides, Roberto thought,
what would it hurt Escobar? He was such a powerful,
wealthy man who was burdened with many people to watch
over and many crops throughout Colombia. How would he
even find out?

The stealing was easy indeed. Roberto relieved the two
gunmen who stood guard in round-the-clock shifts. He
also made it convenient by relieving his daughter, Maria,
who also picked cocoa leaves with two dozen others. Maria
was the eldest of Roberto's children; his one son and three
daughters. Roberto's plan was to encourage Maria to give
the gunmen some friendly company. The three of them
would sit by the shed where the tools were kept. And as her
father instructed, Maria served Escobar's boys a meal of
beans and rice. She was already a spectacle in her prairie
dress and loafers, a sight that her father hoped the men
would concentrate on day after day. Conversations and
laughter grew out of Maria's hospitality. She'd take a short
walk with one man or the other from time to time. Always,
Roberto would nod in approval so that Maria and the gunmen knew all was okay. Within sight and hearing, he'd sit
and have lunch alone.

After a few months, this system of lunch breaks and short walks became routine. Roberto thought he heard laughter at one point, and left his post to see what Maria and the others were up to. From behind a cluster of underbrush, Roberto found what he was looking for, what he was expecting. He watched momentarily as the gunmen manhandled Maria. Their pants were at their feet and they took turns with his daughter. Roberto became erect the instant he heard her muffled screams and, even from his distant position, he saw the apprehension masking her face. He backed away in shame, but just as soon answered his quickening heartbeat. This was his opportunity.

He scurried back to the unattended hut and pulled down a bundle from an unfinished stack. He hurried with it over to a hole he had dug weeks ago behind the shed. He quickly filled the hole and returned to stand guard by the hut. A scream escaped in the distance, but Roberto pretended not to hear. He clasped his hands, looked up, and closed his eyes, half praying that Maria would be okay and half asking for forgiveness.

"Maria!" Roberto gave the threesome another five minutes or so before calling for his daughter again.

"Maria!"

Roberto's call wasn't threatening, nor was it in answer to his daughter's scream. He was calling for her to return to the fields. His objective was complete.

"Si, papi." Maria appeared before the gunmen, as if she was still the innocent daughter Roberto once knew.

"Vamos a trabajar," was her father's direction, and she shuffled off, turning away in hopes that he wouldn't detect foul play.

When the gunmen emerged, it was Roberto who now turned away, hiding his own guilt.

Six weeks after Roberto had begun his pilfering, eventually filling the dozen or so holes that he'd dug behind the toolshed, Escobar's response came swift and lethal.

It was an early, cloud-shrouded morning in Rio Blanco de

Sotara, a village of five thousand, where the Nunez family lived just outside of the cocoa crops. The neighborhood of one-level shanties, including its schoolhouses and churches, sat at the foot of a windswept mountain terrain where illicit crops and their legal alternatives grew side by side. A hint of sun wouldn't show for hours. Yet, in the forefront of such an idyllically peaceful vista, with its inexhaustible contours of exotic flowers, plants, and trees, a team of weathered Toyota pickups rumbled along the dirt and weed covered roads.

A dozen of Escobar's beret-capped guerillas were loaded inside and on the backs of the trucks, armed with their "don't fuck with us" expressions and their arsenal of weapons at the ready. Within minutes, they were deep into the village. Seconds later, they were kicking in the front door of the Nunez home. Some carried machetes in one hand and flashlights in the other. The others merely pointed their assault rifles loaded with fifty-round banana clips.

There was a brief search amidst swinging rays of light cutting through the dark dwelling. Screams from both the young and the old ensued as the armed intruders marched into the different bedrooms. They dragged or prodded the parents and their children into the front end of the shanty. Within moments, a gunman stood behind each of the family members.

Eight-year-old Elsa Nunez was weeping uncontrollably on her knees, with her hair tight in the clutch of the man beside her. Maria and Mrs. Nunez were also on their knees with their hair in tight grips. All three Nunez females were in their nightgowns.

"*Silencia!*" ordered Franco, the leader of the posse. And in that instant, Elsa was released. She fell off balance to the floor. The ominous clicking sound could be heard by all as a gunman positioned his rifle over the girl.

Mrs. Nunez screamed.

Numerous shots blasted into Elsa, with the brief flashes from the rifle leaving a burnt sulfur haze. When Roberto rebelled, a guerilla swung a rifle butt, connecting with his head. He slumped over and moaned, not quite unconscious.

Franco's sarcasm lingered as he eased over to one of his soldiers. He took a machete from his hand and was right back to Maria. "Such a pretty girl . . . how sad." Franco pulled Maria's long hair upward, almost suspending her, while his men held her arms outstretched behind her.

"No! What do you want? Anything!"

"For starters, Mr. Nunez, where is the remainder of the cocaine you've stolen from Señor Escobar?"

"Huh? I . . . uh . . . it's buried. It's buried out near the toolshed where the crops are!"

"Well, well . . . so there is more hidden. Is that all of it? Are you sure? How can I trust you?" Franco spoke while he also threatened to harm Roberto's oldest daughter, pulling back the machete as if ready to swing.

"Yes! Yes! That is all. Please! I put my life on it!"

Roberto's answer danced around in Franco's head for a spell while he stood still contemplating.

"No, that is not enough." Franco hadn't even finished his response before he stretched his arm back, the machete's sharp steel extended with the reflective glints of light.

There wasn't time enough to scream, to appeal, or to think as Franco hooked the massive blade around for a clean sweep at Maria's neck. Maria's body, headless now, dropped to the floor with blood spraying about. Franco returned from his half-spin, stood erect, and looked somewhat caught up in his own dastardly act. Maria's head dangled with a frozen expression, her hair still tight in Franco's hand, until he tossed it into Roberto's lap.

"*Terminalo,*" Franco ordered his men. Then, amidst the screaming, crying parents, the leader pivoted toward the entrance of the Nunez shanty.

In Franco's absence, the gunfire and slashing continued for a senseless five minutes until the cries finally ceased altogether; until the Nunez family was butchered to death.

CHAPTER TWENTY-FOUR

Mario

That fateful night so long ago devastated the village of Rio Blanco. None of the villagers would dare speak out against the massacre, for Escobar's wrath was a frightening one. Still, the neighbors, farm workers, and local leadership endured the horrors and assisted in the burials.

Alberta Nunez-Artega, Roberto's sister, came from Bogotá to tend to unfinished business. Fortunately, she didn't have to see the worst of the carnage left by the guerilla rebels. However, the Nunez shanty would most likely forever be a stained dwelling, forever keeping a trace of that offensive bloody odor.

Fernando, a local priest, accompanied Alberta. The moment Alberta walked through the entrance, Fernando closed the door and escorted her to the back to the bedrooms. They were as they'd been left that night, with death and ghosts lingering. In their language, Fernando went to great lengths in developing a rapport with Roberto's sister. He had to be absolutely certain she was righteous. That she wasn't an impostor.

"There is a photo album here, Mrs. Artega. If you wouldn't mind, could you point some things out for me?"

"Why, sure. I'm surprised that there are any possessions at all. In Bogotá, the locals might have looted the home clean."

"The people of Rio Blanco were deeply troubled by this

senseless killing, señora. We have heard the word that Señor Nunez took cocoa from the hut where he worked. But we didn't understand the purpose for the killings of the women. Most likely, they were not a part of Roberto's acts."

"Yes, I understand. Young Elsa . . . my God. She was only eight years of age." Alberta caressed Elsa's photo.

"And Maria was but sixteen," Fernando added.

"How did you bury the twins?"

"Excuse me?" Fernando asked confusingly.

"Roberto, Jr., and Roberta . . . how did you bury them? In the same space, or separately? We had a burial in Bogotá recently, twins. They were buried in the same spot. They placed one casket above the other."

Fernando was silent for a beat, reading Alberta's eyes . . . and even trying to read her mind.

"I'm sorry. I don't know anything about twins. The family was only four as far as we know."

"*Four!*? How long have you known this family, Father Fernando? How can you claim to know my brother and yet you say you know of only four?" Alberta's eyes shifted from the priest to the photo album. "Look here. Maria . . . Elsa . . ." She flipped the pages. "Roberto and his wife . . . that's me at the wedding . . ." She flipped another page. "Where are the photos from this page, señor? There seem to be photos missing!"

Fernando was convinced. "Please, señora. Please, sit." Both of them found space on a bed. "It was important for me to know that you were truly who you say you are. I haven't known the Nunez family for long, true. Just the last six years since I came to this village. I was the one who saw to the funeral. I delivered the sermon. I—"

"The children, señor. Please." Alberta spoke as if in a trance, perhaps reading between the lines. "Roberto had twins . . . Roberto, Jr., and Roberta."

"The children are alive, señora."

"Aaah!"

Fernando reached out to cover Alberta's mouth with his hand. "Shhh. Señora, please. This is sensitive. You must maintain secrecy about this—the walls are so thin. A scream, a shout could be heard outside in the streets."

"Of course. Of course." Alberta was hyper, finding it difficult to breathe or to suppress her tearful angst. "Where?"

"They are safe with me. They are in the basement at the church. My sisters there are watching over them for now."

"But how?" Alberta wiped a tear from each eye.

"As far as we know, the children were hiding under their bed that night when the rebels stormed the home. It's unclear what either of them witnessed. Both of them were traumatized. Young Roberto seems to have come along. But Roberta is still quiet and afraid of the dark. She hardly eats and cries all the time. Loud noises frighten her."

"Can I see them?"

"Sure you can, señora. You can understand my wanting to protect them, yes?"

"Of course. Of course. Thank you. I understand indeed. Between the rebels, the police, even the villagers and farmers, does everybody work for the drug lords?"

"It seems so. We can never be too careful, señora."

AT THE CHURCH

The priest stood back alongside of Alberta. He detailed the aftermath of the tragedy as the two looked on from an alcove just under the steps that led to the basement of the church. Roberto, Jr., toyed with a set of building blocks, while Roberta was motionless in a fetal position atop a comforter on the floor, staring with watery eyes into space as if lost in time.

"She's so pretty lying there. So peaceful," Alberta commented.

"Yes, señora, but in so much pain."

"Have any doctors looked at her?"

"Not as of yet. The doctor who tends to our villagers, Dr. Obando, has been missing for a while now. It is said that he has moved up your way. Only nurses are picking up the slack now. A nurse who came to see Roberta says she thinks the girl is okay and that in time the shock will wear off. I hope she speaks the truth." There was agreement in Alberta's eyes. "They're not safe here, señora."

"No. I guessed as much."

"Based on what we know, the track record of Escobar's rebels is to leave no surviving family members, perhaps to prevent revenge or to send a message to others. We can only guess at their reasoning for murdering innocent women and children."

Alberta said nothing.

"Don't get me wrong. We would love to keep and care for these lovely children, but it could be disastrous for us at the church. The guerillas are ruthless, señora."

A tear of joy and sorrow fell down Alberta's cheek. Her calling was evident. The children's lives would change, and so would her own.

Alberta's First objective was to protect the identities of Roberto, Jr., and Roberta. She was especially concerned about Roberto, Jr., as a young boy would be the greatest threat to the right-wing guerillas that carried out the orders of the drug lords. To offset any connection to the children's father, Alberta introduced them to the Bogotá villagers as Mario and Roberta Ortega.

Her second objective was to have the children live a normal life, not in a church basement or hidden from other children their age. Since Alberta had children of her own, it was a cinch for the siblings to blend in to what was considered normal. The two were admitted into Santa Librada's Primaria program, the equivalent of elementary schooling, where they completed a curriculum of grades one through five.

Santa Librada also maintained a Bachillerato, the equivalent of secondary schooling or high school. Roberta adapted well there, finding a place among her classmates as Miss Inteligente. She generally picked up lessons pretty fast, and eventually tutored others, helping them to excel as well.

Meanwhile, Mario rejected secondary schooling. He attended classes as scheduled for the first year. However, by the second year of Bachillerato, Mario began to skip class. He befriended boys who were from the barrio, and eventually felt behooved to prove himself in effort to be accepted as barra—part of the gang.

As Roberta was impressive in her schoolwork, her brother was just as impressive to the barrio boys. Mario could get away with stealing cars in broad daylight, as if he were invisible. It was a step up from what the others were comfortable with, stealing fruit or other goods from local merchants. But even then, he could at least escape capture . . . Mario, the fast runner.

The leader of the barrio boys, Antonio Espanosa, Jr., became close with Mario, seeing as his new compadre outdid him in most every way. Since he couldn't beat him, he felt it was best to join him. Antonio introduced Mario to his family, who accepted him as one of their own. Outside of the barra activities of stealing and protecting their turf, the two boys often joined Antonio Espanosa, Sr., (Antonio's father) on his boating trips, braving the waters of the Pacific Ocean on his mega yacht.

Each week, Espanosa and his eight-man crew would take the *Quindio* out from where it was docked on the harbor at Cape Corrientes. One of Espanosa's men taught the two boys to catch catfish, bocachica, and the small, brightly colored tropical rainbow trout. They spotted electric eels and crocodiles, which inhabited the inland waters, as well as one or two carnivores at the coastline, such as pumas and jaguars that were said to be endangered species.

It never dawned on Mario while he was fishing, sightseeing, and carrying on in the vessel's small sundeck pool that Antonio's father was out on the water to do his own brand of fishing.

Antonio Espanosa, Sr., made weekly excursions for more than mere leisure. He was on the payroll of Cali Cartel, Colombia's other cocaine goliath, who was considered to be more political but less violent than Escobar's huge and brutal Medellin empire.

Because of his affiliation, Espanosa, Sr., always had the protection of the Colombian Coast Guard for those outings where the *Quindio* would rendezvous with cargo ships, cigarette boats, seaplanes, as well as other mega yachts. Mario learned later into his teens that Espanosa was one of many couriers who owned their own vessels and who worked for one cartel or the other. But it was Espanosa who was aggressive in both trade and politics. He knew the truth: that it was always who you knew that could make or break you.

As a teenager, Mario was mature and streetwise. He recognized that Espanosa's way of life, with his big home and his luxury boat, was a life soaked in money. It was a lifestyle that Mario could look to as a reference, something to aspire to. In their native Spanish language, Mario asked Antonio questions that he felt, up until now, might be out of line.

"Why do you stay in the barrio if your family is living so good?" he got up the nerve to ask.

"That's my family, not me. I want my own. Plus, the barra are my boys. I proved myself as a leader. I won't just quit like that," Antonio answered.

"It just doesn't make sense to me, Antonio. To be stealin' cars one day, and to be on a rich boat the next. It doesn't even sound right."

"I know. But I'm having a lot of fun, too!" This was Antonio's response as the two hung out on Bolivar Street in downtown Bogotá. It was a place where the barra could spot tourists and other targets who would be their next victims. This was the ritual, to loiter in rough clothing, to smoke, and to survey the turf.

"That's a nice one. I think I could take that." Mario pointed out a yellow sports car that looked to be worth twice the average catch.

"I don't think you should. It might belong to somebody important. Who else would have a fancy car like that?"

"I guess. It sure looks good, though," Mario told his friend.

Carlos and Poppo were a few feet away from Mario and Antonio, also smoking, acting like adults, and talking about the yellow sports car. Carlos already had a deep scar under his left eye, and Poppo was getting a lot larger than the average teenager. All of the boys were beginning to develop facial hair, wearing their own brand of cool and vigilant and unfuckwithable attitudes.

Just a few days later, Antonio didn't show up on Bolivar, and the rest of the barra dared Mario to try and take the yellow sports car when it happened to show up on the turf again. Mario mentioned Antonio's opinion, that he should not try this particular car, that it might belong to someone important, maybe powerful. But the boys continued to question Mario's courage, even if he had already stolen four other cars on the block. He continued to resist until the boys finally sighted the driver, a woman—brunette, with a short skirt and a healthy bosom.

"See? Look! It ain't nobody important. Just a woman. See?" Poppo helped to change Mario's mind. He encouraged him to think past Antonio and to turn his inhibitions to action.

"I'll do it," Mario said. "Watch my back." Then he swaggered over to the vehicle. It was across the street and the woman was about to load some groceries in the back.

The barra watched from a distance as Mario performed as an innocent. They watched as he convinced the woman to accept his help. Then he took her bags and put them neatly in the car. Finally, Mario stepped ahead of the smiling woman, being a gentleman and offering to open the driver's side door for her. The door seemed to be locked and Mario held his hand out for the key. Before any of them could blink, Mario unlocked, opened, and then shut the door once he was inside. He locked the door, and the woman stood screaming and yelling for help. None came in time. Mario left nothing but a dust cloud in his wake.

When it came to getting paid for stolen cars, there was little to be expected. Many of the cars were raggedy and worthless, and stealing them was merely for sport. But the yellow sports car which Mario took, an imported Porsche, had to be worth hundreds of thousands of pesos. He was only able to make a few hundred pesos for the earlier takes, money which he shared with the barra. The Porsche, however, was an entirely different story.

Mario took the car to four chop shops that same day he jacked it. Yet, nobody wanted it. It was hard to figure out if they couldn't afford it or if there was some other reason. They wouldn't say. Eventually, Mario was forced to keep the car parked behind a fix-it shop where Poppo's father worked as a mechanic. Mario had to promise he'd remove the car before the week was up.

Antonio heard about the carjacking and couldn't decide whether to be proud—in anticipation of a landslide payoff—or to feel disrespected—because Mario went against his suggestion. Hesitantly, he chose pride. It was Carlos who delivered the bad news to Antonio.

"The word is all over the streets," Carlos told the barra leader. "The car belonged to a low-level lord on the left." Carlos spoke in a low volume, knowing the alley's echo.

"The Communists?" Antonio asked.

"You said it. Some guy named Batista."

Antonio rubbed frustration from his face and it wouldn't go away. "Shit!" he exclaimed. Then he asked, "Do they know who?"

"They're sayin' barrio."

"Oh, shit! I told that fuck not to take that car. I had a feeling."

"You had a feeling what? How was I supposed to know it was a drug lord's car? A woman was drivin' it." Mario had snuck up and overheard the gang members.

"Too late for that now. They sayin' barra did it. They comin' after all of us."

"You scared?" Mario asked.

"Fuck yeah, I'm scared. You ever see them guerillas? You know what they do to people who steal from them?"

"Pussy!"

"Your momma!" Antonio shot back.

Mario snapped at the thought of Antonio playing all high

and mighty, disrespecting his deceased mother. He charged at him and the two crashed into an arrangement of trash cans. In a swift move, Mario pulled a knee up into Antonio's groin and followed up with a right cross to the face. Carlos ran to pull the two apart. Poppo ran over as well, finally restraining Mario from further assaulting Antonio. Mario and Antonio cursed each other until they were out of each other's eyesight. Mario felt like an outcast of the barra, and never went back to Bolivar Street.

It was a mystery to him what, if anything, would result from his poor judgment. Within two weeks, Mario had forgotten about the issue. He became a fixture once again at his Aunt Alberta's home and was surprised to see how his sister Roberta had developed into a smart and attractive schoolgirl. For now, at least, he set the barra, the stealing, and the Espanosas out of his mind. He began escorting Roberta to school, and if he had time, he escorted her home. Having been around Bogotá's undesirables had made him concerned for his sister's safety.

But Mario soon learned that was the least of his worries. Not five minutes away from his aunt's home, on the way to Santa Librada to pick up Roberta, Mario was cornered by a team of older men who abducted him, tied and gagged him, and then drove for miles to a hideaway on the banks of the Carare River. It wasn't a challenge for Mario to realize that this had to do with the yellow sports car he'd stolen.

Two of the men grabbed Mario and half-carried, half-pushed him until they reached a cabin that was isolated amidst tall palms.

"This skinny kid was the one?"

There she was, the big-breasted brunette driver, nodding at some guy in a safari outfit.

"And he probably doesn't have the slightest idea who he's crossed."

Mario, the quick, street-smart orphan, couldn't come up with a getaway plan now. He was out of his league. The moments escalated quickly with an ever heavier burden to bear.

Mario soon found himself bound to an armchair, gagged, and at the center of attention. The woman had a look of satisfaction on her face before she left the cabin.

"This will be a painful lesson, kid. But you will be an example to all of your barra buddies. Nobody steals from Miguel Batista . . . nobody."

As soon as Mario saw the hedge cutters, muffled pleas fought to get out of his mouth past the gag. However, his efforts were futile and had no bearing on the realities at hand. One of Batista's men took hold of Mario's wrist. Another stood behind him, hands heavy on his shoulders. Still another stood behind Batista, reaching in to grab the target hand. The hedge cutters were now sharp against Mario's pinkie until the finger was wedged in beyond the second joint.

"Stupid kid can't be more than twelve or thirteen."

Mario's hand trembled despite being held. His whole body shook. There was a silence, and urine suddenly flowed in Mario's trousers. Batista squeezed the arms of the hedge cutters together in one snapping motion. The severed pinkie fell to the floor while the youngster bellowed loud and hoarsely, struggling within the grasps of those around him. The nub on his left hand pumped steady squirts of blood to the rhythm of his heartbeat. The men stood and watched Mario buck and jerk in concert with the pain and torment. One minute seemed like ten.

"Wrap him. Put him in the back. You're lucky I got a soft spot for teenagers. I usually take three fingers off for stealing." Batista never mentioned that he intended to have Mario's pinkie delivered to the rest of his gang from Bolivar Street.

Mario never returned to his Aunt Alberta's house. No longer a brother to his twin sister, he stayed in that same cabin for a year after that painful day when he lost his finger. His body went numb for weeks following the trauma, with only the brunette to nurse him back to sanity. Batista was against her involvement, but Marisol felt guilty, almost adopting Mario as her own. She even began to like him.

During the first year, Batista had his men teach young Mario to break down cocaine into kilo bricks. He'd man a plastic wrap machine, and he'd keep the bricks tight and neatly stacked for pick up. This was a job Mario did daily in two five-hour shifts, morning and afternoon. In between, there were meals that Marisol fixed, popular magazines she brought, and a small black-and-white TV to watch. Of course, Mario slept like a baby, not affected by the horrors of his past like his sister Roberta, who often woke up screaming in the middle of the night.

From preparing cocaine kilos and cleaning up the cabin, Mario progressed to playing outdoors. There was little to do alone as a teenager, but Mario found his own joy in catching fish and swimming. Marisol was told to watch Mario when Batista and his men were away. Many more years of servitude were expected out of the teen, and although he seemed to settle for what was his consequence, nobody wanted him to leave.

For Mario's fourteenth birthday, Marisol convinced Batista to buy a gift. He was almost like family now, and very little concern was given to him possibly wanting to flee Batista's stash house. Batista bought the boy a video camera and a few cases of blank videotapes. By now, there was also a color television and a cassette player in the cabin for Mario to view his camera work. He found new energy with this hobby, capturing footage of various birds, wild animals, and scenes of the riverbank. When Marisol took her daily swim, Mario recorded her, too, an objective that made him even more creative with his angles and the steady use of the camera.

Nobody else had this revelation, but Mario—in his puberty stages—was becoming attracted to Marisol. Those scenes of her swimming became his sole subject matter. The recordings he made were his latest pleasure, something to look forward to, and he kept them hidden under his bed, under a floorboard where only he'd know about them. The only times he could watch the tapes alone, when he could masturbate, were when Marisol was swimming and the others were away. Otherwise, his days of observance stimulated many nights of untold fantasies. On occasion, he'd toss and turn in bed, only to leave his ejaculate in the sheets. There were also occasions when Batista stayed the night to have relations with Marisol. Mario could hear their passionate sounds in the solitude of his own room and it kept him awake with discomfort. Always, Batista would be up and out again in the early morning hours when it was dark. It painted a mysterious image of the man, and he became more and more of an idea than a presence; more like a ghost.

"Come with me, Mario," Batista ordered one late night, leaving Marisol alone with one of his men to package kilos. This was becoming less of a rare occasion for Mario to go out with Batista on one of his—as Batista called them—adventures. "And bring your camera with you."

Mario loaded up into one of three pickup trucks that were at one time white and clean. Each of the pickups had five or six men packed in, and they formed a motorcade, sandwiching the Land Cruiser that transported Batista in typical drug lord fashion.

"He wants you to record everything. Make sure you get all the blood, too," one of the men said.

"Blood?"

"You'll see. A fiesta of blood!!!"

The death squad lumbered along paths and dirt roads until they were deep into the forest where another cabin was located. Other pickups were parked outside of the cabin, and a light was on inside. The men disembarked from the vehicles, Mario and his camera with them, and they all spilled into the entrance of the cabin. There was already laughter filling the common area where four men stood around two captives. The captives were seated with their ankles tied back to the rear legs of the chairs. Their wrists were tied back as well, and their bodies were propped up so that they were arched.

Mario began to record the activities, the men drinking and laughing, as well as those bound and helpless. A closer view showed that the men had chunks of logs on the seats behind the smalls of their backs, making it so their asses were close to the edge of the seats. Mario understood why they were arched now. They had no choice. Mario got close-up shots of the prisoners, right down to the beads of blood and sweat that drenched their bruised faces and chests.

One of Batista's men urinated on the prisoners and another joined in. Another wielded a dagger, holding it a hair or two away from their eyeballs.

This was a party unlike Mario had ever witnessed. He zoomed in on the dagger. The blade was pressed into the space between an ear and the man's head. The man cried out loud.

"Dare me!" the man said in Spanish. And just as soon, a chorus of voices dared him.

In the eyepiece of the camera, Mario was dumbfounded by the image of a hand stretching the ear out and the dagger slicing it off. The butcher waved the bloodied dismembered ear in front of the yelling victim, who was heaving around, tormented within the restraints. Mario captured the victim's uncontrollable jerking . . . the shock his body was experiencing. Meanwhile, he was also experiencing the thrill; that strange contradiction of excitement and horror combined.

Soon a subordinate cut the clothing away from the genitals of both captives. With gloved hands, he tied a noose around where the penis and scrotum meet the groin. He then tied the free end of the twine around the handle of an empty metal bucket, suspending it so that it was hanging between the legs. He repeated the same for the second torture victim while the guerilla holding the ear tossed the severed flesh into the bucket of its owner. The camera also captured a man with cable cutters as he clipped off the toes of the other victim.

Eventually, the deafening cries died down to mere murmurs as there were no more fingers, toes, or ears to slice or snip off. All of the body parts filled the buckets that were hanging and weighing down on the genitals of each victim, who were both reaching unconscious states.

"Salts!" shouted a drunken rebel. And someone waved smelling salts below the noses of the bloody bodies. Salt was thrown on them as well, soaking into and reviving the pain of their wounds, causing them to wake up in even more pain and torment.

One of Batista's goons had gone out amidst all of the carnage, and he returned to the cabin with a bucket mixed with stones that were as small as golf balls and as large as oranges. A contest began. Each rebel took a handful of stones and tossed them carnival-style into the buckets of flesh, bone, blood, and urine. All the while, the weight of each bucket increased, making it more and more unbearable for the organs of each man. Mario captured every moment, every tear, and every scream on videotape, including how the testicles eventually ripped from the battered bodies.

The party came to an end once the floor below the victims was doused with kerosene and a line of the flammable fuel was streamed across the floor to the outside of the cabin, where the gang all convened. A match was lit and the flame raced along the trail of fuel until the cabin grew into an uncontrollable forest fire.

This was Mario's first "adventure," but not his last, as snitches, detractors, and others who violated cartel rules were maimed regularly. Tortures took place as frequently as Batista and his men wished to scratch their itch for a thrill . . . the thrill of watching another human being endure pain. There were those that were stuck with needles, disfigured with acid, or other such tortures that made hedge cutters to the genitals seem boring.

There was the time that a man's stomach was gutted, enough so that he was still alive, even with his intestines hanging outside of him, bloody and exposed. The man's cavity was then filled with worms and dirt, and he was left to the crocodiles. Mario taped it all.

There was the time a man's wife and teenage daughter were gang-raped by a dozen of Batista's guerillas and then butchered with chain saws. The videotape was then prepared so that the husband and father of the victims had to sit and watch his family violated and shredded to pieces.

The recording continued as the snitch was then tortured himself, his penis severed from his body and stuck in his mouth until he bled to death.

All of these images of torture and pain were not only recorded for Batista's video library, they were also permanent scars on Mario's memory . . . images that he'd forever have to live with.

Mario was a backseat driver and a second eye for Batista and his death squad for the rest of his teen years. He grew up as the "baby," a loyal follower of Miguel Batista, as Batista himself evolved into a powerful, feared leader of his own vigilant empire. They called his empire a "cartelito," one of hundreds of copycat cartels that grew like weeds following the downfalls of both the Medellin and the Cali cartels.

Some cartelitos took the left-wing point of view—the Communists who sought to take over the government by force. These groups were operated by the most lawless groups; some of which acted like Batista's, with death squads, torture sessions, and home invasions.

Other cartelitos adopted the right-wing (anticommunist) perspective, with armies of revolutionary guerillas that fought to protest the business. Still, other groups benefited from both the right and left wings, or just their purpose of maintaining their profits by any means.

All of these activities had once been the deeds and decisions of Pablo Escobar. But now that Escobar had met his brutal demise, and since his competitors were subsequently jailed for life, ethics, honor, and other such scruples were history. The game as it was known could be played by anyone, and it was. Twists of fate in the dangerous, evil, multitrillion-dollar illegal drug trade (which included crack cocaine, marijuana, methamphetamine, heroin, and ecstasy pills) and the production, transport, or distribution of these substances, created new constitutions in what was already considered the drug war.

CHAPTER TWENTY-FIVE

Roberta

Abigail and Brendan Novick had been happily married for nineteen years and lived in a six-bedroom colonial in Manhasset, Long Island. Abigail had graduated college with a master's degree in art conservation and acted as the preservation manager and conservator at the Museum of Natural History's Rose Center in New York City. Brendan was the vice president of mergers and acquisitions at Solomon Smith Barney on Wall Street, and had received his MBA from Stamford University in Connecticut. The two had met at an art gallery in lower Manhattan where Abigail was an intern and where Brendan's college class visited during a bus trip to see a half dozen such galleries.

Abigail had given birth to one child nineteen years earlier, a baby girl named Marcella. As an only child, Marcella grew up in her mother's footsteps. There were the local and regional beauty pageants that she won and lost during her preteen years. There were the slumber parties, a sweet sixteen party, and a high school graduation party, all of them hosted at the Novick home. Marcella made a splash at Long Island's most notable debutante ball. And eventually, she was accepted into Stamford, where both parents agreed she might be expected to learn her father's trade.

Brendan bought Marcella a brand new Toyota 4-Runner as a send-off gift, and it served the purpose for her return home for holidays and college recesses. For the Novicks,

Marcella was a storybook fantasy child: extremely attractive, a 3.8-grade-point-average student her first year in college, and once she finished school (or indeed before), Brendan would make certain that Marcella was positioned into a promising position on Wall Street. Maybe she could even intern with her mom at the museum, just to round her out and get her in-the-know with all the board of directors who made things happen. It could come in handy once she began managing big accounts. Brendan understood that it was college and hands-on experience that would take care of the "what you knew" part of the equation, but he lived by the theory that it was who you knew that ultimately made the difference.

I t was just two years earlier that Marcella was travelling home for the holidays, braving both the snow and the reckless driving that was normal for Interstate 95. The Novicks received a cell-phone call from their daughter during which she anticipated arriving in Long Island within two hours' time. That was the last they heard from Marcella. The next word they'd hear regarding their daughter would be from state troopers.

Brendan had already realized that Marcella was more than four hours late, and he took the family's Range Rover down the Long Island Expressway, over the Throgs Neck Bridge, and up I-95 until he reached Stamford. In Connecticut, Brendan stopped at police headquarters and learned the worst. Marcella was involved in a pile-up that caused her 4-Runner to do a rollover right off the thruway and down an embankment until it slammed into the wall of an underpass.

The Novick balloon (that perfect storybook lifestyle) busted that day. Their only child, Marcella, died before emergency response teams reached her.

Abigail was hit the hardest by her daughter's death. No psychiatrists, no trauma victim support groups, and no heavy doses of sleeping pills could erase her pain. Marcella was more than her mom's mirror image, more even than the best friend who joined her for all the society events. Marcella was a big chunk of Abigail's living and breathing. She was her lifeline, an investment into her own immortality.

Although Brendan was as devastated as any parent would be about their daughter's passing, he was also the realist in the family. Marcella had lived a prized life while she was here. She touched a lot of people with her existence. You eat, you shit, and then you die. There was little else except memories left. Brendan hated to think so bluntly about the situation, but life had to go on. It's what Marcella would've wanted.

Plus, these monthly visits to her gravesite were getting a bit out of hand. Sometimes it was good to go there . . . to cry and release. But most other times, Brendan realized this was for his wife. The visits to the graveyard; to places they would often visit when Marcella was alive; and, of course, the way Abigail kept Marcella's old bedroom just as she left it—except for the candles, photos, and a piece of the wall that chipped away where the 4-Runner had hit—were all that was keeping their daughter alive.

Brendan wanted so much to pull the plug on all of this "keeping Marcella alive" business. He wanted to smack some sense into Abigail . . . to have his wife back, even if it was as childless parents. But he couldn't bring himself to pop her balloon. It was already painful enough. Their lives were already taxed enough, and the family was all but lost. He just didn't want to be the one to tip it over all the way.

Today, the Novicks were headed for JFK Airport, with Brendan driving too cautiously for the Belt Parkway, keeping to the right lane so that most other drivers could pass them. This was just another Marcella-thing, where Abigail made him take extra precautions in memory of "her." Any more than 45 mph made the wife a nervous wreck. "She's watching us, Brendan," was what Abigail would say if he dared inch up to the speed of 50 mph. Just to keep her from that god-awful and eerie statement, Brendan complied. He didn't mind it now anyway, because he had a resolution in mind. If this didn't work . . . this bit with the foreign exchange student . . . if this didn't help ease the pain and misery Abigail was experiencing, Brendan figured he would have to do at age forty-nine what he didn't want to do, even what others were suggesting. He'd have to cut his losses and move on. Divorce.

"I know this will work out, darling. You'll see." Abigail was touching up her makeup in the mirror behind the passenger's sun visor.

"Oh, happy day!" Brendan told himself in order to keep a good attitude about this whole deal. Aloud he said, "I think it will too, darling. A little company never hurt anyone. Just let nature take its course." But to himself he was thinking, Just let the girl live her own life, and don't try to make her into another Marcella. There's only one Marcella . . . or, there was.

"Do you think we have everything she needs?" Abigail asked with concern.

"More than enough, darling. I mean, what more can we do? We got her into the country club, the intern program at the museum, and a half dozen other activities that you've set up for her. We've even opened a bank account for her, and she hasn't even landed yet."

"I guess you're right. Maybe I'm overdoing it . . . ya think?"

Brendan wanted to say, "Glory be to God! She's waking up!" But his heart was controlling his mind again. Instead, he said, "It'll be all right, darling."

"This is our exit," Abigail nearly sang as she flipped the visor up and put on her sunglasses.

It was now July, and there was a month before the Novicks' new guest would be registered into classes at St. John's University, giving them plenty of time to get to know her better than mere letters and phone calls.

"And remind me that I have to call the agency to let them know she arrived safely." Abigail was jittery, with her twitching foot.

"How can I forget that," Brendan said shortly, but finished to himself, "You've only said that five times in the last hour."

At Kennedy Airport, they parked in a no loading zone. When an attendant came over to chase him from the space, Brendan slipped the worker a hundred-dollar bill under the guise of a handshake. The attendant quickly made a U-turn and walked away.

Once inside, Abigail asked a skycap which gate Air Colombia arrived at, and the skycap made a face, pointing the Novicks to a television monitor that listed arrivals and departures.

"Air Colombia . . . Gate thirty-two . . . Flight four-o-four . . . arriving on time . . . ten fifteen A.M. We've got about five minutes, hon. Let's hurry."

Abigail held Brendan's hand as they stood near the arrival gate under a closed-circuit color television that was fed by CNN, programming catered especially to travelers. Brendan noticed that Disney, Coke, and Viacom stocks were up. It made his smile much more genuine than it might have been otherwise. Just in time, too, since the travelers on Flight 404 were now disembarking in orderly fashion, streaming out through a doorway where a stewardess thanked everyone "for flying Air Colombia."

Abigail spoke out of closed lips now, as though she didn't want anyone to hear her. Abigail, the ventriloquist. "There she is! She's so bea-u-tiful!" She said this to Brendan as she squeezed his hand to smithereens.

"Relax, darling . . . just relax."

"Hi! You must be Roberta. I'm Abigail Novick, and this is Brendan."

"Yes. It's good to meet you."

"Oh, darling! And she speaks such good English!"

Brendan ignored Abigail's comment because they had already been hearing the young lady's voice at least once a month up until days ago. Their long-distance bill was through the roof.

"It's getting there," Roberta said. "I've been in a lot of language classes for this exchange program. It's the slang I can't seem to get yet."

"Oh, don't you worry about that, darling." Abigail was closer to their new friend now. "You'll be just fine with proper English."

Brendan was fixed on Roberta's eyes, her perfect cheeks and lips, the shoulder-length hair—such a silky texture it seemed. The girl was stunning, and Brendan was suddenly inspired by the whole idea. Sure, the Novicks had the photos to go by, and her paperwork was impressive as well. But not in a million years did Brendan think he'd come face-to-face with such unblemished beauty. Again, Roberta smiled as Brendan took her shoulder bag. Abigail, in the meantime, took Roberta's arm, pushing buttons of intimacy, of friendship, and of parentage.

"Obviously, the flight had absolutely no burden on your radiance, darling," Abigail continued with the compliments.

"Oh . . . thank you, ma'am, I—"

"Please, please, please . . . call me Abby. It's what all of my friends call me."

"Okay, sure. The flight wasn't too bad. It was my first, you know. Well, my first in a long time. There was the time when I was real young . . . like almost fifteen years ago. But it wasn't so bad. I could use some sleep, though."

Beauty sleep, I bet, Brendan thought, but aloud he said, "We're not too far from home. Maybe forty-five minutes with good traffic."

It was either homesickness or jet lag that kept Roberta numb and light-headed during the first twenty-four hours at the Novick home. And the living! This was the best she'd ever known. Her very own bedroom with two pillow-ridden window bays, a computer and personal library, a vanity made for a princess, and a closet filled with designer labels.

"If there's something there that doesn't fit, or if you don't like it, let me know. I can always have Anna change it."

"Oh, Abby . . . I couldn't—I mean . . . I can't accept all of this. This is just . . . oh, my . . ."

"I'll hear of no such thing. I want you to be as comfortable as possible here in the United States. I want you to blend right in at school . . . and besides, I have a few other surprises for you. Places we'll be going."

"I just don't know what to say." Roberta lowered her head. A tear raced down her cheek and bounced right off of her oversize hockey jersey. The jersey was a gift from a boyfriend back at Nacional University in Bogotá. He explained that it was representative of a sports team in New York. Roberta figured that to be the significance of the "Rangers" name that adorned the jersey.

"Oh darling! Is everything all right? I haven't overdone it, have I?" Abigail rushed to sit by Roberta on the bed.

"No. I'm just silly, that's all, and very overwhelmed. I never had such luxuries—a housekeeper to answer my needs, a comfortable bed, a pool, and, my God, a computer! I feel like I've been born again, only . . . in another world."

Abigail smoothed her hand against Roberta's hair, petting her. "Well, you just enjoy it all, my dear. Our home is your home. I don't want you to need, or beg, or want for anything ever again. Mr. Novick and I labored all of our years for what we have just so . . . well, it will be nice to share this with our . . . I mean, with someone special like you." Abigail had to stop herself before her big mouth got her in trouble. "Now, I've been dying to ask you: where in heaven's name did you get that Rangers hockey jersey?"

"Oh. This?" Roberta blushed. "From a guy-friend at school back in Bogotà."

"A guy friend? As in . . . love?" Abigail made the quotation marks gesture to emphasize.

"Well . . ." Roberta blushed again. "Not quite. I never really got that far."

"Kisses?"

"Uh-hmm."

Abigail adjusted to a skeptical expression and said, "Sex?"

"Oh no! Why . . . I've never had . . . sex, Mrs. Abby. I'm just nineteen years old." Roberta said that as if the idea were taboo.

Abigail was instantly reminded of Marcella and how she'd be nineteen this year. At the same time, she thought it to be so cute how Roberta had some scruples about her. No sex by age nineteen?! She really isn't of this world, Abigail concluded.

There hadn't been time to show Roberta around the day she arrived. Instead, Roberta had slept like a baby. However, Abigail decided that now was the time to show Roberta the rest of the house.

The Novick home wasn't just any ole house. It was an estate, with its circular driveway that led up to the 10,000-square-foot brick colonial. It sat on three acres. Of the six bedrooms, three of them were full bedroom suites, while the three additional bedrooms still had amenities such as walk-in closets, skylights, and window-bay views of the property's lush landscaping.

There were wraparound terraces, eighteen-foot ceilings, fireplaces in the master suite and the family room. Some of the more extravagant details included gold-leaf wallpaper, sun-motif carvings, and the porte cochere entry right into the large sunken living room with its vaulted ceiling. Surrounding the house itself were patios, a beautifully landscaped garden, a tennis court, a vanishing edge pool, waterfall, and gazebo area.

Abigail walked Roberta through the entire home, and they circled the property in a golf cart so that the two could view its entirety without tiring.

"I thought your family history . . . your background, et cetera, was quite tragic, Roberta. I didn't want to just go on with these living arrangements, being so close and all, without opening up about a few things. I didn't want things to stay so bottled up if it's not necessary. Hope you don't mind me saying something."

"No. It's fine. I've had to learn to live with it, ya know? Sometimes it doesn't hurt when you don't know what you've lost. I was so young, ya know?"

"I guess. You're really taking it well. I just wanted to share that we've also had a bit of tragedy in our family."

"Oh?"

"Our daughter . . . Marcella's her name," Abigail said, as if there was a young woman that was still very much alive, "she was in a terrible car accident. We lost her a couple of years ago. She was about your age, as a matter of fact."

Roberta said nothing as Abigail pulled a locket out from under her top. It was attached to the end of a long chain that Roberta quickly realized was made of gold and which fell gracefully between the forty-something's cleavage.

"She's beautiful," Roberta said, looking closer at the photo that was set within the shell-like opening.

"Thank you. She was such a sweet girl . . . so smart and excited about life. A lot . . . a lot like you."

Roberta was unsure of a response. She simply wandered with her eyes, as if she were daydreaming.

"Oh, well . . . I'm glad we got that out in the open. I can breathe a lot better now that I understand your pain, and now that you understand mine."

Roberta nodded, thinking she understood as well.

"I'm sure you'll have a busy curriculum once the school year starts, Ro—you don't mind if I call you that, do you?"

Roberta was amused by the idea . . . her with a brand-new nickname. "Of course not. Whatever works for you," she told her, suddenly ready for fun and games to come with her new moniker.

"So . . . Ro, before school starts, I thought we'd do the town. I'll take you by the museum. It's a marvelous spectacle. Really, you'll be floored by the exhibits and how the developers re-created the world as we know it—all contained underneath one massive roof. Then, I was thinking of one of our favorite five-star restaurants, a play on Broadway, and maybe a horse-and-buggy ride through Central Park."

Roberta's eyes lit up at the mention of the horse. "Horses? In New York City?"

"Oh yes, dear. All over the place. And we must, must, must stop by the club and meet the girls."

"The girls?" Roberta asked hesitantly.

"Oh, just women like me who have husbands in high

places, with deep pockets and big homes." Abigail gestured, as if to say look around you . . . this is what I'm talking about. Get used to it. "And we'll get to play a round of golf. Have you ever played?"

"No," replied Roberta, trying not to make a face.

Abigail was thrilled by the way they talked and the rapport they were creating. "Well then, shall we get started?"

Already, the Novicks had a daughter again. Abigail made it as if six months were squeezed into just one. For Roberta, there were too many faces to recall and too many names to keep track of. This is Mr. and Mrs. So-and-so, he's the vice president of this, her father is the sheriff over in whatever township, and . . . on and on it would go. All of the status, names, and titles danced around in Roberta's head like a soupy mess. It was as if status and titles were purchased with college degrees, a person's descent, or else some other lottery-like luck. Here and there, Roberta could sense that people she met had earned their positions from the ground up.

These realities were all a bit above her head. They were there, but then they weren't. For her, all of it was an illusion. Not because it was indeed an illusion, but because none of it mattered to her. None of it meant to Roberta what it meant to others. And being so grounded helped her to look at whomever she met from the standpoints of character, posture, expression, and attitude. She could keep things in proper perspective. Otherwise, she just wasn't impressed. Was the man or woman insecure? Did the person seem uncomfortable in what they wore? Was their smile painted on or genuine? Again, these ideas, while part of Roberta's psyche, were not to be spoken of, even though she was not conscious of how she came to such conclusions. This was simply an inherent ability. A sixth sense or foresight that came built-in with the package she came into existence with.

Unfortunately, Roberta had all that going for her and still suffered in her sleep. Sometimes, she woke up screaming. Other times, she cried to herself in long, uncontrollable bouts that left her damp in her expensive gowns and sheets. There was tossing and turning, and there were nights she just lay there with her eyes open and glassy, recalling images that she couldn't leave behind in Colombia. It followed her wherever she went, year after year . . . from Rio Blanco to Bogotá, from Bogotá to Manhasset, Long Island, in some rich, white family's home. The horrific images Roberta kept with her always involved blood. They always included the severed limbs and those ugly men's faces; the horrified expressions of her mother and father, and the decapitation of her sister Maria.

For a long time, Roberta couldn't understand these images. She was too young to comprehend what it all meant. It just scared her. These dark, gruesome images really scared her. And as she got older, they became a movie that kept rewinding . . . kept replaying . . . in many instances, with slow-motion effects that the big screen could never project, something that she couldn't even explain herself.

There she goes again, Abby . . . Abby?" Brendan nudged his wife into consciousness. "Want me to go this time?"

"No, no, I'll go." Abigail said this with an audible sigh as she rose up from their bed. After months since Roberta's arrival, the misery was beginning to set in. Abigail had to keep telling herself that this would work out. It had to, especially since the Novicks were expecting to adopt Roberta and have her stay with them for good.

CHAPTER TWENTY-SIX

"You're doing good, Coco. Just keep it up and keep it safe. And remember, we're with you all the way. All we need is ten more bodies."

"Ten?"

"Yes, ten. And make sure to keep the buy—"

"I know, I know. Keep it over five grams."

"Right." Carson was with Coco Love in the room adjacent to the MET satellite office. Confidential informants, such as Coco, were always kept separate from the technical side of operations, and were generally exposed to few agents. It made things more relaxed if she happened to run into undercover agents during the operation. This way there'd be no unusual expressions or comments. Coco would continue with her modus operandi as planned.

Carson finished attaching the body mic and was now draping the necklace around Coco's neck. At the end of the chain was a pendant that had a miniature camera within.

It was now 5 P.M., and going on week number three of Operation Snowfall. Coco was setting up the buys with Nightfly's subordinates. She was becoming a regular at all the hot nightspots, wearing all of the clothing that she'd eventually call her fringe benefits. Tonight, she'd be rocking the hip-hugging jeans cut below the waist, dipping far below the belly button. Other nights, there were the flimsy halters and tube tops, the edgy Band-Aid–size shorts and skirts, the lizard pants, leathers and other slacks that left room for navel gazing. Coco was a walking promise of breathless lust. She promoted the magic that erupts when people first meet—before people got to know one another enough to recognize habits and faults. This was Coco's edge when she cozied up to the ballers, players, and dealers.

It was known already that Nightfly had almost two dozen salespeople, and it was Coco's job to tie as many of them in as possible to the overall conspiracy. Many of Nightfly's people were women, which Coco thought was smart because the DEA usually targeted men first. Men were the typical pirates in the drug trade.

But Coco soon saw right through that myth. It was even easier for her to overcome erstwhile barriers because of who she was on the outside. Her skin tone, first and foremost, was the complexion of a suntanned Asian. It wasn't too dark or too light, and so she appealed to a broader audience, overcoming those initial racial stereotypes which people were accustomed to pushing or pulling at. Coco's facial features were, however, ethnic enough that she could be mistaken for Italian, Puerto Rican, Brazilian, or even a very light-toned woman from the Caribbean. You just couldn't peg her from a distance, except to realize (at once) that the woman was gorgeous, with her headlights beaming at you—the first thing that people noticed.

That's what Coco figured to be Candice Gordon's fault. Candice was a twenty-something, creamy-white beauty with Egyptian-cut blonde hair. Candice sold Coco two grams on a Thursday night, then two more grams on the following Saturday night. Coco had only to buy one more gram to complete her quota on Candice. Only thing was, Candice had pushed up on Coco from the start, except Coco wasn't reciprocating, not yet anyway.

On the second buy, Candice said, "I thought I'd never see you again, girl! Can we get together? You know . . . chum around?" Coco was smart enough to feel Candice's intent down in her loins. Especially by the way Candice looked at Coco's cleavage. The intensity caused Coco to bite the lower corner of her lip in consideration.

"Sure!" Coco said as a reflex. It was what she was used to saying. She had become accustomed to lying; anything to make the buy. But neither the wire she wore, the agents who watched her back from afar, nor her own common sense could control what was happening in her heart . . . how she was feeling a certain type of way about Candice. She really *did* want to "chum around" with Candice. She did want to explore some things. If not for the tight schedule she had to keep (to get around to all those South Beach clubs to buy her second and third grams at one hundred dollars a pop from Nightfly's other subordinates), Coco would've taken up the proposition already.

Then there were the other women, all of them in their early or mid-twenties. Farrah . . . Daniela . . . Alcira . . . Cathy . . . Anita . . . Star . . . a transvestite named Legend . . . a snobbish redhead named Melissa . . . and Roxy, a dirty blonde with hair that reached her lower back with obvious implants that appeared to walk in the room a few seconds before she did. All of these women were selling blow for the same prices, in the same one- and two-gram amounts, and all of them were so comfortable in their little worlds of nightlife and two-hour highs; even comfortable enough to use their real first names.

The list of Coco's catches was growing rapidly. She could already count the thousand dollars that she'd make per body. And with two dozen of them to catch, with twenty-four grand to look forward to, Coco had little time for the bullshit and the phone numbers that club goers, both men and women, slipped to her. No time to dance or get her drink on. No hard drinks, only a juice or soda to make it look good. And shit, if one more hand reached out to grope at her, she was gonna slice a mothafucker's face open.

The objective was simple. Get in the club, make herself at home, and get out. Ten clubs in one night meant ten buys. If she was able to do a two-gram buy from any one person, then that was one less time she'd have to see their face. That was the only part she hated: the exposure, showing her face to all of these people.

All of them, she was sure, had lives outside of the night-clubs. All of them had family, friends, and even jobs who counted on their contribution in life. She could see how a lot of these salespeople were violating one of the ten crack-commandments: don't get high on your own supply. She could also see how others were straight-up business, concerned only about the bucks. Maybe there was a child to take care of at home, same as Coco had. Maybe the sales helped to subsidize some other enterprise. Or maybe they were just so caught up in their own fanciful lifestyle that they were sucked in to the point of no return.

Still, Coco couldn't help wondering what if. What if after the sweep, after their day in court, after a stretch in prison . . . she ran into any of these men or women again? It was enough to keep Coco knee-deep in camouflage of various hairstyles, clothing, makeup, and accessories, anything to hide who she really was. Besides, this was Florida. Coco was from Philly, halfway across the world as far as she was concerned.

"Okay, Coco, tonight we hit The Left Bank, Mango's, Shooters, and Velvet Lounge. They're all in Fort Lauderdale. Then we head back down to Miami. There are at least a dozen spots we could get to. What do you feel like tonight? Two?"

"I'm okay with two. It just depends, Carson. If my energy is up, I'll even go till three."

"That's my girl. Now here's the list to glance over. There are a lot of guys on this go-round. Trinton . . . Carlos . . . Alan . . . Renee . . . Slick. Also Rex—remember him? That was the one—"

"Don't remind me. I can't believe he smacked my ass like that. I swear, if I didn't have to go back to see him to get him to the five-gram mark, I'd have cut his fuckin' ass!"

"Easy, easy, Coco. We'll be sure to give him his. Trust me. Remember, you have the power, babe. It's all on you. Sign these people up for a nice jail term. That's where your head should be. I don't want you to catch an assault charge."

"How the fuck am I gonna catch a charge if you are sending me in and setting me up with these punks? I'm working with you all, remember? A team?"

"Right, right. Just don't get crazy on me, Coco. Stay in charge. No kidding."

Coco took in a deep breath. She reviewed the rest of the list. Shareef . . . August . . . a club promoter named Tommy . . . a hunk she recalled by the name of Jive . . . a cowboy named Noah. The list was enough to make Coco say "Wow" to herself. All these people were about to fall into the black hole, and all within thirty days' time. She had to admit that it was a trip to see how a person's life could change so quickly, from marvelous to mud. And "Yes," she considered, "I do have the power."

From one South Beach hot spot to the next, Coco's mission was going smoothly. The Mobile Enforcement Team figured they'd have her working another week and a half before they pulled her out and sent her home. She had already bought up to 75 percent of her goal, the product that was now sealed, tested, and shipped to Washington to be held as evidence. There were thirty-something more buys to do, and one which was larger than all the others . . . a buy which Coco wasn't even aware of yet.

"Has she done a ten-gram deal yet?"

"Nothing more than five . . . the operation before Seattle. You don't remember that, Steve?"

"Carson, if I could remember every takedown we've done . . . every arrest and the amount of junk we stopped, I'd be better than a thousand-gig Pentium. I can't remember all that stuff."

"Well, for the record, I know Coco can handle this. Piece of cake."

"All right. It's your call. But we've got an unsolved homicide down here, with people and suspects we hardly know. Skeletons we haven't even been introduced to yet."

"So we put extra agents on her. A cinch."

"Again, it's your call, Carson."

Both agents were in the hallway at the World Class Motel, speaking in confidence outside of Room 216, where the dozen other agents prepared for the day's events. Agent Stevens stuck his head out.

"It's Van Dyke on the hotline."

"Be right in."

"Actually, he wants Agent Brown, but . . ."

Masters knew that his supervisor was across the street having that full body stuff done, with the nails, the facial, and all the womanly stuff.

"Okay, I'll take it." And Steve Masters followed Stevens into the room.

"Agent Masters here, sir. Is there something that I can help you with? Agent Brown isn't available just yet." Masters was quiet, listening to Van Dyke. His expression was one that made even Carson curious.

"You don't say. You don't say. Hmmm . . . interesting. This morning, huh? Sounds like a situation. Thanks, I'll tell her you called." Masters hung and said nothing. He just held his chin and stared at the wall where a map of the South Beach region was posted, with pushpins indicating the buys already done and those to be done.

"You're joking, right? What the hell, Masters? Spill it."

"It's our man—Nightfly. I don't think he'll be selling those ten grams. Well, at least not in this lifetime."

There go the stakes, shooting right through the roof," said Agent Brown. She had Agents Joel Green and Steve Masters with her. The three stood off to the side as the various authorities performed their duties along the Julia Tuttle Causeway. Miami Beach police officers had the bridge closed off at both ends, while both the Emergency Response and Miami Homicide units worked out the procedures of retrieving Nightfly's body. It was suspended, hanging down at least fifty feet from the centermost area of the bridge. The rope was as thick as a half-dollar's circumference, with six officers in all tugging and pulling in the body as if it were some spectacular catch.

"No matter who does this investigation, I'll never believe that this doesn't have anything to do with Charlucci," Agent Brown added.

"Oh, I'm sure of that. I'm just wondering with the Coast Guard and the cruise lines on one side of the bridge and with the series of islands on the other, how many people could've been exposed to this? Who saw what?" Agent Green queried.

"I'm with you one hundred percent, but they tell me this took place at maybe three or four o'clock this morning. It's dark as a black hole around that time," Agent Masters said.

"And the toll is paid by incoming traffic—one way. So, it's anybody's guess which way the culprits might have come or gone," Green added.

"Well, boys, you know what this means. We've got to find a link between the sales and Charlucci, otherwise Operation Snowfall is gonna become Operation Slushpile."

"I say we complete whatever buys we can today before the targets run out of product . . ."

"Before they get with a new source."

"I doubt it. Charlucci's not gonna want to lose the business he's been doing in the clubs. He'll maybe send in a secondary front man," Agent Brown calculated.

"There's Mr. Big," Masters said.

The state troopers were moving a barricade, allowing the Chief U.S. Attorney of Miami to drive through.

"Business as usual, boys. Don't let on that this is detrimental to our operation. We can't afford digression at this juncture." And as if in the same breath, Agent Brown greeted Peter Van Dyke. The two went private and discussed the latest accounts.

In the meantime, the other two agents had a second thought: would a new front man mean that the first set of buys, those while Nightfly was alive, would have to be done over? Or could the operation still be waged against Charlucci as is?

. . .

Charlucci was at home now on the cell phone on which he conducted "business." The ISN code and phone number were changed weekly in the event the authorities tried to get heroic. So far, the Kingpin was able to evade conviction, whether it was by bribing individuals within the grand juries or by his connections within the Justice Department. For now, there had been no indictments and no arrests. His record was clean . . . crystal clean.

"Are you sure we'll be okay? Based on what you're tellin' me, there's a lot of heat in Miami now. Don't you think they'd be watching the airports and the harbors?"

Charlucci listened carefully through his earpiece, but kept a steady pace on the Fitness One running machine. At this rate, which was seven miles per hour, he figured on completing four miles by noon.

"Yes, of course, I'm familiar with him. He moves almost fifty keys in a month. That's big business . . . for you and me . . . you're wondering if I ordered the hit. Come on. You think I'd be that stupid? My operation is bigger than a twerp named Nightfly. I'd never risk all of this on scum like him."

A beep sounded amidst the call.

"Hold on. Yo. Yeah, what's up? Well, well . . . my favorite hoodlum. Good job. The calls are already comin' in. No, no—nothin' you did. They're just guessin' out there. The cops watch the TV news and the TV news comes from the newspaper reporters. It's the newspaper guys that are making all these assumptions. Of course my name is gonna pop up. And that same damned high school photo they got . . . remind me to send 'em a new, updated flick."

As Charlucci addressed Ortiz, he suddenly felt a presence behind him. He looked to the window out in front of him, but instead of the Miami cityscape, he looked at the reflection. It made him change modes with his call.

"So, the bottom line is this, Lincoln. By the way, I never asked you why they call you that. Is it because you're a good real estate agent, or a bad one? Yeah? I can tell. Anyhow, I'm not ready to make a bid on the Portofino Tower. To tell you the truth . . . I'm kind of happy with what I've got. But when it comes time for me to buy into a second property, you'll be the second to know. Listen, I have another important call. Can we close this out? Talk another time? Cool . . ."

Charlucci switched over to another call, or so it seemed. "Sorry, Sam. These agents, I'll tell ya. They are just a nuisance." He looked at his watch. Thirty seconds till twelve noon. "Hold on for thirty seconds." He pressed a button on the cell phone lodged in the caddie in the front of him. His call went mute, and he began to sprint at a faster pace . . . faster . . . wildly faster. Then it was over. The conveyor belt under his feet slowed to a stop. His breathing was erratic as he leaned over for the towel.

Bianca eventually made her presence known.

"Oh. Hi. Did I wake you?" Charlucci asked.

"Mmm-mmm. I have a few errands this afternoon. Plus, I have to pick up Jason from preschool."

"Cool. You okay?"

"Ah . . . yeah," Bianca's voice dipped, wondering what Charlucci meant. "Did you expect that I'd wobble out of bed?"

"No, but I thought that maybe you might not be able to sit down . . . for a while at least." Charlucci withheld a smile.

"I'd throw something at you right about now, Mr. Funny-man, but instead, I'll just have you know that you're not the first one I let do that to me."

"O-hoooo! Damn! Touché!" Charlucci turned his attention back to the call he had put on hold. "Sorry. You caught me at the end of the run. I'm here for good now. So . . . the bottom line is that we're on for tonight. Good. I'm gonna have my guys down there to handle things." Charlucci's breath was beginning to return to normal . . . a heavy normal. "When they tell me it's clear, I'll drive in. We'll talk then. One A.M., right? Good."

"So you think I'm stupid, huh?" Bianca had been eavesdropping, only Charlucci couldn't be sure for how long.

"Shit! Goddamn you, Bianca. Why can't we just be lovers without you worrying about my business?"

"Your business? Jason thinks he's your business. You had me thinking that I was your business. But really? All I see is you thinking about you. This is Charlucci's world, and everybody else comes second."

"Bianca, sit down. You're uptight."

"Don't tell me—"

"*Sit!*"

Bianca was startled by Charlucci's tone. He shouted at the top of his lungs, and he pointed, too. This was a first. She eased her behind to the couch, suddenly wishing that it was softer. It reminded her of the last time she participated in anal sex. It wasn't so much the penetration and the pain that accompanied it—that was a pain easily overlooked, a good pain. But it was the aftermath that killed her. It made her vow that she'd never indulge again, just like she had said the last time.

The Spider was the latest technology when it came to listening devices. The microphone was the shape and size of an actual spider and was generally placed on walls, under furnishings, and even outside of windows. It was powerful enough to pick up audio through glass up to a quarter-inch thick, as long as the conversation was no farther than twenty-five feet away. The device sent digital signals to a receiver, generally placed somewhere within a hundred feet. The receiver sent its signal either to a stake-out team or to a satellite, which would in turn send audio anywhere it was required. Charlucci hadn't noticed, but a Spider was affixed to the outside of his penthouse window. And Agents Simpson and Evers were on the morning shift, not far from the gated Utopia, taking notes as they saw necessary.

"The hell with the operation," Evers joked. "This here's the real juice to record on tape."

"Gotta take the good with the bad," said Evers.

Then Simpson jotted down, "Heat in Miami. Don't you think they'll be watching the airports? Harbors? Fifty keys a month! Hoodlum. Good job? TV news, reporters, real estate? Portofino Tower? Bluff? Sam."

Simpson and Evers were scribbling fast and furious. Their minds were spinning like turbine engines . . . revelation upon revelation. "Tell you what, Evers. You listen in on the juice, and I'll call downtown. I think we're finally about to secure an indictment here."

CHAPTER TWENTY-SEVEN

The wheels of the judicial machine cranked on as agents worked to answer Van Dyke's questions regarding their investigation. It seemed like he was working for the other side as hard as he was making it to move along from the complaint to the impaneling of a grand jury. But Mobile Enforcement understood him taking an objective position. It's what the defense attorney would do—attack the investigation. So, instead of being embarrassed in the courtroom, better to get it all concrete upfront. This is how MET saw it. Nonetheless, the investigation rolled forward.

It was clear by the recorded notes gathered from the Spider tap that a deal of some sort was going down at one in the morning. However, it wasn't clear where the rendezvous would take place, or with whom. The best Pam could do was to have her team focus on this sole issue of the 1 A.M. meet. One agent was enough to assign to Coco and her nightclub tour.

Agent Green was low in the driver's seat of a pickup down in the Utopia's underground garage. Charlucci's muscle car was already fixed with a tracking device, and Green confirmed by two-way that the device was showing up on the radar only two blocks away. It was midnight now and the level of anticipation was as thick as oatmeal, as if it could be seen in the air.

"He's in the garage now," Green mentioned into his body mic. "Get ready."

And everyone was ready. This was the first stakeout since the Bronx Terminal Market about a month ago. The funerals were still very fresh on the agents' consciences. They'd be extra careful tonight.

P am was having her own problems. She was in a backup unit with Simpson and Carson. Simpson was confirming what he'd heard at the Utopia.

"Charlucci must know about us. What else would he mean by 'heat in Miami'? And who in God's name was he talking to? Who is all this good information coming from?"

"It has to be from our side."

Pam shook her head, not wanting to believe it. Her people? Miami DEA? It was a puzzle for now. But she figured if Charlucci was gonna meet this caller tonight, it would help to clear things up.

"Hey! He's not taking the—everybody listen up. We're not tailing the Oldsmobile. I repeat, no Oldsmobile. The Snowman is in a black, four-door Nissan Maxima. I repeat, a black, four-door Nissan Maxima . . . and he's moving now. Over."

"Gotcha, Green."

"License number four, six, seven, two, one, niner."

"We're on him at the gate."

Harbors and airports . . . that was what MET expected. However, they hadn't the least bit of detail of where or which ones. They had to tail the Snowman. And now, since he'd chosen an alternative vehicle to remain inconspicuous, agents would have to tail the Snowman without the tracking device. Bigger than that, Charlucci was already aware of an ongoing investigation. He would most likely be looking hard for tails, surveillance, and the like.

"All units . . . drop the pursuit. I repeat, all units . . . drop the pursuit." All at once, everyone with a radio knew that was the supervisor speaking. "Remain in your current positions until you're clear. Then, meet me at the Miami Arena parking lot. Over."

"What's up, Boss?" Carson questioned.

"I have an idea." Pam pulled out her palmtop, and after powering it up, punched in an unlock code. Then, she scrolled through phone numbers. She pressed another button and the palmtop proceeded to dial. In the meantime, Pam connected her cell phone to the palm device.

"Communications, this is Agent Pam Brown, number zero, four, two, six, one—Mobile Enforcement Team. Yes, thank you." Pam waited to be connected to a representative that would serve her immediately. "Hi . . . I have a plate number. I need dedicated satellite tracking on license plate four, six, seven, two, one, nine, black Nissan Maxima. Yes . . . last known location is Ocean Drive, Miami. Thank you."

Carson immediately put two and two together. Pam was arranging for a global satellite trace on the vehicle's plates. It was the same technology that some cities instituted, taking instant digital photos of traffic light violators. If you ran a red light—and it could be at four in the morning in the middle of nowhere—you'd receive a moving violation in the mail, complete with a photo of your vehicle and a close-up on your plate.

Federal law enforcement agencies had another version of the same technology available 24/7. Only difference was, instead of a camera up on a street pole, satellites high above the earth's surface had long-distance cameras pointed at the earth. With the plate and location, the dedicated satellite could scan the part of the earth where the vehicle was last seen. That was enough of a lead to zero in and pinpoint the whereabouts of the plate down to the sector, region, state, and street. All Pam had to do was have her agents lie back; once the Snowman stopped moving, the agency's communications devices would display the vehicle's whereabouts on their monitors.

"Yes, thank you. Can you transfer the video to us? Or am I asking too much at midnight?" Pam crossed her fingers. "Oh, I sure can. Just a moment." Pam pulled the cell phone from her face. "Carson, I need a dedicated line for the video upload. Sounds like we'll be able to keep an eye on Snow-man with a laptop."

Carson had a handbag with all kinds of equipment, but it was in the back of the vehicle. "We've gotta stop the truck. The stuff's in the back."

"There's time for that. Just give me the number so they can set it up."

Carson flipped a few pages on his notepad. When he found the number, he jotted it down and passed it to Pam.

"Okay, ready?" Pam gave the number to the agent on the line and waited. "Thank you." She jotted down an authoriza-tion code and the phone call was over.

When they arrived at the Miami Arena parking lot, there were a few cars still there, straggling out after the big Sade concert.

"Look at these guys . . . smoking junk right out in the open." Agent Evers was speaking of the two men and two women standing outside of their car, passing a stick of weed around.

"Pull up, Evers. Nothing aggressive." Evers wheeled the Tahoe till it stood a few yards away from the foursome. "En-joy the show?" asked Pam.

"Awesome, babe. Real awesome. How 'bout you?"

"Oh . . . we were a little busy tonight. Big investigation, ya know. We're looking for—I'm sorry, I'm being paged. Go." Pam suddenly had her two-way radio in hand, visible for the stragglers to see.

"We're almost there, Boss. Which side of the arena are you on?" The radio chirped and hissed with its authoritative sounds, but the voice came over crystal clear.

"The east side, Agent," Pam said with emphasis.

"Two minutes," the agent said. "Over."

Pam nodded, not overlooking the stick of weed that one of the four had smothered in his palm. She had seen him wince in the process.

"Sorry, busy night for us DEA agents, ya know. So, as I was saying, we're looking for a group of thirty-somethings. We got an anonymous call that some drug use was taking place out here at the arena. You wouldn't know about anything like that, would you?"

Both agents in the Tahoe held stone expressions, there to back up their supervisor no matter where she was going with this.

One of the concert-goers coughed the smoke out of her lungs. She'd been holding it in for as long as she could.

"Say . . . is she all right?"

"Oh, Joanne? She's fine. Just a little sick, that's all. But . . . I'm sorry, officer, I—" Just then, two vehicles, a sedan and another Tahoe, were approaching with their headlights on blast. "I—uh—listen, we were about to leave. I hope you find who you're looking for." The bespectacled man was speaking to Pam, but he was also pushing his three friends, encouraging them to get the hell in the car. "Gotta go." And just like that, the weeded quartet disappeared.

"What was that about?" asked Agent Simpson, who pulled up beside the Tahoe, driver's side to driver's side, with the window down. A few chuckles escaped the Tahoe's cabin.

"Oh nothing. Just a few Sade fans blowing hot air."

Now, four other vehicles pulled into the eastern end of the parking lot and all of the agents congregated. Carson was still in the back of the Tahoe, fixing up the laptop and cell phone link in order to see the video feed.

"I'm glad we could all get together out here in the open—no phones, no closed rooms. I have a little bit of a problem that I want to share with all of you."

Other than an airplane flying in the distance and the passing traffic on nearby Dolphin Expressway, there was silence in the late-night air.

"The Snowman knows we're on to him." The agents' faces turned concerned and confused, looking for answers. "Don't take this personal. I'm not indicating any of you blowing cover . . . I'm just telling it how it is. He knows. So, instead of doing crisscrosses all over Miami—instead of the whole peel off–peel on deal—I figured we'd get some help. I should be getting a call in a few minutes that will give us

Snowman's exact location. What's more is that we'll have live video fed to us.

"In the meantime, I want you boys to help me out by thinking hard about how we've been made. Think also about the fallout that could take place . . . our informants endangered, our salespeople suddenly disappearing, evading our traps . . . This investigation is dependent on what we do or find out in the next six hours. And that's no shit.

"Now, I've been in situations before where I've had mud on my face, so of course I'm wholly willing to take the heat if this operation fails. I do too much good for the agency to go sour with Washington. But I know we've got something incredibly large down here. It's right in our reach. And I want it." Pam had her arms folded and her eyes were cold steel, with determination streaming from their depths.

"Boss, we have the upload!"

"Gather 'round, fellas. Let's check out the marvels of technology." The dozen agents joined Pam, circling around the laptop that sat in the back of the Tahoe, with its hatch door opened to the sky. "These are the coordinates down at the bottom of the screen, changing with every foot the vehicle travels. Somebody pass me a map," Pam directed. But Carson was prepared.

"Already gotcha on that, Boss." He flipped open a second laptop. A map of Southern Florida lit up the color monitor. "The Snowman is headed up Route 953, crossing Miami Springs Golf Course . . . here's City Hall . . . Ninth Street, and so on. He's doing the city speed limit, and my guess is he's not going far because he'd maybe take the expressway."

"Any airports or docking up that way?" Pam inquired.

"Well, here's Opa-Locka Canal, here. There are a few lakes, but nothing for a ship. I reviewed this possibility earlier. Opa-Locka Airport. It's a small area with just one runway, but it closes after ten P.M."

Pam turned her head up toward the moon and, without a sound, mouthed the words, "Oh my God." A moment later, she was on her cell phone, and (as he'd done to her on too many occasions) Sol Goldridge was now the one wiping sleep from the corners of his eyes.

"Sorry, Chief. It's me, Agent Brown. You know . . . your golden girl?" Pam said it as though her voice was wincing. "Yes, it is big, sir. Okay. I'm down here on the Snowfall operation and we got a good lead on our man . . . some rendezvous he's supposed to have at one in the morning. Yes, I know it's twelve-thirty. I only just figured out that this might be a large shipment coming in. I figured that with Snowfall being so big, and add the airport being closed at ten in the evening, there's no better way to bring the coke in. I was just thinking . . . exactly, sir. Air support." Pam meandered along the blacktop, not far from where the others stood fixed to the laptop monitor.

She listened while the DEA chief explained how difficult it was to get air support over there so soon. Yes, she was in need of something within the hour. But, no, he couldn't arrange anything until maybe an hour tops. It would've been easier if this was a DEA operation. In that case, Goldridge explained, air support would be available from right where Pam was situated.

This was one of the difficulties that came up with Mobile Enforcement. These operations were kept separate and apart from the local and regional DEA offices in an effort to avoid exposure. Many an agent now worked for both the agency and the cartelitos. It was a reality that reached back to Escobar and beyond. It was just that the money, the insider's perspective, and the ease by which one could maneuver inside and outside of enemy lines was an intoxicating position to have. It was a position that was considered above the law . . . untouchable.

"No, you're right, sir. We must keep this operation quiet . . . or as quiet as possible, especially now." Pam suddenly realized her boss didn't know about the breach—that Charlucci knew about an ongoing investigation—and she caught herself before she said anything stupid. "But, of course, if we get over there and . . ."

Pam made a gesture to the other agents, swinging her extended forefinger in a circular motion, directing and informing them that it was time to go and bag the Snowman. "If there is an airplane, I'm gonna pull every string. Every available agent and officer will be on it. Thank you for your blessings on this, sir. I'm gonna go get our man."

As soon as Pam flipped her cell phone shut, her foot was in the door of the Tahoe and the Mobile Enforcement was in full motion, racing up Route 953, sirens and all. When they were less than a mile from Charlucci, they shut down the emergency lights and such.

"He is going into Opa-Locka," one agent said. However, that didn't change the adrenaline and heartbeats, all of it still racing frantically, of everyone involved.

Pam was on the cell again. "Yes, this is Agent Pam Brown, DEA. I have an authorization code . . ." She ran off the nine-digit number, reading it directly form the Post-it note on the dashboard. "Thank you. I need a second feed. Yes, I need a visual on Opa-Locka Airport in North Miami. No, I need a video feed. Sure, I can get that for you." Pam was about to ask Carson for a second dedicated line, but he was already on it, having listened to her and reading between the lines. He jotted down a phone number.

"Here we go," Pam said into the cell phone, while her eyes appreciated her agent's sharp foresight. She gave the phone number to a dedicated line and waited patiently for a confirmation. In the meantime, Carson was preparing a third laptop computer, wiring it to a cell phone.

"Holy Moses, Mary, and Microsoft!" Agent Evers reacted to the visual that came in on Opa-Locka. It was just like the picture received on the Snowman feed, a bit grainy with dark, night vision imagery. Clear enough still to recognize the details. "There's a plane there! Looks like it recently landed or it's about to take off—one or the other."

"Look at the manpower in there," Carson said, as if the airplane and the people were inside the laptop itself. "They're armed to the hilt." The laptop showed a bird's-eye view, yet from enough of an angle to see some of the faces, if even from a distance. "There has to be like sixteen men standing on the runway."

Pam was the silent one, her mind confirming what her heart told her. Then, she spoke as if the words were an unconscious utterance, as if she had no control over what she was saying. "Wow. This is big." She shook her head. Then she reached to her side, pulling a 9mm from its neat nylon holster. She wasn't the only to check her firearm, as both Carson and Evers did the same. Evers did so with his knees and forearms controlling the steering wheel, juggling both objectives.

Pam was back on the two-way. "We're going in. Strap up." As the vehicles raced along 8th Avenue, passing City Hall and the Hialeah Race Track, they cut off onto the LeJune Douglass Connector, a stretch of road that was isolated and free of traffic. Out of nowhere, a motorcade approached 135th Street, cutting them off.

"What's this?" Carson asked no one in particular.

"What seems to be the hurry, friends?" A Dade County trooper was standing at the driver's side of the Tahoe, taking it slow, while his partner moseyed along the opposite side, somewhat impressed by the vehicle as he strolled. The police cruiser was one of five that now semi-ambushed the Mobile Enforcement Team's three Tahoe SUVs and four sedans. Each police vehicle had the authentic emblems, colors, and overall presence that was typical of a cruiser, and the emergency lights spun relentlessly, with the halogen lamps almost illuminating the dark road to daylight standards. In other words, these were official police authorities.

"I'm Agent Brown, officer," Pam spoke up, lending her authority over to the team. Her badge and credentials reached out past Evers like a branch and leaf.

"Dee-Eee-Aayee? In livin' color." The trooper took the identification, marveling at Pam's photo and how attractive she appeared in it. "Cut your hair, did ya?"

"We need access here, officer. This is official federal business."

"I'm sorry, ma'am, about your official federal business, but the big man says nobody but nobody enters the airport at this time."

"Oh, really? And who is this big man?" Pam asked matter-of-factly.

"That might be confidential, ma'am. I'll need to speak to the boss about that."

"Oh really? Well, who's the boss?"

"The big man," the trooper said after he looked over at his partner. Then they both broke out in laughter.

"Okay, here's the bottom line, officer. If you don't free our right of way, I'll have you arrested for interfering with a federal investigation."

"Arrest? Me?" Again, he looked at his partner, and now they were laughing hysterically. "Imagine that—her . . . arresting me!" The laughter grew.

Pam realized that the challenge was well supported, with more than ten state troopers now standing about and around her mini-motorcade, guns drawn.

"Ma'am, no disrespect, but did you ever consider auditioning for that there *Def Comedy Jam*? 'Cause you tell some funny jokes." Again, he continued with the laughing, holding his belly.

Carson nudged his supervisor. He had a new revelation that Pam couldn't very well know about, being all involved in the back and forth with the officer. Pam turned to Carson, irritation washing her face in red.

"I'm sorry, officer. We probably have a misunderstanding here. Maybe we should go through proper procedures. Tomorrow's another day," Carson said.

"See? Now that there is one smart nigga-agent." The trooper and Carson shared an instant of deathly silence, their eyes wrestling with ego, malice, and fury. The trooper dared, and Carson surrendered to the man's raw power, ignoring the shame he felt.

"Evers, let's go," Carson said, still in the trooper's eye. Evers made a U-turn and the other six vehicles followed suit. As they rolled away, all kinds of shouting ensued. Pam yelled at Carson. Carson was cursing the trooper, and Evers was swearing to God.

"Look! Look!" Carson was pointing at the laptop screen.

On it, he'd managed to zoom in on one of the men shaking hands with another, the interaction being done in the center of all the gunmen. Pam could've swallowed her tongue when she realized who it was.

DEA Chief Sal Goldridge was nearing his twentieth year with the agency. Within his circle of law enforcement colleagues, he was the most adamant when it came to swearing he'd seen it all. As they always said, though, there's a first time for everything. And this was also a first, for Goldridge to order up three Blackhawk choppers, load them up with eleven of his prized Washington agents—all within an hour and a half—and to be down at Miami International in record time. All of this speedy movement was making him young again, making him feel like he did back in the good ole days when he was a rookie in the agency.

Before Goldridge even arrived in Miami, Pam and all of her agents had packed up all their equipment and all their belongings, and had vacated The World Class Motel with no warning to the management. Even the receptionist at the front desk was unaware of their leaving through the back entrance—the door which led to the pool and beach area.

For now, everything was packed into the vehicles which were now parked in the fire lane outside of the passenger's terminal. Pam took Agent Carson with her. Both of them were now passengers on a baggage cart that taxied them out onto the tarmac. Goldridge was stepping down from one of the Blackhawk choppers. Both Brown and Carson advanced to shake the Chief's hand, and the entourage was escorted into one of the hangars where an office awaited their use.

"I need to see this for myself," Chief Goldridge directed.

Carson had the laptop in hand for just that purpose. The images had been captured as stills and arranged in a slide presentation.

"I thought you'd never ask," said Carson as he powered up the laptop.

Pam said, "All this time, Chief, I'm bustin' my ass down

here . . . putting my agents' lives on the line, only to find out that our own people are in on it . . . from the top down."

The laptop was ready. Carson turned it so that the Chief could see. Then he stood back so that his supervisor could explain the details.

"This is a shot of Charlucci's Maxima. We ran his plate. It's registered in the name of one Lu Anne Montalbo on Delray Beach. I've got two agents on that now. This is a snapshot of the trooper we ran into at Opa Locka Airport. These are shots of some of the others with him."

Pam took these guys seriously, her voice trembling, bordering on angry. "Now, here's a shot of the airport, Chief. Mind you, it's closed after ten P.M. But as you can see, it's very much open for business at one in the morning. I should point out that these men holding automatic rifles have half their police uniforms on, like they just came off of an eight-hour tour. We checked out this guy here. I recognized him from the homicide scene on the Julia Tuttle Bridge, too . . . the dealer they called Nightfly? Remember I told you about that? His name is Wild . . . Chief Wild. And those two near him are Chief of Detectives Todd and Detective Banks." Goldridge was awestricken. "Oh, it gets better. This is our outstanding lawyer—representative of the rights of Floridians— the Chief U.S. Attorney for the state . . . Peter Van Dyke."

"Well, I'll be a son of a—"

"Oh, hey, I'm saving the best for last. See this man here . . . with the goatee and the Uzi under his arm? That's Mario Nunez. He's the son of a slain cocoa farmer over in Colombia. There's a series about him in the *New York Times*, a part of which was in the latest Drug War Report. Did you see it? It talked about him coming up in a gang in Bogotá. And now, here he is in our country, shaking hands with the good ole U.S. of A's Chief U.S. Attorney." Pam had laid a mouthful on Goldridge. It was enough to make him sick to his stomach. When the worst of the shock passed, Goldridge made a call.

"Silver, good morning. This is Chief Goldridge. I'm in

from Washington. Need to see you ASAP. And you're gonna need a dozen of your local agents with you."

MET and the local DEA were expected to convene at the State Attorney General's office to discuss the investigation and the latest revelations. On the way, Pam shared other vital details with the Chief—stuff that was secondary to the priorities.

Number one, Van Dyke had set the team up with a snitch, so how valuable was Joey Pickle's information now? Number two, Van Dyke set the team up at the World Class. Once the agents found out that the Chief U.S. Attorney was involved, on a hunch, they checked the rooms for bugs. Six transmitters were found before the agents vacated. Number three, nobody could find Coco Love. She had been out on her own when agents were rounded up for the drive to Opa Locka. Now, before agents could get to her, before they could usher her to safety, she was gone—checked out of her hotel room.

CHAPTER TWENTY-EIGHT

Can we get together? You know, chum around?" The words stayed warm on Coco's mind ever since that night she met Candice Gordon, the creamy-white twenty-something with the Egyptian-cut blonde hair. Coco had gotten Candice to sell her four grams so far, a gram away from the goal of the five-gram mark, which would guarantee a five-year prison sentence.

With other dope pushers, Coco had to sling around her stories and lines and lingo, the act that made her believable. "The creative shit," Coco called it. But that wasn't necessary with Candice. The woman's entire image was an aphrodisiac for Coco. The way that woman's eyes slanted just so—something like Coco's—and how the clothing she wore molded to her thin, sculpted body. Great tits, a sensational ass, all of it calling out loud to Coco.

Since the agents called off work for the night—for what reason, Coco didn't know—she felt adventurous enough to go out alone and to do some of that "chumming around" that Candice talked about.

Cameo was the type of nightclub experience that couldn't be described by advertisement or pictures. It was an old theatre space first of all. That meant that it was spacious. That meant the people had enough room to run wild. That also meant over 9,000 square feet of dance space. This was beyond a nightclub. This was an all-out experience. The atmosphere was a mob scene outside of the entrance which became a hormone-rich, DJ-driven house of nirvana if a person was fortunate enough to be admitted past the velvet ropes.

Coco didn't have a problem getting past the rope when she was "working," so she didn't really expect a problem now. Although, even to herself, she had to admit that there was a naked feeling tonight. Maybe it was her outfit. She'd wanted to wax this apple-red leather dress for the longest. The leather was more like a free-flowing drape than anything else, how it dropped low enough to expose her healthy cleavage, how it could be unzipped to allow the calves, thighs, or even the hips to breathe, how it promised—access. To complete her look for the night, Coco strapped up some red-laced boots that reached high on her calves, a gold-beaded choker necklace, and some tinted eyewear.

It wasn't hard to spot Candice, hobnobbing with the club's owner. She was decked out in an all-silver sleek halter that couldn't be more than six inches wide, covering just enough of her breasts to keep it legal, and the same color and texture made her bell-bottom pants sparkle against her ass, hips, and thighs. Candice had many spaghetti-thin silver hoops that made up a necklace lying against her naked collarbone. A silver earring also dripped from her left ear like tinsel. Coco couldn't help staring at the woman's midriff and the small jewel lodged in her navel.

"You are simply sex, baby. Nothing but sex!" Candice bounced up closer to Coco and kissed her cheek. A slight hug as well.

"Me? You! You're glowing with sex!" Coco replied, knowing that to call a person "sex" was the highest form of flattery amidst the club set.

For an hour, Candice and Coco dazzled and smooched with the famous and the infamous. It was an eclectic crowd too; very hands-on.

"Wanna get out of here?"

"Sure. Why not?" Coco answered. And the two took off, practically dancing their way out of the club.

When the valet drove up with Candice's sky-blue Porsche, it made Coco's eyes practically do loop-the-loops in their sockets.

"You like?"

"Oh, I really like." Coco replied in a tone that came more so from deep down in her loins.

Candice pushed the Porsche like it was nobody else's business, whipping down Biscayne Boulevard with her 18-karat, white-gold, bejeweled Cartier watch all but blinding Coco's senses. They stopped by the China Grill and indulged in equal plates of Shanghai lobster, knocking hunger on its ass. Then they breezed up to Bal Harbour to take the cruise down Collins Avenue at ten miles per hour—the wind combing through their hair—sightseeing until reaching La Gorce Drive.

"This big house is yours?" Coco's jaw dropped to her crotch.

"Mmmm-hmmm. A Mediterranean, four bedrooms, and I'm about to put a pool in the back."

"The business must be doing you good."

"It is, love, really it is. I can call you that, can't I? Love?"

"That's my name, Coco Love." Coco said her name in a quick one-two combination.

"Well, I kinda like the 'Love' part. Like, it's so ultimate, just like love really is."

"Mmmm." Coco did one of those sensual nods that started from the back of the neck and rolled. It made Candice look at Coco as if she was caramel or honey; soft; sweet; enticing.

"Shall we?"

"We shall," Coco said with more than enough innuendo. Candice gave her guest a tour that bespoke her lifestyle, lush and contemporary. "Did you hire a decorator, or is this your taste talkin'?"

"All me, baby."

"I like the palms, the furniture, and *dang* . . . You have so much space to work with."

"I like to keep it simple, ya know. Like life. But no matter what, it's got to be comfortable."

"Wow!" Coco was led into the master bedroom and had hardly crossed the threshold before she gushed with emotion. "This is like . . . like Cinderella's fantasy. It looks like something right out of a romance novel."

Candice had a queen-size bed that could've been carved from a tree, its four sculpted posts pointing to the ceiling like chunky spears. The white comforter and pillows were fluffy as luminous clouds, bright against the brown wood. A nightstand to the right had a mirror, a lamp, and seven bulky candles in a tight cluster. The other nightstand had an arrangement of fresh flowers lying in and around a large, woven basket.

Coco was lured to the flowers. "Tell me these were cut today and I'm gonna melt." She said this and then inhaled deep, taking in the aroma with a wide smile. Candice was at the right of the bed now, lighting the candles.

"This morning. I don't go a day without fresh-cut flowers."

She took another deep breath and released a helpless shudder with her exhale. "So, you live here alone?" Coco asked, suddenly at a loss for words. Her hands were on her hips and her eyes were still wandering. "And is this you?" Coco noticed a framed photo on the wall above the headboard.

Candice finished with the candles and nonchalantly went for the dimmer on the wall. "Mmmm-hmmm. That's how I grew up. Like a sugarplum fairy. I spent three and four days a week in leotards, tights, and wooden toes. Dancing was the only thing I had to keep me feminine, growin' up with five brothers and all."

"Five? Dang, your moms was a busy so-and-so."

"Yeah, and Dad, too."

"Man, I always dreamed about being a ballerina. You still do it?"

"Oh no. I stopped the ballet dancing once I discovered nightclubs. Only dancing I do is in crowds."

"I saw you, too. Like Madonna or somethin', only sexier."

"Sexier than Madonna? Stop it." Candice screwed her face.

"You were a mess." Coco crossed her arms.

"As long as you were lookin'," Candice said, and now had her hands on her hips, standing just two feet from Coco. It made Coco a little uneasy, a bit like gelatin. "You were looking, right?"

"You're beautiful, Candice. How could anyone miss you?"

"From now on," Candice said as she pushed Coco's tendrils of hair aside, combing them so that an ear was exposed, "please, call me Candy."

"A pet name? But we only just met."

"You'd be surprised"—Candice let her finger travel from behind Coco's ear down the side of her neck and along the front of her leather dress—"what you can learn about a person when you first meet."

Again, Coco shuddered. Her eyelids fluttered as well.

"Scared?"

"A little."

"Ever been with a woman before?"

"Kinda, but it was just, like, this girl-girl show I did for my boyfriend. We didn't go all the way. I was too much in love with him I guess."

"And now? You still in love?"

Coco chuckled under her breath, with Mustafa's image suddenly in mind, tarnishing the moment.

"With my daughter. She's like the only person . . . the only one, really, that I love in the world."

"Been hurt, huh?"

"Hmmm . . . don't bring it up. It'll just make me sick."

"Nothing a little . . . companionship can't fix."

Coco took a long breath. Her nostrils flared. She wasn't conscious of how she curled her lips in a little, moistening them. Candice had her palm against Coco's cheek now. She eased closer, increasing the warmth between them. Their eyes searched each other for meaning and aim. Coco swallowed when Candice fingered her cleavage.

"Relax, baby. Everybody loves a little candy." A chirping sound pierced the air and the silence in the bedroom. "Sorry to shake you. I should've put it on vibrate. Hold on, I'll do it now. No interruptions, ya know?"

Candice reached into her purse on the bed. She couldn't help her curiosity as she pulled out the pager to flip the switch to the vibrate position. The digital readout on her two-way pager was glowing. An emergency call.

"Just hold that thought, babe, one eensy-weensy second." Candice trotted across her carpet to the cordless phone on the vanity in a darkened adjoining room. She could still see Coco from where she made her call.

"You know, this reee-ly better be an emergency. I'm talkin' an eee-merge-en-cee." Candice turned her head downward as if to look the caller in the face. "Yeah . . . yeah, but how do you know her? Trust you?" Candice looked back into her bedroom. Coco was out of listening distance, now sitting and trying out the softness of the bed. "Get the—" Candice suddenly lowered her voice to a hush, making extra sure not to be heard. "Get the fuck out. Get the fuck out. You're shittin' me."

A minute or so passed while Coco waited, immediately falling in love with the bed and how soft it was under her behind. She figured this was the moment of truth for her. She'd never done it with another woman, a stranger at that. But if there was anyone more appealing, if there was anyone who made her feel tingly all over, it was Candice. The chemistry just seemed to answer all of the questions. How would they do this? What was Coco's role? Candice's? And did this mean she liked women more than men? And what would this mean to Asia? Hell, she was too young to understand. I need! Coco thought to herself. I deserve! she demanded. Her leg was shaking now—nervousness beginning to set in. Why was Candice taking so long?

"Sorry, babe. Business, ya know? Now, where were we?"

"Oh. I'm—listen, this is really hard for me, being the first time and all."

"Relax, baby. Love," Candice added with emphasis. Her eyes were wide and excited. She stood between Coco's legs now. Her hand on Coco's cheek again. Her eyes were more condescending now, more authoritative. Now, Candice had her hands on her hips, as if she had an idea all of a sudden.

"You know what? I think that underneath that sensual image of yours is a sweet little girl just dying to be brought out, someone who is hungry for some discipline." Coco uttered a lighthearted laugh, as if part of what Candice guessed was absolutely right. Candice was now barefoot. She lifted one leg up and put her foot on the bed aside of Coco's thigh. She moved ever closer, preying on her guest with a purr and then a growl. "Can I have it, Love?" Candice spoke in a soft, breathy tone. "Can I make love to you? Experience you? Touch you and hold you like no one ever has?"

A shiver went through Coco, having heard ideas that her body beckoned to realize. Candice was closing in for a kiss, which made Coco fall back on the bed. There was a hard kiss against the lips, and then Candice toyed with Coco's neck, cleavage, and earlobe. All the while, she made claims that could've made Coco cry. Instead, Coco just moaned with want and desire.

Candice kissed Coco. She also undressed her until she was totally naked. Coco totally surrendered herself, both mind and body, to whatever Candice had in store. Coco sighed underneath the hands that roamed her curves and the kisses that explored her folds.

"Oh yeah," Coco cried. "Oh—yeah."

"Can I have it now?"

"Oh yeah."

"Can I?"

"Yes . . . yes."

"Turn over on your back for me," Candice instructed.

"Oooh, whatever you say, Candy." And Coco flipped over like a pancake.

Candice was on top of Coco now, still with her tube top

and bell bottoms on, outlining Coco's body with her own. Candice ground her body against Coco's, still making promises in her ear.

Out of nowhere, Candice had a scarf and affixed it, blindfolding Coco.

"Oooh, kinky, are we?"

"Shhh, enjoy the moment. The pleasure I'm about to give you is out of this world." With the blindfold in place, Candice made sure to extend Coco's arms and legs until she was spread-eagle on the bed.

"Mmmmm," Coco hummed her appreciation.

Now Candice was kneeling over Coco, securing her wrists and ankles to the bedposts until the sheets were as tight as ropes.

"Ouch," Coco uttered once Candice pulled the first sheet into a knot. She swiftly did the same three more times, ignoring Coco's pleas.

"Oh, don't you worry, Love. You're gonna love this." Candice dragged the pet name now in a deep, sarcastic way.

"But you're hurting me."

"No, that's your imagination. Shhh." Candice grabbed a candle and started dripping hot wax on Coco's naked back. Coco bucked and jerked, but Candice was mounted, sitting with her weight on top of Coco's ass. Coco began to scream in sharp spurts.

"Oooh, I didn't think you'd like it this much, Love." Candice held the flame an inch from the skin.

"Let me loose. Damn it! Get offa me!" Coco screamed.

"Huh? You undeserving little bitch! How dare you talk to me that way?" Candice smacked Coco's ass three times hard. "I told . . . you that you needed . . . some discipline." Candice noticed that one wrist was coming loose. She dismounted Coco's behind and went to fix the makeshift restraint.

"Why are you doing this to me?! Let me go! I'll scream again!"

"You're already screaming, Love. That's the beauty of my little home. It's comfortable, but it's also far enough away that my neighbors can't hear you." Coco screamed anyway.

"Gag that bitch." Ortiz was standing in the doorway with a gun in his hand. Candice was startled at first, until she saw who it was. She now noticed the gun and held her hand to her chest. "What's the face for? I heard the scream and thought you were in trouble." Ortiz put the gun down.

"Omigod, omigod, omigod . . ." Coco said, and then let out her loudest scream yet.

"Could you shut that bitch up?"

"The parties that the Versaces have are louder than this, Ortiz. Plus, I'm getting off on it."

"Well, I'm not." Ortiz went to get the red leather dress. He flipped open a switchblade and cut a strip off about four inches wide and long enough to do what he wanted. Then he grabbed Coco's panties from the floor, snatched her head back, and said, "Scream now, bitch."

She did, but she was still blindfolded and couldn't see that Ortiz was ready with the panties. He balled them up and stuffed them in her mouth as soon as she opened it. Then he wrapped the strip of leather around her mouth and head, tying it in a knot. Coco's noises were now muffled.

"What were you doin', freakin' the bitch?" Ortiz finally got a real good look at Coco lying there naked on her stomach.

"I don't discriminate," said Candice.

"Well, I do. I don't like no confidential informants. Now, you wanna turn your back? Or you wanna watch this? It ain't gonna be pretty. I promise you that," Ortiz said as he unbuckled his pants.

Candice went to sit on a sofa by the wall. "Indulge me. I'm still a little horny myself," she said under the glow of the candles.

CHAPTER TWENTY-NINE

"Baby . . . Sheryl . . . pick up. It's me, Ted." There was a second or two of silence, and then the feedback squeaking from the answering machine as Ted's wife of eight years picked up the phone.

"Hold on, babe. I'm shutting off the machine. You know, we're too technologically advanced to be havin' this dinosaur answering machine still. You so damn cheap. Anyway, how you doin', baby? You okay? We miss you."

"I'm good. I just needed to hear your voices. Work's got me tense."

"You don't need a voice. You need one of my nasty sessions and a massage to go with it."

"You always know how to make a man feel wanted. How're the children?"

"Kendra's got the flu."

"In May? Damn."

"It'll go away. Nothing to jump off a cliff about."

"And how's the little one?"

"Keisha's okay. She asks for you, Teddy."

Carson inhaled. "As soon as I can, babe, I'll be home. It won't be long now."

"You always say that."

"I know. But I—listen, I gotta go. Love you." Carson returned his wife's audible kiss and hung up the phone.

He rushed across the street to where agents were grouped, preparing for an early morning sweep.

The Mobile Enforcement Team, the local DEA, and the Broward County Sheriffs Department as well as dozens of U.S. Marshals created a battalion of armed law enforcement. They were organized in teams, all with a list to target (photos in some cases) of those identified as part of Charlucci's organization. It was an extensive list, starting with Charlucci himself. He was the easiest to locate as agents descended on Utopia. The "Snowman" surrendered peacefully. Agents couldn't find Ortiz for now, but the arrests were adding up. There was Nightfly's crew, ten of them now, who were under arrest. The transvestite, Legend, gave agents quite a problem. He/she had been surrounded at Opium, where some of the biggest sushi snobs hang out amidst Japanese décor. Legend was seated at a table alongside one blonde, three brunettes, and a fella whose hair seemed as starched as his shirt, and that was unbuttoned all the way down to his pants.

"One of those punks," an agent whispered to another agent as they stood nearby to evaluate the situation. It was the procedure, before advancing, to take account of a target, the target's state of mind, and who the target had for company. By all accounts, this was a lightweight arrest. They'd wait till Legend stepped off for the bathroom.

"They do go to the bathroom, don't they?" one agent asked.

"Maybe not, especially if they've cut it off," the other agent replied as a joke, amusing themselves while waiting. "Which bathroom would that freak use if he, er, she did have to go?" That question evoked a shrug.

Legend had such outrageous features; the broad lips, big teeth, giant forehead. Legend's nose and eyes were the largest parts of his face. The nose looked like an awkwardly grown bulb of garlic, and the eyes were set inside of what looked like inflamed eyelids. The bottoms of the lids weren't there at all. It was the top lids, all painted up with clown makeup, that looked like three-dimensional sacs. Of course, the eyelashes were an additive, as were the eyebrows that were exaggerated into swooped-up arches on his head. His earrings looked like they might belong on a chandelier somewhere. Bigger than all of that, Legend had on a catsuit. The agents made play-wagers, some saying Legend would be well-hung, and some saying Legend wouldn't be hung at all.

After a half hour of evaluating, agents got uneasy. "I think he made me," one said to another. But before that bit of information could be shared with anyone else, Legend did the craziest thing.

First, Legend sat up on the wall behind the booth where the group was stationed. Apparently, there was about to be a toast, because the others joined in with the raised glasses. Next thing the agents knew, Legend was standing, and seconds later, hopping from booth to booth and table to table, destroying the meal for a whole lot of screaming sushi lovers.

The agents launched their pursuit, making a mess them-selves, running into waiters and busboys and patrons. Agent Seager was the fastest, almost tackling the maitre d' before he dived for Legend's lanky legs. The agents behind Seager piled on top of Legend until one of them finally got out some cuffs. Cuffing one wrist was a cinch, but Legend was incredibly strong, not giving in a bit. Maybe it was an accident, or maybe not, but the other end of the cuff ended up attached to Leg-end's ankle. That's when the agents raised up and brushed themselves off, exhausted and embarrassed by how extremely mismanaged this capture had become. Seager knew that Pam would have a fit if it was just MET at work. She'd bitch about all the possibilities of controlling the capture before it got out of hand. But since the posse Seager was with included a vari-ety of law enforcement, blame couldn't be placed.

Sure enough, the women who were arrested were either ex-tremely emotional or they were too passive to be believed, perhaps to draw compassion from the agents. Melissa, the snob who Coco set up buys with, got all indignant, talking about calling her "friends in high places," and how she wanted her "one phone call . . . *right now!*" The agents found her laughable. Roxy, the dirty blonde with the fake tits, cried and cried and cried. She claimed that her life was over now and that she wouldn't last a day in jail. Farrah, Daniella, Alcira, and Cathy all went along quietly.

When it came to the men being arrested, agents bulked up on the manpower with six agents per subject. Trinton was caught red-handed, selling someone a two-ounce bag in the bathroom at The Forge. Agents arrested the buyer as well.

Alan, who pronounced his name as Al-aine, was found at the Heavy Maintenance Salon on Collins Avenue. He was having his toenails manicured while a beautician moussed up his hair. Agents waited and made jokes about how long those good looks would last before some prison beast named Mo put a cucumber up in Alan's salad.

Carlos was at home, dressing up for the hair and fashion show at Liquid. Canceled.

Renee was living out of his luxury bus, which he kept parked in the parking lot at Denny's during the daytime and in the alleyway beside The Shore Club at night. When agents showed up, knocking at the window at the front of the bus, Renee poked his head out like he was about to give someone a beat down. Weapons were already drawn and pointed, and Renee came along uneventfully.

Agents spotted Rex dipping into the men's room at the Crystal Club and followed him in after a moment or so. Rex seemed to occupy a bathroom stall for much too long. His legs and feet were positioned facing the toilet, with no sound of pissing to be heard. Broward's Officer Kamenstein didn't even announce police presence when he pushed open the door to the stall. Rex was standing there, pants on the floor, with a sexy little dope fiend sitting on the toilet, legs crossed and Rex's flagpole in her mouth.

Kamenstein couldn't help it. He had to say something sarcastic. "Surprise!"

• • •

When agents arrived at Candice's place on La Gorce Drive, there was no answer at the door.

Candice heard the knocking and immediately ran upstairs to peek out of a bathroom window. It was small enough, with curtains, so nobody would see her.

Ohmigosh! she said to herself. Then she hurried to a window at the back of the house. Cops, she told herself. Quietly, she descended the steps, both sets, until she reached the basement.

"It's the cops. Ortiz, it's the cops! What are we gonna do? Whatarewegonnado?" Candice, the distressed ex-ballerina.

"Keep it down, bitch, 'fore they hear you."

Candice didn't have a mind to challenge Ortiz's audacity. After all, he didn't know her that damned well.

"What're we gonna do with her?"

"Just cool it. Let them figure out that you're not home, and when shit is clear . . ."

"But my Porsche! And what about your jeep?"

"I didn't think about that." Ortiz turned to Coco, who was semiconscious, with her hands bound to the beam at the center of the cellar floor.

"Damn, Ortiz. You really made a mess down here." Candice had been busy up in the bedroom. With the quilt all bloody from Ortiz violating and assaulting Coco, she had to strip the bed down and clean up. The quilt was already going through a second washing. Meanwhile, Coco was bruised, with her face swollen where it had once been camera-ready. She was bunched up on the floor next to the beam she was tied to. Ortiz had just urinated on Coco—in her hair, on her face and body—and it was stinking up the basement.

Candice twisted her nose and lips at the sight of Coco, nothing like the woman she'd been preying on only hours ago. Then she climbed the steps to peek out the window again. Cops were convened out on her lawn, probably wondering why there were vehicles and nobody home. Candice went to look out back. Two officers were situated there.

"They're still here. We're cooked. I just know it."

"Probably waiting for a warrant so they can come in. Take your Porsche."

"My Porsche?" Candice didn't even get the words out before she drifted off, falling out of balance from right where she stood. Ortiz was quick to catch her.

"Oh, no, you don't. Don't faint on me now, bitch." Ortiz popped her on the cheek a couple of times to keep her awake. He hadn't indulged in so much female assault, in so short a time, in quite a while.

Coco was moaning now.

"Asia . . . A . . ." This was the result of being coked-up from the injection Ortiz put in her arm.

"Hold on, girl. We gotta get out of here some way."

Candice was in and out of consciousness with Ortiz holding her, shaking her, and beginning to worry.

"Uhm . . ." the sound escaped Candice's lips and Ortiz thanked God.

"That's it. Shake out of it, babe. Let's find some way outta here."

"I . . . I can't just . . . leave my—oooh, my head."

"Okay . . . water. We need to get you some water." Ortiz helped Candice to the basement sink, doused her face with some water, scooped some into her mouth, and managed to get them to the side door. Ortiz checked for cops and saw none. "Here's the deal. You gotta move with me—we're gonna slip out to the Porsche. The cops are in front . . ."

"There's a couple out . . ." Candice was drowsy and her voice drifted here and there. But Ortiz was determined to get out from under the gun. Nothing was gonna get him back behind bars. Nothing.

"You just stick with me." Ortiz felt his side to be sure his gun was still there, or maybe that was just to boost his confidence.

"Wait. My . . . my keys."

"Where are they?"

"Upstairs. My purse is in the bedroom."

"Hold tight. Don't go nowhere. I'll be right back." All of

a sudden, Candice was left there in the basement to gaze at Coco. Coco was slouched there, naked on the floor. Her eyes had an unfeeling, mortified, frozen sense about them. But they were directed at Candice like a curse.

Hey-hey-hey! Somebody's in the Porsche!" a cop yelled out after hearing the car's motor.

"Shit!" another officer said.

Like water bugs suddenly hit by a light, the federal agents and local police officers sprayed out from their lil' gatherings and sprinted to their vehicles. A few of them drew their weapons and began shooting for the sky-blue sports car. The Porsche was able to swerve around Ortiz's jeep, now holed up by bullet slugs, and shot out past two cruisers that tried to form a mobile barricade a second or so too late.

Now, the cruisers and unmarked sedans formed a broken arrow along 5th Street, Route 41, and then Alton Road. Support was called for, and soon enough, additional vehicles skidded into a roadblock at the intersection of Alton and Dade.

The Porsche did a 180-degree spin and charged back down Alton away from the roadblock, but against the team in pursuit. Now the driver of the Porsche was firing shots. Two of the cruisers were frightened into wayward tailspins after hitting their brakes. The vehicles behind them swerved outward to avoid collision. Still another pushed forward. The Porsche was facing a dilemma, apparently; the gunfire stopped, if only momentarily. The two vehicles continued advancing at top speed, neither of them giving in or hinting at submission.

Less than thirty feet apart, the Porsche shot left and onto the sidewalk. A collective of coin-operated newsstands were taken out along the way. Pedestrians had already witnessed the chase when it passed them the first time. So they were ever aware now, scurrying out of the way as the sky-blue blur downshifted, picking up speed.

When the opportunity presented itself, the Porsche cut back onto Alton, made a right onto MacArthur Causeway, and left the others behind.

• • •

Shit! shit! oh shit—yes!!!" Ortiz shouted as he realized a certain freedom. There was no sign of cops in his rearview, and nothing but virgin road up ahead. The energy raced through him like a free-fall dive, and he was still pushing ninety miles per hour.

"My God, can you slow down now? I'm like . . . dizzy."

"You were already a dizzy broad. In a few minutes, we'll be somewhere safe. For now, close your eyes and enjoy the ride to freedom, trick."

Candice took a deep breath and covered her eyes.

Got 'em, Chief!" The pilot squeezed his throttle until the pressure stung his palm and fingertips. Chopper 12 picked up the chase back at the intersection of Alton and MacArthur and was now carving its way through the sky, dropping close enough for the sniper onboard to make the call.

"Steady. Steeaady." The police sniper was talking to himself, but the pilot could also hear him in his own headset. "Just a little closer and I'll be able to take out the . . ." The M-16 jerked in the sniper's arm, with its sounds drowned out by the helicopter's scissor-sharp propellers. "Got 'im!"

The sniper had hit the left rear tire of the Porsche, causing it to lose control. Within seconds, there was black smoke from the tire, which was now shredded and left on the road, and then sparks as the naked rim skated along the concrete. The vehicle wiggled. It bounced off of another car and lunged right. Then it tore into a line of bright orange cones. Other cars in the Porsche's path swerved in every direction in order to avoid its wrath. Finally, the Porsche ripped into a spastic spin-out, leaving the roadway and then cartwheeling into a series of violent end-over-end flips until it came to rest in a ditch.

Within minutes, authorities spilled onto the scene of the wreck. They found Ortiz unconscious and Candice dead, with her head lodged through the front windshield of the car.

• • •

Pam couldn't wait to meet the Snowman. She wanted to both see this man and get an idea of how he coped with captivity. Would he be miserable like most others, willing to tell all to save his miserable life? Pam also wanted to push all of his buttons; she wanted to get him to stoop to his lowest without his world of money and power to protect him. She wanted to milk him for everything he knew, and she'd pull every card to do so.

"You're not my lawyer," Charlucci said, sitting behind a table in his new orange jumpsuit and iron bracelets. Nowhere near the jewelry he might otherwise be wearing.

"Right, I'm not. I'm better than a lawyer. See, your lawyer is gonna try to maintain control of your future. Me? I'm already in control of your future—total control. Right now."

Charlucci made a doubtful face and turned away.

"I'm Ms. B—"

Charlucci huffed under his breath at the thought of what the *B* should stand for.

"—and frankly, you're no longer Mr. Big, or 'the man,' like your underlings might call you. No. You know what you are now? You're a goose that's cooked. We've got you for more than twenty violations, including organizing a criminal enterprise, and importation and distribution of over five hundred kilos of cocaine. Furthermore—"

"I want my lawyer."

"Fur-ther-more, we've got you for murder one in connection with your ongoing criminal enterprise. In Florida, that's the death penalty."

"Awesome. Truly awesome," Charlucci responded; Pam's expression revealed that she misunderstood him. "Your game . . . your presentation," he explained. "Bravo!" Charlucci did his best to clap with the handcuffs on. "And in the category of best actress, with the prettiest ass and the nicest set of tits, the Oscar goes to . . . Ms. B!" Again, he tried to clap.

"Oh, a comedian, huh? Well, let's see if this makes you laugh." Pam unfolded a sheet of paper that had been in her back pocket. She had jeans and her DEA blouse on. The embroidery was in yellow thread, standing out against dark blue. "I got four women who want to return to the streets. They want to be able to have children. I've got a transvestite who says he—or should I say she—can't go another minute without hormone pills. Some pretty woman named Roxy, who . . . ahh . . . also has nice tits, well, she says she's known you since high school. I know shit about you that your momma doesn't even know. But there's more."

"I want my—"

"There's a certain club promoter named Tommy and a very misunderstood fella named Rex who knows something about you knowing a certain U.S. Attorney. And the cherry on the shortcake is this: Ortiz? He's alive and talking. He's mumbling now, but I don't need an interpreter to make out what he's saying . . . something about Nightfly and a murder." Pam rose up from where she sat on the table. Her back was to Charlucci. She moistened her lips and turned her head.

"So what's it gonna be? You still want your lawyer? Or do you want to breathe fresh air again someday?"

Charlucci seemed to be making the biggest decision in his life.

"Okay, it's your life. Lock his ass back—"

"Wait! I'll give you somebody."

"Somebody?"

"In New York. His name is Freeze."

"Uh-uh, we already know about Freeze. He'll be sitting where you are shortly."

"So whaddaya want from me?"

"I want Van Dyke. And I want your Colombian connect."

"I can't do that! You're outta your fuckin' mind, lady!"

"Maybe you're right. I have been feeling a bit beside myself lately. Tell you what. I'll make you another deal." Pam was up in Charlucci's face now. "If you can hold your breath long enough for your eyes to pop out, I'll let you go home." Pam spun around and left the room while the guards at Miami Correctional Center took Charlucci back to deep lockdown—segregated for his own protection.

BOOK FOUR

BOOK FOUR

CHAPTER THIRTY

A number of Southern states, especially Virginia, the Carolinas, Mississippi, and parts of Georgia, were built on the backs of slaves who survived the brutal crossing from West Africa. And although this was so many years ago, some of the naiveté, miscommunication, and lack of available resources still lingered today. Granted, the walls of ignorance crumble constantly, but until knowledge, information, and resources become readily available, the middleman would continue to play the field. Some will hustle. Others will prey.

For thrill-seekers living in Fayetteville, North Carolina, Charlie "Junebug" Johnson and Danny "Preacher" Williams were those middlemen who played the field. They were important, essential to negotiate with (for some more than others) only because they controlled the food which fed those who were dependant or addicted to powdered and crack cocaine.

Junebug was the first to stake a claim when it came to serving up the white man's high in this area. He grew up in The Grove projects; those one-, two-, and three-family prefab houses that were rent-controlled and paid for as part of the government's Section 8 housing program. Of course, there was the holdup of Jay Jay's Grocery during which his gang buddy, Stretch, got his arm blasted off, which led to Junebug spending all of his teenage years at Stonewall Jackson Training School for Boys.

By eighteen, the age when residents of the school had to be released, Junebug was back at home with his mom, turning The Grove projects into his headquarters. Junebug changed his mind about going back to hold up Jay Jay's Grocery. He'd grown sensible enough to know that such an endeavor would send him not to a boy's training camp, but to prison next time. Holdups were out of the question.

On the other hand, Junebug was not about to spend the rest of his life on a nine-to-five job, either. There was just one easy answer to survival. At Stonewall, Junebug had learned a little about the dope game. So he took that seed and ran with it. He made fifty bucks a day as a lookout for Blade, another drug dealer who lived in The Grove. From lookout, he went to "hooking"—luring sales from out on Merchants Road. As fate would have it, Junebug returned home one day to learn that Blade had been arrested. Word on the street was he'd been caught with a smoking gun, so to speak: in possession of ten kilos. Nobody expected his return. Not for a long, long time anyway.

However, the cops who bagged Blade apparently knew little or nothing about where the dealer lived or that he had a stash of two kilos left behind.

So Junebug acted quickly. He broke into Blade's crib. He grabbed up what drugs and money he could find, even a 9mm, and was immediately in business for himself. The clients were already established, coming from different corners of Fayetteville for their twenty- and fifty-dollar fixes. Within a week, Junebug had his own hooks and lookouts. The only part he was missing was a connect to buy future product from. To prolong his good fortune, Junebug added more Mannitol, a baby laxative that he was told would stretch the amount of cocaine. Now, the two kilos magically turned into four kilos.

Soon, one of Junebug's runners came back to tell him, "The customers are complaining. They say the stuff is weak this time, that you stepped on it maybe one time too many."

Junebug's answer was, "Take it or leave it." As far as he was concerned, his was the only game in town. His competition was none. His customers were lowlifes anyway. All users are, he determined. They'd just have to hang in there. He'd get in touch with an out-of-town connect in due time.

If Junebug thought he was the only one selling, that he was the big fish in a small pond, he had another think coming. He probably assumed as much because his mind had been isolated for a number of years in confinement. But, his mind was just as confined now, localized in the worst way, to the point that it slowed him.

Hey, Skinny! Lemme holla atcha!" Junebug shouted across the playground at a woman who had been one of his most frequent customers.

"Whatchu want, Junebug?"

"How come you ain't been comin' 'round in a while? You usually come like three, four times a week. Now, you ain't come in a whole month."

"I . . . ain't been usin'. I'm tryin' to get clean."

"Yeah. And I'm an altar boy for the Pope." Junebug grabbed Skinny's wrist.

"Oooowww! You hurtin' me!"

"Tell me who you gettin' yo' stuff from, dopehead."

"Oooowww-ooowwch! Okay, okay. 'Cross town. The Preacher."

"What preacher?"

"Not what preacher. Preacher ain't wit' no church. He called Preacher, that's all."

"Oh, and you just gon' switch up—just like that."

"Everybody say you step on the stuff too much. They say your stuff turnin' soft," Skinny said, trying to pull away from him.

"Oh yeah?" Junebug let go of Skinny's wrist. She was rubbing it now, lookin' like two sticks trying to make a fire.

K-oss was at the other end of the playground, with his eye in Junebug's direction the whole time. It was the sight of Skinny snatching her wrist away so abruptly that made K-oss come over.

"'Sup, June? Skinny outta line?"

"Naw. Ain't shit. I'm just pressin' her. Git outta here, you crackhead bitch." Skinny scurried away. "K-oss, why ain't you been true to me?"

"Huh?"

"I'm talkin' 'bout some preacher dude on the east end."

"Far as I know, he been sellin' junk as long as dudes from The Grove has. He just keepin' low key."

"He do much business?"

K-oss shrugged. "I hear he work them clubs like The Hideaway and Kamikaze. Your girl might know him. She use to—"

"Peaches?"

"Yup. She worked over there."

"Doin' what? When?"

"Easy, playa. Ain't sure what she did over there, but I know she was there, prob'ly way before you got wit' her."

"She ain't never told me that."

"Come on, dog. You only just got with Peaches since you come up in the game. Whatchu think? You think she was just layin' around in her own bedroom waitin' for a nigga like you to come along?" Junebug had an expression that was unsure of whether K-oss had just dissed him. "Ease up, dog. Why don't you ask Peaches, 'steada 'ssumin'?"

"Think I won't?"

A s if it was a trend, runners and lookouts courted young women with the excesses that the drug trade provided. There wasn't one low-level player who didn't spend his money on a fly ride, fly clothes, and jewelry. Sure, others might spend tax-free earnings on investments such as real estate or on inspirational activities. But for the ghetto fabulous, a hot car with sparklin' twenty-inch rims and a beastly sound system was an investment. It was their inspiration. The bottom line: this was the only life they knew.

The young women were just as focused on these frivolous expenditures as those who accumulate them. They knew the cars by name, the clothes by the label—and naturally, they had their own concepts of what was hot. After all, that's what their video icons were rappin' and singin' about on TV, wasn't it? Wasn't Foxy rappin' about Cristal, Moët, and Gucci? And wasn't Lil' Kim droppin' names like Dolce & Gabbana, Prada, and Versace? And if they were rappin' about it . . . if they were wearin' it . . . didn't that mean it was the *"in"* thing to have?

Whether or not these colors, flavors, and sounds of the streets were important in the big picture was neither here nor there. These were the things important to them—those who bought into these trends—and to follow the crowd was to be accepted. To be accepted was all that mattered.

Peaches was indeed one of the girls now, especially after her breakup with Preacher. She had been his assistant, his money-counter, his secretary, his sex slave, and damn near his wife for all of three years. Ever since switching from North Carolina University to Durham Central, and then quitting college altogether, Peaches had been a dope dealer's wifey. She'd met Preacher back when she was eighteen. He was nineteen, and frankly, the beginning and end of her every waking day. Aspirations of getting her degree in communications and of launching a career in broadcasting were dead, buried, and gone.

Peaches was twenty-one now, still young and energetic, still lookin' like a juicy peach, not yet succumbing to the baggage of failed relationships, abuse, and dead-end promises of dreamers. She didn't have any children yet, and had little other responsibilities other than to dress good and to look good for her man. Junebug was her man now. She was considering something substantial with him, too. But maybe she'd give this one a little more time before she dived all the way in, before she gave up everything . . . as if she had account of what "everything" was. Maybe she was thinking of her heart as everything.

Junebug parked his BMW behind the building where Peaches lived. He enabled the car's alarm and slipped in the back door. He saw the nosey-ass super peeking out of his window, and told himself that the guy had better mind his own business.

The corridors along the basement were painted in semi-gloss sky blue and the floor was like polished slate. Pipes and wires riddled the ceiling and were just out of reach. Junebug took the stairway to the second floor and headed for apartment C. There was a determined sense about him, issues that he already had answers to.

First and foremost, he'd have his own key for 2C within a week or so. Second, Peaches already fit into the shoes she was expected to wear. She did as she was told. So there was no doubt in Junebug's mind that she'd tell all regarding what she knew about this preacher-dude. Most importantly, was he hittin' that ass?

Bop, b-bop, bop, bop.

That was Junebug's signature knock. And Peaches was at the door within seconds.

"Hey, daddy," she sang, all loose in her oversize T-shirt and short-shorts. "I thought you'd never get here." Peaches now had her arms draped around Junebug's neck. She sucked at his cheek first, and then went for his lips. He pushed her away, although not as hard as he wanted to.

"What's wrong, lover? You stressin'?"

"Naw. I just got issues I'm fittin' ta discuss wit' you."

"Sure, baby," Peaches replied as she shut the door behind him. "What's up?" Her hands were propped on her hip now. And the stance she assumed made her breasts stretch the limits of her T-shirt.

"Sit."

"Dag, baby. What's wrong?"

"Nothin's wrong. I just wanna have this talk."

"No problem." She sat. "Talk to me."

"Who was you fuckin' before me?"

Peaches seemed to brace herself, taking a deep breath. A slight shiver ran through her, as well as her eyes were dilated and surprised. "Wooeee, baby. You don't waste no time gettin' to the point, do you?"

"Why should I? You didn't waste no time in gettin' with this dick, did you?"

"That's cold, Juney." Her eyes showed a hint of offense.

"Whatever. Who?"

"Just some guy from college." She sucked her teeth.

"Which college? You went to two."

"NCU. Just some guy. It wasn't nothin', really."

"Who else?"

"Huh?"

"Who . . . else?"

"Nobody."

"So you sayin' you was only fuckin' one guy in college, huh?"

"Why it gotta be so gutter? He was my boyfriend for a minute."

"So what's that? Love?"

"Juney," Peaches said, not really wanting to get into it.

"Was the dude's name Preacher?"

"Huh?"

"Oh, you wanna play stupid now."

"I don't know no Preacher, Junebug." Peaches said this with a no-nonsense mask on. But Junebug didn't change his penetrating stare. "Junebug, I don't know what got into you today, but I don't like it. I've been doin' right by you for a few months now. Anything you ask, I been there for you . . . as your wifey. But, Juney," Peaches got up from where she sat, crossing over until she stood between his legs. He was still slouched there on the couch. Now she lowered herself, eventually kneeling before him. "Do me a favor, please? Please don't take my love for granted. Don't abuse me."

" 'Buse you? Watch whatcha sayin', woman. I hope you ain't callin' me no wife beater."

"I'm just sayin' treat me like I treat you. I do right by you, Juney. So do right by me." Peaches' whole presence was submissive. Her eyes turned saucy and her hands smoothed along Junebug's thighs. With Peaches all wide open like this, Junebug could smell sex in the air. He just hoped that this do-me-like-I-do-you bit that she was talkin' wasn't her way of wantin' him to make things equal between them. Ain't no way that was gonna happen. Not while he was a livin' breathin' man. No matter who it was, Peaches or any other woman,

Junebug was always gonna be the shot-caller. He was always gonna be the big money side of the relationship. And for sure, he wasn't gonna have no lyin', dishonorable bitch by his side.

At this level in their relationship, although Junebug never laid out his specific demands, Peaches was expected to "understand" his way of doing things. She had that woman's intuition goin' on—so let her read between the lines. This was the unspoken truth that ruled their time together. It was the way things were so long as he was buying her clothes, paying her rent, and keeping things convenient for her. Not another word was said about the possibility of a Preacher-Peaches thing. It was simply one of those instances where Junebug had a lot to say, and a lot more to ask, but never got to complete his thoughts. Peaches made all of those concerns melt away. That was the thing about her. The way she smoothed out his rough edges, the way she calmed him in times of stress, the way she sucked his dick like a Heather Hunter protégée.

CHAPTER THIRTY-ONE

Tabitha Miles thought it was strange, at first, for this guy to come into her shop requesting "the best stylist in the house." Who was this guy, a playa or somethin', with his rings, his diamond Rolex, and medallion hangin' around his neck? Was she supposed to believe that stuff was the real thing?

"Listen," she said when Preacher first came into her shop with a couple of his boys as shadows. "We ain't got time for no games in here. There ain't no party, no dancin' stripper-girls, and no room for hangin' out in here. We're here for a reason, to do business. So, please, take your boys with you and find a pool hall or somewhere 'fore I get to callin' the police."

"What is it? You jealous of my money? My jewels? My ride outside?"

Tabitha had a hand on one hip and the other on the desk where her clients made appointments and paid their money. A telephone was also there within her reach.

She was the sole proprietor at A Little Magic Hair Salon, one of six shops that were scattered along Merchants Road. The shop was busy for a Thursday evening. Women were all over the place getting their Jheri curls, perms, weaves, and wash-n-sets. Kendra did the African braids in the back corner of the salon. All seven hairdressers, or beauticians (as they called themselves), were in tonight, not including Tabitha, who served as proprietor, troubleshooter, teacher, advisor, and social worker, which was the case in dealing with these street types who often wandered into her shop. And now, it's final, she decided. She would indeed have that door buzzer system installed that a vendor had been soliciting her about for all these weeks.

With a "you must be kidding me" look on her face, Tabitha turned away from Preacher, her eyes canvassing the entire salon, asking nobody in particular: Do you believe this fool?

Preacher pressed on. "I'm for real, ma—what? Do I stink or somethin'? Like I ain't washed? Or do my clothes offend you? My forty-eight-hundred-dollar outfit too much to look at? Or is it my money?" Preacher made a thick wad of bills appear in his hand. There was a gold-and-diamond money clip securing what looked to be a few thousand dollars. "My money ain't no good in here?"

Tabitha shifted her weight now and copped an attitude, thinking he wasn't all that. Meanwhile, her eyes reviewed Preacher, maybe now putting a different perspective on things. However, her lips were still pursed, unsure of where this was going or who this guy was.

Preacher didn't want to sound like he was there to diss the woman, so he made an effort to smooth things out. Activities in the salon had come to a screeching halt a half minute ago when Preacher began listing his material possessions. Somewhere in the shop, Denise Williams' voice was fluttering over an orchestra.

"Listen, ma, I—"

"I ain't your momma."

"Okay, so . . . Miss?"

"I'm Tabitha. I own this salon. And I'm the one who'll be filing that police report." By this time, Tabitha had her hand on the telephone. Preacher made an unthreatening advance and put his hand on hers, firm but affectionate.

"Listen, I just want to get my hair done. That's all. I ain't here to give you no problems." Preacher's hand was still on top of hers, until he realized hers was shaking. He removed his hand. "All them shops down the way—the men's shops, I'm talkin' about—they can't do my hair like a woman can." Tabitha heard the respect in Preacher's voice, and it didn't hurt that he used the "woman" bit in his rap, either.

"Who was doin' your hair before?"

"A woman down at Stacy's Wondercurl, but I just found out she's in the hospital. Havin' a baby, that is."

"Didn't you know she was with child, and that you'd be needin' a new hairstylist to fill in?"

"Mmm-hmmm . . . but I was—how you say? Procrastinating."

"Hmmm. Likely story," Tabitha said in a friendlier tone. "But I got bad news for you, playa."

"Name's Preacher. I ain't no playa."

"Okay, touché on the name-callin'. Bad news, Mr. Preacher. We're all booked up tonight. Busy like a Saturday up in here." Tabitha stretched her arm out as if she was a magician's assistant. "As you can obviously see for yourself."

"I see," Preacher said, noticing that a few women were waiting on a couch scattered with magazines. He checked his watch. It glistened for the audience.

"It's only seven now. Any chance I can wait, or come back to see you later?"

"I don't know," Tabitha started to say, knowing that the evening was already expected to stretch into her sleep time.

"I came here because they say you the best."

"Well, my shop does have some of the best—"

"They say *you*, Tabitha, are the best. And no disrespect to your staff here, but my wig gotta be right for the weekend. It can't wait. I'm not gonna let it wait. What would it cost to make it worth your while?"

A bit overwhelmed and proud, Tabitha maintained a stance of integrity and dignity, if not for her own conscience, then for her lil' audience. Even though that money did look good.

"Money isn't the issue here, Mr. Preacher."

"Just Preacher. Call me Preacher. It's my name."

"Okay, Preacher," Tabitha said, now more at ease with the man and his lil' entourage. "The issue is really about me, my sleeping habits, and being awake enough to do the best possible job for my clients." The statement was enough that it should have commanded applause.

"Well, can you at least tell me it's a possibility? 'Cause I'm a patient man when it comes to getting the best service."

Tabitha couldn't help giving in, even if a little bit, to Preacher's compliments. She was flattered. Someone behind her murmured, "All right then," in a praise-the-Lord kind of way. Tabitha turned again to her clients and beauticians, a different expression on her face now: Maybe I was wrong about this guy.

It was a long night indeed. The stigma that came in the door with Preacher wilted away to nothing. He made it convenient for the women in A Little Magic to accept him, too, ordering Domino's Pizza and a case of sodas for all to share. One woman declined on the pizza, the soda—all that. She simply finished with getting her hair done and strutted out of the shop with a chip on her shoulder. She probably sensed that Preacher was dealin' dope; either that, or she had a thing against disposable income. As Preacher came to realize long ago, you can't satisfy everybody, so the woman's attitude did not affect him in the least.

Eventually, Tabitha got to Preacher's hair. She noticed that it didn't need a full relax, just the roots. Therefore, it wouldn't take as long as she thought.

"You got nice hair," she told Preacher, having already handled and touched the visitor enough to feel some kind of way about him.

"I try to keep it up. I really need someone in-house to handle it so I wouldn't have to bother people like you so much."

"Oh, it's no bother. Really. I'm kinda glad you came by. The pizza and all was nice of you. My staff and clients really enjoyed it."

"Tab, I'm gone," said Jan. "Kendra's still back there with the braidin'. I tell ya, I don't know how she does it. That woman got patience like a rock to be spendin' all that time on one person's head."

Tabitha smiled at Jan. "Good night, baby. Do me a favor. Hit the outdoor lights on your way out."

"You got it." Jan flashed an appreciative look at Preacher, with the cape covering his upper body and his hair all gooked-up with relaxer. " 'Bye, Preacher." Jan merely batted her eyes at Preacher's buddies, but she was hopin' one of them would read between the lines and maybe come back to see her sometime.

That impulsive pizza party was months earlier. Preacher left the shop that day with a sharp-ass do and a new lady friend. He felt somethin' for Tabitha, too. He even sent her two dozen long-stemmed roses that following Saturday for her to share with what she had said would be a busy shop. Tabitha answered the roses with a phone call since Preacher had written his number on the inside of the small card that merely said, "To a lovely lady."

Once she called, he asked to see her. She agreed.

All of that—the first day he came to the shop, the flowers, and then their dates—was a blur for Tabitha now as she lay there naked by Preacher's side. It had to be close to daybreak. Why else would she be awake like this, propped up on an elbow and just staring at Preacher like she was? Or maybe it was all of the second thoughts she was having.

Tabitha had always vowed to keep her legs closed . . . to be all about business until the day that A Little Magic was the full-fledged salon she dreamed it would be. She worked such long, hard hours to get to a position of independence and financial freedom, to be able to know when and where her next dollar was coming from.

There was her thousand-hour course at beauty school; there was the apprenticeship that she took up under the original proprietor of the salon when it was called Carolina

Hair; there were the many sojourns to attend the out-of-state beauty shows; and finally, Carolina Hair was going up for sale.

Tabitha gathered up her resources, the money she'd squirreled away, some commitments from other beauticians and clients. Soon, she had a deposit big enough to be taken seriously. And now, the money she was making more than helped to pay off the balance of the buyout and the current salon expenditures. She could see the light at the end of the tunnel—when she'd truly be financially free, when she'd have her own disposable income, be able to take vacations, and have a family.

So, if she hadn't yet reached that goal at the end of the tunnel, why, she wondered, was she giving her milk up to this guy? What was it about him that was any more special than the other Tom, Dick, and Harry who made attempts to get between her legs?

"And, oh my God! The sex!" Tabitha was telling her friend, Kendra. "The man was just filling me until my spine was about to give! Never. Nev'r-nev'r-nev'r-nev'r, in my wildest dreams did I think a man could do for me what Preacher did last night. What Preacher has been doing—*shit*!

These were the types of thoughts that sometimes had Tabitha delirious . . . suspended in time. They were thoughts that made her say to herself, "Oh well," "Whatever," and "If it ain't broke, don't fix it." It helped that Preacher was fine, in good shape, and kept himself well-groomed. Just a few of the things that Tabitha saw now while lying there and inhaling the aftermath of the sex they had only hours earlier.

"Boo!" Preacher came out of nowhere with the snap expression. It scared her out of her mind. She screamed short and loud.

"You scared me!"

"You supposed to be scared. Why are you all up in my grill so early in the morning?"

"Just . . . just thinkin, that's all."

"Oh yeah? 'Bout what? 'Bout what we talked about last night? The drugs?"

"Well . . . that, too. But I was just thinkin' about everything, ya know? Girl stuff."

"Really?" Preacher yawned up and away from Tabitha. "So, what, uh, conclusions did you come up with? Don't tell me you 'bout to leave me or nothin', 'cuz I'm the only one who does the leavin' 'round here," Preacher said with a phony smile.

"Hmmm . . ." Tabitha rolled her eyes, but somewhere in the back of her head that remark was put on the shelf of "Things to Remember." "No, I'm not leavin'. Any woman would be a fool to leave this." Tabitha's eyes indicated Preacher's body. "I just wonder how . . ." She sucked her teeth, and then changed her mind. "Oh, I shouldn't really go there."

"No, no . . . go 'head, baby. Speak yo' mind."

"Well . . . I was just wonderin' how secure a future would be with you. I meet so many women from day to day who either have a man in jail or in the game. A few been killed, and even fewer are doin' well. But in most cases, there are problems. I hear about their trials every damn week. My man this, my man that. It's like every woman . . . her whole life is all about that man. So, if he's in the game riskin' his life—or liberty—he's really not securin' no future. 'Cause you never know when they comin'. You heard that song, didn't you?"

"Which song?"

"Erykah Badu. The one where she said, 'Whatcha gonna do when they come for you?' She said, 'Me and my baby got this situation . . . brother got this complex occupation.' That feels so real right now. That's you and me, Preacher. It is."

"You shouldn't live your life by no song, girl."

"Hmmph, just like a man. Play down what I'm tryin' to say. Besides, that's just the point. I don't wanna be the subject of no song or no talk show shit, either."

"No, I feel you. But the dudes who really have risks are the stupid ones. My game is deep, baby. You wouldn't even know I was dealin' unless I told you. I hardly see the stuff. Besides, you shouldn't really worry yourself so much. I got this."

Again, Tabitha settled with the self talk: Oh well, Whatever, and If it ain't broke . . .

The beauty of having a working woman for a wifey (for some) was that she was away for significant periods of time. It allowed for breathing room when it was necessary or, in Preacher's case, it kept her out of his business. And that sense of ignorance was the best place for wifey to be.

Preacher had his own crib, like Tabitha did. But he enjoyed hanging out at both places. It lent him a sort of illusive state of being, which was fine because "his people" were out in the streets handling business, feeding the need. So it didn't matter where he was, or with whom. Besides, if there was something really important to talk to him about, they had his two-way pager number, and he had a cell phone on which he could call them back if necessary.

The two-way was going off now while Preacher was checking himself, standing naked in front of the full-length mirror in Tabitha's bedroom. He had just finished showering, and she had run off early to get some errands done before opening the salon. He returned the call, unsure of who it was. He couldn't remember all of the codes he had given to the women who had his phone number—only the most important ones.

"Who's this? Well, well, well. Is this the number one rooster comin' home to—well, you seemed to think so not too long ago . . . Yeah, you right; a lot has changed since then. So then, why you gettin' at me? You must need some money . . . Oh, well that's somethin' I'm used to. What kind of problem?" Preacher listened for a time as he balanced the phone and dressed all at once.

"That sounds like a problem that I can surely help you with. You know where Peachtree Street is? Yeah . . . it is ironic . . . well, lemme give you the address. Bring it over here now, before I change my mind."

Preacher hung up. He was still for a moment. Then he smiled to himself.

• • •

"**H**ow'd you get here?" Preacher asked Peaches after she slipped in the door. She dropped a bag on the floor.

"Taxi."

"Did he know you?"

"No."

"Good. I don't want anyone puttin' two and two together."

Peaches looked around and then turned to her ex-boyfriend, ex-lover, ex-everything. "So, this your new spot?"

"Not really."

"Who is she?"

"Nosy."

"Who-is-she," Peaches pressed.

"None of your business."

"She ain't here, is she?"

"Pssshhh—girl, you ain't changed a bit. You wanna know everything."

"No. I just wanna know whose ass I gotta kick if she gets in my face with some jealousy shit."

"Oooo-weee . . . has Peaches become a monsta since she was kicked to the curb?"

"Call it bitter. Call it upset. Call it—oh, daddy! I miss you so much." Peaches gushed with emotions, running to hold Preacher, sparking up those old coals, reminding him of her scent. He embraced her, cuddling her head with one hand, the other positioned against the small of her back.

"You women are too much. You act like you know what you want, but when you find out that's not good, you fall to pieces. Chickens."

"Whatever, Preacher. Can't you just hold me? I really need to be held right now."

After a moment, Preacher asked her, "How did it go down? Tell me."

"I did just like you said. I tore up the apartment, I broke some things, and I left the door wide open. Then, I slipped out the back through the basement. It was late at night, so nobody saw me."

"Nobody?"

"Not even the super. Nobody."

"And you got it all?"

"Right here."

Peaches handed Preacher the shoulder bag. Being so caught up in seeing him again, in holding him after so long, she almost forgot the business at hand.

"Damn. He keeps his money neat, don't he?"

"Not really. That's my work. I counted it, stacked it, broke it down, and wrapped it in groups of five thousand."

"Hmmm, just like I taught you."

"Mmm-hmmm."

"How much is here?"

"Oh, all of it. A hundred and seventy."

"Shit! That mothafucka is gonna have conniptions when he hears about this."

"Be-lieve me, he's definitely gonna flip."

"Good work, Peaches. I'm glad you got smart and contacted me—even though you ain't wifey no more."

"I wanna be wifey again."

"Yeah, I'm sure you do. Maybe we can work something out. Maybe. But we gotta do this first. We gotta go to Plan B."

Peaches deflated a bit, not exactly thrilled about this part. "You about ready?"

Peaches inhaled, suddenly with fear in her eyes. "Can we at least make it real? I mean, if I was gonna be kidnapped, robbed, and beat up, wouldn't the guys rape me?"

"Maybe."

"So . . . before you . . ." Peaches swallowed. "Before you beat me up . . . can you—rape me?"

"You want me to rape you?"

"Well, a *good* rape . . . you know, like we use to do—playactin' 'n stuff."

Preacher wagged his head, telling himself that bitches go for the strangest shit. Then he stepped up and snatched Peaches by her shoulder-length auburn weave. He snatched her head back and bit into her neck enough to make an impression. After that, he threw Peaches on the floor, undid his robe, and reached for his leather belt nearby.

"So you think this is a joke, huh? This is all fun and games for you." Preacher turned into another person right before her eyes. She wasn't sure if he was playing, or if he was really gonna hurt her. Until now, Peaches didn't know pain.

CHAPTER THIRTY-TWO

If Junebug didn't keep his hair braided, he might have pulled it out. He was that vexed in response to the news regarding competition in his neck of the woods. And now, he was on the hunt for that skinny bitch, Brickhouse.

The day that Rose and Tucker came down to Fayetteville from New York City was a godsend to Aunt Julia's neighbors from The Grove. The woman that folks called High Yellow along with her buddy—the one with the outrageous head of Tina Turner hair and varicose-veined legs—both tried to keep their new contact a secret. But it was their friend Skinny, the woman everyone else knew as Brickhouse, who couldn't keep her mouth shut. Now, a swell of folks wanted to meet Tucker—who called himself "T"—in hopes of buying some blow. Many bypassed the usual visits to the video store on Merchants Road, and they bypassed visits to Preacher and his people who camped out at Kamikaze and at The Hideaway. The attitude that folks had was simple: find this man, and find him quick.

"A new king in town? Sheeiit, I gotta meet him. No, not tomorrow. Now."

"Yo, Brickhouse, you betta put me down with that good shit. Please?"

"Brickhouse!"

Everybody, it seemed, wanted a piece of Skinny lately. She was suddenly a liaison—maybe the only person who was willing to answer the impulsive hunger that Fayetteville addicts and recreational users had for Tucker's quality cocaine. But Brickhouse was also a very inconsistent woman; the same bone-thin, big mouth, drug addict who bought drugs from Blaze, and then Junebug, and then Preacher, and now Tucker. All the while, just to pay for her habit, she'd break into homes and cars, and she'd steal from the mall, to a point where the mall security banned her entry more than a dozen times. All of Fayetteville was open game for Brickhouse, the woman who even gave up her house for a high.

"That's about the last of it, Tuck. Soon as I load up the Dodge, we can get back to the city."

"Man, just when I was cleanin' up down h're." Tucker was weighing his product on his digital scale when Rose returned from his last outing. "Do you know how hungry these people are down here for good shit? For my good shit?"

"How hungry?" Rose responded, not as devoted to the game as Tucker was.

"The same gram that I sell in New York for twenty-five and thirty dollars is goin' for a hundred fifteen to one twenty-five down here. They're payin' cash. No questions asked. No consignment or credit. I even have Aunt Julia's friends returning two and three times a day." Tucker reached to his left, picked up a stack of money, and tossed it up in the air. "It's rainin' money down here."

"Maybe you should come back down and set up shop or somethin'."

"Are you kiddin'? Maybe I shouldn't leave at all! Only thing is I'm gonna run outta shit by tonight, or tomorrow morning at the latest."

"So we'll head back at noon tomorrow."

"Bet."

Rose took his bag of guns into the guest room and fell asleep while Tucker broke down the rest of his product, knowing that Brickhouse would be at the screen door within the hour. This was her third stop today, and Tucker already figured she was reselling the stuff. But it didn't matter to him.

• • •

Brickhouse took the bus across town—six times so far—until she had the resources to eventually catch a checkered cab to Ridgeway where Aunt Julia lived and where Tucker was making money hand over fist. Only, on this visit the skinny woman was not alone. Junebug and his boy, K-oss, were low-riding in a recently purchased white Mercedes CL600 with a convertible top. The two were parked far enough away where they could see but not be seen.

"Whose house is that?" Junebug asked K-oss.

"Pssshhh, shit if I know. I don't be hangin' out in the suburbs."

"Suburbs?" Junebug sucked his teeth. "This ain't no suburbs, only down the way from The Grove."

"Well, whatchu call it then?"

"Just a buncha houses. Ain't shit."

"Look." K-oss pointed as a bald-headed guy opened the screen door to let Brickhouse in. "Some dude I ain't never seen before."

Junebug sucked his teeth again, then said, "Well, new nigga or old nigga, that's gonna be a dead nigga if I see Brickhouse bounce outta there in the next two minutes."

"Why two minutes?"

"'Cause that's about how long it takes for a deal to go down. She takes out the money, he gives her the shit, and boom—done deal."

"I guess you right. There she goes."

Brickhouse skipped down the steps from the front porch and headed down Ridgeway. After a block or so, Brickhouse cut into a driveway where a rusting van was parked. Junebug slowly pulled out of the parking space. He and K-oss both gave the house a brief once-over. It had aluminum siding in an off-white tone. A closer look told Junebug that the house must be vacant as well, with its unkempt yard, tall grass and weeds, and piles of newspapers and circulars that hadn't been retrieved.

"That trick done found herself a spot to get off, June. Check 'er out."

Brickhouse was in the van by now. It was an old broken-down Volkswagen, one with rounded corners and dirty windows.

"Let's creep up on the bee-atch."

"Bet." K-oss had to smile.

Seconds later, both Grove boys were peepin' in the van window as best they could. Sure enough, Brickhouse was fixin' her high, thinking she was alone.

"Boo!" Junebug shouted.

Brickhouse hopped up in the seat and hit her head on the roof of the van.

"Oh shit!" she called out, holding the top of her head with both hands. Then, when she realized that her cocaine had fallen to the dirty floor of the van, she turned to curse her pranksters. "Junebug! Dang!!! Why you have to do that? Awwwe shit, Junebug! My stuff is all on the floor!"

"That's what you get for takin' your business to the competition, crackhead bitch!" Junebug slammed the door on Brickhouse. She was already on the floor, picking up what she could, even more desperate for that fix.

"Let's see that bitch-ass nigga," commanded Junebug. The two hopped back in the car and made a U-turn. K-oss was in the glove compartment, pulling out a Chinese-cheap 9mm pistol. It merely looked like it had a pearl handle.

"You gotta do better than this, June."

"You got somethin' betta?"

K-oss didn't answer. He just reached into his waistband and presented a larger pistol.

"What the fuck is that?"

"M-1. Got it from one of them army dudes. He said they popular in Israel. He brought it home."

"Damn. I ain't never seen nobody with one of those. I gotta git one."

"Ain't shit. I'll go see him tomorrow."

"But for now, I bet my nine will do the trick, 'cause if that nigga don't pack his shit on a dime, word to my motha, I'm gonna cap his ass."

The Mercedes was back in that far-off parking space

while Junebug and K-oss boldly stepped toward the house. Both of them pulled their Panther caps down low on their foreheads to conceal their eyes as Junebug knocked at the screen door. They stood with hands in pockets.

"Yeah?" the dude asked after opening the inside door. The screen filtered his presence, but he could be seen nonetheless.

"Brickhouse sent us. Said you had some good stuff."

"I don't know what you talkin' about. What stuff?"

"Some . . . you know . . ." Junebug rubbed his knuckle across his nose and sniffed audibly. "Stuff."

"Sorry, you got the wrong place. Bounce."

Tucker was clear and adamant about what he said and what he meant. He didn't expect a challenge from these two, and also felt especially empowered due to the artillery that was stashed in the house and out in the car. He sensed that his response was a little obnoxious, but so what. These dudes had some nerve to just step up like they did—all thugged-out—at a stranger's doorstep. Tucker, however, was totally unprepared for what happened next.

As soon as he said the word *bounce*, the lead thug forced his 9mm straight through the screen. He tore a hole there where his wrist, hand, and gun were now inches from Tucker's face.

"Open it, bitch-ass nigga."

"Hey, easy dog. I don't want no problems." Tucker had his hands half-raised now, trying to calm the gunman.

"I said open—the fuckin'—door!" Junebug insisted, while K-oss turned to scan the street and sidewalks.

Nobody seemed to be around except for the gunman, his tagalong, the broad daylight, and this gun in his face.

"No problem, whatever you say." Tucker was speaking to the two as if they were children or some naïve folk from down this way who might not be as cold-hearted as they appeared. He flipped the latch on the screen door and backed up as the two made their way over the threshold.

"Where's the shit?"

"I told you, you got the wrong—"

K-oss stepped past Junebug, who had the M-1 pressed tight against Tucker's head.

"You ain't from 'round here, is you, boy?" Tucker was shaking his head "no", but it was more of a shiver than a normal response. "Where you from?"

"U-u-up north. U-uh, Jersey," Tucker lied.

"Well you down our way now, boy. And I know we must be a couple 'bammas to you, some stupid niggas who don't know their heads from their ass. But ain't nothin' too dif-fer'nt 'tween you'n us. We thinks the same, we bleeds the same. Nah mean?"

Tucker's neck was craned back some, doing his best to go with the flow. He nodded slowly.

"Now, my dog here asked you where the shit was at. I suggest you git to gittin'. We ain't 'bout waitin'. We 'bout swissin' cheese up."

Tucker swallowed and his eyes suggested that the stash was in another room. Without explanations, the intruders followed him, both with the heat at point-blank range.

"Jackpot!" Junebug said at the sight of the table where cocaine was set in a small anthill, on a scale, and in tiny Zip-loc bags. There was also money everywhere. "See that now? That wasn't so hard, was it?"

There were a few seconds of silence, a time during which Junebug deliberated on what to do. It was this instance that he didn't count on. Some stranger doing the very same thing he did. He was black. He was making money, and probably a lot of it. But Junebug ignored his slight admiration to recog-nize that dude was violating.

"Lemme ask you something. Did you think you was gonna come on our turf, take our business, and that you wasn't gonna get no challenge? No problems?"

"Really, I—I didn't . . ."

"I-I-I . . . really . . . uh . . . er . . ." Junebug faked a stutter, a more exaggerated impression of Tucker. "You probly knew exactly what you was doin'."

"No, I—"

"Ain't nobody said speak," said K-oss with the pistol leveled again. Just before anyone could think of what to do next, there was the sound of gunmetal sliding back and forth, its deadly *clack-clack* grabbing everyone's ears.

"We got problems, Tuck?" The voice was suddenly the most pleasing moment of Tucker's whole life.

As the two intruders turned to see what and who, Tucker leaped forward to snatch the M-1 from K-oss. For some reason, Tucker felt this guy to be more dangerous than the talkative one with the slick eyes.

"Not anymore, we don't," Tucker snapped back. "Lemme get that up off you, dog." Tucker pointed the M-1 at Junebug. Still, Junebug didn't budge. His 9mm was still level with Tucker's waist.

"Naw, that's aiight. I'm keepin' this here. You could shoot me if you want, but the one shot I do get off is gonna be right atcha dick, nigga."

"You's a smart-ass 'bamma, ain'tcha?" Rose said. "See if you understand this." With that said, Rose brought the Uzi up so that the nose was an inch from Junebug's temple. "This here will blast about fifteen slugs in your skull with a single squeeze of the trigger. You could go 'head and shoot my boy's dick, 'cause that shit gets him in too much trouble anyway. But me? I'm gonna paint the walls in here with your brain in about two seconds."

"Rose! Junebug! Tucker! What's goin' on up in here?" Nobody noticed that Aunt Julia had entered the house. All in attendance suddenly realized this was wrong. If Aunt Julia knew everyone by name, if she was just as concerned for one as she was for the next, then something was indeed out of whack. "Put them guns away in my house." She said this as a blanket statement. When they procrastinated, she put her hands on her hips as emphasis that she meant what she had said.

Aunt Julia sat the young men down and made further introductions. She talked about how she changed Junebug's diapers when he was a snot-nosed infant. She spoke on

Rose's father—her brother—and how they grew up and apart before he was sent to the penitentiary for murder.

All of these revelations made Rose and Junebug feel like family; cousins, as opposed to enemies. They talked about the drug game, the gun game, and made arrangements to work together. Why did they have to fight? There was enough money to go around. Besides, why would Tucker even need to come down if Junebug already had Fayetteville in check?

Finally, Rose gave Junebug a 9mm—a real gun, he told him—for his personal stash, and he kissed Aunt Julia good-bye. There was no sense staying any longer. This was Junebug's house . . . his turf. He'd buy his product from Tucker from now on.

Whew.

If it don't rain, it mothafuckin' pours," said Junebug when one of his runners escorted Peaches to his crib at The Grove projects. She was wearing a pair of bulky sunglasses that were very dark and almost resembled the masks that carpenters use to keep sawdust from their eyes. A bandage was over one eye. A piece of it could be seen there under the glasses. Her left arm was in a sling and her lip was swollen.

"What the fuck happened to you?" he asked with absolutely no compassion in his voice or manner.

Peaches dropped her head in guilt. Her speech was slurred, somehow stuck between her throat and blood-stained lips.

"What? I can't understand you."

"I said, I was robbed, I was raped, and they beat me up," Peaches managed to say.

Junebug's head bounced as he asked, "Whatcha mean, robbed? Robbed for what?"

"At home, June. At h-h-home . . ." Peaches began to sob.

Junebug stood with his hands on his hips, looking over at K-oss with a "do you believe this shit" expression.

"Peaches, look at me." He was up on her now, his hand raising her chin. "Tell me they—*whoever* it was—didn't get my dough." Peaches turned her head away, slipping from his hand and back to that certain level of guilt.

"Fuck!" Junebug blasted, reading Peaches' silence as the worst-case scenario. Then he stopped himself from grabbing Peaches, turning away like a babbling, rumbling suppressed volcano.

K-oss was reserved about the whole thing. For one, he believed nothing he heard, and only half of what he'd seen. Moreover, his sixth sense told him that there was a little more to this story than he was willing to believe. He asked himself, who in their right mind would take so much money? Not only that, how would they know to hit Peaches' apartment if nobody but her and Junebug were aware of the stash?

His hunch took him to The Hideaway the following weekend. He made the excuse of wanting to "release some stress for a few hours" so that Junebug wouldn't expect him to hang out the way they usually did. K-oss knew that Junebug was going into Durham on Saturday to a club called The Power Company. Since he'd be going with two carloads, K-oss figured he wouldn't miss the extra man.

On Saturday night, The Hideaway was ass-thick with college students. They ordered pitchers of draft beer and plates of fifteen-cent hot wings, and they were absorbed in the skippin', hoppin', jumpin' and shoulder-rockin' dances that hip-hop music encouraged. A deejay was spinning and cutting prime selections by every rapper from the Dirty South to Brick City.

To a foreigner, this all might seem a bit too reckless—how the young women tantalized circles of men with their shredded T-shirts and shorts that wedged up between their ass cheeks. The men, in turn, were guzzling down beer, smoking weed out in the open, and aiming to outdo the next man for a woman's attention.

K-oss knew that this definitely wasn't what Mommy and Daddy expected of their collegiate offspring. But this was the release, the way to vent after so much pressure from teachers, from parents, and from peers. The college life wasn't all that it was made out to be, not on the surface anyhow.

In a corner of The Hideaway, K-oss noticed a group more outrageous than the next, with every man holding a bottle of Dom P., Moët, or Cristal in hand, either raised high like a flag, swinging in concert to the music, or pressed to his lips. They stood in a semicircle, enough so that others could get a peek in on the action. The action was a couple of bootylicious dancers dressed in thongs and frilly tops. They were barefoot and exhibiting provocative body language, sultry innuendos with their eyes, and all the rest. The guys were obviously closely associated, in each other's ear, trading eye contact, and equally loose with the money.

K-oss recognized Preacher at once. He was passing out money to these guys like an ice machine dropping ice. Endlessly. The guys would tip the girls in the same breath, throwing money away on cheap thrills, encouraging the women to become as loose and raunchy as they wished.

K-oss watched this go on for most of the night. He didn't have to guess what the big toast was about. He didn't have to be a mind reader to see why there was so much elation among Preacher and his crew.

Preacher had that damn money.

And as much as K-oss knew the truth, he also knew to keep his mouth shut. He knew that to say something to Junebug would lead to trouble. It meant that Junebug would want to attack Preacher and everything he called near and dear to him. But K-oss knew that to try something like that—something that the hyper, impulsive Junebug would most certainly call for—would mean suicide. Junebug may have been from the street. He may have lived and breathed the thug life. But Preacher, by his presence alone, was smart. And smart always won over all else.

CHAPTER THIRTY-THREE

If you can look up, you can get up," was a famous quote by a famous man. And even if Junebug didn't read much more than the digital screen of his cell phone, he knew what that famous man meant: that there was a way to come back from this. He could bounce back just as a broken bone heals to be stronger than it ever was.

Now that he had his New York connect, Junebug could outdo any dealer in the Carolinas. Tucker told him that the supply was infinite. He also said he'd consider consigning the product once Junebug showed him some promising numbers. Junebug saw that as his gateway to the promised land. Like going into a bank vault with permission to walk out with whatever he wanted.

Things began to snowball. Peaches was history. No more chickenheads to fuck up his money. She was lucky he didn't rape her and beat her too on top of all else she had endured. Once he relieved himself of that burden, he was free of the boy-girl games; free to expand into other towns like Durham, Raleigh, Chapel Hill, and Lumberton. He set up things the same way he did in Fayetteville. Duplicity, they called it.

From the measly two kilos that he took from the now-imprisoned Blaze, Junebug turned his two-bit hustler's lifestyle into a $60,000-a-week cash machine. And the numbers were just beginning. After months of dealing, Tucker soon introduced Junebug to the meth game—how to mix methamphetamine into the cocaine, creating that dire physical addiction that had folks strung out, paranoid, and shaking uncontrollably. All of his users were now languishing with that incurable medical emergency. The fix had become a priority over eating, sleeping, family, and sex. It was get high or die for literally thousands of people, both young and old, throughout Junebug's network.

But one person's loss was another person's gain. Junebug was now "the man." He had women, as young as seventeen and as old as forty-four, sucking his dick before asking him for money, and never the other way around. He had a number of vehicles now: the BMW, the Benz, the Range Rover, the newest Toyota Camry, and in a few weeks, he vowed, the latest Jaguar. Other possessions included a $90,000 wardrobe, including the leather jackets, slick furs, and the best footwear money could buy. All of Junebug's tastes and favorites were now worn on his back, driven through the hood, or just experienced for the thrills they were. He ran through money like it was drinking water.

For entertainment, many dealers spent their time at the strip clubs and social clubs. They bought their group of thug buddies the top-shelf champagnes, studied the faces and bodies of women, and amidst all the movement, the music, and the marvels of human flesh, agendas were discussed regarding deals done and deals to be done, as well as issues and concerns of the day.

Just as Junebug and his group were part of the underground nightlife, so too was Preacher and his subordinates. Junebug was as familiar with Preacher's game as Preacher was with Junebug's. Fayetteville may have been remote and small in comparison to many other cities, but it was not the home of the stupid. Both groups generally gravitated to their respective spots in the club, whether it was at Kamikaze or The Hideaway. On occasion, they'd send a bottle of bubbly over as a sign of respect: "Champagne, sir. Compliments of the fella in the corner."

Preacher was the first to make such a gesture, and Junebug immediately thought it was a diss. But K-oss read between the lines and told Junebug, "He's really sayin' he respects you. If he wanted to diss you, he'd send you a bottle of Wild Irish Rose or Mad Dog 20/20."

Junebug considered that and said, "I guess. But I'm still feelin' funny 'bout that nigga, like he mighta had somethin' to do with that jack a while back."

K-oss was quiet.

"You agree? Or you just ain't speakin' on it?"

"I can't agree 'cause I wasn't there."

Junebug twisted his lips.

"So, no, I ain't speakin' on it."

"Sometimes I think you know more than you sayin'."

K-oss returned the twisted grin. It made Junebug turn back toward Preacher, wondering if he really did have something to do with the robbery. He also thought about Peaches.

The local police in Fayetteville had been watching Junebug and Preacher for a while now. Over the months, many drug users from the area were arrested for one reason or another. Some were snagged in the course of a breaking and entering, and others thereafter, when they tried to sell what they stole. Users were also infamous for starting or being involved in family disputes and arguments with neighbors. They were violent and abusive to their friends, family members, and children—and to themselves. They were usually unsuccessful in the business of selling dope themselves, which led to someone's murder or someone's arrest.

All of these activities filled the courtrooms, the local lockups, the county jails, the state and federal prisons, the halfway houses and drug treatment programs. All of this was a very routine part of the drug culture, a culture that is sometimes (not always) wrongly confused as a crime as opposed to a social ill. Still, those that professed hatred for the game couldn't help but to see that there was also a love for the economics. From the many who are employed, including judges and law enforcement, to all of the many services and agencies and contractors that depend on this routine, the wheels and mechanisms of the game continue to crank and spin.

As much as police depended on the economics of the trade, they had a bad taste for some of the characters that the trade encouraged. In Fayetteville, detectives saw Preacher as the savvy one. They knew he didn't deal from his home on Hillcrest, and that he had stash houses somewhere. But Preacher, in their opinion, wasn't obnoxious or arrogant with his game. Not like Junebug was.

Junebug created a bad taste with the locals. Perhaps the locals didn't agree that he was deserving of his coming up in the game so fast and furious, and still using The Grove projects, which was government-subsidized housing, as his headquarters. Not only that, there were several overdoses and three homicides that were linked to The Grove. All of it, they presumed, was due to Junebug and his thug approach to the drug trade.

See this shit? I'm not even drivin', and mothafuckas is followin' me," said Junebug.

"Calm down, dog. They ain't pulled us over yet, so don't get all twisted up."

"Yet. You said they didn't pull us over yet. That shit is a prophecy if I ever heard one, K-oss."

"Chill."

"Yo, Twiggy, make a left up here at the corner," Junebug said, and then he reached up to the Range Rover's dashboard panel. Ja Rule's voice and music suddenly went silent. A moment later, Junebug cursed and said, "See. I can't even go out for a fuckin' joyride without them DTs on my ass." Junebug fell back in his seat, somehow defeated. Then, as if a lightbulb went off in his head, he went into his pockets. He pulled a thick roll of bills from one pocket, peeled off three one-hundred-dollar bills, and passed the rest to K-oss. He reached down to his ankle and pulled up his sweatpants. The 9mm that Rose had given to him was wedged in a neat nylon holster, strapped to his skin. Junebug made it tighter.

"Whatcha doin'?" asked K-oss.

"I'm jettin'. I got a funny feelin' tonight's the night."

"Man—"

"Yo, kill that shit, dog. Just work wit' me. Every movie I've ever seen about the game—any game—got motha-fuckas trapped because they couldn't make the right deci-sion at the right time. They ain't follow they instincts. My instincts say jet. So I'mma jet. You'll be aiight 'cause ain't shit in the truck. Lock yo' piece in the floor like usual, just in case. And I'll see you 'round the way."

"I still think you trippin'."

"Twiggy, slow up just enough to catch the red light at Crawford."

When the Range Rover reached the intersection, Junebug took a deep breath, pushed open the rear passenger side door, and strolled off down Crawford. Twiggy was directed to head in the opposite direction. And Junebug already told himself that if the unmarked Chevy followed him, instead of the Range Rover, he was gonna take off.

Without turning around or even looking over his shoul-der, Junebug sensed the dark vehicle tailing him. By now, it was almost sundown. He took long, but not fast, strides while he calculated what his next move would be. The single-family homes along Crawford were so close together it was hard to see what obstacles might face him, but he knew this area well enough to make a go of it.

Junebug shot through a driveway where a car was parked. The area between the vehicle and the home was narrow enough where he almost had to shuffle sideways. He took a glance behind him. The unmarked car pulled over, blocking the driveway. An emergency strobe light had been turned on and flickered throughout the nightscape.

The realization was a rush for Junebug, who was now sprinting into a stranger's backyard. Since he had once been a member of the track-and-field team at Stonewall, Junebug was accustomed to running and jumping fast. The fence in the backyard wasn't higher than his chest, but it was high nonetheless. He picked up speed as he approached, and reached out to leverage his weight so that he'd hurl himself over feet first. A sharp edge of the fence caught Junebug's sweatpants and they ripped. Half strung up on the fence, Junebug cursed and worked himself free. At the time, he didn't even realize that he was bleeding. The backyard Junebug climbed into was riddled with children's toys: a Big Wheel, two bicycles, a kiddie pool, and a dollhouse. He negotiated his way around the dollhouse, heading for a gate, all the while imagining the cops circling the block. Maybe, he thought, one was chasing him on foot as well. Still, he was too shaken to think about that. He just assumed the worst.

Junebug reached the edge of the driveway without incident and guessed which way the police would come. Something in the back of his mind told him he was on Hillcrest. Then he saw the police vehicle rounding the corner way down the block. He didn't think they could see him there slinking up to a tree, but he knew he had to get going, and quick.

Now he knew he was on Hillcrest. A few houses down the way, a turquoise blue Jaguar was parked in the driveway of a brick-faced home. There was only one person who had that car in this town. Preacher.

Junebug knew this because the turquoise model was one of a kind, one that Preacher got to before Junebug did. It wasn't that Junebug couldn't afford it, either. The salesperson at Two Towns, the local dealership that sold luxury cars, sold it behind his back. The guy promised to hold it for Junebug and didn't even extend a courtesy call to let him know to come in and pick it up. Junebug didn't find out about the missed opportunity until he saw the car on Merchants Road, with Preacher in the driver's seat. It was a diss, but not important enough to kill a salesman over.

Preacher paid for police protection. It was the only way to insure his thriving empire. Also, if there was a power-hungry, gung-ho cop about to swoop down on him, he'd get the phone call well in advance. It would enable him to move whatever product or cash that was targeted, therefore avoiding a loss.

Because Preacher had cops on the payroll, the frantic

knocking at his front door was unusual. It was the kind of knocking that indicated an emergency of some sort. It made him stop what he was doing to peek out of the front window. Seeing Junebug outside, fidgeting as though he had to go to the bathroom and knocking as if good sense had gone out of style, was a laughable sight at first. But there was obvious desperation on his competitor's face. Sweat. Worry. He was even calling Preacher's name over and over.

Thinking that this emergency might somehow concern himself, his home, or his car, Preacher hurried to the door with a gun wedged in his waistband.

"What?"

"The po-lice is after me. Let me in. Come on—let me in." Junebug was almost out of breath. Preacher was about to ask what the police had to do with him, about to tell Junebug to step off, but he reconsidered. After all, the guy did send him a bottle of champagne a few weeks back, returning his gesture and all.

Against his better judgment, Preacher opened the door. "Hurry up," he said, realizing that the police were closer than he thought. He quickly shut the door behind Junebug.

"Thanks. Them niggas won't leave me alone."

Preacher told himself it paid to have cops on the take. He was peeking outside again. "Don't thank me yet," he said. "This way." There was a knock on the door as Preacher led Junebug into another room, and hid him inside a closet. "I'll get rid of 'em," he told Junebug. But before he answered the front door, he had one other bit of business to tend to. He poked his head into the bedroom. "Listen," Preacher said in a low tone, "stay put. We have an unexpected visitor. He won't be here long."

"Will do, daddy. Just hurry back. We don't have much time, plus I'm horny." Peaches was half undressed, far past the seduction stage of their little get-together.

Preacher knew she was right, too. Tabitha was expected to close the shop soon, and so far, he'd been doing a good job juggling the two women without conflict.

• • •

Yes, officer?"

"We're looking for a colored kid, about so tall, with braided hair and a blue sweat suit."

"Nobody here by that description, sir."

"You mind if we look around in your yard out back?"

"Of course not, officer. Take all the time you need. We need more dedicated policemen like you . . . keeps the neighborhood safe." Preacher sent the police back on their chase and turned back to Junebug. But Junebug had a suprise housewarming gift for Preacher.

"So it was you," guessed Junebug. He had a fist full of Peaches' hair in one hand and the 9mm in the other. "You ma'fuckas set me up."

Peaches was wincing, but Junebug twisted her hair harder.

"Owww!"

"Shuddup, trick. I can't be-lieve I fell for you."

"Yo, easy, playa. I just saved you from the po-po out there."

"Yeah. Good look. Too bad they can't help ya now. Where is five-o when you need 'em."

Peaches whimpered enough for Junebug to grow irritated. He tossed his ex-girl to the floor and stomped the sole of his Timberland boot into her pretty face—no hesitation.

"Yo, dawg. There gotta be a way we can work this out. Ain't nothin but homies in here."

"True that. One homie who's breathin', and another who ain't."

BOOK FIVE

CHAPTER THIRTY-FOUR

In the shadow of Manhattan's skyscrapers, Bronx County is a brick city. It's a maze. It's alphabet soup, and the residents are the letters. The Bronx is congested with apartment buildings, no parking zones, and multilingual inner-city living. The busiest areas, with their loud subway sounds, offensive odors, and hordes of people, make the borough seem overpopulated. But to the many hundreds of thousands who call the Bronx their home, this is all they know. It's acceptable. For others, the heavy traffic, the puzzle of streets, alleys, and passages, the overall confusion serve as a haven. It provides a sense of security despite the hard, cold image the world might see. For the criminal-minded, the Bronx is one massive illusion; a machine that provides secrecy for evils unknown, for dangers yet to come, and for the city's worst enemies.

Roscoe grew into that very monster. He was the reject, the throwaway, the neglected. All of the oppression, the misery, the hate—all those cats made Roscoe their best friend. He was the scapegoat who didn't die off or fade away. He merely grew corrupt and ready to victimize. The shadiest parts of the Bronx protected Roscoe's activity. Fertile ground for his lawlessness.

Roscoe and his Mo' Money Brothas—Ras-Terhane, Tec-9, and Rook—had the ultimate method for gettin' paid. To say they were merely experienced at robbery was the understatement of all time. The way these four thugs ran up on drug dealers was no less precise than a Special Forces squad and how they executed a rescue or an invasion. Their tools included high-caliber pistols, automatic assault weapons, and duct tape. Their track record was an undefeated forty-one robberies. They preferred to control each heist so that there would be no casualties, but some targets chose to be heroes. Those were now dead heroes.

All four members of MMB were bullshittin' this evening, smoking a thick spliff of weed between them. They were watching a laptop DVD player in the black Jeep Cherokee, parked in the lot at the McDonald's drive-thru where Fordham Road meets Southern Boulevard. It was almost dark now, and the jeep blended in with other vehicles that recently passed through or whose passengers were inside the restaurant getting their grub on.

"I know you ain't buy this ting, Roscoe. Me ain't known you to spend more 'n fifty dollas on nuttin' before."

"You right, Ras. Times is tight. This is from the load we caught comin' out of JFK. If you want one, just say the word."

"Nah, mon. I ain't wit' all dis technology. It look good, though."

Roscoe was speaking on the heist the guys had pulled off weeks earlier. It was an eighteen-wheeler coming from JFK Airport, filled with various electronics. Tec-9 and Ros-Terhane provided additional support for the holdup, but never got involved with the top-level interactions, such as the distribution of the goods, nor did they have an opportunity to see the actual contents.

"You sure?" Roscoe asked.

"I'm sure," Ros-Terhane answered and continued watching the screen.

"Them girls wasn't no joke out there, boy. Check that one, there with the big ass." Tech-9 pointed to a woman walking across the screen, one of many who the guys recorded with a DVD camera. They usually carried the camera with them to capture nightclub events or big gatherings like this one. The event they were now watching was the yearly assembly that took place at Grant's Tomb. The camera mainly recorded hot girls who showed the most skin, or the attractive ones who didn't. The men in the picture were just a backdrop, along with throngs of others and vendors who sold food, drink, and various Afrocentric goods. But Roscoe and his band of ruffians were only checkin' for eye candy, tits and ass, and things to thrill them . . . something to pass time.

"Yo, dog! There's that nigga Freeze." Tec-9 said this even as a sea of ethnic images passed to and fro across the screen.

"Where?"

"Rewind that joint, Rook!"

Rook depressed a button and the images raced by in reverse.

"That's good. Right there," said Tec-9. "Yeah, here it comes, right after the big-hip woman with the baby carriage. Okay, you there in the shorts and tank top. Hold that still, Rook. Can you stop that tape?" Tec-9 didn't have any idea how ignorant his statement was, since a DVD is not a tape at all.

"He's rollin' a little light, ain't he?" Freeze's image was suspended there on the screen. He wore shorts and a tank top. His jewels, the diamond Rolex and medallion draped around his neck, glistened.

"I count him havin' one dude with him. But the way he's dressed, he definitely don't look like he packin'. More like he profilin'. This woulda been a good time to run up on him."

"Nah . . ." Roscoe said. "Then wasn't the time. I wanna catch him when he's home, or in the middle of a business deal. Even if we run his car off the highway, I can get with that. But it gotta be when he least expects it."

"Word."

"So . . . we wait. We watch, and we wait. He's gonna catch it. Believe me, he's gonna catch it."

• • •

Rose and Tucker had just returned from North Carolina, possessed with the fatigue and irritation that comes with long drives. All of that, including the tolls, the traffic, and having to continuously watch for troopers, only to return to Striver's Row, to have to climb all those steps to the fifth floor. It was enough to make a man dizzy. Tucker could've fallen out from exhaustion the first time he climbed these steps. But now that he was by his cousin's side so frequently, the climb became routine.

At the top of the third set of steps, turning to climb the fourth, Tucker jumped back in surprise. Misa was right there in his face.

"Uh-huh. Ain't nothin' like a scared-ass nigga."

"What the—" Tucker had bumped into Rose, immediately triggering a response.

Rose was already reaching for his waist. Then he finally saw that pretty face; the body that he'd already seen naked more than a dozen times. Rose melted into relief. "Bitch, you gonna make a nigga kill yo' ass."

"As long as you do it thorough, mothafucka. Where you been?" Misa was already stepping past Tucker, practically leaping to embrace Rose. She could've been a cat clinging to the side of a tree for dear life.

"Business. But, uh, how'd you get in here?" Rose asked, suddenly remembering that the building was locked to everyone except residents.

Misa didn't point. She merely turned and indicated with her eyes. She wasn't alone. Chanté was sitting there, a few steps up, slouched back with a smug expression.

"Hmmm. I forgot about you and your rebel sister," Rose said, as if Chanté wasn't there. Then he addressed Chanté specifically, saying, "You betta be careful you don't pick the wrong lock one day."

"No, *you* betta be glad we ain't already inside your place, relaxin' like we own it." Chanté was rolling her head with her statement, suppressing a smile.

"Try me," Rose shot back, his eyes obviously enjoying the repartee.

"Bend over, and I just might."

Tucker couldn't help but to laugh.

Misa just said, "Y'all are a trip. Maybe you two need to be fuckin'."

"Naw, baby, I'll leave the dirty work to you."

Tucker laughed louder.

"You got that one," Rose said with submission, still promising some get-back at another time.

The four friends went into the fifth-floor apartment and Wolf was let out of the back room to do his little meet-n-greet before he climbed out onto the fire escape and up to his usual rooftop romp.

"So, what y'all been up to?" Rose asked Misa.

"Maaaan—did we have some drama while you was gone," Chanté answered for Misa.

"Drama, like what?"

"Charmaine, for one," Misa elaborated. "She got into this big fight with her boyfriend. I'm talkin' knives, blood—all that. The nigga ended up with a buck-fifty across his cheek."

Rose didn't change his expression like Tucker did, wincing as if he was the one to endure the cut and the hundred and fifty stitches.

"Trina happened to show up just when it got messy. She got Charmaine outta there before the cops came."

"Where she at now?" Tucker asked, somewhat revealing his affection for Charmaine, with her stolen diamonds and arrogant attitude.

Misa looked over at Chanté before divulging the secret. If she could be truthful with anyone, it had to be Tuck and Rose. "At Trina's place, for about a week now. She should be safe there."

"But what about Iris and Liza? Ever since Liza's man as executed by the Nieta, they've been threatenin' those girls somethin' fierce. Now that's some beef there." Chanté held a serious expression.

"What kind of threats?"

"Iris has a cat named Scruples. Had, that is. One a' them boys killed Scruples. Then they rubbed the dead cat's blood all over her pink Suzuki," Chanté finished explaining.

"I'm even hot about that," Misa interjected.

"So where are they now?"

"Over my spot," Chanté said. "If I wasn't tired of all the company already, Misa woulda come here alone. Sometimes a girl gotta have her privacy, feel me?" Chanté expressed with pursed lips, a little disgruntled.

"So . . . all you big-time gangsta bitches done curled up to hide from the big bad wolves."

Chanté took Tucker's statement more serious than not. She took off her dark Ray-Ban glasses to show him her steel-eyed gaze. Then she said, "Most of our problems originate with niggas like you!" Chanté's head was rolling around on her neck again. "You mothafuckas lean on us for our bodies, our minds, and our good credit, and then you leave a bitch out to dry. Mothafuckin' dogs, alla y'all."

Tucker was about to respond, but Rose said, "Chill that shit, dog. Can't you see they got serious problems here?"

"Listen." Misa wanted to take her visit to the next level. "I appreciate all the concern for us and our problems. But we're grown-ass women. We can handle this. Meanwhile, I came here for one reason—and one reason alone." Misa was hugging Rose again, more determined now. "How about breakin' me off somethin' proper, lover?" Rose didn't look down, but Misa's legs were rubbing together, craving him between them. Now she was kissing him.

Chanté turned away and happened to see Tucker, who had the nerve to look her way. She just sucked her teeth and rolled her eyes at him. Before things got hot and heavy, Misa's two-way pager went off.

"It's Trina. She wants to see me—says it's an emergency."

Rose shrugged. It was his way of approving a visit, although all of Misa's Hot Girls had been up to his place a few times already.

The wait for Trina spoiled things for Misa's physical needs. She took forty-five minutes. When she finally arrived, Rose buzzed her in. When Rose went to let her in his apartment, there was all sorts of commotion outside of his door. Trina had Charmaine and the Fuentez sisters with her. Both Charmaine and Liza were helping Iris over the threshold. Iris was visibly sick, with tearstained cheeks, trying to catch her breath. Rose couldn't tell if it was all those steps or if something else was wrong with her.

Misa asked, "What's wrong? What happened?"

Tucker and Chanté were on their feet now.

"I'll get her something to drink," said Tucker, already on his way to the kitchen.

"I . . . swear . . . it wasn't my fault!" Iris spit the words out, and now the tears were streaming again. Liza tried to control her sister's shaking.

"Oh shit! What the fuck is going on? What isn't her fault??"

"Something went down," Trina said to Misa, her eyes explaining a lot more than her lips were.

"I swear . . ." Iris cried. "He was playin' me! He didn't think I'd do it." Then Iris said to her sister, *"Le juro a Dios que no lo queria matar."*

And Liza replied, *"Tranquila, hermana, tranquila. Tu estas bien aqui."*

Rose was trying like mad to figure all this out, and then Spanish set in. Now, he swore he was about to lose his mind. "Misa . . ." he said in a warning tone. "Liza, please let us know what's going on before I fuckin' explode."

"Iris, she . . ." Liza began, but Trina tapped her shoulder, as if this was a relay race and it was Trina's turn to run with the baton.

"Misa . . . we went out."

"You what?"

"We went . . . out." Trina's eyes dilated to emphasize.

"But, how could you? Without us?" Misa indicated herself and Chanté.

"It looked easy. We wanted to impress you, I guess."

"Well, I'm real impressed. Real fucking impressed. What happened?"

Trina didn't say. She cut her eye as if to need privacy.

"Ain't shit to hide now, chile. They already know most of our business. Might as well tell it all."

"It was easy, Meese. It was—"

Charmaine was by Trina's side, nodding in agreement. "Four of us—two of them."

"Two of who?" Rose cut in.

"Maybe you should start from the beginning," said Charmaine. "Fill him in."

"Baby, we—the girls and I—have been, well . . . doin' stickups." Misa stopped there to see how that would digest.

"You? The girls and you . . . stickups?" Rose blurted the idea in dribs and drabs. He couldn't believe what he was hearing.

"Yeah! What? Females can't do stickups?"

Rose was thinking to himself, Apparently not, but the timing wasn't appropriate. More on that later. Now, all he wanted to know was what happened. Rose looked at Tucker, wondering if he knew about this. Tucker had just handed Iris a glass of OJ. Then he raised his hands as if to say he didn't know jack about what was going on.

"We been doin' stickups, Rose."

"Been. As in, before you met me?"

"No, after. But we did a lot of 'em."

"A lot?! What's your real name? Bonnie???"

"Yeah, and you're my Clyde." Misa may not have meant to, but the way she said that set some blame on Rose, as though it was him who got her into this.

"Oh, so the gun you bought from me that night, the other gun I gave you? They weren't really for what you said? Protection?"

"Yes, Rose, they were . . . at the time. I mean, Iris and Liza already had a beef. Plus, we were gettin' money here and there. Shit was hot. We needed weapons."

"Yeah . . . but?"

"But what? I sold all the coke you and Tuck been givin' me . . ."

"You mean Tuck. Tuck alone. I don't deal drugs, remember? I'm the gun man."

"Oh—right. Well, we sold all of it. We started gettin' more beef. Dealers tellin' us we can't do shit around their turf. So—okay—we backed off. But, we came back. We rolled up on a few of them. Surprise!!!"

"Did you do this on your motorcycles? I mean, how obvious? Six bitches on Suzukis. You'd be the talk of the town, standing out like neon signs."

"Nah. We might be a little dizzy, but we ain't dumb. We got this rent-a-wreck, ya mean? We had masks 'n shit. Duct tape and blades . . ." Chanté filled in the blanks. Rose looked at Tucker again. Tucker now returned the "I don't believe this shit" expression.

"Y'all seriously doubt us, don't you?" Trina added, looking at Tucker with knowing eyes. Was this the one who was hiding his feelings for me? What? Did he think I was soft?

"It ain't like that, Trina. I guess we just—"

"You was just checkin' for tits and ass, huh?"

"Yes, they was," added Charmaine.

"Well, rock-a-bye, baby!" Chanté joined in with her favorite movie line. And even Rose could see now that Chanté was a shoo-in for a black version of Lolita.

"Okay. So now you know," Misa said to Rose. Then she turned to Liza and her sister. "What I wanna know is what went down tonight."

"It was a few hours ago," Liza said, with the whole Spanglish flavor in her words. "We were at the Bay Plaza theaters, just caught that joint called *Smuggle*. So we're chillin' in the lot, passin' a spliff, then we see these Jamaicans, or maybe they was Trinis. I can't tell the difference, but they had that spicy accent goin' on. They was weighted *down*, man! I mean, bling-bling-*bling*! As if they were the most untouchable mothafuckas on the earth. So we was like, yo momi, let's do this. So we followed them bum-bitches to this spot up on Westchester Avenue over near that big subway station."

"Parkchester," Tucker clarified.

"Right. Well, they went into this little spot for a minute, like they had that jerk chicken and shit. We sent Charmaine and Iris in. They started hittin' on them, that whole hands-on bit. So, you know, they suckered them dudes. And the next thing you know, they left the shop and one of them must've lived right next door, 'cause that's where they went."

"Then I signaled Trina and Liza, and I opened the door for them," Charmaine interrupted. "But when I got upstairs, Iris already had the nine on them. Both of 'em had their hands up. And there was just two of 'em."

Now Iris said, "They was on to you, Charmaine. They had some buzzer or somethin' . . . it went off when you opened the door downstairs. That's when I panicked. They started sayin' wild shit, callin' you bitch, and one of 'em reached under his shirt . . ."

"That's when I came in," Charmaine continued, "'cause Iris was like, mothafucka! And she was loud as shit. The dude started laughin', like it was all fun and games." Charmaine wagged her head, as if to say those dudes made a big mistake.

"Iris just flipped on them. I swear, I never saw this bitch act that way; like a whole different person. It was wild. Girl, you scared the shit outta me!" Trina exclaimed, and her hand went to her chest.

"So what happened then?" Rose asked.

"I . . . I couldn't trust it. He . . . he just kept laughin'. He moved—I thought for sure he was pullin' a gun . . . I . . ." Iris said, stumbling on her words.

"Oh shit!" Liza exclaimed. Her sister heaved right there in front of everybody. Vomit shot to the floor, some of it splattering on Liza's ankle. Iris ran to the toilet. Chanté followed closely behind to help her.

"Rose, Iris shot the dude—point-blank. Killed him."

"Shit!"

"Put one right where the wrinkles go. She vomited two times already. Couldn't handle it."

"Damn, y'all are like the six deadly venoms."

"There was only five of them," Charmaine said. "And besides, we're twice as deadly as venom."

"And you said you done a lot of these?"

"Probably a dozen. You remember that story they had on the cover of the *Post*? The bit above the Carnegie Deli?"

"Don't tell me."

"Do tell you."

"But, Trina . . . there was a kid that got shot there, a five-year-old child."

"Hold up, playa. I ain't tell ya the whole story. We rolled in there at just before midnight. We checked three dudes and a woman, four altogether. I swear—to—God. Only four. No kids. We taped up their wrists and their mouths. Then we grabbed six birds and forty in cash, and were out."

"No bodies?"

"Not one of us even fired a gun."

"So what's the paper talkin' about?" Tucker asked no one in particular, recalling how the *Post* featured the "Massacre Over Deli" story. There had been seven dead bodies, four men, two women, and a five-year-old, all shot execution-style four weeks earlier.

Liza shrugged, then said, "Believe me, that's been the twenny-five-thousand-dolla question all this time. The shit kept me awake for two nights. I even wanted to call Channel Four News to tell them that we didn't kill anyone. But you know I kept my mouth shut."

"Humph. I know you did," Charmaine said with a slight attitude. The Hot Girls spoke about their other experiences until Iris rejoined them. She seemed to be recuperating well.

"Hmmm . . ." Rose was seated now, wagging his head at the ceiling. "So we got Bonnie, Thelma and Louise . . . Catwoman . . . the goddamn black Lolita, and who are you supposed to be? Patti Hearst?" Rose was on a roll now, spittin' out all the female gangsta-bitches he knew of.

"Yeah, and I coulda been kidnapped, too, if it wasn't for my girls showin' up an hour ago," Misa replied, still referring to having sex.

Rose whispered something to her. She smiled and asked, "Until I'm hoarse?"

Rose nodded.

And Misa said, "Okay, I feel better now."

"As for the rest of you, this is how we're gonna handle things from now on." Rose went on to lay out preventive measures for the women. To the best of his knowledge, he figured the Nieta threat on Iris and Liza to be nothing but empty. Otherwise, he concluded, they would've "done them" already. "If we're gonna be a family, we gotta look out for each other. It means stayin' alive."

CHAPTER THIRTY-FIVE

Freeze, Squirrel, and Butch were at Manhattan Proper attending another of those Tuesday evening comedy shows that Stacy and Lisa promoted. So far, there was just the after-work crowd, and daylight still saturated the area at the front of the club where the bar was a bustle. Butch recalled the little altercation that Freeze had with Stacy—with her fine self—and this evening he assessed her attitude, wondering if she was still "in her feelings" about how cold the man was to her. Butch almost chuckled at the thought of how Freeze said he had finer hos than her that shine his alligator boots.

While Butch stood guard, assuring that nobody brought harm to Freeze, even so much as to bump him, Squirrel was going over figures for the week. He was sharp enough to do it by memory alone.

"Lucky came through, but he says things could change next week. Them bodegas? The Feds busted twenty-five of them over in Brooklyn, and a few in Queens, too. He thinks they're headed for the city, maybe even Harlem and the Bronx. He expects to cut his distribution by two-thirds."

"Two-thirds?" Freeze threw down a shot of Jamaican rum and cringed as it burned in his throat. "Two-thirds he'll take?"

"No. One-third he'll take."

"Goddamn, how the fuck can distributions go down when

the need is still out there? Ma'fuckin' crack addicts strung out all over town. They ain't even lookin' at the economy, employment, nothin'! When they need shit, they just rob, steal, or bend over."

"I dig it, but our only connect with the street is our middlemen, our buffers." Freeze remembered Squirrel speaking to him about a "buffer zone"—a protective shield that would keep Freeze from any exposure to unproven, low-level functionaries.

"All right, fuck it. What about the others?"

"Ms. Sharon is comin' up big-time. She got all them dignified women strung like dried garlic. Last week, she got fifty offa us. And there's no end in sight."

"She pay regular?"

"Yup, she pays regular."

"How 'bout that boy in North Cacka-lacka?"

"Preacher's usually does good. His last deal was sixty keys. He was back and forth between fifty and sixty. It's still good money."

"Whatcha mean, was?"

"Just that I ain't heard from him in a minute. But that could be anything. You know how he do; droppin outta sight for a week or two."

"Aiight. Who else?"

"De Jesus is pushin' forty keys now. He got the whole club gig on lock. I swear. He had one of his boys knock a nigga out at Roseland the other night for tryin' to sell shit."

"Good. I like a ma'fucka with some ethics."

"My only problems are Pops and Tuck. Pops got shot up over the weekend."

"You mean Mister I-think-I'm-thirty-years-old?"

"Yo! The dude is bangin' like four chicks all at the same time. Got 'em livin' in his Atlantic City suite—he stays in hotel rooms. But the nigga still can't get enough pussy. He gotta go screwin' around with this lesbian's girlfriend . . ."

"What?"

"Check it—he's over the lesbian's house bangin' her girl, and guess who shows up?"

"Get the—"

"No shit! The dike started bustin' guns like she was two-gun Crowley or Ma Parker or somethin'. Pops got hit like seven times. He's layin' up in a hospital somewhere. He's holdin' on strong though."

"So what's up with the money? Don't he owe us?"

"He was payin' good till he got shot."

"Can you reach his bitches? Maybe they can get somethin' together."

"I'm already on it. Tucker is the only one I'm vexed about. Between him and the bodegas, we was pushin' two hundred keys. Now, Tucker is buyin' from somebody else, and I already told you about the bodegas. We gonna be hit this go-round. Outta five hundred kilos we got, I can see more than two hundred sitting idle."

"Shit!" Freeze flipped his wrist and the empty shot glass flew off behind the bar to the floor. The sound of broken glass was only slightly audible with the music and conversations filling the club. Butch braced himself for any response. The few who did notice merely stayed alert. Lord only knew what kind of crazed nigga Freeze would turn into when the money wasn't right. Squirrel was a little shaken himself, but tried to control the others with his gestures and demeanor. His "calm" habit at work again.

"You wanna get out of here?" Squirrel asked Freeze.

"I wanna do a lot more than just get out of here. I wanna go cause trouble for Tucker just like he caused trouble for us."

"Whatever. I'm with it." Squirrel would support Freeze on anything, but this idea got him excited. Whatever Freeze had in mind was okay with Squirrel. Revenge sounded good right now.

For weeks since Tucker reneged on the 100 kilo order, Freeze had wanted an excuse to teach him a lesson. The only thing that held him back was Tonya, Tucker's sister. But Tonya must've called it quits since she hadn't gotten back with Freeze after he slapped her that day at the USA Diner. No visits, no messages, no nothing. The absence of

Tonya felt a lot like rejection, even though Freeze had a few project chicks he could call on anytime; even though the girl Denise from up on Church Avenue was available on the strength of a phone call; even though he had Karen, a white girl from up in Bronxville, who could swallow him three times in one night. All of this sex-to-order and Freeze still felt the scorn of one woman. And now that her brother jerked him, essentially severing Freeze from the Wall Street business, it was as if he'd been rejected twice. Add a few drinks, and there was every reason imaginable to be angry.

They were in the bulletproof Lincoln Navigator tonight, where Freeze had his Tec-9 under the driver's seat, a .45 in the glove compartment, and the pistol-gripped pump-action Maverick shotgun under the floor in the rear. Squirrel brandished his Mac-11 and replaced a conventional thirty-round clip with a concoction that had two of those thirty-round clips duct-taped together, back to back, so that when one was spent, the other would be readily available to pop into place. Butch was driving, but he generally wore a 9mm anytime he was out with the boys. Furthermore, since this appeared to be one of those times when things would get hostile, Butch fully intended to grab that .45 in the glove compartment.

Go away!" Tonya shouted from behind the door of the Wilson residence. Squirrel could see a piece of her face peeking out from behind a small window over the door knocker. The porch light was yellow compared to the moon above.

"I told you, Tonya, this ain't about you. I wanna see Tucker. Where he at?"

"I'mma tell you for the last time. You and that wannabe-James Brown and that other goon got thirty seconds to get the fuck away from my house, or else you gonna have all kinda surprises up yo' ass. Now try me."

"That's aiight. Y'all can't hide in the house forever. You gotta come out sometime." Squirrel turned to leave. Freeze and Butch were sitting in the Navigator, which was parked out in front of the residence.

Just then, the latch was thrown and the front door was pulled open. Tonya shot out of the door with a palm-size 9mm. She pointed it right at Squirrel's head.

"Hide? Hide?" Tonya's brow was furrowed, her head tilted slightly. "Ain't nobody in the Wilson family gotta hide, nigga. Especially me!" Tonya had been about ten feet from Squirrel. Now, she was six feet away. Squirrel was still, his arms down at his sides. "So? You take that bullshit back, or what?"

Tonya had determination in her manners, but there was that one instant where her eyes cast a hint of bewilderment. Squirrel didn't miss it.

"Tonya, now you know and I know that you ain't gonna shoot me in the middle of your front yard. Look around you. There's neighbors looking out they shit. Shoot me, and I'll be dead. But you'll be in prison for the rest of your life. Think about it." Squirrel was at ease now, despite the concern in his mind.

Tonya couldn't help but to look. Yes, the nosy-ass neighbors were all up in her business. And no, she didn't really wanna shoot Squirrel. But as Tonya's eyes roamed the area, they came to a screeching halt. Freeze was there in the Navigator, behind the tinted glass—she just knew it. Suddenly, the sting that had once throbbed across her cheek returned. The impact of Freeze's hand shook her again. It jolted her, and she snapped. Toya swung the pistol and pointed it at the Navigator. Then, she squeezed the trigger, and she kept squeezing. Bullets were bouncing and flying.

Squirrel flinched at the first shot. But once the disbelief was shaken off, he moved on Tonya. Swooping up under the weapon, Squirrel grabbed Tonya's arm and guided the bullets up into the night. He overpowered her and took the gun. In a fit of rage, he threw Tonya to the ground. Then he squeezed the trigger, emptying the remaining bullets into the grass near her body.

Tonya, almost in a fetal position, jerking with each shot fired, covered her head, scared to death.

"How's it feel, huh? Huh??" Squirrel threw the empty pistol at the house and broke a window. "I coulda killed you, girl." Squirrel took a quick look around. Too much attention. Folks were in their windows, blocking the indoor light within each neighboring home. "Tell your brother it's on . . . for real." Squirrel trotted back to the Navigator. He opened the passenger side door and jumped in. The truck raced off into the night.

L*ong after the police had come . . .*
    "Tucker, forget it! Don't even think of going home. Mom and Dad will probably have you arrested. Dad is especially mad right now. He said a lot of shit about a gun in the house, about Rose and his father's influence . . . about you and your dealing. You shoulda seen the police that came to the block. They almost locked me up."

"And how 'n the fuck does he know about me?"

"He already suspected it, Tuck. But tonight, when the shit went down in front of the house, right after the police left? Daddy sat me down and let me have it. And he was worse than the police, Tuck."

Tucker let out some air exhaustively, but over the phone it sounded like the steam pushing out of a hot iron.

"Tucker? You okay?"

"Am I okay? Am I okay? Girl, are you off your rocker? You just had shots fired at you an hour ago and you're askin' if I'm okay? You need a goddamned doctor to check your head."

"Just stay away from the house, Tuck. And be safe."

"What about you? Where you gonna stay?"

"Trust me. I'll be fine as long as there's a man who likes a pretty face and a nice ass."

"Yeah, but that's what got us into this trouble in the first place."

"Good night, Tucker."

Tucker hung up the phone and fumed. That pipsqueak mothafucka Squirrel looking for me? And he had the nerve to bust guns at my family's house? At my sister?

There wasn't much thinking left to do. Tucker stepped out of the bedroom. The girls were cross-legged and relaxed about the living room floor. Chanté had just pulled on a stick of weed. She was holding the smoke in her lungs now and passing the weed to Charmaine. Iris was a lot better now, having resolved her issues about taking a life. Trina was heavy into a tale about a recent sugar daddy she got over on. And Liza was tossing playing cards, trying to aim them for the potted plant against the wall.

Tucker ignored them all, taking stalwart steps to the second bedroom of the apartment. The door was unlocked and when he opened it, a rush of incense fragrance welcomed him. Rose was in the room with Misa on top of him, bucking like her life depended on it. They didn't notice Tucker, or how the candlelit atmosphere suddenly changed. Maybe they didn't care. Tucker knew just what he wanted. The most violent, most fearsome weapon he could find. He snatched up an M-16 assault rifle from the spread of weapons on the floor. It was just like the one they used in the movie *Heat*. Then he took up a box of magazines that he knew were loaded and which he'd seen Rose pop into the rifle's well at one time. The heaving, grunting, and moaning continued as Tucker tiptoed from the room.

Rose was just about to blast off when he opened his eyes. Or they opened themselves. He could see the silhouette of Tucker holding a rifle in the doorway, and then the door closed. With the exhilaration he was experiencing, it was hard to tell if it was a mirage he saw, or if that was his cousin taking a gun from the room.

As if lightning hit and in the midst of unfinished business, Rose swept Misa off of him. She was still caught up in the activity, even though she'd been removed. Her body convulsed and her face went through some torment. All of that while Rose hopped to his feet, wrapping whatever he could find around his naked body.

"Yo!" Rose called out. Tucker was already heading out of the entrance to the apartment. He hadn't yet opened the door. "Where you goin'?"

"I have some business to take care of."

"Business? With a fuckin' M-16 in your hands? Whassup?"

"Just some shit, Rose. I can handle it."

The girls didn't exist as far as these two were concerned. Their conversation was exclusive, as though nothing else mattered. In the meantime, about a half dozen eyes and ears were tuned in to every sight and sound.

"You can handle it. Can you believe this shit?" Rose asked, swinging his head around, finally acknowledging, or somewhat appealing to the others in attendance. Rose raised his voice. "Why don't you fuckin' relax and tell me what the hell is goin' on!"

Rose never had to talk to his cousin like that, but for now, it did the trick. Tucker took a deep breath and explained what happened up in Riverdale. The story got everybody wound up.

"So you were ready to go out with an M-16 and do what? Shoot up every Lincoln Navigator till you got the right one? Did you think this guy would be standing at the corner of one-two-five and Lenox, waiting for you to shoot holes in him? Wise up, cousin. Slow your roll, and wise up. There's a smart way to do things and a dumb way to do things. Let's take the smart way; the stay-alive way."

"What about my parents?"

"From what you've told me, there's too much exposure at your house now. Plus, the police are most likely investigating. Freeze may be a reincarnation of Jimi Hendrix, but he's no dummy. Here's where we use our heads."

$\mathscr{C}$HAPTER THIRTY-SIX

It was definitely too risky to be driving a black Lincoln Navigator around the Bronx, especially for Freeze. So the night of the altercation with Tonya, Freeze, Squirrel, and Butch drove straight to Atlantic City. They planned to stay there for the weekend, time enough for things to cool off in New York. Besides, Pops was out in A.C. and there was some money to see about.

Squirrel was the one to approach the receptionist in the lobby of Atlantic City General Hospital. He told the woman he was in from out of town to visit his uncle.

"I only know him as I've always known him by his nickname 'A.C.' But they call him Pops out here, too." It helped that the woman was young and cute, and that a fifty-dollar bill was slipped to her. Squirrel led her on with an interested eye, even though his intentions were only to see Pops.

"I think I might know who you're referring to," said the woman. She looked through a clipboard full of names and picked up the phone to make a call. Squirrel noticed her pressing 210. "Yes, ahhh . . . I have a gentleman here who says he's looking for Pops or A.C.? Yes. Yes. He says he's your nephew from out of town. Oh, all right. Sorry to bother you, sir." The receptionist hung up, and then with a discouraged way about her, she said, "Sorry, he says he's not seeing anybody. Perhaps he's not feeling too well. Maybe you can try back tomorrow."

"Thanks. See you then," Squirrel said, but his mind was on that number: 210.

It didn't take much to do what was necessary. First and foremost, the trio pinpointed the entrances and exits to the hospital, including those designated for deliveries and what not. They noticed that flower deliveries were constant, and that the drivers disappeared inside of the hospital for five, ten, and even fifteen minutes. They needed to get with a plan.

"I read in this book called *Big Pimpin'* 'bout them dudes from the Army Reserve? They were ready to get gung-ho on those pimps up there in Michigan. So they went to the local florist, schmoozed their way into using their uniforms and truck to make a delivery," said Butch, the reader of the group.

"So?"

"So? It worked. They gained entry to the pimp's mansion. No problem. We could do the same thing here."

The florist idea worked. Only there was some persuasion involved. A hundred-dollar persuasion. Plus, six bouquets of flowers were paid for, compliments of Freeze. The florist explained the procedure at the hospital and within ten minutes, Freeze, Squirrel, and Butch marched into Room 210 with a nice gift for Pops.

"Squirrel! Well, goddamn, boy! If this ain't the surprise of my young life!" Squirrel turned to his companions, wondering if they saw the ghost he had. Wasn't this the man? The one who got all shot up by the jealous lesbian?

"That was us down in reception, Pops. I was startin' to think you were tryin' to hide." Squirrel was speaking directly to Pops, even if his eyes were wandering, stupefied by all of the flower arrangements in the room.

"Shit. If you got shot seven times, you'd be extra careful too." The guys nodded in agreement. "Them bullets don't feel too great once they get past the skin. Outside of the skin, they okay. But once they penetrate, them is some burnin' hot mothafuckas. So, shit, how y'all doin'? 'Scuse all these roses 'n shit. Women, ya know. So, tell me who's all with ya?"

"This is Butch. Butch, meet Pops. And this . . . this is the big man. This here's the head nigga in charge—Freeze."

"Well, shit! Nice to finally meet you, young buck. Now, let me just say that I haven't forgotten y'all's money. If I'm correct there's about . . . two hundred and eighty thousand you got comin'. Ain't that right?"

Squirrel agreed, suddenly encouraged that this wouldn't be another loss. Pops was okay. The money was okay. Those had been the only two things he cared about on his way out to A.C. Fuck the gambling and girls. Business comes first.

"Well listen, I'm feelin' as good as new. The doc patched me up, filled the holes, and doped me up. If y'all would escort me, I'm ready to be up and out of here t'day." Pops and his energy penetrated the consciousness of his visitors. It was his upbeat attitude that grew on them. An intoxicating character he was. Freeze wondered why he didn't get to meet this "old head" long ago.

I never did show you my lil' spot up at Bally's, did I?" Pops was up front in the passenger's seat. Butch was driving up Park Place, following Pop's directions. Meanwhile, the question was for Squirrel, who was in the backseat beside Freeze.

"No, Pops. We always did our deals in the casino parking lot or in the hotel restaurant. But I heard you got a few babes up there. Word is they're kissing your hands and feet." Squirrel was part facetious, part serious. He'd believe it once he saw it.

"Well shit, young buck, you only live once, right? Okay, young buck, make the left here, take the ticket from the machine, and wheel this baby to the third level." Pops called every younger man "young buck."

Butch was instructed to park next to a dark blue Ferrari. "We have our own parking spaces up here."

"Who does that belong to?" Freeze's curiosity was sparked.

"Nobody, really. It sits there every day, all day. The service comes up to wash and wax it every so often. But when a whale comes in, my girl offers it to him as a loaner."

"A whale? Your girl? Did I miss something?"

"Okay, this how it goes, young buck. One of my girls is a salesperson here. She's what you might call a "hook" if she was scouting for drug buyers in the street. Only here at Bally's, they're called hosts."

"And she loans out Ferraris?"

"Kimmy pulls in the high rollers from around the world. Actually, I have a few girls who help Kimmy, but she's the main one. She basically does what's necessary to keep the big fish coming. If they need a car, she's got it. If they need to get laid, she takes care of that."

"You mean Kimmy's your girl? And she's fucking the high rollers?" Squirrel asked.

"Well, Kimmy's got a few girls to handle the job, but if it's necessary, she'll lay down, too."

"And you cool with that?" Freeze asked.

"Shit, if a mothafucka is willing to lose five hundred Gs and not have a heart attack, Kimmy better taste test that man's dick until he begs for mercy. She'll do whatever it takes." Pops uttered a slight laugh, and the others could see that there was still a hint of pain.

Freeze got a kick out of Pops, thinking the old head was definitely a pimp. He was also suddenly interested in meeting this girl Kimmy.

"Kimmy got restaurant and bar owners, real estate developers and stockbrokers, doctors and lawyers, too. And those same whales are the ones buyin' stuff from me."

All three of Pop's visitors were finally enlightened; hip to his hustle.

"I got one doctor who has nothin' but clients who buy coke. When he comes to town, we have dinner, he tells me he's staying for four days. That means I'll have four kilos waiting for him in his hotel room. Five days means five kilos. The system is cut-and-dried. Plus, Kimmy's gettin' them to spend at the high-stakes tables."

Pops continued explaining his game to Freeze and Squirrel as they strolled past a line of other exotic cars, into the hotel's corridors, and through the casino itself. Butch followed the three like a shadow. Pops explained how leading actors, and sports and entertainment icons helped to create the illusion that lures gamblers. He told of the differences between high-rollers, whales, chasers, and pressers.

"Then you got the ones who get in the grease. We say, 'He's gettin' greasy.' Basically, that means he's dipping into his own money instead of money he won. Kimmy's a real pro at this. She gets a signal from the pit boss or someone up there." Pops indicated the video cameras concealed inside of dark bubbles along the ceiling. "That's when she knows to turn up the affection. She might send Sylvia or Gigi or Chastity to see the guy, to whisper in the guy's ear or even massage his shoulders. I'm tellin' you, you'd get a kick out of watchin' these girls operate."

"And, don't tell me," Freeze said as the group passed the blackjack tables, working their way by a sea of slot machines. "These girls—Sylvia, Gigi, and Chastity—they all live with you?"

"Somebody's gotta look after them and protect them."

There was more underneath Freeze's twisted grin than he chose to reveal. Admiration. Envy.

They stepped out of the elevator car directly into the penthouse. The opulence cried out, "Money!" The living room was a monument of marble, flowers, chandeliers, frescoes on the walls, with gold glinting off of the arrangement of plush couches. There was a fireplace as wide as a picture window and six feet tall. A butler was there to take Freeze's fox fur. Both Butch and Squirrel kept their jackets on, not wanting to expose their precautionary firearms.

"It's seven thousand square, with a full-sized kitchen that I hardly see." Pops seemed ready to give a grand tour. But a scream shrieked through the penthouse, and then another. From further back beyond the living room, three· shapely women pranced over to Pops and company.

"Pops! Oooh, Pops. Are you okaaaay? Are you hurt?

Omigod, can I even hug you?" All three women spoke at once.

"Easy, girls, easy. I'm as good as new. Just don't hug too hard. Hey-hey-hey—can't y'all see we have company? Girls, I want you to say hi to my friends, Freeze, Squirrel, and . . ."

"Butch."

"Right. Butch. Now make them feel at home." Pops said this while his head sunk down at an angle, somehow telling his girls that they knew what needed to be done. "Fellas, this is Chastity, this here is Angela, and this is Sylvia." Pops handed off the girls one by one as he introduced them, and they took the arms of his guests, escorting them to a couch. The men were offered drinks and asked if they were hungry.

"Wooo-eeee, it feels good to be home," Pops exclaimed. exclamation. "Now, where's Kimmy and Gigi?"

"They should be home soon, Daddy. Gigi was out with a client. Kimmy went to pick her up."

"Good, good. Then I guess I'll go change out of these clothes. Fellas? Please—" There was that gratuitous smile of his. "Make yourselves at home. What's mine is yours." Pops and his sparkling eyes disappeared from sight as the makeshift couples indulged in small talk.

The guys looked at one another with a disbelief that faded by the second. Angela was stroking Freeze's chest, fingering his chest hairs inside of his shirt. Sylvia snuggled up to Butch, her hand caressing his bald head. And Chastity was turned toward Squirrel, looking more delectable than his favorite dessert, with her welcoming cleavage, her saucy smile, and her breathtaking hazel eyes.

"I see you all gettin' along pretty good," Pops said as he emerged in a set of gray velour sweats. The top had POPS embroidered in black right above the heart. He also had a fresh pair of sneakers on. Squirrel took Pop's appearance as novel, always having seen him in that Cadillac style, all G'd up in the city-slick ensemble that was perfectly pressed to a razor's crease, alligator belt and shoes. Sometimes he'd wear the matching derby.

"I wanna take everybody out for a nice lunch, but Kimmy—oh, this should be her now."

The faint gong indicated the elevator's arrival. The way the three strangers focused on the elevator doors, you'd think the heavens were about to be discovered. Pops had built up such an extreme anticipation for Kimmy—Kimmy this, Kimmy that—that Freeze and company were baited with the need to see this woman. Wondering how she looked. Wondering just how good Pops had it.

"Hey!" Her spirit might've entered the penthouse a few seconds before she did. Kimmy's hair was black, tied back to the side so that it formed an edgy porcupine's tail. A few tendrils fell over her forehead, dangling there against her pine-toned skin. Kimmy quickly realized that Pops was back at home. "Pops!!" she called out, and practically flew across the carpet toward him. For an instant, it looked like she'd knock him over, but he put his hands out, encouraging her to go easy. Gigi was the blonde right behind Kimmy.

"Ho-ho-ho, baby. I'm alive and kickin', but trust me, I'm still healing." Kimmy was unsure of where to touch or hold her leader, but Pops reached out to pull her to him in a delicate hug. She gave him a peck on the cheek, the chin, and then the fully loaded passionate kiss on the lips.

"Oh, Daddy." Kimmy's tears began now. "I'm so glad you're okay. They wouldn't let us in the hospital, and we didn't know what to do. How'd you get out so quick? We heard you got shot more than six times."

"It was seven. The seventh bullet is still somewhere in my leg. I'll be sure to show you all my wounds later." Kimmy had stepped back, her hands were on her hips and her head wagged in awe.

"Same ole dog, huh?"

"Same ole," Pops replied with a slight smile. "Hey, these are some friends of mine." Pops introduced the three guests, two of them sitting with their mouths open. "Now, Kimmy, you and I need to discuss some business real quick."

◆ ◆ ◆

On Sunday night, the Navigator was on the Garden State Parkway again, headed back north to New York City. Squirrel was flipping through some snapshots from their stay. Freeze was knocked out, lying across the backseat.

"Damn, Butch, I can't say I ever wanted to leave Atlantic City." Squirrel appeared to be flustered, having to relive such incredible memories, knowing they had to leave it all behind.

"That Chastity chick turned your ass out, huh?"

Squirrel thought about that at the same time as he peeped a Poloroid photo of Chastity. She was topless, wiggling through a private tabletop dance before an audience of nine as if she didn't have a bone in her body. Squirrel could imagine the photo coming to life there in his hands.

"I'mma keep it real, Butch . . . she turned me out, she turned me up, and she turned me over. And I ain't known the girl for more than twenny-four hours!"

"If I die and come back, I wanna come back as Pops," Butch said just as he tossed another fifty cents into the toll basket along the Parkway.

"What happened with you and Sylvia?"

"Not a goddamned thing, Squirrel."

"What?"

"Yo, I'm keepin' it real, dog. The girl was too freaky for me. I mean, she was whisperin' all this good shit in my ears in the beginning, but when we got to the bedroom, I turned into a punk."

Squirrel cracked up laughing.

"Naw, really—that's how a mothafucka catches AIDS, dog. That promiscuous shit can get a nigga caught up. It looks good upfront, all flowery with fireworks and all. But that's just momentary. The long-term shit? All you gotta do is check the history books, dog. Look at Eazy E, Arthur Ashe, and Liberace."

"Liberace was a flamin' homo, dog. Ain't nothin' right about how he was livin'.''

"Yeah, but just 'cause a dude's head is fucked up don't mean he should die. Plus—okay, you want somethin' that's closer to home? What about that girl who promoted all those hip-hop events in New York? Remember? We used to go to her joints at The Cellar, Honeysuckle West. The Country Club. Essos."

"You talkin' about Maria Davis. I remember, but she ain't dead."

"But she's sick, dog. Can't you feel me? Didn't you check her on BET? I got mad love for sweety, but she looked like a fuckin' skeleton. She use to be a goddamned fashion model. She went from one extreme to the next."

"Yeah, I know. And she was always preachin' at her shows too. Readin' passages 'n shit. Psssh . . . man."

"I'm just sayin' we gotta be careful our here. Can't get all caught up so fast. All the money in the world ain't gonna buy you a new body or a new life."

"Well, don't rub it in now, after I already done twisted a bitch out six ways from Saturday. Like Pops said—you only live once."

"What happened with that anyway? I thought we said we was gonna step to that lesbian who shot 'em up."

"Nah, Pops said he was dead wrong with what he did. He said he should've never slept with that woman's property."

"That's a tough lesson, to almost die over some pussy."

"Live by the pussy, die by the pussy," Squirrel said.

For what Rose was about to get into, he needed a real soldier by his side, a dude who would be ready to gun-clap at the drop of a dime. He had all due respect for his cousin Tuck, but Rose knew deep in his heart that that nigga was a bourgie mothafucka for real. He was already a little frightened at the sight of guns, much less the use of them. This confrontation with Freeze and his boys was inevitable. On such short notice, there was just one person wild enough, only one person who Rose knew that would be fearless when it came to battle. That person was Junebug.

◆ ◆ ◆

Wassup, June?" Rose and Junebug connected with the arm wrestler's grip and the buddy hug.

"I came as soon as I could, Rose. Brought my boy and dealt with the whole ten-hour drive. We like blood, nahmean? This is K-oss, you remember him."

K-oss connected with Rose.

"Tuck'll be back in a few. He went to take care of somethin'."

"So wassup, dog? Let a ma'fucka know what's goin' down."

"We got a little battle goin' on with a dude up here called Freeze. He used to sell to Tuck, but Tuck cut 'im loose a while ago. Then outta nowhere, the nigga shows up at Tuck's house threatenin' 'n shit, lookin' for Tuck."

"How he rollin'? This Freeze dude? That's his name? Sounds like a ma'fuckin' ice cream pop."

"He's rollin' with like two niggas far as I know, but they say he got guns for hire. He even got mercenaries 'n shit. A month ago, the nigga had two gunmen roll up on the DEA, killed a bunch of agents doin' some stakeout up at a market in the Bronx. Both dudes were on motorcycles, strapped with Uzis 'n shit. So check it—one dude goes down right, crashes into a DEA, plus he's all shot up. So the other dude? Man, let me tell you. They say his name was Shorty. He wasn't shot or nothin', but he was surrounded. Do you know that nigga did top speed and slammed into a wall? Some ol' suicide mercenary shit I ain't never heard of."

Junebug sucked his teeth, as if that wasn't shit. As if he could go one better. Then he said, "Had to be a stupid ma-'fucka to do some dumb-ass shit like that."

"I'm just sayin', these are the type niggas we might face."

Junebug sucked his teeth again, saying, "Whatever. I got somethin' for a mercenary ma'fucka. He wanna die, we can help his ass take the expressway to Hell."

"See, I knew I called the right mothafucka," Rose said, and they connected again with a stronger handclasp.

Rose showed Junebug and K-oss his war room. The two

had wide eyes, like they'd hit pay dirt. There was a quick summary of which were the best weapons for which objective. It didn't take a genius to know how to operate the guns.

"Whatever happened with your situation down the way? Remember you told me about some crosstown beef you had?"

"You talkin' 'bout Preacher. He took a vacation. For good. We started to squash our beef after he saved my ass from the police. But then I caught his ass red-handed. Ain't no doubt he was involved with the money that was taken from me."

There was a pause before Rose asked, "And wassup with the girl you was with?"

Junebug sucked his teeth and said, "Peaches? That bitch is history, too. You shoulda seen how hard that bitch begged me not to do her: 'Juney I'll do this for you; Juney I'll do that for you.' But she shoulda thought about that when she set me up."

Tucker came through the door. "Yo, wassup, June. Peace, K-oss." Tucker did the quick meet 'n greet, having just returned from his run. "I took care of that, Rose. And it felt good as shit. Everybody in the world must think I'm a maniac, but at least I got the message across."

"You went out alone?"

"Not quite," Tucker said, turning to look behind him. Chanté and Iris were there, finally making their way through the door.

"Shit. Can't y'all find a first-floor apartment?" Chanté said this, trying to lay the blame of her weight issue on the five-story climb.

"It's good exercise. Don't hate," said Rose, dishing out the sarcasm.

Iris ignored the two, knowing how Chanté and Rose enjoyed dissing each other so often. Then she said, "Where'd you get this guy from, Rose? It's like we were rollin' with a lunatic or somethin'. You shoulda seen him. We went to, like, ten barbershops around the city. He went in there buggin', sayin' 'Freeze is this' and 'Freeze is that.' Whoever

Freeze is, he's gonna be one mad son-of-a-bitch when he hears about this."

Then Chanté added, "One spot—Harold's I think it was, up in Mt. Vernon—I swear we was gonna have to start poppin' gats 'n shit when the owner pulled out a baseball bat from behind a counter."

"Yeah, that was close," said Tucker. "I almost shit myself."

"Well, the bottom line is that word is out there now, and you're safe," Rose said. "Now we wait." Rose simultaneously cocked the slide back and forth on the twelve-gauge in his hands. The *clack-clack* sound assured everyone in attendance that things were about to get serious.

$\mathcal{C}$HAPTER THIRTY-SEVEN

Freeze woke from an incredible dream; nothing like he'd ever had before. There was a harem with wives and concubines and servants traipsing around half-naked, all kissing up to him. There were stacks of money, gold bars, and piles of diamonds in the furthest parts of a wide tent. Meanwhile, one woman fanned him, another filed his toenails, and still another did his fingernails while a more familiar face was feeding him grapes. There was the soft beat of congas, the incense wafting, and the gaiety all fighting for the same air.

Just before Freeze opened his eyes, before his mind was able to focus on the present, he realized that this was not a fantasy. It was a nightmare. That familiar face feeding him the grapes was Tonya. She went from the task with grapes to smoothing a razor-sharp switchblade across his cheek. She was about to sever his jugular vein when he finally shook himself back into reality.

Reality was always supposed to be worse than the world of dreams and fantasies. Not in this case, though. Freeze was actually relieved to be back to reality, whatever that was.

There was a draft in the Navigator, one that was prickly against Freeze's sweaty skin. The chill was troublesome until he became fully alert. Butch had the truck at a standstill, there at the tollbooth—the last tollbooth, thank

God—before they were to cross the George Washington Bridge into New York City. Phyllis Hyman was making a soulful plea to someone over the truck's sound system, wanting him (or her) to meet her on the moon.

"What's taking so long?" Freeze asked Butch once he noticed that the usual transaction, that simple give-and-take bit, was stalled.

"Says he ran out of singles," Butch replied.

Phyllis was yodeling about her feeling someone's symphony deep inside of her. Freeze was upright now, still a little dizzy from the dream, and probably more into the music than he'd be otherwise.

"What the fuck, are they printing the money?" Freeze readdressed the long wait. Then suddenly he broke his relaxed mode. He turned to look left and right out of the Navigator's tinted windows. His heartbeat quickened. His body jerked and his mind raced. Could this be a setup? Did they identify the truck? Had they been looking for the Navigator even now? Freeze turned back to the toll-taker. It was a black man with spectacles and a long face. Probably one of those bourgie mothafuckas tryin' to be a hero, Freeze thought to himself.

"We gotta wait till somebody brings the singles out?" Freeze was frustrated now. Squirrel shrugged, more or less agreeing with the wait being too long.

"Thank you for waiting, sir," said the attendant. And Butch threw the Navigator into gear. Freeze exhaled.

"Too bad she had to go that way. She was a beast with that voice of hers," Squirrel said as the song ended. Freeze would've agreed, but he was too spent from the anxiety that had just overcome him.

"Let's stop by The Shadow. De Jesus is probably there with his crew."

"I ain't in the mood for no party, Squirrel. Pops partied me to death," Freeze said.

"You ain't gotta go in. I just wanna arrange a pickup for tomorrow. He should have a hundred Gs for us."

"Make it quick."

Parked outside of the popular midtown nightclub, Freeze and Butch blended into somewhat of a ritual. A lot of guys did this; double-park, smoke, and look at the line of patrons. It was a little brisk tonight. The radio was talking about a first snowfall coming. So everyone was wearing the leather, the wool, and the faux furs.

"I never did understand how females be puttin' up with the cold weather—wearin' stockings and high heels 'n shit in twenty-degree weather. All of 'em can't be troopers."

"But all of 'em can freeze their asses off though."

"Shit—no doubt. Me? I gotta have on Tims, jeans, thick-ass socks, whatever. I'mma keep that hawk off me." Butch was adamant. "That shit is crazy how females gotta get all dressed up just to show their asses." He was talking to Freeze, but he was facing the crowd—a mob scene really, but orderly—all in that thick line to get in the entrance of The Shadow. "Then, on top of that, they go through labor, have babies, keep the house clean, cook dinner." Butch wanted to add "get smacked around," but Freeze would've differed with that opinion. "And all of that starts right here at the club with that whole boy-meets-girl shit, like they're itchin' for a hard-knock life."

"Yeah, well, life's a bitch, and then you die," Freeze concluded. Squirrel had been admitted into the club ahead of all others. Now he was coming out. De Jesus was with him.

"What the fuck is he doin'?" Freeze said half to himself and half out loud. Then he realized Squirrel had De Jesus wait on the sidewalk while he stepped up to the back door. Freeze lowered the window.

"Yo, I know you don't mix with the mid-level dudes, but I thought you might wanna hear this for yourself."

"Hear what?"

"Dude says—trust me, boss. You wanna hear this for yourself. You ain't never gotta see this guy again."

Freeze thought about it. He gazed past Squirrel at De Jesus. His hair was curly. He was light-skinned. He had on black leather pants and a fitted jacket. The jacket was opened enough to reveal a red silk shirt and a few gold rope chains.

Freeze considered that De Jesus had pushed more than twenty-five kilos of product through a lot of New York's hot spots each month for a year now. That didn't change the rules however. No meeting the mid-level dudes. Have to keep the buffer.

"Whatever. You sure about this?"

"I put this on everything, man. De Jesus is stand up. Trust me on this." Freeze nodded and Squirrel waved De Jesus over.

"No need for introductions, all right?" Freeze uttered this even as De Jesus was approaching. Freeze saw he had a diamond in the left ear.

"Peace," the Dominican said.

"Peace. You needed to talk?"

"Yo, money, the streets is talkin' 'bout this dude name Tuck. Says he been goin' all over the city droppin' your name. He say you a bitch-ass nigga. He say if he catch you, he gonna punk you, then he gonna beat yo' ass. Word."

"Oh yeah?"

"I heard this two times today alone, and once last night. Like this is some kind of street promotion for a new movie or somethin'." De Jesus wasn't talking just to talk. There was some apprehension in his tone, like he couldn't even believe what he'd heard. "Yo, dog, I don't even know today's date, yet I still know more about you and Tuck than I should."

"Really? Like what?"

De Jesus explained, a mishmash about "Tonya," and how "Freeze got a shipment of bad coke comin' in" and worse that "Freeze takes it up the—" De Jesus couldn't get up the nerve to complete the statement.

Freeze didn't change his expression. He just said, "Anything else?"

"Nope. The dude has been tellin' everybody he will be on Striver's Row if you man enough to step up."

Freeze still showed no emotion, but his leg was twitching. His heel was bouncing relentlessly even as the ball of his foot was planted. Freeze shrugged and said, "Peace." Then he pressed a button for the window to slide shut.

Squirrel gave De Jesus a pound and there were some words exchanged before the Navigator sped off.

D r. Pearson is an education professor at SUNY. Charles H. Green is the president of the Harlem Chamber of Commerce. Mrs. Wells survived her husband to own and operate Well's Restaurant over on Adam Clayton Powell Boulevard. Mrs. Ruth Griffin is the Director of Publicity for black music at RCA Records. Duke Simpson is the president for the local chapter of the Democratic Party, responsible for directing the $40 million Harlem Preservation Fund. Renee Bloom is the proprietor of In Bloom Salon management, the company that has been acquiring beauty salons for its collective empire.

All of these folks—Dr. Pearson, Charles, Mrs. Wells, Ruth, Duke, and Renee—as well as many other doctors, lawyers, politicians, and business owners, many who were old enough to remember Harlem's last renaissance and called Striver's Row home. To a cop, an electrician, a plumber, or a cab driver—the blue-collar workers of the city—this was 138th Street. But to many who lived here, this was where the "strivers" lived. This is where you lived or owned property if you excelled; if you were acknowledged or notable amongst "your people"; if you were black folk who had six-figure incomes and four- or five-story homes that were all designed to resemble the existing nineteenth-century brownstones; if you possessed luxury vehicles, potted plants, trees, wealth and opportunity.

And now Freeze was here.

E arly Monday morning, folks began filing out of their residences. Finally, a few parking spaces were made available. Snow began to fall but, so far, it merely dusted the landscape and remaining vehicles. The snow was a curtain for Freeze, Squirrel, and Butch, who were in a black Dodge

Caravan. It made all of the vehicles on the block a uniform white. No one automobile would stand out any more than another. Besides, the dark vehicle was the best they could rent on such short notice.

Butch wondered aloud, "You think they'll be comin' out so early in the morning?"

"If this is the right spot, he gotta come out sometime," said Freeze.

"Oh, this is the right spot all right. See that BMW there?" Squirrel pointed it out.

"By the hydrant?" Butch asked.

"Yup, that's Tucker's. We use to sit in there and count money."

Freeze was reminded that Tucker was once responsible for moving as much as 100 kilos of cocaine on the streets. It only made him angrier to know that he'd lost such a large cash flow in the blink of an eye. Whatever happened to honor amongst thieves?

Pumped up on coffee and, so far, two sticks of weed, the three began to get restless after an hour of inactivity. It was now 9:30 in the morning.

"Why wait?"

"Huh?" Squirrel said.

"Why wait? I say we go right to his door. I mean . . . how rough can it be, some Wall Street fag talkin' shit. He'll probably get on his knees and apologize."

"If he don't, he will."

Squirrel checked his weapon, and then stuffed it back in his waistband. Then he adjusted the strap to the Uzi under his jacket. He enjoyed being the front man for Freeze. In less than ten seconds he was out of the caravan and springing across the street to 414, to the gate, up the steps, to the door, pressing the buzzer.

"Who's there?" a male voice announced after a short wait.

"I'm here to see Tuck."

Not another word was spoken. Squirrel turned toward the

others with an expression as to say, "I guess I'll wait." Then he stood back, closer to the curb, expecting the same face he'd known and dealt with.

Squirrel waited. The snow trickled.

T his is it. I told you they'd come out in the daytime. Pussies. They ain't lookin' for no drama for real. Otherwise, they'd come at night." Rose was fixing the Velcro straps on the Kevlar vest. At least it would protect his upper body.

"I say we pretend it's night and toast they asses," said Junebug as he popped a double clip in the M-5 assault rifle.

"Word up, Rose. If they don't start none, there won't be none."

"I feel you, K-oss. But let's stick with the plan. It's gonna be their call. We bring war only if they ask for it." Rose knew that an all-out war would force him to relocate— something he was prepared to do, but he didn't want to be inconvenienced.

"You the boss, Rose."

"All right, I'm goin' down." Rose made eye contact with both Junebug and K-oss. Then he slipped out the front door. Two Ruger .45s were holstered under his Yankees jacket. Junebug and K-oss went to the fire escape.

Y ou ain't Tucker," said Squirrel.

"No, I ain't Tucker. But I'm speakin' on his behalf. So, wassup?"

"Wassup?" Squirrel twisted his face, wondering if this nobody knew who he was or who he represented. He looked back across the street with the same face. Freeze and Butch stepped out of the van now and swaggered over to where Squirrel stood out in front of the brick-faced walkway. "Apparently, you don't know who I am or what I'm about," said Squirrel. "You new around here?"

"You could say that," Rose answered, his thumbs stuck in his front waistband. "New, but respected everywhere."

"Oh yeah?"

"So, wassup here?" Freeze intervened as he stepped up. "Where's the boy Tucker?"

"Whatever you gotta say to Tucker you can say to me." Rose said this directly to Freeze.

"Oh yeah? Who is this guy?" Freeze asked Squirrel. "Does he know who he's dealin' with?"

"He says he's new around here, so maybe he don't. Maybe we gotta show 'im." The two spoke as if Rose wasn't right there listening.

"Show me?" Rose stepped closer. He was on the sidewalk now, mere feet from the trio. "Lemme explain somethin' to you, all 'a you. Rose don't fear no man walkin' this earth. No man. So, I'mma tell you again . . . you got something to say to Tuck, say it here. But Tuck ain't comin' down—he don't want nothin' to do with y'all, and I suggest you roll out if you don't want trouble."

"Roll out?" Butch got haughty. He marched forward to step to Rose, but Freeze stopped him.

Then Freeze said, "I'mma do it like this . . . you go up and tell Tucker to bring his black ass down here, or we gonna roll up in this spot blastin' everything movin'. That means you, Tuck, women, children, whatever. Now he got exactly five minutes to bring that ass, or we're goin' in."

Rose said nothing. His eyes said nothing. His demeanor seemed to yield to the men before him, and he turned to retreat. To his visitors, Rose had surrendered and Tucker would be frightened; he'd be downstairs in two shakes of a lamb's tail. What they'd do to him then they didn't even know. Maybe Freeze would bitch-slap the guy. Whatever. He'd cross that road when it came time.

Meanwhile, Freeze's statement reached into the deepest parts of Rose's soul, as if the blood flowing through him turned to hot soup. No, of course he didn't have women or children upstairs. But those words repeated themselves in his head. And they stuck like thorns. His back was to them now as he retreated through the gate. He was pacing. He was feeling their eyes on him. And now, he was whipping around with a Ruger in both hands.

"Don't think about it, baldy, 'cause you be the first to catch it." Rose was up on them now. Close enough for them to make out the German manufacturer's logo branded on the barrels. Rose's head cocked sidelong as he demanded, "So what's up now, money? What's that shit about blastin' me, women, and children?" Rose had the right hand and gun pointed horizontally at Freeze's forehead. The left was on Squirrel, then Butch, then back to Squirrel again. Rose was an all-knowing, all-controlling force for the instant. He was God, shifting his eyes with poise and grace, somehow alluding that he had everything under his watchful eyes. "Sounds like you need a lesson in respect." Rose had a nod going that more or less decided how he'd deal with Freeze.

In Rose's consciousness, however, there were many more ideas floating around. Here he was practically on stage, in broad daylight, in a neighborhood just perfect for the secrets he negotiated and the guns he stashed. Rose didn't have to look, but he assumed that there were probably one or two residents already scoping down on the confrontation. They'd likely phone their next-door neighbors first. One might see this as more of a life-or-death situation, place the call to the cops right away, and then phone the next-door neighbor. Now that he had to draw on these dudes, Rose figured, no question, he'd have to relocate. He'd have to move his cache of weapons. But he'd have to handle this situation first.

Junebug and K-oss had made their way down the fire escape, careful not to slip in the snow, and they parted ways in the alley behind 138th. It was an obstacle course back there, with trash cans, sandbox gardens, garages, and makeshift sheds for recyclables; the ugly side of Strivers Row.

As Junebug bolted along the narrow passage, he ignored the many rear entrances, the stray dog and cat, and the heap that must've been a homeless person. He'd been down this path already. Rose had shown him just a day earlier in preparation for this very engagement. But there was no sense of familiarity here. He followed his instincts. He measured time as best he could. He imagined K-oss doing all the same things, but coming through from the opposite direction.

Once Junebug reached the main street he felt a bit exposed underneath the open air, trees, and all of those windows of all of those homes. The specks of snow melted into wetness on his face while he forged on. From a half block away he could see Rose descending the steps outside of 414. He could see the one guy, the same guy who buzzed, standing out on the sidewalk. That alone had Junebug breathing easy. Whatever went down this morning would likely work itself out in Rose's favor.

In the distance beyond where Rose and the visitor stood feet apart, K-oss was creeping—just as Junebug was—empowering Junebug with even more confidence. As close as five car lengths now, Junebug's brow furrowed. He became curious, alert, and paranoid all at once. While Rose was still negotiating a one-on-one war, two others—a bald-headed stocky dude and some freak with long hair and a waist-length black fur—were crossing the street to join the powwow. Junebug cursed to himself for not being able to eavesdrop on the conversation. The situation didn't seem hostile and none of the visitors had weapons drawn, but as Junebug told himself, that's the way it's supposed to be. A victim isn't supposed to suspect the violence that's about to come.

Now the fur-coat-wearing dude was stopping baldy from moving on Rose. Junebug's heart quickened. Someone stepped forward, pointing at Rose—pointing up at the building. Junebug could sense trouble brewing; the interaction had stepped up a notch. It was enough of a signal that Junebug pulled up the handkerchief to cover his face, but not his eyes. He crouched even lower now and scurried across the street in order to come up behind the three visitors. He hoped that K-oss would catch on, even if from a distance.

Having crossed over, Junebug released the M-5's safety, preparing for the inevitable. Just as the shit was about to hit the fan, before Junebug jumped in their asses, Rose backed off. It confused Junebug because of how intense the talks seemed to grow. He was lost for a spell, asking a god, a ghost, or even a snowflake what he should do now. He replaced the M-5's safety.

Then it happened. Rose spun around on those dudes with his pistols drawn. He wasn't firing them. Not yet anyway. Still, Junebug remembered Rose mentioning that he wouldn't pull out unless he intended to shoot.

Safety off and scarf pulled up, Junebug pressed on, using the line of parked vehicles as his protective barrier. The standoff was clearly under control, with Rose holding the weapons to mean business. Junebug eased closer, and he could see K-oss doing the same. However this was gonna go down, Rose's back was covered. For an instant, Junebug thought Rose was about to blast the James Brown look-alike, having leveled the pistol to the guy's temple. Rose seemed hyper too, the way he was shifting his eyes and his head, trying to keep an eye on everything.

Junebug had a perspective that Rose couldn't possibly have. One of the visitors, the big one with the shiny dome, was slowly reaching behind his back. He went under his shirt with one hand while the other feigned surrender.

Junebug's heart superseded his mind. His mind anticipated and calculated, but in his heart, he knew this guy was about to wage harm on his man Rose. Junebug's conscience roared and screamed like an ear-shattering silent alarm. He bounced up from his crouched position and pulled the butt of the M-5 to his armpit. He kept his eye in the rifle's scope as best he could, taking aim at the shiny globe. He was close enough now for Rose to see.

"Nooooo!" Junebug shouted as he pulled the trigger hard. A half dozen slugs must've spit out at once. He didn't wait for results. He just pulled the trigger again, spraying some more lead.

• • •

Rose couldn't tell where the gunfire was coming from. None of his visitors had weapons exposed, as far as he could tell. But the blast echoed loud enough for him to wanna dive for cover. Did these guys have backup? And where were Junebug and K-oss? Unable to see past the big dude, Rose was blind to Junebug's approach. He did hear the yell, but that's when blood and guts started spattering out from the front of baldy's stomach, chest, and then his head. The man was standing there with his body jerking as if electrocuted. His whole body could've otherwise been pelted with tomatoes as gross as it all looked.

On the pavement now, and not sure of who to fire on, Rose noticed Junebug standing behind the big dude . . . the big dude who finally toppled forward to the snow dusted sidewalk. From the other direction, K-oss sprinted up to get a fix on Freeze and Squirrel. Squirrel was on the ground too, hit in the thigh by Junebug's rapid fire.

Junebug helped Rose up off of the ground, while still pointing the rifle at Freeze. At the same time, K-oss was just itching to get in on the action.

"Mothafucka!" K-oss hollered and readied his weapon ever more, wanting to punish Freeze for being the man at the forefront of it all. That, along with the adrenaline rush was about to get Freeze wet-up from toes to nose. But Rose jumped to stop the attack, leaving K-oss to relieve his tension (or empty his weapon) into the pavement and a number of rounds were redirected to the exterior of a building.

"Yo! Easy. Easy, K-oss." Rose tried to instill calm, realizing how severe things had become. Then he addressed Freeze. "See what you did, pimp? I wonder if you the one gonna see that boy's family, tell his momma that he died for your sins. She'll understand."

Rose jerked his head at his friends, implying that there was an urgent situation at hand. In an earlier discussion, the word was clear that if things got crazy, certain moves had to be made immediately.

• • •

Agent Joel Green had been with the Feds for eight years before joining Pam's Mobile Enforcement Team. He started out with the FBI, and he had dabbled in CIA operations, especially in assisting with the compilation of information for the congressionally sanctioned Drug War Report. Finally, there was great promise (job security and benefits) in joining up with the Drug Enforcement Agency. Switching from one branch of law enforcement to another was easy as 1, 2, 3; especially moving within the Feds.

Green's meeting two years ago with DEA Chief Sal Goldridge worked out to be something more than he imagined.

"You're more intelligible than my average agent," Goldridge explained to Green. "You've been places and you've seen things that others haven't. It makes you my most prized operative. As you know, Joel, we can never be too careful in this drug war. The enemy is not only on the other side of the net. They're also among us. If you're reading me clearly, Joel, I'm interested in having you perform duties that are more sensitive than even my MET supervisors are accustomed to. We need intelligence beyond our operations. We need covert performance that is above and beyond the call of duty. You're that man, Joel. I've seen your record. I know your capabilities. I looked through everything from PT scores at Parris Island to your marksmanship at Quantico. And frankly, you're an untapped treasure."

Green wasn't sure at the time if the Chief was setting him up as a fall guy, or if he was really serious about this covert operative mess. But he was flattered enough to take the small steps asked of him. He reported all activities to the Chief—those that were by the book and those that weren't. He tailed certain agents who were suspected to be on the enemy's payroll. He even spent two weeks as an inmate inside of Colorado's ADX Maximum Security, with its electronically controlled gates. Green was aggressive when he had to be, violent when he had to be, and grimy when he had to be. The worst he'd done so far was to visit a snitch at the Reeve's Medical Center in Honolulu, Hawaii. The snitch had ratted on everyone in the ruthless Jamaican-bred Shower Posse. A sweep was done and the posse's leader was indicted.

"We need the leader on the streets," Goldridge explained to Green. "He's an important tool in our negotiations."

Green didn't really need to hear more. This was an indirect order to pay the snitch a visit. Never mind that this Jamaican kingpin had been escaping prosecution over and over again, or that the public awareness was kept at bay with regard to the dispositions achieved on his behalf. None of that was important to Green. He was the man for sensitive situations like this, and he wouldn't disappoint.

At the Reeve's Center, the snitch was under twenty-four-hour surveillance, hospitalized in ICU for gunshot wounds incurred from an attempt on his life. Green flew out to Honolulu. He infiltrated the hospital's security. He completed the task.

The hospital staff and local law enforcement were spooked by the incident, wondering how a man could be poisoned right under their noses. Two weeks later, the Jamaican drug trafficker was released and the indictment expunged. No witness, no case.

And now, two years later, Green was in a van with commercial plates—marked A to Z Carpet Cleaning. The van was parked outside of 396 138th Street, also known as Strivers Row. He had been tailing Brian Carter, also known as Freeze, for one week now. Green had noted everything from the altercation outside of the Wilson residence, to the visit at Bally's Casino in Atlantic City, to the rendezvous with the Dominican at The Shadow in midtown Manhattan. He met with everyone from Riverdale residents—neighbors to the Wilsons—to hotel security in Atlantic City, to the manager at The Shadow.

This activity, however, he didn't expect.

"Goldridge? It's Green again. Well, you ready for this? Okay, here goes. I didn't get involved. Not in the slightest. It got a little bloody out here." Green was still in the van watching as police, paramedics, and news reporters volleyed for their own elbow room. Strivers Row was closed off at both ends of the block. Residents were being interviewed. A body was being loaded into a coroner's vehicle. "No, they didn't get our man. There was a leg injury besides the homicide, but he got away with the others. They all just left the one body lying there. No. No, I didn't make the call. I didn't have to. People were home, and it's broad daylight out here. Yes, I got photos of everything. And I mean everything."

CHAPTER THIRTY-EIGHT

The *New York Times'* Monday morning edition read:

GOVERNMENT OFFICIALS MAY BE A PART OF INTERNATIONAL DRUG TRADE
by Scott Deville

South Beach, Florida—Until recently, the very tip of Miami Beach, with its concentrated nightlife, its high-end real estate, and its homes to Versace, Stallone, and Estefan, has attracted the young, the rich, and the hip from all over the world. It is here that money is no object, and where Floridian hyperbole is still an illusion of sorts. The shameless luxuries, the paradise-like living, the electricity-charged nightclubs, and all of this South Beach experience, with its fantasies, real and imagined, had been the stomping ground for Charles Burns, otherwise known as "Charlucci," Florida's most notorious drug kingpin.

Charlucci's rise to power was featured in a five-part exclusive last week (see *NY Times*, Sept. 2–6) that detailed the extents of his operation as alleged by the Drug Enforcement Agency and with the Florida District Attorney's Office. It was also noted (see *NY Times*, Sept. 4) that cases of this magnitude, especially those investigated by federal law enforcement agencies such as the DEA, FBI, and ATF are ordinarily handled and prosecuted by the Chief U.S. Attorney's Office on behalf of the federal government.

Now it appears that extraordinary measures have been taken in relation to the designation of Charlucci's indictment, his case, and the jurisdiction of court proceedings. These measures are so incredible, in fact, that they could be deemed a misuse of authority and an abuse of office. To trace the burden of responsibility, it is necessary to know first that there are indeed benefits to Charlucci's current jurisdiction as a state case and not a federal case. Most importantly, such efforts and decisions would serve to protect Charlucci from the severity of federal prosecution.

This latest turn in the case, labeled as Operation Snowfall, came about when reporters met with Charlucci, who is presently being held without bail under protective custody at the Miami Detention Center. Charlucci indicated that he might be willing to cooperate in exposing high-ranking officials who he says have been a part of protecting his trafficking activities as well as assuring his immunity from serving serious jail time. When asked why he decided to cooperate now, since such immunity had been "assured" him, Charlucci replied that he was finished with his life of drug dealing, of being labeled "the Snowman," and that he only wished to have back his liberty and the possibilities of having a family. Evidently, Charlucci seeks to avoid any and all terms of imprisonment whatsoever. In his quest, he seems to be willing to go to all extremes.

Investigative reporters have met with members of the DEA who have requested anonymity, and who have confirmed Charlucci's allegations. In fact, these agents themselves alleged misconduct by both Dade County and Broward County police departments, the Florida U.S. Attorney's office, and within their own agencies.

However, in this climate where drug lords and their underlings control everything from politics to law enforcement, it is unclear (at least) who is telling the truth, who is passing misinformation, and who is doing both.

Ever since Congress empanelled a commission, and ever

since the release of the commission's 250-page Drug War Report, the document that details the impact of cocaine from A to Z, the DEA has been launching widespread no-holds-barred street sweeps and interceptions. This year, there have been a dozen such sweeps across the nation, including operations in Seattle and Virginia, where commando-like missions have been carried out in an effort to sever cocaine avenues between Colombia and the United States.

But this week, a private research group has found that the activities mainly resulted in the arrests of low-level functionaries, including runners (those who lure drug users), dealers (those who service the users), and lookouts (those who help to secure transactions).

So far, the research group revealed, various "mobile operations" have netted tens of millions of dollars in confiscated money, drugs, and property, as well as the arrests of hundreds of mid-level supervisors, classified by the DEA as Class 1 Violators. A Class 1 cocaine trafficker is defined by the DEA as one who has the capability of distributing at least fifty kilos of cocaine monthly, and who manages at least five subordinate drug traffickers. These violators, for the most part, have been indicted and prosecuted under federal laws which threaten a twenty-to-thirty-year prison sentence and multimillion dollar fines if convicted. These same sweeps have earned even fewer arrests of principal administrators, who are otherwise known as "kingpins." A "kingpin," under the well-known 848 statute, is "any person who is the organizer or leader of an enterprise that involves three hundred kilos of powder cocaine or three kilos of crack cocaine."

In our five-part report last week, Charlucci's alleged scheme was shown to include more than a dozen such mid-level supervisors, most of whom are currently in custody. In the report, he had an operation which served to distribute more than 1,500 kilos per month from the gulf coast to New York to Washington, D.C.

"There's no doubt that Charlucci falls under the Kingpin

Statute," an agent noted. However, the early processes of Charlucci's arrest and indictment have placed him under the umbrella of the state's judicial system. "That would imply that Charlucci and people like him are treated special; that they're needed in order to continue with the ongoing passage which drugs must take to reach this hungry market. It's almost a form of maintaining job security," the agent said.

When the Chief U.S. Attorney for the state of Florida, Peter Van Dyke, was contacted for comment, he explained that the arrests related to Operation Snowman were executed by a combination of agencies. "The joint effort was necessary for the sheer volume of work to be done. To date, there have been more than four dozen arrests in this case, not to mention the real estate we've confiscated, the vehicles we've impounded, and bank accounts we've seized. We've shut down a clothing boutique and a nightclub. We've launched a second wave of investigations that continue today, even four weeks after the first big sweep. All of these involvements require labor, manpower, and a community of contributions. This is no small endeavor," Mr. Van Dyke said.

He also explained about the various addresses of various subjects and about seeking search warrants for the safe houses and other businesses used within the scope of the criminal enterprise. "Furthermore, Mr. Charlucci is a legend and a liar. He should be glad that we have not taken the case from the State Department. And that's still an option."

Indeed, state jurisdiction has its benefits, such as less stringent statutes and no consequences of life in prison, or worse, the death sentence. There's the possibility of parole, state prison camp, and conjugal visits. But each day that Charlucci spends at MDC, with twenty-three hours to think in his one-man cell, he is forced to face certain fate. And as he reflects on the past ten years of his life, he says he can guarantee one thing: "A few more heads will roll if I have to rot in prison."

Scott Deville is a staff writer for the *New York Times*

• • •

E ver since Scott Deville's years at Albert Leonard Jr. High
School, he was interested in being a writer. It wasn't even
that he dreamed of a profession as a reporter, author, or
columnist. What Scott loved most was the actual act of writing itself. How the pen would glide across a nice pad of lined
paper, the ballpoint pen partly sinking into the page like a
waterbed absorbs the tension of the human body. This thing
he had for writing was closer to a habit or a hobby. Not labor, and certainly not a job.

Even before he graduated from elementary school, he enjoyed the ebb and flow of writing. Scott would constantly
take notes in class, copying what he saw on the chalkboard
or in the textbooks. Not that the notes were an assignment or
part of his studies, just that he loved it. He loved how
thoughts from his mind could ooze from whatever instru-
ment he used, to the point that his longhand cursive strokes
were creative enough to feel like art.

At Albert Leonard, Scott ventured into journalism by
submitting a story for publication in the *Purple Rose*, the
school paper. It didn't matter that he'd copied the story word
for word from a local college newsletter. It only mattered
that he was acknowledged as a writer. The paper's editor
questioned Scott about the article, pointing out that he was
impressed.

In keeping with his newfound talent—or the one which
he'd projected—Scott searched back issues of magazines
and newspapers for similar articles that would both appeal to
a ninth grader, but which would be considered popular subject matter. In Scott's research, he found that most publications usually visit the very same subjects in their own unique
and random ways, just in order to satisfy a corresponding
base of readers.

One form of research led to another, to the point that he
became skilled enough to at least feel capable of finding
out most anything about anybody. If Scott wanted to find
an individual's Social Security number, address, or even

their medical files, he could do it. If Scott wanted to find dirt on a company and perhaps some illicit activity that helped the enterprise to take shortcuts in order to facilitate its growth, he could do it. And if Scott wanted to, now that the Internet was a fact of life, he could get access to bank accounts.

But Scott never crossed that fine line where the unethical became the unlawful. He simply kept doing what he was doing, and in that respect, he kept getting what he was getting. Notoriety and acknowledgement in school soon turned to local popularity and job offers. Scott passed on those initial offers at the *Standard Star*—his hometown paper—and a local magazine. Instead, he freelanced for these publications, therefore furthering his exposure without marrying to any one entity.

This routine made him enough money to increase the memory on his hard drive and to build a small lavatory, complete with a reference library and twenty-four-hour access to the Associated Press newswire. Scott's apartment doubled as a virtual command center of information.

The ruse turned serious the day the *Times* called him. The senior editor wanted to meet with Scott and negotiate his joining the editorial department. Scott took the position of staff writer and vowed to himself that he'd no longer engage in the false representations. This was a serious job, he told himself. And he wanted to make a career out of it.

"Great story, Scott. I don't know how you do it. Over and over again you come through, stories that no other reporter could possibly get a hold of." Tina Worthy was one of those reporters.

"Thanks, Tina, but I don't deserve the credit. I . . ." Scott took a deep breath before saying, "I'm just a channel, a vehicle. A higher power is using me as a tool."

Tina thought to herself, Yeah, right, the instant Scott made that statement. She somehow sensed something behind his eyes. Some lack of authenticity. It didn't help that Scott couldn't mention God instead of "a higher power." It was as if he was afraid to be specific, maybe for fear of being struck by lightning.

"By the way, I wanted to ask you about that assignment you took yesterday," Scott said.

"The shooting?"

"Yes, have you started on it?"

"I've got the foundation. Saw the police report and the coroner's report. I'm going up to Harlem later for interviews with some of the residents. I expect to have a story by press time."

"Any chance it could be drug-related?" he asked.

"I don't know. Anything's possible. Why?"

"Just curious. There's a series of follow-ups I expect to do on the South Beach story. It's kind of a trickle-down effect that I wanna do; show the cocaine trail from the leaf to the grave."

"The grave?"

"The grave. It's a rough sketch now, Tina, but what I'm finding out so far is that this whole drug game is a lot like a boxing match. There's a winner, there's a loser, and there's a whole bunch of folks in between that depend on both as their livelihood."

"What's that got to do with the grave?"

"That's where the losers are."

Tina told herself that maybe Scott was good for something, after all. But he'd have to show her more before she could see the truth. She'd have to see what he was made of. "I'll let you know what I find out," she said.

Since Misa lived closest to 138th Street, she could shoot over in time to help. So, Rose called her. Misa had showed up on her bright yellow Suzuki, and Iris was doubled up with Liza on their hot pink model. When the girls pulled up around back, Rose, Junebug, and K-oss were already rushing down the fire escape with bulky shoulder bags in tow.

"Where'd they come from?" asked Rose when he reached ground level, slightly breathless and breaking a sweat.

"They're with me now. Some shit with Chanté. So what happened? What's up with all the people out front?" It was just ten minutes earlier that Junebug cut Butch down with the M-5.

"We gotta move the guns, Misa. I can't get into it too much. No time. Just help me out, aiight?"

"Whatever. Tell me what to do."

"There's a bunch of stuff bagged up there. Take what you can. We're loadin' up the beat-up." They all referred to the Dodge Dart as "the beat-up." It was parked on 137th and could be accessed through a narrow passage. Even as sirens closed in on the scene where their victim was gunned down, Rose and his four helpers were able to remove what weapons remained. Meanwhile, for the want of somewhere safe to relocate, Rose moved in with Misa, Iris, and Liza.

Damn threats! Goddamned threats!" Pam Brown was back in Washington, D.C., when she received a faxed copy of the *Times* article. She was already heated that the article didn't mention names. She so wanted Van Dyke's name to show up as the one who "protected Charlucci's trafficking activities as well as assured his immunity." But now, Pam read further between the lines. She saw how Van Dyke used the interview to his benefit, virtually telling the prisoner to shut his mouth or else he'd "take the case from the State Department."

Pam saw the bluff, however. There was no way Van Dyke would supercede state jurisdiction to take the case. It would turn out much too messy in the courtroom with Charlucci pointing fingers and naming names. Law enforcement and its blue wall of silence would be tested to the fullest extent once defense attorneys put agents on the stand.

Then there was Charlucci's threat that "heads would roll." She thought that to be a hearty statement, clever and gutsy, too. It made her chuckle at Charlucci's psych game.

"Overall, it was good publicity for us, Chief. The story last week, too. They literally convicted the guy in the newspapers. But what I don't understand is why Van Dyke hasn't been indicted or arrested. I mean, we all sat there and watched the satellite view of him at the airport, actually over-seeing the illegal shipment. I mean . . . you have a copy of the signal, for God's sake," Pam said to Chief Goldridge over the phone.

"There's just no solid evidence, Pam. Do you realize what a circus act we'd look like if we indicted a U.S. Attorney, only to have a grand jury laugh in our faces? And worse, what if the grand jury did return an indictment? If the man was proven innocent, if the evidence wasn't as obvious as a smoking gun? The press would punish every agency and every agent in the investigation. More importantly, the events—all of them—would tax the integrity of law enforce-ment. Integrity would be at an all-time low for years to come. Years to come. Think smart, Brown."

"So, Chief, does that mean we ignore the bad guy be-cause he happens to be a U.S. Attorney and because he hap-pens to represent blind justice?"

"Solid evidence, Agent Brown. We must have solid evi-dence."

Pam allowed the words to resonate in her mind. *Solid ev-idence*. She had to wonder if that satellite image of Van Dyke wasn't solid enough. Bigger than that. The Chief had hung up after those words. Just like that. What? He didn't want to discuss the subject further? Was this too sensitive a subject? Or was he just frustrated with me, trying to discour-age my interest in the issue?

So much for Pam to consider, and yet she had to stay the course and continue her job as if everything was A-OK.

They blindfolded Roberta and escorted her from her room, through the house, and out to the circular driveway where a brand-new 4-Runner was parked. It wasn't terri-fying at first, when the blindfold was tied. But after a mo-ment or so, Roberta was getting faint flashbacks of darkness and violence. She began to perspire. Was this all a setup? For her to come here as part of a student exchange program, to get all comfortable with this new family, in this new home, all of that to finally be kidnapped? And what would be next?

The fact was that Abigail and Brendan Novick had set this up over the past two weeks, making sure their schedules would permit this most important moment. And finally the time had come.

Abigail untied the blindfold and said, "Voilà!"

Roberta took a few seconds to adjust to high noon's sunlight, but when she did, there was suddenly more justification for her watery eyes.

"Oh my," Roberta said through a sigh. "It's . . . it's . . . it's not. No. It's . . . it can't be . . ." Roberta stuttered her response, looking first to Brendan, then to Abigail, then back toward the 4-Runner.

"Yes, Ro, it is. It's our gift to you—your very first car."

"Oh my," Roberta sighed again. From watery eyes to tears, she gushed in response to this latest show of Novick generosity. Without premeditation, she'd been building up for this moment as well. So much pent-up appreciation for all the love, the gifts, and the sense of belonging. Overwhelmed was an understatement. Roberta got in the truck and immediately felt out of place. Even after eighteen months of settling in to the Long Island lifestyle; into the Novick household; into their daughter's shoes; all of the luxury and status at her fingertips, she was still affected by this latest gift.

"There's another surprise we have for you, darling."

"Abby, I can't take this. You're killing me with all the gifts. Even at school in the dorm, they're calling me Cinderella." Roberta had a little smile going, indicating that the nickname wasn't a problem—not even the girls who snickered behind her back, calling her a nerd. And they thought she didn't know.

"But I see it all as a blessing, maybe poetic justice in a way. One of my teachers talks a lot about Universal Law. How what you put out there comes back to you, good or bad."

"Something like the saying, you reap what you sow?"

"Mmm-hmm," Roberta answered, and Abigail reached

through the driver's window, dabbing the tears from Roberta's cheeks. "So, what's the surprise now?" Roberta asked this, feigning a sinful expression with a squint and pursed lips.

Abigail looked on at Brendan, who was leaning in the passenger's side window. It was his turn to do the revelation. "Yes, well, the Mrs. and I are quite proud of you, dear. You're excelling in school. Abigail tells me that you're extremely helpful at the museum. Of course, the internship you filled at Solomon Smith Barney turned into a part time position, and actually, I should add to this little surprise party that the board has decided to offer you something permanent at the office; something substantial enough to introduce you to the world of finance."

"Wow," Roberta exclaimed, and she turned from Mr. Novick to the Mrs., as if for confirmation. Abigail widened her eyes, the silence saying how exciting this must be.

"Wait a minute, that's not the good part." Brendan had to clear his throat. "Mrs. Novick and I have had long conversations about this. She also tells me that you both touched on the subject at least once or twice. Well . . ."

"Stop beating around the bush, sweetheart, and tell her already."

"Really, doll, this isn't easy. Roberta, Abigail and I would like to . . . adopt you. We'd like you to become a permanent part of the Novick family."

Can you believe? Me? Here for good? One of the family?" Roberta spilled this incredible news before her friends. All of them—Roberta, Janice (head of the St. John's cheerleading squad), Maureen Talbert (the kiss-ass), Catherine Stockman (with the red hair and the daddy who owned a car dealership), Jill Hamilton (aspiring actress), and Summer Johnson (with the dazzling personality)—were spending the weekend at the Novicks' house up in the Hamptons, about an hour away from Manhasset.

"Come on, babe. You belong here. You are family—please!"

"She's right, Ro. You're like one of the girls, ya know." Maureen affirmed Janice's proclamation. "Who else could own a whip like that?"

"I really like the 4-Runner, Roberta," Jill said, having joined the party late. "You think I can ride with you some-time? An errand? A doctor's appointment? What-ever. I just wanna be you for a day."

A few of the girls chirped with laughter. They were all in sleepwear now, slouched, melting into the thick carpet and vegetating on the plush contemporary couches. The fire-place was alive with heat in front of them. Random songs were playing low enough for the girls to hear each other.

"Oh, this is, like, my fave." Janice rolled her eyes at Mau-reen's taste. She wanted to tell her how unhip her thoughts were. "Don't we have a routine for this song? Only they speeded it up." Maureen directed her question to Janice, em-barrassing the hell out of her.

"Ahhh, Jillian? Maureen? Ahhh, Roberta was talking about something important. Like her adoption this week. Can we, like, give her the floor here?" Janice rolled her eyes again.

Roberta suddenly felt as though she'd been put on the spot. From a mere expression of joy to, now, being prompted to give a speech. Her complexion reddened.

"It just feels good to be loved, ya know? You'd have to be in my shoes to really understand. In my whole life, well, so far anyway, I never had a family I could call my own." Roberta's eyes watered fast. It pooped the party a bit.

"Awww, Ro." Summer got up to hug her friend. She was a little teary-eyed herself.

"Ooookay. In an effort to keep this party afloat, why don't we indulge in some truth or dare," Janice suggested, and the evening eventually changed into fun and frolic.

They ate roasted marshmallows, toying with them to see who could be most raunchy. Jill won that role, taking sticky and gooey to a whole 'nother level. Janice and Maureen taught some dance moves to go with the more upbeat music. They watched a bootleg copy of *Smuggle*. And finally, they dozed off to sleep one at a time.

Saturday morning brought in a snowstorm, and Roberta was the first to rise. She was joined by Summer, and they both worked on a big breakfast of pancakes and eggs for the rest.

"What's it like in Colombia, Ro? I mean, is it like they say with poor farmers all worshipping rich drug lords?" Summer asked with the after-movie inquiries.

"The worst of it was when Escobar died. They have these copycats now, they call 'em cartelitos. A whole bunch of 'em, trying to be big and powerful like Escobar was. They're more dangerous I hear because they lack the ethics and discipline of their predecessors."

"How can people with death squads and people who sell cocaine have ethics or discipline?"

"It may sound crazy, but look at the mafia and how they have certain codes. The police department even has a code they go by. These guys today who run with the cartelitos? I read that they're merciless, uncontrollable, and more violent than ever."

"You seem to know a lot about that stuff, Ro."

"I can't help but be aware. The only way I really stay in touch with my roots is by reading, watching CNN, and stuff like that. And every day—somewhere—there's something printed about the illegal drug trade in relation to Colombia. Besides that, you already know that my family was murdered in that climate—the drug lords and all that."

Summer was unsure of what to say, not intending to go as deep as the conversation had. "Sorry I even brought it up, Ro. Really, I'm sorry."

"It's cool, Summer. This should be the last batch. Pull out the plates and silverware, the glasses are in the cabinet over the sink."

Summer accepted Roberta's abrupt shift in subjects, and she headed for the cabinets.

"What's your second year look like?" Summer asked, hoping to avoid talk of family, Colombia, and death squads. "You give any thought to the sorority?"

"I did. And you know what? I'm gonna decline. It's my

schedule. I'm taking a position at Solomon. I'm organizing the Atlantis exhibit at the museum. It's coming to town during the second semester, but it'll take all of my free time during the first semester. Besides that, I'm in the student government at school, there's the book club, and if I have any time left, I visit the country club with Ab—" Roberta had a sudden loss of words. "Gee, I suppose I can call her my mother now, huh?"

Summer shrugged with a smile. Then said, "Well, as long as I can spend time with you, Ro. I really like your company. Miss Roberta Novick."

"Summer, I like your company, too." Roberta smiled.

The second night's slumber party was fixed; Janice had a surprise for the girls. She made everyone hide their eyes. That alone was exciting—to have to hide so that Janice could surprise them. In their sleepers, their furry slippers, their oversized T-shirts, and with pigtails, ponytails, or curlers in their hair, the girls complied. They either sank their faces in the couch, in the carpet, or in the giant throw pillows.

The next thing any of the girls knew, someone smacked them playfully on the ass. It was a guy named The Rod who wore a fireman's uniform, or a guy named Silver who had a police uniform on, or it was Kevin with the Rambo fatigues. Janice had hired three male strippers to bless her group of girlfriends with an exclusive show.

Six blossoming college girls and three worldly men, naked down to thongs and negligees filled the night with thrills and anxieties. Hampton heaven. The next morning nobody got up. The girls ended up having brunch delivered and they ate and they talked about guys. There was some male bashing, some infatuations, and a lot of fawning over actors and sports celebrities.

As night number three fell over the weekend slumber, the girls took an oath. They each agreed that as long as they breathed, they would be friends, they would share resources, and they would come together for gatherings once in a while. They promised that no matter what post-college involvements there were, no matter what the future had in store, they'd maintain their sisterhood. Roberta had a gift for all of her friends as a reward of sorts.

"Congratulations on a successful first year, and here's wishing you never-ending success for your second." A miniature card was taped to the present, a must-read before the gift was even opened. It was obviously some trinket or jewelry, according to the size of the box. It turned out to be a gold friendship bracelet. A chorus of "Ohmigods" were called out. Hugs and kisses and tears followed. There was enough girl-to-girl affection to last a year.

oberta's second season of holidays was spent in regal, Novick form. Brendan and Abigail took her on vacation with them to Switzerland where she learned to ski, twisted her ankle, and spent the rest of the two weeks shopping, learning about Swiss watches, or eating chocolate to soothe her pain.

Back in New York, Roberta juggled a heavy winter schedule with all the classes, her responsibilities at work, and setting up the exhibition coming in the spring. So absorbed was she that her twenty-first birthday, May 1, crept up on her without notice.

Abigail arranged a surprise party with Summer, who summoned Janice, Maureen, Catherine, and Jill. Together, the sextet drew up a list of folks who knew Roberta personally, or who knew of her contributions. The list grew past 125 guests, all of whom were invited aboard the *Triumph*, a boat-for-hire that transported the large party up and down the Long Island Sound.

The Novicks footed a bill that included a champagne toast, a plentiful hot and cold buffet, and the jazz musician Marion Meadows, whom the young women absolutely adored.

By the end of Roberta's second school year, she'd grown into a regionally celebrated society chick. News photos included her with the daughters of dignitaries, icons, and tycoons. She made the society pages more than a few times. As a result, men began to call on her.

After just six months at Solomon Smith Barney, someone had to notice Roberta's karma and charismatic skills. Not only could Roberta manage and organize, and not only was she fluent in both English and Spanish, but she was an attraction—a saleswoman—in her own right.

"Good afternoon," a stranger said to Roberta as he strolled around the mezzanine that formed a circular walk-way around the perimeter of a replica of the planet earth. "Roberta, is it?"

Roberta was sparked at the sound of her name on the man's lips, but then remembered that she did wear a name tag.

"Yes. Are you enjoying the exhibit?"

The man looked at the globe again and replied, "I'm impressed. What part do you play in all of this?"

Roberta wanted to say "conservator" or "preservation manager" like Abigail could, especially since Roberta was taking on a load of Abigail's responsibilities.

"Part?" Roberta had to chuckle a bit. "I'm like you, somewhere down there, a pin in that exhibit, an organism trying to become somebody."

"Oh, but I beg to differ. May I introduce myself?" The man pulled out a business card that read Branch Manager, European American Bank. The letters EAB were prominently combined in a neat logo.

"Oh? If this is a business solicitation, sir, then the business manager up in—"

"No, no, no, I'm uninterested in museum business, Miss Novick. I came here to meet you. I'm Vick Stone."

Roberta's name tag did not note her last name. Now her interest was triggered all the more.

"Yes, I know your name. I read about you in the museum directory. That was just today, but I've also seen the newsletter from your other job."

Roberta said, "Oh?" knowing that Solomon had a

newsletter which credited employee performance, a four-page monthly that was only distributed amongst staff.

"Yes, ma'am, I have a friend or two that work there." Roberta looked again at the off-white business card, with its raised print in gold. "And quite frankly, I've wanted to meet you for some time now. Can we go somewhere to chat just for a moment?"

"I really have a busy schedule, Mr. . . ."

"Just call me Vick, Miss Novick."

"Okay. Well, Vick, maybe we can set up an appointment. Say, what is it you're so interested in anyway?"

"I'd like to make you an offer."

CHAPTER THIRTY-NINE

Where have you been?" Tracy asked the instant she recognized Coco's voice, or the trace of it. But Coco was already choking back tears and about to experience a psychological breakdown. There was no way she was gonna get into a whole nine-yard explanation of the where, the why, and the what. Coco wanted to curse her sister for not realizing, for not having the intuition enough to know that she could very well be dead right now. But how could she know?

"Listen, Tracy, not for nothin' but I've really been through a lot in the past few weeks. Could you please let me speak to my daughter, please?"

Tracy put Asia on the phone, and mother and daughter went back and forth repeating I love yous and I miss yous. Coco kept her tears hidden under a fabricated joy and excited voice. And when Tracy got on the line, she felt a bit better.

"So, talk to me, girl. What's goin' on with you, huh? Asia's second birthday is in a week—next Tuesday. Will you be here?"

"I'm gonna try, sis. Just let me get myself together here and . . ."

"Where are you?"

"I'm not supposed to say, Tracy. But I can tell you I'm coming home real soon. Real soon. And I don't think . . ."

Coco let it out now. The emotion was out of her control, bubbling inside of her and pushing against her heavy heart. She snorted and moaned into the phone. Her voice turned hoarse and breathless. She finished what she wanted to say, sobbing throughout. "I don't think I'll be doing this anymore." And then the phone went dead in Tracy's ear.

Coco had been an ICU patient in Miami Dade Medical Center for a few days, but she was doing better now, healing from trauma, rape, and assault. She had been stuck repeatedly with a needle, sodomized until she bled from her rectum, and urinated on, all at the hands of Orlando Ortiz.

"At least they got him," the officer who provided protection said. Then the doctor brought back negative results from the blood test, and the same officer was at her bedside saying, "At least he didn't give you AIDS."

Coco wanted to tell the guy to shut up with his weak attempts at consoling her. The last thing she wanted to hear was how good things were, considering that she lay there with a black eye, swollen lips and throat, pains in her ass if she even budged, not to mention how filthy she felt.

Sure, the urine had been washed from her and she'd had an antiseptic bath, but the thoughts and images were what made her cringe every so often. Even when she cringed, her ass hurt. No, it wasn't a time to feel good about anything. It was a time to pray for forgiveness. The pains, the torment, and the nightmares had to be a punishment of some kind. Was it being away from Asia? Was it how she treated Mustafa? Was it all the people she helped to bury in the jaws of the justice system? For what reason, she wasn't sure. She just knew that it was time to make some changes. Thank God, she could still make changes.

Joey Pickle had become something of a local legend down in South Beach after much ado about the electronic murals and the still images which flashed on the walls of the Crack House, a gallery-turned-nightclub. Porno film directors were calling on him more often now. They wanted those facial expressions that he provoked from the actresses. If he did it once, they figured he could do it over and over again.

Late Monday night, there was a video shoot going down in the back office of 3-Way Auto Body Shop. The producer's name was Oz, who already earned praises for *Jailbait Sluts*, volumes 1 to 4. Now he was working on volume 5. He figured he could make the most out of a West Miami auto body shop that already had an attractive neon sign as a marquee. Oz booked Holly and Tawana in order to keep the flick interracial, and he booked "The Pickle" because of the reputation he got from the *Backdoor Thrills* flick. The concept was only thought up the night before in the producer's dreams. And now, on the spur of the moment, he was walking his crew through his vision.

"I see Pickle and Holly doin' it in the back office. They're alone. Holly, you're makin' enough noise to be featured in a torture scene from *Planet of the Apes*. You feel me? I'm talkin' screaming as if there's a bloody murder happenin'." Oz pointed at Pickle. "And you, all I want you to do is fuck this girl like your life depends on it. She's a customer and you just finished fixing her car. Problem is she can't pay you. She's complaining about her college tuition . . . her rent is past due, you get my drift?"

"Sounds like this chick needs plenty of help," said Joey.

"Right, and you're gonna help her." Oz turned to Tawana. "Now, you're coming to the shop to have a, uhh . . . a dent. Yeah, you're wantin' to have a dent fixed. You're hitting the bell at the desk in the front office, but nobody's answering. In fact, these two think that the bells are ringin' in their heads from all the hot sex." Oz looked to the ceiling for clarity in his vision. "So, Tawana, you begin to hear all these strange sounds, you get curious, and you creep to the back of the shop. You end up like a peeping Tom. You get excited. You start playing with yourself and making your own noises. Next thing you know they hear you. One thing leads to another, and bang-zoom. Pickle is doin' you, he's doin' her, you're doin' her, she's doin' you. Fuck it—you all are doin' everything and everybody. Got me?" The actors agreed amongst one another. "Now, I want plenty of vile language, sound effects, and all the raunchy shit. Got it?"

Oz had two cameramen on hand. They were sitting there awaiting commands. "You two—I need close-ups, close-ups, and more close-ups. Just like last time and the time before that. Get in there until you can smell it. Hey Pickle, you don't need no fluffer today. Tawana's gonna get an extra hundred to take care of that for you. So you two, go on and get started. We'll be shooting the sex first. Move it."

There was a bell ringing.

"What the fuck is that?" Oz asked no one in particular.

"Sounds like the bell up front," Holly said, already disrobing and preparing to oil her skin.

Oz marched out, expecting the owner of 3-Way to be out there ready to interfere with production. "Who the—oh. Hey, Pete, what brings you out here?"

"I know all things, Oscar. Did you forget who I am?"

"Right. So, what can I do you for?"

"You're about to lose a porno star."

"Huh?"

"Is the Pickle here?"

"In the back," said Oz. "Wait, Pete. Where you goin'?"

Peter Van Dyke stopped and looked down at the hand holding his arm.

"Sorry, I didn't mean to. Pete, please lemme finish this shoot before you see Pickle. It took a lot to set this up."

"Oz, this is important—a matter of life and death. Mine." Van Dyke stepped ahead while Oz cursed and stomped.

At Van Dyke's inquiry, Holly pointed to the room where Joey Pickle was preparing with the help of Tawana. Van Dyke didn't even knock. He just pushed open the door and stepped inside. Pickle was sitting back against a desk with his pants down. Tawana was down on her knees, eyes directed up at Pickle as she pulled and sucked on him.

"Get dressed, Pickle. We're going for a ride."

"Dag," Pickle said after sucking his teeth. "Just when things were gettin' exciting. Sorry, babe," he said to Tawana.

"And how old are you, miss?"

"None a' yo' business, asshole." Tawana was up from her knees now, going to find Oz.

"Where we goin'?" Pickle asked.

"*We* aren't going anywhere. But you? You're going on a long trip, Pickle . . . a long, long trip. Things are a little hot around town. A bunch of guys with questions of all sorts."

"This gotta do with the story in the papers . . . with that Charlucci?"

"Just get dressed. And cancel Christmas."

Honey! Could you get the door? It's probably a traveler!" Lu Anne Montalbo was in the kitchen, stirring a pot of candied yams with one hand and handling a cordless telephone in the other. "Yes, yes. I'm sorry. Did you say Flight three-eleven? Okay, at six P.M.? I got it. Flight three-eleven at six P.M. Thank you." Lu Anne hung up the phone, working to memorize the details given to her by the travel agent who made arrangements for all of the travelers—the Colombian women who traveled with deposits of cocaine inside their stomachs. There were three women staying there at the Del Ray Beach cottage currently. One of them, Lu Anne knew, was out catching some sun. She'd have to come in to eat soon.

"I got it!" Paul called out and took his short duck-walk to the front door. Through the screen door he could already sense a problem.

"Mr. Montalbo? Mr. Paul Montalbo?"

Paul didn't answer. It was a response that he knew, for all these years, would stick in his throat.

"I'm afraid we have a warrant for your arrest."

Paul's lips quivered. His head sank. And for an instant his eyes shut. Almost thirty-one years on the run and it had finally come to this. Four federal agents stood with suits, badges, and (he was sure) guns. In many a dream, Paul pictured this moment, but all the while, he denied the worst. And now, as he stood frozen stiff, he didn't know what to do with himself.

"Honey? Who was it?" Lu Anne came out from the kitchen. The kitchen utensil dropped along with her jaw. Paul had the screen door open.

"Mrs. Montalbo? You're gonna have to come with us as well. You'll be charged today in Federal District Court for harboring a fugitive," the female agent announced.

"May I ask how you found me?" Paul Montalbo asked.

"Don't sweat it, sir. Charge it to good ol' fashioned police work," an agent said. "Somehow, somewhere, the criminal-minded always mess up."

U pon searching the Montalbo home, agents met Cristina, Celia, and Tania. None of them could speak a lick of English, and agents had no reason to believe that they were a part of harboring the fugitive. Conveniently enough, Detective Banks was called. He drove up from Miami to pick up the three visitors and said that he'd see to their proper handling. On his drive back to Miami with the travelers in tow, Banks phoned Van Dyke.

"I got 'em," he said without as much as a hello, hi, or how ya doin'. "They should be safe and sound in the motel by noon."

"Good, detective. Make sure to give them instructions, and let them know if anything is missing they might not ever get back home."

"I gotcha, Boss. What's up with Pickle?"

"He's on the next plane out of here. Now we only need to find Jimmy Z."

"As soon as I drop these broads off, I'll be on that, chief."

"Good. Call me later."

A gents Simpson and Stevens were left to tend to the post-sweep interviews. It would be a lengthy endeavor considering all of the visits to MDC-Miami, to the nightclubs where Nightfly and his subordinates operated, to the homes that would be confiscated if it was determined that they were purchased or subsidized by drug money. Joey Pickle was at the top of the list, and so was Jimmy Z, but neither could be found. They also needed to find Charlucci's girlfriend, Bianca, to see if her hands were dirty at all.

Simpson was the first to follow the MDC procedure. He signed the logbook, removed the Glock from his holster, and placed it in one of the small wall lockers provided. For Stevens, this prison visit routine was a first, so he simply watched and followed suit. A buzzer rang out, as if horses were now off and running. A heavy door was simultaneously unlocked and the DEA agents were signaled to step through. A corridor or two later there were a few inmates doing menial labor, and finally a few glass-enclosed rooms.

"These places are pretty much all the same," Simpson told his colleague. "Like a standard model that's been duplicated in every metropolis. I've been to at least twelve of them and they're all set up with these same steel doors, electronics, video surveillance, and all. No guns inside federal prisons. State is another story. Those are just like the movies, with the watchtowers and the guards pacing along catwalks with rifles."

"Scary. I've seen a couple of those flicks—*Attica, Shawshank Redemption*. A few of those big-name actors. Stallone, Van Damme. You know the ones," Stevens said.

"Too well. Ain't it crazy how universally known those films are? Almost like points of reference."

"Yeah, like if you're giving me directions, I'm gonna ask what's the nearest landmark? So movies are like the landmarks of life."

"I can agree with that. Every time a movie premiers it's discussed on most every radio station in every state. More important than the topics you hear on, say, NPR."

"NPR?" Stevens asked.

"You never heard of NPR? National Public Radio."

"Oh, like PBS? Like that?"

"Sure," Simpson replied, realizing that to get deep with this guy was probably fruitless. "Here's our guy."

◆ ◆ ◆

Ortiz was feeling like shit this morning. It wasn't that he didn't know the feeling, because he'd certainly been there a few times before. Federal, state, local, it was all the same to him. One way or another, from this way or that, someone was gonna test him. The federal detention center, known as MDC-Miami, was overcrowded these days. This world of the innocent-until-proven-guilty, the political prisoners, the immigration violators, and the others already convicted at trail and waiting to be assigned to one of dozens of federal prisons throughout the country, was a human warehouse. A kennel, Ortiz believed. He knew he could count on one thing there if he couldn't count on anything else: three meals; access to a sink, toilet, and shower; the ability to send and receive mail; and, naturally, the interaction (on some level) with other prisoners like himself.

This was an isolated community where Ortiz was sure he'd cohabitate with hucksters, con men, and weasels. He knew there'd be snitches nearby, ready to drop a dime as soon as they witnessed something that would benefit them. He knew he'd have to size up jokers quick. He'd have to decide right out if he'd be able to take another man in a one-on-one, because if he couldn't, he'd need to be ready for alternatives. He already knew to sharpen the handle of his plastic toothbrush. He always filed his fingernails to be weapons. And for the biggest, baddest monsters in the prison, there was always the microwave oven to boil water. A few squirts of baby oil in the water and the motherfucker would get the hot oil treatment of his life. That shit would have his skin melting off his bones regardless how many muscles he inflated; no matter how cocky he thought he was.

Ortiz was ready for all of that. It was a normal, everyday way of life for a prisoner. He wouldn't walk around asking for trouble, but if it came his way, if he couldn't avoid it, he was prepared to be the victor at all costs. "Don't start none, won't be none" was his motto.

But this morning was miserable. The two pancakes he got were ice cold. The syrup that had been poured over them had dried up. There was a banana, but it was nearly green and no longer than his dick in shrivel-mode. Ortiz turned down the coffee, to the joy of a fellow inmate who apparently looked forward to anything that anyone else didn't want. So the container of milk and the orange was what he had to rely on until lunch.

Beyond the food, he had to make do with the one pair of underwear, a T-shirt, and the bright orange jumpsuit he was issued. He wouldn't receive a fresh change until the following week. Some of the inmates who had been there longer— some for as long as two years—were able to amass a few underwear and T-shirts, which they washed in the bathroom sink. The bathrooms were consumed with odors. Odors that fought one another, odors that wouldn't go away. The showers—there were only three of them in the dorm where Ortiz stayed—had to accommodate all forty prisoners on that floor. You needed slippers to go in the shower, or else the crud that built up on the floor of the stall might connect with your skin. And that would mean possible health problems.

When the correctional officer called out for Ortiz, he was already on line for twenty minutes for the morning's shower. The guy before him, he already knew, would take fifteen or twenty minutes at least. Not to mention the sound effects that he made in there. The inmates called him Showtime, as outrageous as he got in there. But Showtime didn't care. A year on trial is a long wait without sex.

And now the CO called.

"Shit!" Ortiz exclaimed, wondering if it was the Legal Aid chick again. Moments later, after the customary strip search and the application of handcuffs, Ortiz was escorted by two COs to an elevator that traveled to the first floor. Already, he could sense trouble by how important the COs were treating this visit. Number one, they were taking him in a different direction than where other visits were held. And number two, the COs always said who was visiting, whether it was lawyers or family. These guys were hush-hush. Some secret agent type shit that was annoying him with all of its phony pretension.

"Mr. Ortiz? Orlando Benedict Ortiz?"

"Listen, if I gotta talk to you suits, the least you can do is call me Orlando or Ortiz. That name Bene—you know the name—that shit pisses me off. I'm still lookin' for my pops so I can stick his ass for namin' me that."

"Have a seat, Ortiz."

"Who you guys with? You got badges? Metals? A cigarette?"

Simpson pulled out a pack of Newports and looked at Stevens at the same time, wondering if this was allowed. Simpson acquiesced by expression alone.

"DEA, Ortiz," Simpson answered.

"Oh. You guys. Whatcha got? Some more charges to lay on me?"

"I wish, Ortiz. I really wish. No lie." Simpson waved off the cigarette's offering. Then he said, "You really hurt that girl, man. You hurt her bad. If I had my druthers, they'd plant you so far into the earth that you'd be able to see how the center looks."

"What girl? I don't know what you're talkin' about."

Simpson lost it. He jumped up from his seat and went for Ortiz's neck. A struggle ensued as Simpson squeezed the color out of the prisoner. Stevens rushed to stop Simpson.

Eventually, Simpson let up, brushed off his suit, and regained his composure. None of the COs who passed by the room caught the altercation, so Stevens could breathe easy. The interview wouldn't come to an abrupt end. He gave Ortiz another cigarette and Agent Simpson tried again to communicate with the prisoner.

"I'm gonna start again, Ortiz. You'll have to excuse me. I have a daughter that girl's age."

Ortiz had to steady himself and his trembling hand in effort to take a toke from the Newport.

"I'll just keep this brief. You're in hot shit. We have a man who's willing to testify against you. According to him, you organized his pickup of five hundred kilos of cocaine. He took the stuff across state lines. The amount was well over three kilos, so that means a guaranteed life sentence. But that's not all of it, Ortiz. We've got these."

Simpson took some photos from his pocket. He set them in two rows on the table. Twelve photos total. Ortiz and Nightfly going in a club, coming out; both of them in a yellow Humvee; Ortiz meeting Nightfly at Charlucci's beach house; Ortiz amongst a group of others and their motorcycles; a photo of Nightfly hanging off of the Julia Tuttle Causeway.

"I believe you know this fella here." Stevens pointed to the hanging man. "His name is Robert Jones, aka Nightfly. I'm sure these photos can refresh your memory."

"What about 'im?"

"Well, the thing about him, Mr. Benedict Ortiz, is that we're about to add murder one to your list of convictions." Simpson pulled a few sheets out from a folder. "On your rap sheet we've got assault, assault with a deadly weapon, breaking and entering, another B and E . . . oh, here's an armed robbery—you got off on this one, though, thanks to a missing witness—there's a grocery list of possession charges, and even a gun charge."

Simpson put down the papers. "Funny thing is you've never done any serious time, Ortiz. A slap on the wrist here and there. Probation. A one-year stretch in the Glades. You haven't yet tasted the inside of the big house . . . the Federal Pen. You know . . . that's like the Hotel California in there, Ortiz. Remember? The Eagles? Or the Heartbreak Hotel. Remember Elvis?"

Now Stevens said, "We're not here to bust your balls, Ortiz. We're here to offer you a deal. A take it or leave it deal. Maybe you can see the street again. Someday."

"What kinda deal?"

"The biggest deal of your life. We want you to testify against the Snowman, the big man."

"Charlucci? Have you lost your goddamned mind? Or maybe you need a doctor, 'cause you talkin' crazy."

"Crazy? You ain't seen crazy yet, fella," Simpson said. Then he looked at Stevens and the two got up to leave. With their backs turned and moving toward the door, they made sure their mumbling was overheard. Ortiz caught some words about a re-indictment for murder one and the death penalty.

"Whoa! Wait up! What death penalty? For what?"

"You're kidding, right? I'm not from down here, bubba, but even I know what the Bush family put in place down here. You're gonna fry," said Agent Simpson.

"Hey"—Ortiz had lowered his voice—"come on, man. We can do somethin'. You ain't gotta just write me off like this."

The agents looked at each other, wearing expressions of doubt.

"Whaddaya need from me?"

"Now you're talkin'," said Agent Stevens.

The convenience of the interviews at MDC-Miami was almost too good to be true, how all of those arrested in Operation Snowfall were detained under the same roof. The men and women were warehoused in separate areas of the fortress of an office building. However, all of the interviews could be done right there in that same room. Correction officers would escort the prisoners down at the whim of DEA agents, FBI agents, and even U.S. Marshals. For now, DEA Agents Simpson and Stevens were well into their tenth interview. They figured to finish up by 2 P.M. and resume again the next day.

"Farrah, you've been here for a minute now . . . and, ahh, here we are. Your landlord told us he'd be placing all of your personal property in storage. But he also said if he didn't get paid by Monday of next week, he would auction off your furniture first, your clothes next, and then he said something about jewelry and photos. Now—"

"How can he do that? Oh my God! I just can't believe this. Am I not supposed to get bail? I'm not a known killer or a threat to the community. I go to college, for Christ's sake. I have a life."

"Correction, Farrah, you *had* a life. That would be more appropriate to say," Stevens said.

Then Simpson added, "It doesn't have to work this way,

Farrah. I know you and the other girls have been talking up there in the dorm. Six of you have already agreed to cooperate. And we know all about the theme here . . . 'keep your mouth shut,' they've been saying. 'Stay quiet and stay alive,' they told you. But you know what, honey? There is no more organization. Nightfly is dead. Charlucci is here, locked up in this same building with you. And all of Charlucci's people—people like you—are turning over one by one."

Stevens then said, "Six of them, for sure, will get bail today. They're going home."

"So you have one chance to make one choice, Farrah," Simpson continued. "You either cooperate, or you sink with the ship. And I know a pretty girl like you wants to pursue a life, a degree, a family. Make the right choice."

Then, the interview with Star:

"This is simple, Star. You can pull out of this whole experience right now, get your life back together, and maybe even save your day job. I show here that your mother is sick . . . lung cancer, is it? Well, I can promise you, Star, if you cooperate with us, you'll be able to see her again. You can be at her bedside in her last days of life. But if you don't work with us, and if you stick with this 'all for one and one for all' business, you'll stay here for two years of court appearances. I can assure you that. And furthermore, our conviction rate in these types of cases is ninety-seven percent. So, whenever you saw Mommy last? I hope you kissed her bye-bye."

And with Legend:

"So, you're the famous Legend, huh?"

"What's it to ya?"

Stevens slid his foot into Simpson's, an under-the-table indication that he'd like to say something.

"Legend, I'm sure this isn't the most pleasant situation for you—to be locked down twenty-three hours a day . . . to be taken from your natural environment of the clubs, the people, and the excitement. I know you miss your injections."

Legend was looking especially gross these days. The transvestite had to be kept in solitary confinement, away from men and women, because of conflict that the facility has experienced in the past with she-males. Legend ordinarily maintained an image out on the South Beach club circuit . . . shaved bald, makeup, earrings—the whole fabulous fashion statement. But here at MDC, Legend's hair sprouted unevenly about the scalp. The high cheeks that were once dazzling were sagging now, along with the bags under the eyes. What had been breasts were now empty, hormone-deficient sacks hanging in there somewhere underneath the orange jumpsuit. The eyebrows that had been shaved off in the street and replaced with painted-on, high arching substitutions were now growing in a bushy unibrow. The mustache, rough beard, all of this reality set in over the course of weeks without hormone pills, injections, and all the rest of what maintenance Legend required to stay "fabulous." There was no perfume for prisoners, so Legend's manly body odors corrupted the clean air.

"This is the kind of ugly that frightens horses away," Simpson said to Stevens just before Legend was escorted into the interview room. The handcuffs and shackles were still on, because Legend had been a behavior problem from day one.

"I don't mean to sound harsh, Legend, but this is what will happen to you if you decide not to cooperate with us. After your conviction—and trust me, you will be convicted—you'll be put on Con-Air to Springfield, Missouri. There's a place down there for freaks and queers and others with mental problems. It also doubles as an AIDS facility. People who commit crimes and who are dying go there. They do their time, as much of it as they can, until they expire—one way or another. That's what'll happen to you, Legend. It's very real.

"But on the other hand, we can get you bail. We can make a recommendation to the judge, and depending how helpful you are, we may even be able to reduce the charges so that you get off with probation."

"Probation? Honey, I may be crazy, but I'm not stupid. I seen the press conference . . . they got a TV up on PC. We gotta look through the door to see it, but we see it. Y'all are tryin' to satisfy the public. Y'all need convictions to satisfy your little quotas 'n shit. Tryin' to pacify the taxpayers 'n all. Don't con me."

"Legend, I'll be honest with you," said Simpson. "You don't have a chance in hell of getting out of prison, not for the next twenty to thirty years, unless you help us. That'd make you, what? Fifty? Sixty? When you get out, it'll be just in time for Social Security payments and Viagra. You make the choice."

"Wait a minute. That's it? There's no written agreement?"

"No. You take our word, or you don't. Simple as that."

CHAPTER FORTY

Bianca." She said her name with a lil' singsong twist whenever she answered the phone. It was a signature of sorts. One that callers expected to hear . . . anticipated hearing.

"Baby, it's me."

"Oh. Hi." Bianca's voice changed. Now it lacked energy.

"Baby, don't be like that. I called to give you good news."

"What? They're dropping the case, you're coming home today, and you're out of the game for good—is that what you called to tell me?" Bianca said in total disbelief.

"Actually, you're close."

"What are you sayin', Charlie?"

"I'm sayin' that if there was ever a time when I needed someone, it's you and it's now."

"Talk to me."

"They're about to strike a deal with me . . . give me bail and everything."

"Really? That's great!"

"Thing is, my lawyer is pressin' me for more dough. I can pay him, but I need to talk to you first. It could mean me being on the street tomorrow."

She didn't have to think, 'cause Charlucci didn't give her a chance to. He said all the right things, enough to make Bianca come to visit him once more at MDC, a visit that she vowed to never make again.

In her pink Volkswagen Bug, Bianca rushed downtown

and found a convenient parking spot across the street from the detention center. She was feeling vibrant since Charlucci's phone call, and got all dressed up to fit her mood. She sported a red skirt that barely covered the knees, a red top that stretched over her healthy pair of tits, heels, a purse, and her hair in a ponytail.

The processing for her visit had become easier to deal with. The guards seemed to know her now. Or so they pretended. She took a number, waited for them to approve the visit, and then stepped through the metal detector. A couple of steel doors and buzzers and a short wait later, Bianca sat watching prisoners emerge from that door in the corner of the visiting room. There were other prisoners and their visitors in the large room, but they were in a larger area. Charlucci was designated to a section where protective custody prisoners have visits. So that's where Bianca was expected to wait.

Finally, Charlucci came through the door with two guards escorting him. Bianca noticed his hair was cut and his facial hair was groomed. His appearance was much better than the last time.

After the kiss and the hug, the two sat side by side.

"Thanks for coming. I know we said 'no more,' but this is important."

"Mmm-hmmm . . . who cut your hair?"

"An inmate. They only come up to PC every so often. That's why I looked so bad before."

"You never looked bad, Charlie. So what's up?"

"How's Jason?"

"Good. Thanks for asking. He asks for you, too."

"Well, you tell him that his best friend in the world will be back sooner than he can say abracadabra. So listen, I'm working some things out with the government in my case, but I need more money for my lawyers. Plus, they wanna make me pay a fine. They say they'll drop the case . . . everything."

"So what can I do? What kind of money are we talkin' about?"

"It's nothin' really. I have the money already. I just need you to get it for me."

"Where?"

"At the Utopia. I have a couple of safes hidden."

"Okay."

"There's a remote control stuck in the cushions of my couch. All you need to do is get the remote, point it at the bearskin rug, and the safe'll come up. Then you do the same thing for the bathroom tub."

"You're kiddin'."

"Nope. There's about eight hundred thousand dollars all together. Grab it. Bag it. Stash it at your place. I'll have someone call you to get it."

"Why can't I pay the lawyers, babe?"

"I don't wanna mix you up in this, sweetie. Let's just do it this way and I should see you in a few days."

"I thought you said tomorrow?"

"Give or take . . . I mean, you never know with these people." Charlucci was rubbing Bianca's thigh, arousing her by his touch. "Can I count on you?"

"Sure, I just want you out of here, Charlie . . . and out of this business for good."

"Don't worry. I love you. So I have no choice but to do the right thing. For you and Jason." The words were music to Bianca's ears. Her eyes watered at the thought, how it took all of this to get the man of her dreams to go straight.

As Bianca left MDC, her thoughts had her floating. It was on the way to the detention center that Bianca wondered how Charlucci could go from being Miami's biggest drug pusher, with the big newspaper articles, the six o'clock news, and the press conferences, to now becoming a free man within forty-eight hours. But now, after seeing his confidence and hearing him say I love you, she didn't have those questions. She just followed instructions.

There was a reason Charlucci was permitted to make phone calls for up to an hour at a time, at no cost to him, whenever he asked for them. MDC's Protective Custody wing was sealed off from all other areas of the facility, with one-man cells that were each equipped with a toilet-and-sink combo, a bed that was bolted to the wall, and a buzzer to make requests of the correction officer on duty.

When meals were served, an inmate worker would push a cart into the PC block, and the officer would hand a tray through the opening in the steel door to each cell. It was during these meals that the traps were left open and prisoners would talk amongst each other.

On PC Block 2, Charlucci was housed with eight others, like the homosexual named Trixie, the Mafioso named Mickey the Finger, and some guy (Charlucci didn't know his name) who punched the cement wall in his cell for an hour, twice a day. Charlucci made the guy out to be a mercenary of some kind. There was a Wall Street type who was thin as a flagpole, wore glasses, and was being held for contempt of court in an ongoing civil case. Because his case wasn't criminal, the prison had to keep him separated and protected. There was some kid there who was barely eighteen, imprisoned for some computer-hacker case, and scared to death of all things prison. There was one cell way down on the end whose inmate never came out. If he took showers, it was when Charlucci slept. And finally, there was Legend.

"Hey, Legend," Charlucci called out while the trapdoors were open.

"Wassup, baby? How you hangin'?" Legend said in an effeminate tone.

"What'd they say to you?"

"Oh, you know. Same ole shit, Charlie baby. Tryin' to flip me over. Tryin' to make me sing."

"Well?"

"Well, what?" Legend sucked those big teeth. "I just know you ain't questionin' my loyalty, baby."

"That's my girl. Sound like they have a good case? Or are they bluffin'?"

"Can't say. We really didn't talk about no case. They talked. I kept it tight, that's all."

"You did good, girl. I'm gonna take good care of you when we hit the street," Charlucci said, feeding Legend's ego.

"Mmm, sounds good, lover." Legend said this while

rolling his eyes. Since Charlucci couldn't see Legend, he couldn't very well know that there was a performance going on.

Later in the day, Charlucci made the call to Bianca. The CO brought the phone as they usually did, stretching it across the hallway on a long wire, with the receiver wedged inside the trap on the door. Little did Bianca know that Charlucci was putting on an act much like Legend was . . . pretending in order to keep her happy. But what Charlucci didn't know was that this visit was the one the DEA was waiting for.

I hope this is the one, Dugan," Simpson said as he got in Dugan's vehicle, an unmarked Toyota Camry. Dugan was the one to call Simpson and Stevens off of the MDC interrogations.

"I hope so. What's up, Stevens?"

"Hey, Tommy," Stevens said while climbing into the backseat. "I just wanna know how you worked this one out."

"We've been monitoring his calls, number one. But number two, we arranged to release the penthouse through Snowman's lawyers. I think the guy got all excited and called his girl today. I'm more than certain she's goin' to the Utopia. Could be for a key to a safe deposit . . . money or whatever. I do know she's gonna be—wait, there's our girl in the red."

Stevens whistled. "Jesus! The criminals get all the good trim."

"That's her car there, the pink Bug. We tail her. We let her get whatever. We take her down." Dugan said this as he wheeled the Camry in position to follow Bianca.

"Did we ever do any follow-up on Dillow?" Simpson asked.

"The dead gigolo? Just what we could learn about the stash house where he was killed," Dugan answered.

"You mean executed," said Stevens.

"Right. Well, I picked up something today. When we interviewed the girl with the pretty face and fake tits," Simpson said as the party pulled off into traffic behind Bianca in the pink Bug, "I get the idea that there's more to the Dillow murder. Something we haven't been told."

"Whaddaya think it is?" asked Brown as he concentrated on keeping a few cars behind. Bianca wasn't hard to follow at all.

"I can't say. But I wanna pursue it more. See what I can find. Family. Friends. His residence."

"Guy's been dead for a while now—maybe a month. You think the trail is stale?"

"We'll see, won't we?" Simpson said. "Hey, you're right. She is going to the Utopia." The agents watched as the pink vehicle turned into the gated community where the high-rise sat prominently beyond a few others.

"Okay. Once she goes in, we give her a moment, and then go through the motions with the guard at the gate." Dugan eased over to a curb and under the shade of a palm tree.

Bianca's heart was beating fast. For some reason, this felt deceitful. Her intuition said that the money that Charlucci needed was dirty money. But then, she considered that if it was, the law wouldn't have returned the penthouse. It wouldn't be back in Charlucci's possession. They'd still have the door taped off with that DO NOT CROSS tape that police put up to keep everyone out. There was none of that now, so Bianca's mind was somewhat at ease.

She greeted the building's concierge and didn't worry one way or another about the strange look on his face. She entered the elevator and pressed *P*. As the car rose to the top, she inserted a key that would allow exclusive access to the top floor. And now, the tiny circle, (the *P*) which had been illuminated in bright white was green. The doors eventually opened to the penthouse foyer.

"Okay, okay . . . the remote. Find the remote." Bianca was talking to herself. Repeating what she could recall from Charlucci's directives. Her heart still thumped hard in her chest, but it was more like in anticipation of the money, Charlucci's freedom, and their family together once again.

To Bianca, this was one of the last steps in her quest to establish that solid foundation . . . for her and for Jason.

Sure, she had her good business sense, her track record as a successful promoter . . . sure, she had her magnetism, her charisma, and an intoxicating energy about her, but this was just another kindhearted, selfless act—nothing different from things she already did. Yes, Bianca was a woman who was self-made; a woman who could succeed on her own. But it was always nice to have that partnership, that camaraderie, that convenience of steady companionship, which was the reason why she was really doing this.

Bianca found the remote and, pointing it at the bearskin rug, she did as Charlucci had asked. Sure enough, and to her surprise, the safe lifted up out of the floor, with the rug forming a perfect rectangle, draped over the sides like a furry tablecloth. Bianca was instantly fascinated that they even created something like this—a sub-level safe.

She went over to the safe and turned the dial to the combination. A moment later, she pulled open the front. Inside, there were neat stacks of cash wrapped in amounts of ten thousand. Alongside of the money was a package, shrink-wrapped in a shiny brown paper. Bianca was so excited at this point, she didn't even begin reaching for the money. She just came up from her knees to head for the bathroom, telling herself that the tub was next. This she had to see.

Like magic, the tub lifted up from the tile floor. Bianca let out an exhaustive sigh and said, "Whew!" Then she proceeded to open the safe.

"Bianca George?" A voice startled her and she turned around in horror. She shrieked. "DEA. Stay right where you are." Agent Dugan said this, and also braced himself for any sudden moves. These days, women could be just as much—or even more—of a threat as men. His automatic pistol was drawn and at his side. He motioned for Bianca to step aside, wagging his weapon slightly.

"Look what we have here," Dugan announced as he crouched to handle a stack of money. "It never fails. Someone always comes back to the stash spot to pick up loose ends."

"But—"

"Ah, ah, ahhh . . . save the excuses and the alibis for the judge, baby." Dugan took a deep sniff at the money in his hand. "And lookie here! A nice little package, have we?" Now Dugan handled the square similar to the one in the first safe. Bianca was too grief-stricken to see that there were a few more of these packages in this spot under the tub.

"Oh my God! Oh my God! I'm gonna die. I'm gonna . . ." Bianca began to lose consciousness. She started for the floor, but Dugan hurried to catch her.

"Hold it right there, girlfriend. Don't you fall out on me now," he said. Bianca was in Dugan's hungry hands now as he held her against his body. Then he swept her off of her feet, carried her into the next room, and laid her on the bed.

Bianca was woozy, but she wasn't without feeling. The agent seemed to be in a hurry. He asked her where more of Charlucci's stash might be. She felt her lips moving, telling him that she wasn't part of this.

"I'm not part of this. No . . . I'm not part of this," her voice said faintly and more or less on its own.

She heard what sounded like the agent's voice echoing. "Where is it, girlfriend? Where's the rest?"

Then she shivered as he hovered over her. Her lips let out a staccato cry of fear as his hands roamed her curves, her breasts, and the softness under her red skirt.

"Are you gonna tell me where it is? Or am I gonna have to fuck it out of you?" The man's hands violated Bianca in a way that was foreign and unfeeling. Then he suddenly stopped and said, "Come on up. I found what we're looking for. Over." There was the weak squelch of a radio on the agent's person. Bianca was dizzy, but she could see the man standing now, putting away the mic he spoke into and pulling out a pair of handcuffs from his waist. In an instant, he had her flipped over on the bed and cuffed. He smacked her ass. "Stay there. I got business to tend to."

Agent Dugan hurried from the bedroom, pulled free his vest and shirt, and slid as many $10,000 stacks of cash behind the vest as he could fit. He made sure to flatten the money as best he could and tightened the Velcro again. The Windbreaker he had on would help to conceal what he took. There were sounds out near the foyer now.

"In here!" Dugan shouted from the bathroom. "Two of 'em! Floor safes. Hydraulics and the whole nine."

"Good work," said Simpson. "Where's the girl?"

"On the bed in there. I had to hit her. She tried to attack me."

Stevens was already in the bedroom. "Damn, Dugan . . . she's out cold."

Dugan shrugged as though he had no choice.

$\mathscr{C}$HAPTER FORTY-ONE

Bianca George was arrested, interrogated, and detained until further notice. Agents counted and recorded $450,000 in cash and a total of four kilos of uncut cocaine that had an estimated street value of $500,000. Processing Bianca and going over Charlucci's penthouse with a more intense search was an all-day affair.

By 3 P.M., Agent Simpson decided to follow his hunch on Dillow. He called MET Agent Ted Carson, who had worked on the initial Operation Snowfall sweep, in order to share notes.

"Your hunch is good, Simpson. I had the same idea when we were down there, but the Nightfly homicide came and we had to . . . well, there were other problems. If I was you, I'd start with Dillow's family, his crib . . . you know . . . the usual. And see if the name Jimmy Fears, aka Jimmy Z, comes up. He's supposed to have a band called Da Bomb. We didn't pick him up on the sweep. Seems he was a here-and-there type of guy. But he's still wanted. The locals down there wanna talk to him about the murder, I'm sure."

"You mean the execution."

"Right. It sure was."

"All right, Carson. Tell Miss Brown we're gonna cross our *T*'s and dot our *I*'s down here until we figure this all out."

"Just look out, Simpson. Everything isn't what it seems down there."

"I understand."

◆ ◆ ◆

Agent Simpson went alone to the late Joshua Dillow's luxury apartment. He wondered if it was just coincidence that Robert Jones, aka Nightfly, lived on the same street. Simpson turned onto Arthur Godfrey Road where luxury apartment complexes and palm trees decorated the coastline. A chat with the building manager earned Simpson little information, except that the apartment was paid for six months in advance.

Furnished with a master key to the two-bedroom suite, the agent went in and was at once taken aback by the grand layout. He expected that this was how Dillow left the place, a big contradiction. Sure, the residence was an abundant one, with panoramic views of the Atlantic; endless beachfronts and a horizon where the blue sky seemed to meet the blue water; a living space that boasted twelve-foot ceilings; a double-sided fireplace; a kitchen with state-of-the-art appliances; and the dramatic wall of windows wrapped around the southeast corner, with three balconies and all.

But despite all the luxury, the place was a mess. Someone had to have been here before Simpson. Maybe they ransacked the place in search of valuables or a safe. Or maybe they were looking for something else.

Simpson wandered, stepping through scattered books, feathers from one of the couches, broken glassware, and exquisite art that had been destroyed. It was a pity to see such lavish surroundings in a ruin like they were. Potted plants were broken with the dirt spilled about the fine wood floors. A baby grand piano had been smashed with one of the Italian chairs. In the end, Simpson's effort looked to be fruitless. And then the telephone rang.

"Dill? Are you there, Dill?" a voice sounded over the answering machine. Simpson immediately made out the caller as an older woman, a distinguished voice that paid special attention to pronunciation and diction. "I miss you, Dill. I need you, Dill."

Simpson's eyes widened in light of the desperation in the voice. It was almost amusing to know that the caller—

probably some woman with heavy moneybags—was in need of a dead man.

"They won't let me go, Dill. They won't. I need to get out of here. Please come and rescue me. Please."

Simpson considered those words. A prisoner? One of Nightfly's pushers? No. Too old for a college gal. Obviously a former client of Dillow's. The pet name and all . . . Dill. Simpson wanted to pick up the receiver, but he also didn't want to. Let her keep talking.

"I'm still at the home, Dill. My son did this to me. I must get out!" The woman's voice turned erratic. "They're coming, Dill. I gotta go." The line went dead.

Simpson was in the dark for a moment. He quickly went to pick up the phone and called the operator.

"Operator, my name is Agent Simpson, with the Drug Enforcement Agency. Do you need my badge number? Okay . . . well, a call just came in on this line and I'd like to have its origination—the number and address if you would."

A half hour later, Agent Simpson was at the Bell Isle Home, a residence for addiction recovery. He arranged for a nurse to give him a quick tour of the facility—nothing too difficult for a man who projects some authority. And the badge didn't hurt.

"I figure we'd start with the most dramatic areas of the residence and work our way down. The local hospitals have been overwhelmed with drug abusers." The nurse's name was Bonnie, with a nose, chin, and pockmarked cheeks that were chiseled enough to be featured in a video game. She wasn't an ugly woman, but she'd never win a beauty pageant, either. Somewhere underneath that white outfit she had on was a thin frame. But beyond Bonnie's appearance, she had a most pleasant attitude.

"These emergency rooms began to fill up with tweakers and addicts who experience paranoid schizophrenic breaks . . . uncontrollable shaking, chest pains, heart problems, brain seizures. See that patient there?"

The man had an outrageous Afro and was tall like a pole, except that he was horizontal now, strapped down to a bed in what looked like a hospital room. Simpson cringed as he watched the man shake and jerk under the leather restraints. The man's expression was one of fright and alarm. He foamed at the mouth, and at times, it seemed he might break free.

"Isn't anyone gonna do something for him?" Simpson asked, looking to Bonnie and then back at the patient.

"We are doing something. We're saving him from destroying himself. Harold is a tweaker. He's been in and out of the hospital. Problem is his medical emergency is incurable. The hospital can't do a thing for him. That's why he's here. We'll look after Harold by affording him shelter, food, and attention. But unless he completes the addiction program we have here . . . unless he makes a big effort to change his habits, he'll continue to torture himself. He's lucky he's here, really. These guys rob and steal to support their addiction, or they kill themselves trying."

"These tweakers . . . are there many of them? Or is this an isolated case?"

"Let's keep walking, Agent Simpson." And they did. They passed five more rooms where other patients lay strapped down just like the first.

"All of 'em? Tweakers?"

"That's right, and these are just from the last few hours. But they eventually come down from the worst, like this patient. See her arms? How they're flopped off of the bed? That tells me the drugs are wearing off. We'll be removing the restraints shortly, and she'll be moved to this section over here. This is where our residents recover slowly from the tweaking stage. As you can see, a lot of lounging, watching TV, and reading goes on. This is the time when a lot of these residents should be thanking God they're still alive."

Simpson couldn't help wondering which one of these patients was Dillow's caller. He focused on the older women in the room. There were four. All the other residents in the area were too young or male. One of the four women was sitting in a corner by herself, feet up on another chair. She had graying hair, the front of which swept back in a creative swoop. Her hands were clasped and still in her lap as she looked out of the window at the garden.

"The woman in the corner, with her feet up . . . what's her name?"

"That's Mrs. Carole," Bonnie answered after checking her clipboard. Bonnie had a peculiar expression.

"Something wrong?" Simpson asked.

"It's just that I don't know this patient to be a regular. She must've come in recently while I was on vacation."

"Does she have a last name?"

"We don't use last names in here, Agent Simpson. It helps to protect the patient. The whole confidentiality bit, you know?"

"Would it help if I said please?" Agent Simpson turned up the charm, something he was sure Bonnie hadn't experienced in a long time.

"Well . . . since you are an agent . . . here to protect us, are you?"

Simpson nodded.

"Then I suppose I could help you out. Hold tight. I'll be right back." Bonnie stepped away for the records department while the agent parked in front of a soda machine, checking his pocket for change.

" 'Scuse me, sir, got a dollar? I'm really thirsty. I could use a soda real bad." The woman before him wasn't taller than five feet. She was old about the face—even her skin was blemished with age. But the voice. She was speaking like a child. Sounded like those little blue cartoon characters he watched when his children were younger.

"I guess," Simpson stuttered, more or less out of mild shock than fear. He pulled a dollar from his pocket, gave it to the short woman, and she walked away looking at the money like a good book. Simpson looked at the soda machine, then back at the woman drifting away. Then he chuckled under his breath, figuring that he'd been duped. Simpson finally put four quarters in the machine and pressed the button to dispense a ginger ale. A red light flashed near the "Out of Stock" print. He chose a V8 instead, twisting his lip some.

"'Scuse me, sir, got a dollar? I'm really thirsty. I could use a soda real bad."

Simpson froze. He was dumbfounded. The little woman with the miniature voice was back. She spoke to Simpson as though she'd never seen him before. Her demeanor was just as convincing. Simpson wondered if this was déjà vu or if he was going crazy. He eventually shook the stupid from his expression. He looked again at the woman as if she was the bubonic plague, said nothing, and walked away from her.

"She botherin' you?" Bonnie asked as she approached Simpson. Already the nurse was casting a disciplinary eye at Simpson's solicitor.

"Nope. Just discussing . . . V8 . . . yeah. Want some?"

Bonnie looked at him with a doubtful expression. "Anyway, her name is Mrs. Carole Fears."

Simpson's head sank into his shoulder some and he studied Carole Fears, his mind doing all the calculations. Agent Carson's words repeated in his head. "See if the name Jimmy Fears, aka Jimmy Z, comes up . . . we didn't pick him up . . . he's still wanted . . . the locals wanna talk to him about a murder . . ."

"Where are they taking her?" Simpson asked as he watched a staff orderly escort Mrs. Fears away.

"Could be for medication, a call, a visit—for a number of things."

"Listen, Bonnie . . . you've been very helpful. Very helpful. Would it be an intrusion to find out her schedule? And possibly when or where she's permitted to make phone calls? I also need a visitor list—if there is such a thing." Bonnie had her hands on her hips, likely questioning Simpson's nerve. Then Simpson added, "Here to protect you, Bonnie." The agent gave her cheek an affectionate pinch. She instantly blushed and went about her missionary duty of fulfilling Simpson's requests.

Meanwhile, Simpson meandered in the same direction as Mrs. Fears. She was escorted down a corridor and through a set of sliding glass doors until she sat at a table tucked to the rear of a courtyard. There were a number of tables out there, all with large umbrellas to keep the sun at bay. Simpson stood by the sliding doors to watch from the corridor.

Mother."

"James, I wish you wouldn't come here to see me like this."

"Believe it or not, I give a damn, Mother."

"Oh. That's why you had me committed?"

"I didn't commit you. I saved you. You were out of your mind."

"Says who?"

"Mother, you were out on Thirteenth Street!"

"So?"

"You were trying to sell your body for drugs, Mother. Wake up. If you didn't come here, you might be with some stranger. Maybe he'd give you AIDS. Maybe he'd—"

"I don't wanna hear anymore!" Mrs. Fears got up to leave.

"Mom—please." Jimmy reached out fast enough to grab his mother's elbow. He sat her back down. "I don't wanna discuss that stuff. I just came to see you . . . to be your son."

"My son wouldn't turn me in."

"Dad says hi."

"You want me to leave again?" his mother threatened.

"Okay, okay, okay. Well, what do you wanna talk about, Mom?"

"Where's your friend?"

"Who?"

"Dill . . . I mean, Dillow. Joshua Dillow. Uh . . . how's he doin'?"

Jimmy's face turned to stone. His complexion reddened. "Forget him, Mom. He's no friend," he said.

"You really should try to keep your friends, James. You never know when they might come in handy."

Jimmy was sick of the idea as it invaded his thoughts again. Dillow had turned his mother out. She was strung out and desperate for him. Jimmy couldn't wait to say what he had to say. Maybe it would inject a dose of reality.

"Mother?"

"Yes, Son."

"Joshua Dillow? The guy I brought over the house? Well, he's dead. He's been dead for weeks."

"No . . ." Carole Fears said this in one long breath. "I don't believe you, James. You're lying to me."

"Haven't you been reading the newspapers, Mom? Or watching TV?"

"No, I'm too busy being miserable. I need . . . I need to be around some real people. Some freak with a bush Afro keeps screaming all day and night. Another midget woman asks me for money every single hour. The nurses won't give me the . . . the stuff I need."

"You'll be okay, Mom." Jimmy said this as he looked around at other patients and their visitors. "Are you eating yet?"

"I guess . . . a little," she responded in a frustrated tone. "I could use a nice pizza with extra cheese."

"Like we used to have?" Jimmy hoped he could get his mother to reminisce about old times.

"Mmm-hmm . . . in the good ole days."

It was hard to look at his mother and see what she once was: the distinguished woman of the world, chairwoman, coordinator, community leader . . . mother. Now, all he could see was what his eyes picked up. She was withdrawn, and the color was missing from her skin. She didn't stay still for more than ten seconds, always shifting around, looking here and there as though someone might see her. Her eyes were bloodshot, sunk deep in their darkened sockets. The only bright effect was the hair. It was well kept, as though a beautician had just been at it. But so was every woman's hair at the home.

Jimmy remembered that hair care was one of the services offered at this place—which his mom's health insurance didn't cover. That expense came out of his pockets.

However different his mother appeared didn't change Jimmy's desire to spend time with her. It was a different story weeks ago, before Diane had been arrested with all those others from South Beach. It was Diane who had filled that void for him, mothering him and keeping him as her houseboy and sex toy. But the bottom fell out from under her financial gains. She was in MDC now, being held without bail. And her Juki boutique had been closed, confiscated by the Feds. On top of that, Jimmy heard they wanted him. It seemed, in light of all this drama, that it was time to go back to his foundation. No matter how messed up his mother was she was still that for him; his foundation.

The way Jimmy Z carried himself, with the baseball cap pulled down deep over his eyes, and a pair of dark shades to boot, he wasn't looking to be noticed. Moreover, Simpson figured, he might not be interested in being arrested, either. Therefore, Simpson pulled out his Glock, safety on, in order to keep Jimmy scared straight. He expected the young man to come out to the parking lot, and so he waited until he was within a good distance.

"Jimmy Z? Stop right there. I'm Agent Simpson with the Drug Enforcement Agency. Would you step this way please?"

"I ain't got no drugs on me."

"This arrest is part drug related and part murder related. Either way, you're gonna need to come with me."

BOOK SIX

CHAPTER FORTY-TWO

MAJOR SHIFT IN COLOMBIAN DRUG WAR
by Scott Deville

Bogotá, Colombia—Mario Nunez, Jr., is becoming the next Pablo Escobar. Those are significant shoes to fill, considering that there have been many types of drug lords on the planet, but none were like Pablo Escobar.

Now it seems that Escobar's violent legacy has served as a measuring stick by which others have been groomed and influenced. It is here in Bogotá where one of those followers, the notorious Mario Nunez, Jr., grew up as a child of the drug war. And his father, Roberto Nunez, literally planted the seeds.

HIS ROOTS

Born Roberto Nunez, Jr., Mario was orphaned when his father was found to be stealing from the crops that he helped to plant and maintain for Pablo Escobar. The consequence came swift and gravely when one of Escobar's death squads came early one morning to massacre the Nunez family. But while Maria (age 16) and Elsa (age 8) were slaughtered alongside their mother and father, the 5-year-old twins, Roberto and Roberta, managed to escape unharmed. The children were subsequently swept far away from their Rio Blanco village to live new lives with a close relative. Roberta became engrossed in her schoolwork, while Roberto (whose name was changed to Mario in order to avoid association with his late father) ran with the infamous barro boys of Bogotá.

"He started out like the others, stealing fruit, and then he moved up to stealing cars," said a merchant who has owned a fruit and vegetable stand on Bolivar Street in downtown for years. Bogotá Street lore paints Mario Nunez as a fast-running, impressionable young man who easily caught on to the dirty deeds of his peers.

"That's how he got in deep trouble," a local told reporters for Colombia's leading newspaper, *El Tempo*. "He stole the wrong person's car and they kidnapped him and cut his left pinkie off. That's why he always wears that black glove."

Mario also grew fond of chewing on narcotic leaves to keep him pain-free, doped up, and trigger happy. Through his teens, Mario ran with Miguel Batista (his kidnapper) and videotaped the many grotesque activities of Batista's death squad. Some say that by witnessing such heinous acts of torture and violence, Mario became a next-generation practitioner of the same. Experience alone would give Mario Nunez license to advocate the same perils, and with the fuel of drug wealth, it would be that much easier to fill Escobar's shoes. Now, the international drug war would have a new wrath to bear.

HIS RISE

By age 18, Mario Nunez had organized a small gang and waged his own war on anyone in his path. His first target was Miguel Batista, who not only severed Mario's finger, but also held Mario captive until his daily routine of bagging cocaine and videotaping tortures was a way of life.

After chopping Batista's body until he was unrecognizable, Nunez and his men ambushed river patrols along Colombia's 1,021-mile border. They destroyed patrol boats and stole weapons to support their waves of violence. Nunez targeted government-sponsored efforts, such as spraying campaigns that were set to eliminate cocaine traffic. He also clobbered rival cartelitos (cartel copycats).

El Tempo reported that Nunez and his renegades would infiltrate the more powerful, well-financed cartelitos by posing as independent contractors. He'd assisted traffickers by shooting down government planes to protect and control the sky above the jungles where cocaine was processed. In doing so, Mario Nunez proved himself valuable, helping to guarantee these operations. However, once they became trusted, they'd betray the trafficker, often killing him and his associates, and they'd collect whatever drugs, guns, and money they could find. This was repeated over and over again.

Consistence and the inevitable growth of his own guerrilla army bolstered Nunez with an empire that overpowered all others. He bought local police forces that didn't have the money to go against him. If they didn't give in immediately, they were frightened into submission. They had to gun down at least one police chief, which showed all of Colombia that this was serious. Nunez wasn't afraid of killing those in high places.

In some instances, all he had to do was set deadlines for competitors to surrender their operations. This is a testament to how violence rules the drug war, encouraging every government from Panama to Venezuela and on down to Brazil to strengthen defense forces in every way possible. But things got worse.

What have we done to deserve this?" asked a villager, holding a photo of his three-year-old daughter, whose belly is scarred from machete wounds. Most of her left arm is missing, severed at the elbow. "They just went house to house and threw our families on the floor. They chopped and chopped. A hand. An arm. Always the left. Always the left," he said of the Nunez rebels who went on mutilating whole villages, including infants, by hacking off limbs, all in some maniacal wrath. A second photo showed an attractive woman, maybe nineteen, with stumps where her hands had been.

Mr. Higuera Duque, an American Embassy official in Bogotá, described these acts as overwhelming. "I was dumbfounded when I heard about this. I thought someone made this up."

This latest outrage was a revenge for his country betraying him. Late last year, following the U.S. Drug War Report and the $1.3 billion in emergency aid, Colombia's major most left-wing guerrilla group, the Fuerzas Armadas Revolucionarias de Colombia (FARC) joined with U.S. Special Forces commandos to go after Nunez. It is said that the preying on helpless villagers is Nunez's own malicious brand of retaliation. The only kind he knows.

HIS REIGN

Today, experts estimate that Mario Nunez is responsible for trafficking twenty tons of cocaine per month into the U.S. That does not include what Nunez does in Europe and other countries. This means that he is not only supplying 10 percent of the drugs that make it here, but that his gang-turned–death squad has now grown into a monster of a cocaine empire, one that may reach Escobar proportions. If the Escobar legacy is any measure, then elections, government, law enforcement, and the future of Colombia may well be under the control of a wanted man . . . a new wicked warrior.

Meanwhile, polls show that a majority of Americans are willing to have their taxes raised, plus give up some constitutional freedoms to help eradicate the flow of drugs into the United States. "We need a martial plan," said the president in his most recent address to the nation. "We've gotta do a lot more than 'just say no.' What sounded good way back in the eighties is no longer relevant today."

But indeed, a lot of things like violence, like lawlessness, and like death still are.

Scott Deville is a staff writer for the *Times*.

I f I was crazy like they say, I'd kill this Deville character just because he underestimated my worth. Imagine . . . after so much work, me moving just twenty tons of product.

Twenty tons! That's only half of what we're moving on a bad month . . ."

Mario Nunez was settled into a plush cushioned couch on his ultra-quiet Challenger 3000, one of three private jets he owned. The sky was light and cloudy. Mario was perturbed about the story in the *Times*, but he had more on his mind, like the issues with Van Dyke in Miami and the queasiness he felt from looking down on the Atlantic Ocean so endless below the jet.

Yet, what was really taxing his intelligence was keeping tabs on his empire. It had grown so big in just ten years' time, like a tornado with plenty of dead bodies in its tracks. But so much was going on at the same time . . . the farming, the guards who watched the farmers, the convoys that moved the uncut product to labs . . . the stash houses, huts, and secret warehouses . . . the transportation of the product on barges, cargo planes, concealed in suitcases, and in the bodies of travelers.

"I can't even say I'm mad about comparing me to Escobar. Shit, Escobar's dead! I don't wanna be like him!" To Nunez's subordinates it was obvious that something bothered him.

Carlos—with the bushy mustache, the ponytail, and the gashes on his right cheek and under his left eye—sat by, not intending on saying a word to interrupt. He was accustomed to this fuming and ranting, just as Poppo was.

Poppo was in a lounge chair, within view of both Carlos and the boss. It didn't matter either way to Poppo; kill the reporter or don't kill the reporter. He'd be there by the boss' side. Besides, Poppo was getting a kick out of this job . . . this position. It more or less legitimized what he was from adolescence—a bully. Always hungry for action. Always in hot water. Only now he got paid for it.

"But what really gets me? What makes me most upset about this story? It's the goddamned photo. They could've picked a better one." Mario lied about what bothered him. He wouldn't say that the story reignited images of his past—

his family being murdered and butchered, his pinkie being snipped off. To speak of such pain might show weakness. It might show the misery that still bubbled within the bowels of his consciousness. The things that made him tick.

This wasn't the first time Mario read the article, but it was the first time he had a chance to internalize it. It was a five-hour flight from Bogotá to Miami, which gave him more time to focus.

"And look . . . they talk like the United States isn't in on this. They keep saying the government. The government? Isn't Van Dyke the government? Isn't Brooks and McLean and Quinn and Stroman part of their gov-ern-ment? What about the DEA agents on the payroll? Are they government? Oh! And let us not forget the judges! Don't we have one in most of their districts? Aren't they government?"

"And don't forget the military."

"Oh shit, Poppo, you right! All those fuckin' guns they sell us . . . their entire so-called surplus. What's the last deal they did with us, Carlos?"

"A hundred mill, Boss."

"A hundred fuckin' million dollars we pay the U.S. government for their M-16s and their grenades. Shit they can't use unless the big man says I declare war."

"I like that M-60," Poppo said to Carlos. "The mothafucker shoots right through the wall."

"They know damn well where the money comes from. And yet, they speak about me like I'm the devil."

"It's, how you say, po-lit-ical," added Carlos, finally feeling like a part of the conversation. "They must tell lies to cover up what they do under the table."

"With me as the target," said Nunez. "And you should read this here about us killing poor people in the villages." Nunez folded the paper and tossed it to Carlos. "Did we do that?" he asked sarcastically.

There was a moment of quiet. Carlos flipped through the paper, shrugged at the photo of his boss, and passed the paper to Poppo. After a few pages, Poppo lit up.

"Damn!" Poppo's exclamation woke the others—Mario

from his stupor and Carlos from the video he was watching on the giant screen. Then Poppo mumbled something in Spanish to mean "pretty mothafucka."

Carlos took the paper, as though he had a right to it before Poppo did. "Oooh . . . she is a looker. Got one of our names, too. You think she's Latino?"

"No doubt."

"But with a name like this? Novick? Roberta Novick?" Carlos emphasized the last name, but it was the first name that rang a bell for Mario. His sister was named Roberta and he hadn't seen her in close to fifteen years.

"Gimme that," Mario said, snatching back the paper.

"Maybe she married into the name," Poppo said.

"Maybe," Carlos replied.

Mario Nunez stared at the photo of Roberta Novick. Here she was in the United States, hobnobbing with high-society types; celebrating some appointment she received in the banking industry. His eyes started to mess with his head, drifting out of focus, then back in. He felt dizzy.

"You all right, Boss? Hey! What's wrong?"

Nunez was on his feet by now. The newspaper was in hand and at his side, then it fell to the floor. He meandered and stared like a zombie. He stopped. He turned. He said nothing. But if Carlos or Poppo could read his mind, they'd know that Mario Nunez had just found his twin sister.

Mr. Van Dyke," Nunez said as he stepped down from the jet and onto the tarmac of Opaloka Airport.

"Mr. Nunez. I didn't expect you to come along for this transaction. Usually you send someone."

"I thought I'd surprise you, Mr. Van Dyke." Mario put a hand on Van Dyke's shoulder and they stepped ahead of the others who scurried to and fro, handling business as usual. "Besides, I wanted to discuss this that I'm hearing about you at the center of some investigation."

"Oh that. It's nothing really. Or . . . it's about to be nothing."

"That's good to hear. It wouldn't be in our best interest to have to go and change everything now."

"If anything has to be changed, it'll only be on my end of things. I assure you, Mr. Nunez."

Not many things change on PC Block 2, the protective custody wing of Miami Detention Center. Not unless there were extenuating circumstances, like a person being released suddenly. Or a prisoner might be sentenced in court, and soon thereafter, transferred to a far-off prison where he'd serve the majority of the prison term. There were only two other ways to leave the block. Death was one of them. The other was for the safety of the inmates and staff.

"Where they takin' you, Legend?" Charlucci was speaking through the portal in his cell door. Legend was in the common area outside the cell with a set of handcuffs on and a few belongings in hand.

Legend shrugged in response to Charlucci's question.

"What's that supposed to mean? You must know where you're going . . . you got your shit with you." Charlucci could see the toothbrush and toothpaste, the pillow and a Bible in Legend's hands. He also knew that court appearances wouldn't come around for weeks, maybe a month or two. And you didn't take stuff like that with you if you were going home. Charlucci was left to draw conclusions. "Tell me you didn't make a deal, Legend . . . Legend! Look me in the eyes! Tell me you didn't. You did, didn't you!? Legend! Answer me!!!"

"Hold it down, Charlucci," said the correctional officer escorting Legend from the tier.

"Fuck that! You hot mothafucka, lemme see you again. Ever. Nothin's gonna stop me from gettin' at you!" Legend was almost out of earshot, almost through the doorway. "You mothafuckin' freak! Rat mothafucka!!! You're dead. You hear me? Dead!!!" Charlucci banged his palm against the steel door, a fruitless effort at breaking something.

So this is it. This is my fate. Sitting in some man's jail cell while the whole world turns on me. Goddamned snitches. They can do all kinds of dirt with me, but they can't stay honorable when the pressure's on. Weak-ass mothafuckas, all of 'em. Charlucci's venom was for his ears only.

The thoughts of who he wanted to kill and how were useless and ineffective threats within those cinder-block walls and the steel reinforcements. He could only imagine what all those freaks and queers were saying. They were probably all pointing the finger at him . . . Charlucci, the scapegoat.

There was a snitch. Charlucci understood now. Legend must've requested to be moved from PC 2 so as not to have contact with Charlucci. Scared mothafucka. No more than ten minutes later, the CO returned with another prisoner in an orange jumpsuit.

"Oh shit, Pauly!" Charlucci couldn't contain his excitement. "They got you, too?? Awww, fuuuck!" Charlucci said this while he considered all the burdens. All this time he'd been careful to keep Paul and his wife Lu Anne hidden and out of sight . . . all this time keeping them content, well-paid, and still busy as old-timers. All of that careful planning had all gone up in smoke. Charlucci could only imagine that scene at the cottage: the stash, the travelers . . . the Feds probably confiscating the home.

The officer locked Paul Montalbo in the cell where Legend had been and asked if he'd need anything and if he'd be all right. Then he left the tier, flashing his suspicious eye.

"Pauly . . . it's me, Charlucci." Charlucci didn't have to exactly shout, but he was loud. "You okay?" The cells weren't far from one another, yet still out of eyesight.

"Yeah . . . I'll make it. I'm a big boy."

"How'd they get you, Pauly?"

"Your guess is as good as mine. They just pulled up to the cottage and arrested us."

"Us?" Charlucci was thinking about the travelers, those women who came from Colombia with their stomachs full of coke-filled condoms. He didn't consider Lu Anne.

"Lu Anne. They arrested Lu Anne, son."

"Fuck! Shit! Damn!" The reaction was only appropriate. "I'm sorry to hear that shit, Pauly. Really. These are some ruthless mothafuckas." Charlucci wanted to, but he couldn't dare ask about the women from Colombia—at least not now.

"She'll be okay. She's a strong woman. Don't take no shit from nobody, she don't."

"Oooh . . . a newbie. Welcome to PC 2, big boy. If you need somethin' . . ."

"Kill that noise, Trixie. That man don't want no parts of you."

Trixie sucked his teeth and said, "How you know? You just mad 'cause Legend gonna tell on yo' ass."

"Anyway, Pauly . . . you got a lawyer? Somebody good?"

"To tell you the truth, I met with a public defender, somebody from Legal Aid. I got her card here with me. But . . . I don't know, Charlucci. I've been on the run for thirty years. I'm tired, son. Tired. Maybe I ought to just lie down. Ain't much left to me . . . maybe five, seven years."

"Don't talk like that, Pauly. You're just depressed right now. We can lick this thing. You just have faith." Charlucci may have talked his pep talk, but it merely bounced around the tier. Pauly was far past depressed.

The days passed. Pauly learned the ropes: how the schedule worked with the showers, feeding time, the one hour of freedom that was given for prisoners to walk the tier alone. Pauly could even count on hearing the guy down the way who punched his cell wall twice a day. He negotiated his one hour of phone time with Mickey-the-finger in return for Mickey's dessert. Since Pauly didn't really have anyone to call, he could count on an extra cake, piece of fruit, or tub of Jell-O pudding every day. In the meantime, Charlucci passed notes back and forth, depending on who happened to be walking the tier. They only irritated Pauly.

The eighteen-year-old computer hacker was getting on everybody's nerves with his singing. The prisoners were permitted to purchase Walkman radios, among a few other things, from commissary. So now, the kid was acting like a stereo system, singing every damned song that came on. Pauly could make out some of the songs by James Taylor,

Billy Joel, and Elton John. But the way the kid was singin' them sounded horrible—the type of singin' that made a crying baby sound like sweet music.

Everybody was tellin' the computer geek to shut his mouth, but he was ignoring the whole tier. It didn't matter who was sleeping. As far as he was concerned, he could get as arrogant as he wished. Nobody could touch him with all this maximum security in the way.

It was clear that the wall-punching mercenary dude had been on the tier for quite a while by the long conversations the guy had with the CO, as if they were lifelong friends. And one day, Pauly noted that the CO left the eighteen-year-old's and the mercenary dude's doors unlocked at the same time. That was a big no-no in this wing of the jail.

When the CO left the tier, the wall-puncher eased out of his door and eased into the eighteen-year-old's. He didn't spend much time in there, and there was nothing to indicate the assault and battery that the kid deserved. But ever since that day, the singing stopped altogether. Not a peep was heard.

P aul Montalbo finally met with Fay Joseph, the Legal Aid lady. He could tell she was wet behind the ears with this legal game. On her first visit, it was mere introduction. But her second visit was for Paul to review the discovery material for his case.

"Discovery material?" he asked her.

"That's the evidence that the government has against you. We call it discovery."

"You mean I get to see that?"

"Absolutely. It's in the rules of criminal procedure." Paul still had a hard time accepting that idea; him, a criminal. "Mr. Montalbo, let me just say this for the record, because I sense just a hint of apprehension here. This case is an uphill battle—I won't lie to you—but I intend to fight for you all the way. I'm here to represent you . . . to fight for your best interests."

"You make it sound like a boxing match, just that you're

wearing the gloves and I'm the one who's gotta take the punches."

"That's a good analogy. Really. And it's ninety-nine percent correct. That is, for everybody else in the courtroom. The prosecutor is probably the reigning heavyweight champion. You might be the number one contender. The judge? Well, he could be the referee, to see that it's a fair fight . . . to make snap judgments when there are questionable maneuvers—like hitting below the belt. Like keeping both fighters well informed. Me? I'm your corner man, er, corner woman, I should say. I'm gonna lay out the strategy . . . consult you the whole way through. I gotta use my knowledge and experience to help you pull this off . . . to make sure your rights aren't violated."

"Experience?" Paul said, hearing only what he wanted to. "Doll, not for nothing but I'm probably fifty plus years older than you. If there's anyone here with experience . . ."

"Mr. Montalbo, you're fifty-eight years older than me, to be exact. Number two, I'm not intimidated by the age difference, or whatever experience you have. Frankly, sir, your experience is in the area of smuggling and of being a fugitive—with all due respect. But whatever little experience I have? It's the experience that's important right now. The *only* experience that's important." There was a second or two of deathly silence between the two, allowing the reality to marinate. "Sir, I'm not here to bust your balls, for lack of a better phrase. I am here to help you win. Believe it or not, I want to see you back home with your wife."

"How is she—my wife?"

"She's good. She's not the happiest woman right now—I can tell you that—but she's holding up a lot better than a lot of women I've seen in these situations. Now . . . how 'bout we make use of some of this knowledge that I spent long hours in school to learn."

Paul had to respect Fay Joseph's iron-fisted approach. It was probably all he had. The two of them, lawyer and client, went over the discovery. It reached back into his thirty-year-old smuggling case, how he impersonated a U.S. Customs

Agent to help cargo get by the bloodhounds. There were the mug shots taken then and now. A Wanted poster with his different profiles was the same one the Feds had in the various post offices all these years. Finally, Paul noticed a familiar item in the list of vehicles and license plates he was said to have used to evade authorities through the years.

"This isn't mine," Paul said, pointing to a Maxima on the list.

"It says here that . . . lemme see . . . the Maxima was registered to your wife Lu Anne."

"I've never owned a Maxima in my life. Neither has she."

"Lu Anne told me the same thing. But how would the FBI link the car to you?"

The meeting suddenly froze in time. Montalbo's brow furrowed as he recalled a Maxima stopping by the cottage one night. He remembered that some woman—he believed her name was Diane—left the car there and took a taxi home. He remembered a couple of Charlucci's gringos coming by to operate on the car within the solitude of the garage, welding and hammering and whatnot.

Montalbo never asked about it, because after all, Charlucci was the boss. He was the one who even added on the garage in the first place.

"What did the Feds do? Follow the Maxima to my place?"

"Could be. Let's look at the three-o-twos."

"The three-o-twos?"

"Yes, written witness accounts. They're like testimonies on paper. Maybe there's one from an agent." Fay shuffled through pages. "Oh . . . here we are. You ever heard of a Detective Banks?"

Paul shook his head.

Fay made a face, studying thin air. Then she flipped through her personal notes.

"Funny. You had a couple of guests at your home when they came to arrest you."

"Okay." Paul didn't agree or disagree. He merely heard Fay. "So what's that mean?"

"Don't read me too deep, sir. What I wanted to mention is that the DEA report also notes two women in your home. It said that a Detective Banks came to pick up the women."

"Really?"

"Yes, really. It seems pretty peculiar to me—this Detective Banks submitting a three-o-two saying . . . look here . . . he says he spotted a Maxima at a funeral parlor. And that he was staking out the parlor in search of known felons."

Paul rubbed his face like he wanted to erase it with his palm. Bobby's funeral, he told himself. Damn. But Paul suddenly shook the spell. "Wait a minute. I never saw Bobby at a funeral parlor. I went to his funeral—it was outdoors at the Glades Cemetery. I remember it well."

"So why would the detective say a Florida funeral parlor? See here?"

"The hell with the three-o-twos!" Paul was all upset now. "I'm tellin' you I went to a cemetery, not a funeral parlor. He's lyin'."

"So how could he know about the Maxima?"

"I'm wondering the same exact thing." He gritted his teeth and considered all the angles. There was only one person who could tie all of these things together. And it wasn't any Detective Banks.

Pam Brown disembarked from the agency's Gulfstream jet and nodded at a couple of agents standing there on the tarmac of LaGuardia Airport in New York. It wasn't much of a greeting, but it would have to do. Pam was busy thinking; busy trying to make two cents out of the penny's worth of information she had to go on.

She knew that there was shady business down in Miami. She just didn't know how extensive it was or just how deep the involvement reached. Why was Goldridge trying to protect Van Dyke? It was clear to her that Charlucci was a major player in the operation . . . a point man even, no matter how much money he was making. Just as Ortiz was a front man for Charlucci and Nightfly for Ortiz. This wasn't hard to figure out. Everybody had somebody else who was dirtier than them. That's just how it was in any industry.

Pam was headed for 43rd Street now, with her escorts in one of the agency's supercharged luxury Suburbans, with its black monochrome exterior and level 2 bulletproofing. An agent hipped her to a *Times* article that claimed an A to Z account of the "Cocaine Express," and Pam went ahead and set up an appointment with Scott Deville. The name hadn't rung a bell with her when she first read the article, and she wondered even now how the reporter was able to put together such extensive details, more so than any other reporter she'd heard of.

Fully aware of the power that a press pass affords a no-body, Pam was curious. Maybe he had some other stuff that didn't make the paper. Why wouldn't he? She did.

Now she was taking a call from Agent Simpson, who was in Miami. He explained about Montalbo and about Jimmy Z's arrest. Jimmy was singing like an injured crow—Simpson's exact words. He indicated Nightfly as Dillow's murderer, telling about the phony heist at the stash house. He also said he thought Ortiz was the one to kill Nightfly, but the Feds already suspected that. Plenty of surveillance photos to back it up, too.

"Did he happen to know anything about Van Dyke?"

"Unfortunately not. But this chick he was banging named Diane? The woman who owned the Juki boutique? She says she's the one who literally introduced the two—Charlucci and Van Dyke. She says she and Van Dyke were an item. Obviously, she wants to cut a deal, too."

"His mistress."

"Basically. The police aren't talking down here, either. The detective I told you about? Banks? He keeps avoiding me. The guy at the roadblock? Chief Wild? He denies everything."

"Likely story."

"But get this. I visited air traffic control and met with a lady operator named Moss. She handled the radio navigation on the night you all hit the roadblock at Opaloka."

"Yeah?"

"She brought out the logbook and the details on the flight. You know, how many people, the color of the airplane, single or multiengine, the weight, the flight plans—all of it. And guess what?"

"Bring it," directed Pam.

"Nothing matched the satellite photo you sent me. They have a Cessna four twenty-one noted. One pilot. No passengers. Red plane. But the photo shows four men getting off the plane. It's a Challenger—one of those new three thousand models. And the jet is white. It had to cost a ton."

"What's it all mean?"

"Huh . . . nothing, until I checked out Miss Moss. Would you believe if I told you that's her married name? Her name at birth was Joanne Van Dyke . . . his sister."

"No shit!"

"I think we've got a family affair goin' on down here. I just need to thread it together."

"Well, you keep up the good work, Simpson. I have a couple of tasks up here in New York. Then, I think I wanna come and pay Mr. Charlucci one last visit."

"I wouldn't miss that for the world."

Pam picked up the *Times* story again, this time reading it with a closer eye. The traffic on the Grand Central was hell . . . so there was time to kill.

CHAPTER FORTY-THREE

There's a first time for everything, Pam figured as she waited in the lobby of the *Times* building. Never had she gone to meet with a reporter for the purpose of discovery. If there was any discovering to be done, she had access to Interpol and the entire FBI database, as well as her connects in other arms of intelligence, such as the CIA and the Secret Service. What could a reporter possibly tell her that she didn't already know? Or that she couldn't already find out?

Fueled by curiosity, Pam stood by as messenger after messenger rushed into the marbled lobby. Others approached a bank of in-house phones, probably to give what they thought was a story, Pam guessed.

"Agent Brown, it's a pleasure to finally meet you."

"And you," Pam said as she shook Scott Deville's hand. Soft, she thought of his grip. She second-guessed that perhaps he was discounting her value.

Scott showed the agent around the editorial department, the business office, classified, and the presses. Finally, he introduced Pam to his editor before stepping into a conference room. She figured Scott to be the occupant of one of the sea of cubicles out beyond the glass windows of the conference room. He probably shared the room with other reporters for moments like this.

"Thank you for coming down."

"Thank you for being receptive. Can we get down to business?"

"Sure." The two sat across from each other at one of ten conference tables in the room. Scott picked up the phone and tapped out an extension. "I'm in conference. Yes . . . ahh . . . four twelve." Scott then hung up.

Pam noticed the number 412 printed above the touchtone buttons. Her cell phone bleeped and she pulled it from her waist. "Sorry," Pam said. "Excuse me," she whispered inaudibly as she stood up to stroll toward the window with its towering perspective of midtown. "Yes, Simpson. I'm just beginning my meeting." Pam could see the reflection of Scott before her. A woman was approaching him. "Really?" Pam said, responding to the sudden news. "Oh yeah? Him, too? You're kidding. What, did he sense that I was about to come down and get in his ass?" Pam chuckled. "Okay. This is sensitive. Take statements from Montalbo and Ortiz. Save the Snowman for me. Whatever information he wants to give, it better be soup to nuts." Pam listened to Simpson as she looked on at the reporters, both of them with an eye toward her. Pam flashed her forefinger, indicating that she'd be a moment. "That sounds doable. Talk to the prosecutor and see if they'll give her bail. We don't need any heart attacks on our hands. That's not what this is about." With that, she ended the call.

Tina, you'll have to look into it, really."

"It could be serious, Scott. That's why I came to you."

"It could be frivolous too, Tina. I mean . . . a neighbor calling to drop a dime on a senator's wife? Suspecting that she's part of a male prostitution ring? Sounds a little too sensational to me."

"That, or Pulitzer Prize material."

"Yeah right, but I'm into this big coke story. Look yonder. DEA lady stage left."

"I'll see if I can get to it. I was really counting on your help, Scott. Something came up on the Harlem story . . . sounds like a volcano about to explode up there and I just don't have the time to pick up senators' wives stories."

"Get a rookie," Scott said, nearly pushing Tina away. He kept a forgiving grin and addressed Pam again.

"That shouldn't happen again, Mr. Deville. Shall we?" Both of them sat again. Conversations ensued outside and around the conference room, but so many hungry reporters were all out of ear-hustle range since the door was now shut, isolating its users from the entire editorial department.

"Alrighty then, Ms. Brown. We spoke briefly, but I have an idea of your interests. I just don't know how deep you're looking to go. I mean . . . am I gonna be investigated because of what I know? Because of what's in my head?"

"Not likely, Mr. Deville. Actually, if I read your work correctly, you're an advocate of goodwill. Maybe you even have ulterior motives. In either instance, sir—and I don't mean to frighten you, but—you're involved with some very dangerous subject matters . . . the kind that could get you in trouble."

"I've heard the stories, Ms. Brown. For God's sake, I write the stories. If there's anyone who should know, it's me. I guess I'm just not sold on all the violence. I sell it, yes. But sold on it? I don't think so. Charge it to too much *Gunsmoke*, *Bonanza*, and Dirty Harry. I guess I'm jaded."

"I've gotta respect your position—can I call you Scott?"

"Please."

"And you call me Pam. Scott, it's just that you never truly get a grip on this stuff until it's right up in your face . . . until you look death right between the eyes."

Scott's better judgment agreed with Pam. But his silly side thought of a joke he heard from one of those old Richard Pryor videos, something about John Wayne looking death in the face and saying: Get the fuck outta here, Death.

"When you start speculating and forcing your opinion as if it's fact . . . when you start putting folks' photos in the paper . . . it gets serious, pal."

For an instant, Scott was caught up in Pam's eyes. He was far past her attractive features and the feminine image. Even beyond her essence that seeped from her gaze, her lips and aura. No, Scott was looking into Pam Brown's soul, her heart, and her spirit.

On the other hand, Pam could see that the reporter—if he had earlier—no longer took her for granted. She could see that he recognized and acknowledged her power . . . her personal power. "Tell you what. Are you with me that drugs are evil? That they're hurting America?"

"Oh . . . heck yeah, I'm with you. Didn't you see the story I did on the Hale House in Harlem, its founder Mother Hale, and all the crack babies?"

"Sorry, I'm from Georgetown, Scott. I don't get the *Times* unless someone brings it to my attention."

"Well, I covered the subject like I was tracing my own family tree . . . a feature on how cocaine and crack has come to stomp on the less fortunate. I showed how a wealthy family virtually exterminated themselves form existence because of using. I even covered the epidemic in Philadelphia, where ten to twenty percent of all births this year were crack babies."

"I'd like to see that sometime. So . . . not to get sidetracked, but I believe you and I are on the same page."

"Yes, Ms. Brown, er, Pam . . . I strongly oppose coke, Ecstasy, meth, heroin especially, and frankly, I couldn't care less about marijuana. Despite the war of words going on about it being herbal or its medical use . . . you know the story."

"Too well. They can be all the advocates they want about the natural high, but I know of folks who caused pileups on the highway because of weed. I know of people who've leaped off of buildings thinking they can fly because of weed."

"The argument is, at least the one that stumps me, that alcohol and tobacco have killed more people with drunken driving, heart disease, and lung cancer than marijuana. And yet, those are legalized . . . controlled by the government. In other words, the government legalizes what it can control. What it can make money from. Who can stop people from growing marijuana plants in their backyards or even indoors?"

"I know that argument, too. And maybe a lot of this controlled addiction is backward. Maybe even controlled gaming is backward. But I'm not an answer person, Scott. I am an advocate for the good of human beings . . . the preservation of life and the law. I'm sure there are more thin lines between love and hate, more than you and I could discuss in a million years. More gray areas and red tape than we can imagine. But let's deal with what's on our plate . . . the things that we can change."

"You think we can change something? I mean as big as this monster is? Don't get me wrong . . . I'm not the pessimist. I just wonder how."

"First and foremost, Scott, we've got to trust each other. We've got to believe in this thing. We have to want change. Nothing but nothing happens unless it is first desired."

"Or unless it's a reaction, like with the chaos theory or evolution."

Pam made an expression to say that Scott was reaching way over her head. Still, she knew they were off to a good start.

"Have you been to Colombia, Scott?"

"Whoa. Get right to the point, don't you?"

Pam offered her matter-of-fact smile.

"As a matter of fact, I have. That's how I learned about the Nunez family. I went to Rio Blanco de Sotara and spoke with villagers."

"You know Spanish?" Pam asked.

"No. The U.S. Embassy assigned me an interpreter. I met with a few older folks who came to despise the Nunez name. They put their lives on the line to save Roberto and Roberta, his sister, when they were children . . . they hid the children in a local church in case the death squads came looking to finish the unfinished. Their motto is to leave no witnesses, you know."

"Oh—I know, all right."

"Well, they watched and they heard how Roberto, aka

Mario, grew into a maniac. Those were their words. He hurt a lot of people down there. Then I went to Bogotá."

"You and the interpreter?"

"Mmm-hmm."

"No protection?" Asked Pam.

"Afraid not."

Pam shook her head, not believing Scott's nerve. "You could've been killed, Scott. Tortured. Balls. You got some real balls on you, pal."

"Maybe . . . or maybe I just didn't know any better. Like when I was younger . . . I just took risks . . . threw the basketball from half-court. Chucked it. And swish! People thought I was crazy, but I made a lot of baskets that way. I guess I had a good eye."

Pam uttered a smirk now, realizing that Scott was clever. The two shared notes . . . Scott more than Pam.

"I did wanna show you this," Scott said. He unfolded the newspaper in his stack of research. Pam recalled the front page immediately. This was the paper that featured the reporter's "Major Shift in Colombian Drug War" story. The same one she'd left in the Suburban parked out on 43rd, where two agents were still waiting for her. Scott opened the paper to his story. He pointed to the photo of Mario Nunez.

"This is Mario Nunez." Now Scott pulled out another paper—it was the metro section of the very same edition—and leafed through a few pages. "Here . . ." Scott's finger was on the first in a row of six photos. "This is Roberta Nunez."

Pam knew this section of the paper—just like every metropolitan paper, with a collection of prized photos featuring the elite in that city. Pam's hometown paper, the *Washington Post*, had the same thing . . . the politicians, the jet-setters, the high society broads with their golden hair, gowns, and the good ole boys who loved them.

"But it says Roberta Novick."

"I know. It was a coincidence that I even spotted this photo. That it was in the same edition as the drug war story.

But look at the two photos of Mario and Roberta. These are the twins. The same ones the villagers saved back in Rio Blanco."

Pam marveled at the images. She brought them together, side by side.

"Damn, Scott. You're right. Coincidence?"

"Before you came here today, I did some more checking."

"I can believe that."

"Roberta Nunez was a student at Nacional University in Bogotá. She arrived here in the United States a few years ago, part of a student exchange program."

Pam was still as stone, but her heart was beating in double time.

"And get this." Scott didn't stop spewing information—stuff that Interpol would never have. "See the third photo?" Pam ignored the photo with Roberta and a bunch of her friends, all with that debutante flair the newspapers loved. "Here. This is Abigail Novick, a conservator at the Rose Center at The Museum of Natural History. And this here is her husband, Brendan . . . married nineteen years. Brendan is . . . you're gonna die when you hear this . . . he's the VP of mergers and acquisitions at Solomon Smith Barney, Wall Street." Pam tried to read between Scott's lines. "The couple lost a daughter in a bad car accident four years ago. All of a sudden they adopt a Colombian woman who is the same age as their dead daughter, giving her their last name and everything. I checked with the Department of Vital Statistics. They adopted Roberta just months ago, and gave her a good job. Look here . . . it says she's celebrating an appointment to Account Manager at European National Bank. It's like their daughter—their *real* daughter—never died." Pam took in the wealth of details, trying to put the pieces together.

"Do you mind if I offer a theory?" Scott suggested.

"Go on."

"Twins escape a slaughter back in Colombia. They grow old enough to realize what happened to their family. They plot revenge. He does the drug lord bit. She works her way into the mainstream . . . to a position in a bank . . . on Wall Street. This doesn't seem the least bit coincidental to you?"

Pam propped her elbows on the conference table with her chin in her cupped hands, thinking hard.

"What's the biggest problem drug traffickers have here in the United States?"

Pam answered that in her head. Me, she told herself.

"Money. How to get their money . . . how to legalize it." Scott sifted through some more research. "Did you happen to hear about this story?" Scott found the article. "About the pesos?" Pam gave the paper a once-over while Scott summarized. "The drug money is picked up here. They purchase legitimate products and whatnot . . . washers and dryers, cigarettes—anything that Colombians can use on a day-to-day basis."

"I might've been busy in Seattle when this story broke," Pam suggested.

"Well, the trick here is to make the deals with corporations that are already doing business down in Colombia. They buy, say, a million packs of Marlboro up here for, say, a million bucks. The cigarettes are drop shipped down in Colombia to the lords and their associates who sell them at, say, seventy-five cents a pack or even fifty cents a pack. It doesn't matter, as long as they get something for it. As long as it brings in more than their cost to pick the leaves, ship the product, et cetera."

"You broke this story?"

"More or less. When I was down in Colombia, I saw that a pack of cigarettes was dirt cheap. It made me curious. Man, if I could only cash in my curiosity. I'd have more money than God."

Pam ignored that. Too much was going on in her head for jokes and laughs.

"As soon as I broke the story, the *Wall Street Journal*, the *LA Times*, the *Post*, all of 'em ran with it . . . like lil' ole' me didn't exist."

"Well . . . I'll tell you what, Scott. Share some more of your theories with me and all of those papers might end up begging you to come and work for them," Pam said with a raised eyebrow. "I think you might be on to something here." Pam took out her notebook and listed an order of importance. There were about to be some surprises in the drug war.

CHAPTER FORTY-FOUR

The admissions office at St. John's University was busy with students filling out applications for PEL and TAP grants; others answering for bounced checks that were expected to cover tuition fees . . . any and all things financial it seemed.

Roberta Novick was there at the front desk, part of her "volunteer time," a contribution that many students were encouraged to give as a form of school pride. There were other choices like food services, the college bookstore, and the school library, but those positions really sounded labor intensive. So, Roberta picked the admissions office, assuming that, at most, she'd get to meet some new faces. Volunteer time only amounted to two hours per week, and already Roberta was well into her second hour of this charity work.

"Hi. I'm Carl Paine. I called earlier today? About your postgrad program?" He spoke to Roberta as if she might be the one he contacted.

"Sorry, I don't even deal with the phones. But I'm sure I can help you. You're wanting to apply today?"

"Yes, ma'am, for your political science program."

Roberta multitasked a few things: reaching for a new form, keeping with the friendly conversation, and pointing out where Carl should be sure to fill in.

"One other thing. Is there some way I can sign up for a tour? You have them, don't you?"

"Sure . . . no need to sign up. That's my job." Roberta said this with her usual glowing personality. "You wanna do it now?" she asked. And he digressed with his thoughts, momentarily imagining that she meant an activity other than the tour. "Oh . . . uh . . . why not?"

"Summer, I'm gonna step away for a tour. Would you cover me?" Roberta asked.

"Not a problem," Summer replied with something other than college applications in mind. Roberta returned a look that called her friend jealous and escorted her new applicant out of the admissions office.

From the administration building the two followed a path to the various halls. One building housed the student activities center with its lounges, cafeterias, and faux nightclub. "That's the student hangout at night. No liquor, but fruit drinks and shakes." There was a sign on the door that said CAFÉ TOGA, and promoted a few bands with their appearance dates. "It doesn't open till five, when most classes are out. They also change the name of the club like every other week. Just something to do, I guess."

Across from the student activities center was Jefferson Hall, where a massive library was housed. There were banks of computers there as well, complete with Web access. "The library stays open till nine, and Internet access is somewhat limited. Like, you wouldn't be able to access gaming, gambling, or sex sites. Academics only, ya know," Roberta said with knowing eyes.

Another path took them to Franklin Hall, where assemblies, dances, and large career day events were held. The Einstein Building was one of three that housed three floors of classrooms. The school's radio station was also headquartered there. There was the Recreation Center, with the regulation-size basketball courts and the Olympic-size pool on the lower level.

"This is the liberal arts building . . . music classes . . . the college band . . . a recording studio. The works," Roberta explained. "You into music?" she asked, hoping to break the wall of silence this guy had up.

"I guess I'm a soul brother down deep. But I can go for some variety now and then, like hip-hop, classic, rock, jazz, easy listening."

"Get out! Nobody I know is that much into music."

"Try me."

"Okay," Roberta dug in, finally finding more rapport with the stranger, "Carl, right? Okay, Carl . . . I name the song, you name the artist."

"Ooooh, I like this already." Roberta started to think of a song, but Carl interrupted. "Wait a minute. What's my prize for naming, say, seven out of ten?"

"Prize?"

"Of course, prize. You can't just peek into my most intimate thoughts without some sort of tax."

"Tax? Intimate thoughts? I asked you about music. Not your shoe size." Roberta didn't hide her smile too good. Carl could see it through her eyes.

"Okay, well . . . how about a mediocre prize?"

"Like what?"

"Lunch—on me."

Roberta made a face. The likely objective of a man. "That's if you answer seven out of ten, and that's a big if."

"I'm game. You'd better make them hard selections."

The two were near the fountain now, something like a monument in the center of the college grounds. Roberta squinted as she forced her mind to crank.

"Do I have to name the year or the album?"

"Nope, you don't even have to tell me the format. Just keep it as we said; jazz, hip-hop, soul, rock. I'll tell you right now—I'll lose if you name any of the punk rock or grunge stuff."

"How 'bout house?"

"Are you kiddin'? Shoot."

" 'I'll House You.' "

"Too easy. That's the Jungle Brothers. And that's one."

Roberta agreed that it was too easy. "Okay. 'Bennie and the Jets.' "

"That's another easy one. Elton John."

" 'Eyes Without a Face.' " Roberta said it as if to describe her current expression.

"Uh . . . is that Devo?"

"Gotcha! It's Billy Idol!" He looked at Roberta with peculiar eyes, questioning the answer in his mind. "And by the way, Carl, what do I get as a reward if you lose—because you will lose."

He shrugged. "I don't know. What do you want?"

Roberta suddenly felt how one-sided this little contest was, but she was still determined to prove Carl wrong.

"Okay, smarty-pants. 'Rosalinda's Eyes.' "

"Whoa! What's that, Mozart?"

"Aha! That's two!"

"Hey! I didn't give you an answer."

"Too late. Billy Joel did 'Rosalinda's Eyes,' not Mozart."

"Oh, I get it. You and the classic rock, huh? Okay. Hit me!"

" 'After the Lovin'.' "

"Huh?"

"That's right. 'After the Lovin'.' I'm waiting." Roberta whistled the *Jeopardy!* theme while he deliberated. "Time's up! Your answer, sir?" She already presumed her victory.

"I give up . . . Mariah Carey?"

"What? That's three. You lose."

"Uh-uhhh . . . we said seven out of ten. That means I need to get four wrong to lose. Lemme find out you skipped mathematic classes."

"Ha-ha, very funny." Roberta folded her arms over her breasts. It was a gesture that could be read as off limits, especially now that the loss was inevitable. "I have one. This oughta finish you. 'Love Come Down.' "

"Now you know you shouldn't go there. That's my girl, Evelyn Champagne King."

" 'Our House.' "

"Oh really? Crosby, Stills, and Nash."

Roberta pursed her lips, and her hands went to her hips. " 'In a Sentimental Mood.' "

"Which version? Coltrane and Ellington? Or Abby Lincoln? You know she put words to the song."

Roberta's brow creased. " 'Human Nature.' "

"Michael Jackson or Miles?" Now he had his hands on his hips.

And Roberta grew frustrated. " 'We Got Our Own Thang.' "

"We do, don't we? Heavy D."

" 'Olivia.' "

"A wolf in lamb's clothing. That's me. And that, my dear, is number eight. As performed by The Whispers."

Roberta offered her thanks to the waitress and suddenly she didn't feel as tricked into the date. The effect that food had on her was at least enough to settle her nerves. It was at least enough to get her through this little consequence of her latest decisions in life. To think that she was naïve enough to fall for the trap. But now there were the second thoughts. Carl Paine, or Carlton as it read on the student application: he was obviously a bit older than her. Maybe by five years, she guessed. However, now that she was sitting across from him, about to indulge in her veggie burger, lunching with a black man didn't seem so bad. He was good-looking, too. Nice skin, a tapered haircut, a light mustache and hint of a goatee. What was it about him that pulled her in? Lured her?

"So tell me, Roberta, how in the world did you come to know Engelbert Humperdinck?"

"It's my parents. My adopted parents."

"You adopted them?" Carl asked with a smile.

"Might as well. I mean, we came together just a few years ago. It's not like they picked me out of a Pampers commercial."

"Mmm . . ." Carl responded with a laugh as he simultaneously sipped from his water. "So they got you into ole Englebert."

"It's kind of what they listen to . . . Englebert, Sinatra, Streisand, a load of Broadway tunes." Just as Roberta was listing the Novicks' soundtrack to life, she realized that she never gave Carl the Englebert answer. Did he actually know the name of the artist? But as soon as she thought of that she also forgot it. His charm sort of dizzied her . . . relaxed her.

Carl jumped in to say, "So you not only picked up parents, but their tastes in music, too."

"And food, and trades, and where my leisure time is spent. Funny . . . I feel as though I walked into a life that was jump-started well before I got in the car."

"Speaking of which, nice vehicle you got there. I felt like I was floating on air."

"Because it's new. I'm sure there are kinks in that thing somewhere. It drives too smooth. Makes me nervous."

"Insecurity?"

Roberta took in extra air, considering that. "I dunno. Maybe I don't deserve it. But I like it."

"Can I be honest with you?"

"Are you gonna tell me you knew the answer to 'After the Lovin' '?"

"Oh, that. I guess that's part of it. So since this is the moment of truth, I might as well tell you this, too." Carl cleared his throat and started singing just enough for Roberta to hear.

"Crazy Latins dancing solo down in Herald Square . . ."

"Hey! You knew that answer, too!"

Carl continued on. And to Roberta, he was as melodious as if in any play she'd seen on Broadway or any concert she'd attended at Radio City.

Carl finished the verse and Roberta was flattered out of her mind, not even realizing that he had taken her hand during his little performance.

"Oh. Excuse me for being forward. I guess I just got all soaked up in the moment." Carl had set Roberta's hand neatly in his.

"Wow. You can really sing. I guess you are into music, huh?"

"Music . . ." Carl looked up to the ceiling of the diner. His eyes were dreamy. "Sometimes I wish music would adopt me. But you don't seem to be music's stranger, either. Heavy D? The Whispers? And Crosby, Stills, and Nash?"

Roberta smiled. "Charge it to my ability to retain information. That, and the variety of people I associate with. But I do like music a lot."

"Do you have favorites?"

"Stevie Wonder, Sting, and I'm learning a lot about Steely Dan and ELO."

"So where does hip-hop come in?"

"My friend, Janice. She's the head of St. John's cheerleading squad. They do routines to everything. Plus, she lends me her CDs. Isn't it wild how some songs seem to say exactly what you're feeling? Exactly what's in your heart?"

"I dig it. One of Macy Gray's songs did that to me once. It had me in tears and the whole nine. Like someone's been following me all these years, peeking into my bedroom window the whole time, and listening to my prayers."

"Ooo-kay . . . so now, back to you wanting to be honest."

"I give up." Carl's hands were in the air. "I'm a music connoisseur, Roberta. So there wasn't too much you could get by me. 'Rosalinda's Eyes' was my favorite from Billy Joel's *52nd Street* album and I liked 'Flesh for Fantasy' more than 'Eyes Without a Face' from Billy Idol."

"So I didn't stand a chance. I was gonna lose either way."

"Basically," Carl expressed with a guilty laugh. "Now, before I get myself in trouble, let me say this. I was hoping you'd offer me the tour at school today. The moment I saw you in the admissions office, I was attracted . . . at the very least I wanted to get to know you better. When you brought up the subject of music, it made it easier for me."

"Easier?"

"Well . . . it just softened the whole getting-to-know-you process. The whole boy-meets-girl bit. Would you forgive my slight dishonesty?"

"No harm done. Actually, you were creative about it when I think back. So many men have come up to me at my job . . . my few jobs, and they rarely say the right things. That or they're, as you say, insecure."

"Wow. You're taking it different than I could have ever imagined. I could swear you were about to get up and just diss me."

"Why? It's just a harmless date."

He was taken by her down-to-earth attitude. "It's just . . . I've always received a . . . a cold shoulder from Latin women, the ones who are bright."

"I don't see why. You're not a bad person. Good karma and all." Roberta casually forked up a slice of cucumber.

"Maybe it's me, but a lot of Latins tend to play the white side of life, especially if they're smart or educated, and if their complexion is light rather than dark. And they act like they're better than blacks . . . condescending and all."

"Wherever did you get that information from?"

"Living, experience, watching and listening . . . learning. Especially in New York, there's so much classism here. There's so much that light or dark skin tones represent . . . whether we like it or not."

"Sometimes you Americans make me sick with all of these conclusions . . . all of these presumptions. I've seen a lot of that in college as well."

"Ah-ah-ah . . . didn't you say you were adopted? That means that you're an American, too." He said this as if it was a tablespoon of castor oil that she had no choice but to swallow.

"Well, don't think that because you can take the girl out of Colombia, that you can take Colombia out of the girl."

"Ooo-weee! A patriot down to the genes! I like that. Now if I could only find out about my roots." His response corresponded with Roberta's conscience. And she had to at least accept his reasons for thinking the way he did. "Does that mean that a guy like me could possibly stand a chance to spend time with a woman like you?"

Roberta's eyes fluttered before they became glassy and fixed on Carl. "Is that a proposition, sir?"

"Moi?"

"Yes. You."

• • •

Mike was his name, the mercenary guy who punched the cement wall and set off that vibration on the PC block at least twice a day. Charlucci finally learned his name after a month on lockdown in MDC. Eventually, the two became friendly enough that Mike even shared why he punched the wall every day for about an hour. It was some kind of tai chi exercise, Mike told him. And Charlucci could see evidence of the pain involved, how the larger man's knuckles were larger than normal, like golf balls, only a lot deadlier.

Correction officers came to the block to count the prisoners five times during the day and night. For the general population, the 4 P.M. count was a mandatory stand-up count. If you didn't stand up next to your bed, you'd be interfering with the orderly running of the institution. And disobedience would have you placed in cells that are similar to the PC lockup; only no phone calls, no visits, and no such privileges.

On the PC block, prisoners were not disciplinary problems. Therefore, visits were okay. Phone calls were okay. Prisoners didn't even have to stand up for the 4 o'clock count. The CO simply peeked through the grated window of each cell door and moved on.

Charlucci grew accustomed to the counts. There'd be the sound of the officer entering the PC block. There'd be the sound of keys. And when the officer got to his cell, the keys always jingled against the door.

At the 3 A.M. count, all was quiet on the block. Everyone was usually asleep or reading, including Charlucci. And all of these sounds, even the lack thereof, had become a way of life in the PC block. After a while, they're built into the consciousness. The officer's footsteps; the keys again. Perhaps he was going crazy, but Charlucci could swear he sensed the flashlight's ray shooting through his cell so the night officer would confirm that it was more than just a heap on the bed.

It was sometime after the 3 A.M. count when Charlucci felt a slight draft. However, he wasn't conscious enough to question it. He merely pulled his blanket up more until it was up near his neck. He was in that deep sleep, returning as always to the highlights—his times with Bianca and with the actress, Tara. He imagined the both of them together in the same bed with him. If that were only doable, then he'd be able to stop going behind their backs. He could be out in the open with how he felt about each.

And always, his dreams included the perfect crimes . . . all of those shipments he took in from Nunez; all the money he dealt with; all the money that he spent. His mind went back to the sex, back to the money, back to all the cars and yacht trips.

Images of his penthouse raced throughout his thoughts, as if he were lying there right now, lying there in his bed getting that championship blow job for all times. He could hear Tara's breathing. Bianca's breathing. He could smell his own musky odors mixing with theirs. All of these thoughts were driving him wild. Before he realized it, he was tossing and turning. Breathless even. He remembered almost exploding—as if he had to piss. And then suddenly, everything went black.

P am questioned all of the extra attention to detail this morning. Why everyone seemed so sensitive about every little thing.

"The region's coming today."

"Oh, big deal, is it?" Pam signed the clipboard and handed it back.

"Oh yeah, I'd say it is. Usually, we'd have the place smellin' like fresh paint, and you'd be afraid to step on the floors because they'd be so shiny with the whole wax and buff routine."

Pam remembered the last time she'd been through MDC. The tiled floors looked like they had water on them, as glossy as they looked.

"But this is a special visit. Spur of the moment, you might say. Usually, it's a lot of kissing ass to keep jobs. But today? It's a whole lot of kissing ass."

"What's the occasion?"

"There was a . . . er, a problem last night."

"Oh? Is everything okay?"

"For most of us? Oh, sure. But for that dope boy they called Charlucci . . . let's just say, things don't look too pretty."

When Pam found out that Charlucci, the prisoner she came to see, was dead—that he hung himself—she couldn't believe it. She had a million questions about how the PC block was run. Who was on duty? Why didn't anybody sense this could happen? So many questions spit from her lips to the point that the warden had to address Pam. And still, as far as Pam could see, there was no way Charlucci killed himself, since he had called Agent Simpson to make a deal. If anything, he had high hopes; and people with high hopes don't just kill themselves.

While weeks of investigations were ongoing down in Florida, with the regional office of the BOP digging into MDC, with the FBI digging into the BOP, and with the Attorney General of the United States holding everyone accountable, Roberta was floating on air up in New York. She was a woman who could claim to have it all—or soon she would. The jobs at the bank, at the museum, and at school kept her quite busy and always meeting new faces. Sure, she had the status, the good name of the Novicks behind her, and even a membership at the Crescent Country Club. But even with so many resources, she had to admit something was missing. Being all over the place didn't necessarily account for something grounded and exclusive.

Carl was Roberta's only challenge in this new world of hers. How would the Novicks, the folks at the Crescent, and the coworkers at her job feel about Roberta's dating a black man? Would it all fall out from under her? Would the Novicks disown her? And, more importantly, why should it matter?

Roberta's favorite movie became *Guess Who's Coming to Dinner*. She found herself watching the film over and over again, until she could figure out how to break the news. She figured she could force life to imitate art.

"I don't think you should say anything. Besides, I like these secret rendezvous we've been having. It kind of makes things a bit . . . naughty," Carl said mischievously.

"As good as that sounds, Carl, I don't wanna live as if I have something to hide when I don't. How can we be serious if we're sneaking around like this?"

Carl stroked Roberta's hair. He moved in to kiss her and she accepted him. It was both a sweet and a sour kiss.

"You have to admit . . . the sneaking . . . sure does . . . taste good," he said as he savored Roberta's lips.

"Carl? I'm serious about this." Roberta hated to pull away from Carl. She hated to be away from him at all. "I wanna tell them, and I wanna do it as soon as possible. I wanna introduce you to my friends, everybody. I don't care what they say, or if they do turn against me. I'm here to make a life for myself. I want you to be a part of it."

So that's what's going on. Our Colombian friends are selling to Charlucci, and the good ole U.S. Attorney is protecting the shipments all the while. In the meantime, everybody down here is going to bed with everyone else—your mother and Dillow; you and Diane, the boutique chick; Diane and Van Dyke. It's a regular freak fest down here . . . only now there's a wrench in the machine. We stop the load at Bell Glade and come down, not only to do our little street sweeping, but we happen to stumble on a little greed. Your Nightfly wants some extra money, so he sets up someone to be the dead body—that would be your good friend Dillow, who you wished harm on anyway—and lies to Charlucci, telling him that a heist went down . . . that all the drugs and money were stolen. Only Charlucci doesn't go for it. He uses Ortiz to finish Nightfly."

"Pretty much. Only I never told Nightfly to kill Dillow. What kind of power do I have? I'm just a band leader. I do gigs, for Christ's sake. I didn't do anything to deserve jail. I don't belong here." Jimmy Z had done his share of crying for Pam. He was believable and the story seemed credible.

"No, you probably don't. Your boutique owner friend asked about you, too. She says hi."

"You saw her?"

"She's here with you, Jimmy. Everybody's here."

"She in trouble?"

"If she doesn't testify, she's gonna be in a heap of trouble. As a matter of fact, if you don't testify, you're gonna be in a heap of trouble."

"How? What do I know?"

"You know enough. Trust me. How Diane takes the little trips with the Maxima every so often? The fifteen hundred that Charlucci paid her? Oh yeah, we know about that. Then there's the stuff Nightfly told you about Dillow . . . the bit about the safe-house heist. And of course, a jury is gonna want to know all about the various connections down here. Who knows who, and how, and what makes the whole South Beach coke ring tick. Now, of course if you don't want to testify—"

"No. I do," Jimmy's response gushed from his mouth, like a busted pipe. "I will. Anything. Just get me out of here. I got some greasy black guy in my dorm that keeps lookin' at me like I'm dessert."

I don't care if you do or if you don't know who this is," Pam said this as slowly and as clearly as she could into the phone, wanting Peter Van Dyke to comprehend the message despite it being two o'clock in the morning. Her tone was low-pitched and guttural, as if she was miserable and depressed.

"Whah??? Hunhhh?"

"This isn't a courtesy call. I'm just calling to let you know that your ass is gonna fry. You're gonna do so much friggin' prison time that calendars won't matter to you anymore. You won't give a damn about the time of day, the seasons, or who's president."

"Who is this?" Van Dyke asked. "Do you know who—"

"You won't even care about holidays or the weather. You know how you're gonna measure time? By degrees . . . when you go to hell, you sonofabitch."

Pam hung up the phone and allowed the exhilaration to set in. She let her heartbeat come back to normal, and she could breathe easier. She told herself that he was on notice now. If he didn't already know, he knew now that he was the hunted. And hunted people get nervous. They make mistakes since they can't think straight.

Fed up with the excuses from the higher-ups, Pam was through with trying to convince the agency that Van Dyke was one of the bad guys. She was tired of having the evidence looked upon as questionable. She also realized that if there was to be a significant impact in the so-called war on drugs, if anyone was going to set up a roadblock on the cocaine express, it would have to be done now, and she'd have to be the one to do it. She no longer wanted to hear excuses. She didn't care any more about rank, title, or jurisdiction. Her devotion was to the people first and the agency second. It was time to change the game. Time to take this personal. And let the chips fall where they may.

Roberta decided to begin this awakening at her job. Since she was down on Wall Street, and since Carl was working part-time at City Hall, they were close enough to do lunch. The Wall Street lunch crowd was diversified and multinational enough that no one would pay particular attention to them as a couple. It was only amongst society's elite, in better parts of Long Island, that such a concern would surface about the Novick girl and her black boyfriend.

After a series of rendezvous where he picked up and dropped off Roberta, they felt it was time that Carl met the girls. They were already familiar with him as an acquaintance since he came to meet Roberta at St. John's. Only now, they'd find out about the romantic involvement. Roberta chose to make the announcement at the Novicks' Hampton home since her friends were already comfortable there.

Summer followed Roberta into the large living room carrying two trays of snacks, including raw shrimp, chips, cocktail sauce, dips, and veggies. Janice and Maureen were trying out a new cheer routine for Jill and Catherine, their audience. Jill was responding with overdramatic facial expressions and strong handclapping. Catherine was filing her nails and looking up now and then.

"Munchies," sung Summer.

"Thank God," Catherine said under her breath.

"Come on, Janice . . . you can do your cheers later. I have a little announcement to make," said Roberta. She checked her watch, looked in the direction of the front door, and then made herself busy, stalling a bit as she passed out glasses.

"Champagne? Ooooh . . . this is a special announcement, isn't it?" Jill shivered her shoulders and sat up on the couch all excited, ready to be blessed with news.

"I think so," Catherine said. "Maybe it's about this secret admirer she's been keeping from us."

The doorbell rang. Roberta closed her eyes with a deep breath.

"Ladies, I'd like to introduce you to my . . . ahem . . . secret admirer. My man friend . . ." Roberta drew stares, giggles, and anticipation as she reached for the doorknob. "Meet the man himself—Carl Paine."

The awe in the room could've vacuum-sucked all of the oxygen out of the air as Roberta's friends went through varying reactions.

"Get out!"

"No way!"

"Waaaay."

"Ooooh . . . you got you a Mandingo!" Maureen exclaimed to everyone's amusement.

And while Roberta embraced Carl, giving him an affectionate kiss for all to see, the "ooohs," "aaahs," and "awwws" filled the air.

"Do it again!" Jill said, trying to capture a Kodak moment with her camera in hand.

Janice finally smiled. Catherine was still dumbfounded. Nobody said so, but everyone wondered what Roberta's parents would say.

• • •

B aby . . . hi," he whispered into the phone, loud enough to be heard, but not overheard. "I really can't be long here. I just wanted to tell you I love you. I wanted to tell Kindra and Keisha I love them, too. I know. I know they're sleeping. Give them my love, would you? No, everything's okay. It is. I don't know, doll. Maybe another couple weeks or so. I'm not really supposed to be calling now, but I just . . . I needed to hear your voice. Okay. 'Bye, and I love you, too." Ted Carson hung up the phone and his nerves steadied. He felt as though he got away with murder, to be sneaking in a phone call during an undercover operation. But this wasn't too difficult. It wasn't as if his life was in grave danger.

"Well . . . that's the last of 'em, baby. Summer just left." Roberta pulled up to him with open arms. "You think we went over well?"

"Sure. It's your parents who we've gotta impress."

"For real. Mmmm . . . but don't you feel a little better now? I mean, like we're finally freeing ourselves?"

"Uh . . . yeah, of course."

"Mmmm . . ." Roberta moaned. She backed out of his embrace. "That's what I wanna do now. I wanna free myself. I wanna give myself to you without any limitations." Roberta had unexpectedly crossed her arms low and pulled her blouse up, stretching it up and off of her head. She'd been braless and suddenly stood there half naked, ready to shimmy out of the skirt she had on. As she did, she approached the man of her dreams until all of her clothing was on the floor next to her bare feet.

"Make love to me, Carl." Roberta's voice trembled.

Agent Carson swallowed hard, while considering how far to take this.

CHAPTER FORTY-FIVE

The old warehouse on Broadway had been another of Harlem's eyesores for a long time, up until the politicians set up that $40 million preservation fund. A group known as the Renaissance Artists was the first to recognize opportunity. There were six artists in all—four women and two men. Three were painters. One was a fashion photographer, and another made jewelry. Celeste was the only sculptor in the collaboration. She also helped to manage the building and screen any potential residents.

Since Celeste knew Misa Stewart from as far back as their days at LaGuardia High School, one hand always washed the other. With more than two dozen empty spaces, Celeste made it possible for Misa to live rent-free. Just handle your electric bill and make yourself at home, Celeste told her. The building was a home fit for refugees, with lofts, corridors, storage spaces, and stairwells. Misa had a tremendous second-floor space that, beyond the large living area, had four separate rooms all to itself. The floors were cement, the walls plain sheetrock, and the ceilings high, with simple electrical wires and plumbing running to and fro. Misa had two black futon couches and an entertainment center in the main room, which in itself was big enough to accommodate a party of thirty. At present, Liza and her sister, Iris, were occupying the room at the far left, and Misa was with Rose in the room to the far right. Wolf made his home in a corner of the loft on a blanket.

Misa understands, thought Rose as he inhaled the fragrance fed by a recently lit incense stick. At the same time, he was relieved by her hands and how they were all over him, massaging his sinewy arms, his chest, and shoulders. There was a lot of tension in his mind and body; thoughts of the man cut down out on Strivers Row. Thoughts of who might have seen him, the apartment they abandoned, and the news reports he caught on television. He wondered how knowledgeable the police were. All of this was weighing on Rose, and yet, it felt incredible to have Misa there to cause him friction, to accept his muscle, and to ride him hard, until his anxieties were but a memory; until it all seemed to be washed away.

The way she performed, aggressive and determined, was too thorough. Too satisfying. And that's why Rose figured she had to understand his needs. Misa was loud, too. It was a wonder how these girls weren't all up in each other's business, considering how the sisters were just across the loft.

But then, Misa didn't seem to care at all about that, so caught up in her own bucking atop of Rose, her body kicking up and down on him so erratically. Her senses cursed him for just lying there, looking at her like that. In her panting she asked, "What's wrong? Why you lookin' at me like that?" But the words hardly made their way out of her mouth. That, and her words were drowned out by the slapping noise their skin was making on contact and her moans that filled the air. It was her busy breathing, that futile effort of drawing in air that kept her lightheaded and dizzy with rapture. All of this was consuming Misa, driving her crazy with the—Oh God, yes!—while Rose merely lay there like a tool.

"Do that shit, baby," Rose said. And the words seemed to energize Misa all the more. His arms were folded behind his head now. Here and there, his eyes would close in response to the surges of pleasure, but for the most part, he watched her. He watched her carry on with the ugly expressions; her mouth and nostrils opened wide and her eyelids squeezed together in painful, dire need for release. Misa gripped his sides to support her rhythmic pounding and she gritted her teeth.

"Turn around," Rose said out of nowhere. "I don't wanna see your face." Misa continued on, not really hearing him. "I said, turn around," Rose demanded. She made a face in the middle of her thrust and maneuvered so that she could keep him inside of her. Now, with her ass facing Rose, she went at it again. This was a pretty sight . . . way prettier to look at. And it helped Rose to go the distance until he was finally exhausted. He let out a growl and Misa joined in with a cry until she too was spent. She arched over, still sprawled atop of him, with her face to the bed.

For some strange reason the rush of jubilation that shot through Rose ended abruptly. A real bad feeling overcame him; the feeling that only prophets experience.

Late that night as Misa snuggled there in Rose's embrace, Wolf began to howl. Rose automatically opened his eyes and slipped out from under Misa's arms. He set her gently on the bed before throwing on his clothes and grabbing his guns.

He checked and saw that Iris and Liza were okay, both lying there in the same bed. Rose woke Iris, thinking that she was having nightmares again, asking if she was all right.

"Yeah, I'm fine. Whassup?" Iris was still half asleep and groggy.

"Wolf is going off," Rose said. Now Liza came out of her slumber. "You okay, Liza?"

"Mmm-hmm. What's going on?"

Rose left the girls behind and crept out into the loft. Wolf was near the front door, whimpering and wanting to get out. Rose opened the door and allowed Wolf to lead him out into the hallway. Nothing seemed out of place, nor did he sense any danger. But he went on following the dog. Down the hall was the only window with a view of the street below. At the front of the building, Rose could see a few people gathered by the doorway. A couple of cars had pulled over on the street.

More than curious, Rose stuck his guns in his waistband and hurried to the stairs. Iris and Liza were there by the entrance to the loft. He encouraged them to stay put. When Rose got to the ground level, the aroma hit him first. Then he came within view of the commotion. The glass door at the entrance of the building was shattered and a person's head was stuck through it in still life. What was left of the glass door was bloodied. The rest of the body was slumped outside of the door.

"Oh shit!" Rose exclaimed as he came closer. Wolf was barking now. Seconds later, Rose had to turn away from the sight. His cousin had been shot. Tortured. The body, it seemed, had been slammed through the front door. Tucker was dead.

For many who have been shot, or who have some kind of metal embedded in their bodies, it's easy to tell that rain is coming. There's that annoying sensation—like hitting your funny bone—they feel. Mario Nunez had a similar frustration. His wound, where the left pinkie had been cut off, had long since healed. But there was that awkward feeling he got, as if it were still there throbbing with pain, whenever he caught sight of children. They could be at play, or they could be in a photo, or even on the television. The sight of children . . . the mere idea of them, caused his anguish to resurface. It set off the throbbing. It even got painful.

The only other time that the throbbing acted up was when there was great risk. And tonight was one of the riskiest times of his life. The mega yacht that Mario named *The Pioneer* moved steady at six knots, a speed that he felt could be achieved just as well on a bicycle. Only, this was his boat and they were approaching the Yucatan Channel, about to exit the international waters of the Caribbean Sea. It wasn't the time or place for Mario's painful imagination. This was serious business. He was out on the deck with nothing but stars overhead and dark ripples of water as far as the eye could see. Mario had been sunning out on the deck earlier, admiring the views of Jamaica and the Cayman Islands as they passed.

"Some vacation, huh?" Carlos commented in their native dialect as he joined Mario on the top deck.

"Yeah, I just don't want it to be the last one—if you know what I mean. Drink?" Mario offered as he stepped along the aft bulkhead and behind the bar. This was the most prominent part of the yacht—right at the top—where guests or crew members could look out over the bridge, the cockpit, and the bow of the vessel. Carlos declined the drink.

"Don't worry about that. Everything is in order. I just spoke to our people at the channel. They tell us six units will be out tonight, ready to close in on anything moving."

"You think we'll have to go through a search?"

"They say to be ready just in case. There's always a hot dog in the Coast Guard who wants a promotion."

"Things are getting tight out here. I can feel it. I can almost smell it."

"But that's nothin' new, Boss. It's always like that with you. I guess it goes with bein' top man."

"I guess." Mario poured himself a half glass of cognac. "You sure?" he offered again.

"I'm sure. Somebody's gotta be alert out here. Gotta make sure this load gets through."

Mario didn't respond. He already appreciated the devotion of his soldiers.

Carlos noticed the newspaper on the bar. It was the very same one, the *Times*, which had been brought to Mario's attention a few weeks earlier on the flight into Opa-Loka.

"You thinkin' about her?" Carlos asked.

"More and more every day. She's my only family. My only blood family. She probably doesn't even know I'm alive."

"Are you kiddin'? Your face is all over their newspapers. You are a wanted man all over the world, brother."

"But she's . . . a whole different person today. Different

family. Different name. She doesn't even look Colombian anymore." Mario picked up the newspaper to show Carlos again, as if he hadn't been one of the first ones to see her. Carlos considered how important this was to Mario and he put both his hands on the bar, leaning in to make a point.

"You wanna see her, don't you?"

Mario stared into the dark waters ahead of the boat. "And if I do?"

"It can be arranged."

An hour later, Mario and Carlos went down to the lower deck, met with the entire six-man crew, and then headed inside the yacht. Downstairs, the two crossed the mahogany wood floor, the lavish dining room and lounge area with its wraparound couches, heading for one of the four guest staterooms.

"Well . . . this is it."

"Yup. Make the call and let's get this thing over with."

"Gotcha."

"Good luck," Mario said to Carlos and reached into a panel on the wall near some air-conditioning controls. In that instant, the platform where the bed was positioned began to rotate away from a mirrored wall, allowing entry into a hidden spare room with its own small bed, toilet, and shower. This was where Mario would hide as the vessel sailed through the sensitive waters, where the Coast Guard inspected ships for drugs. In the same space was enough room to hold the ton of cocaine being brought to the United States on the trip.

The procedure was pre-set. Carlos was to phone the authorities, pretending to be an informant, and he'd let them in on the details of the shipments—the decoy shipments that were moving across the same waters as *The Pioneer*. The decoys had been easy to arrange; nothing but a couple of gringos from the States who came to Colombia—as many did—in an effort to buy coke at rock-bottom prices. The one with the ponytail was a fast-talker who acted like he was doing Nunez a favor by transporting product into the States. He claimed to have been this route many times over without anyone suspecting him or stopping him. He had a cigarette boat that was white with a blue racing stripe.

Carlos lied to the motormouth, saying that the waters belonged to Nunez . . . that any authorities out there were on the payroll, and if they weren't then they were supervised by those on the payroll. All you have to do, Carlos told the gringo, is travel a mile out and parallel to *The Pioneer*. The cigarette boat would get through the Yucatan Channel safe and sound, he said.

And now, just twelve hours later, Carlos could see the cigarette boat's racing stripe across the great waters of the Yucatan, and the ponytail smuggler was its sole operator, pushing the boat (and fifty kilos of coke) at fifteen knots. Carlos lowered the binoculars and shook his head, knowing that the guy was moving too fast; he was as good as an overcooked hamburger. Then Carlos turned to his left and looked through the binoculars again. If his timing was correct, there'd be patrol units moving about a mile off, heading in the very same direction.

The channel was coming up. The sky was beginning to show signs of daylight coming in. The call had been placed, and there was little left to do but let cause-and-effect take its toll.

Minutes later, a band of patrol boats formed a wide arrow of lights, approaching from ahead. Emergency lights and sirens ate at the atmosphere. The unit on the left of *The Pioneer* cut over and across to join the effort. Carlos could see the cigarette boat weave off course, trying to race away. But the authorities had him surrounded with no way to escape. In the distance, one could see the gringo was standing with his hands up. Carlos couldn't make out his expression; he was too far away. But it was also anyone's guess that he wasn't happy.

"Oh well . . . another one bites the dust," Carlos said to Poppo. "Okay, Joe, take it up to fifteen knots. It should be easy sailing from here on out." The yacht picked up speed with its mirror-white finish gliding through the dark waters. Carlos could breathe easy now. As soon as *The Pioneer* cleared the channel, he'd go and get Mario. He'd get him ready to enter the States with the help of a slight disguise.

The sirens were coming closer now, and Carlos presumed them to be the authorities tooting their horns about the catch they made.

"Police!" the amplified voice called out. "Stop the vessel now. Shut it down, or else we'll have to use force!"

Carlos looked back at Poppo, who was on the bridge now with *The Pioneer*'s captain. The yacht complied and a dozen camouflaged men with automatic assault rifles soon climbed aboard. In the distance, Carlos could see the catalyst of this sudden interference. The recently apprehended prisoner was pointing and carrying on about the setup.

"Do you know him, sir?" the commander asked while pointing out the troubled man.

"No, sir . . . can't say that I do," Carlos answered, pretending to want a better look.

"Maybe he's lying; probably to avoid his own troubles. Caught him with fifty keys. The nerve," said the official.

"Really? A pity how these guys abuse God's wondrous waters," said Carlos in an attempt to control the conversation. He then asked, "Are you with the Navy of some kind?"

"Name's Ferdinand Maldonado," he said with more than a little dramatic pronunciation. "Honduran Naval Sergeant."

"Well . . . nice to meet you, Sergeant. I didn't know you all policed these here international waters." In the most subtle way, Carlos was telling the sergeant that he was knowledgeable of the laws at sea, one being the sovereignty of international waters. Literally, a murder could take place out there, and it would be no one country's responsibility to prosecute or prove such an act.

"It's this big war on drugs, ya know. Something the United States organized . . . gave so much money to this country and that, financing all this new policing of the waters, of the air. Say, you don't mind if my men look around, do you?"

"Sure . . . I mean, of course not. Go right ahead," Carlos replied, a bit concerned that his men were already doing that.

"Thanks . . . yeah . . . this is such a high traffic avenue for smugglers trying to pass through the Yucatan Channel and all that we have drug details night and day. The Army, Navy, Coast Guard, and others from Colombia, Peru, Cuba—all of the coastal nations—have joined forces with the DEA from the United States."

"No kiddin'. I didn't know that," Carlos said, trying not to show nervousness as he watched bloodhounds being led aboard *The Pioneer*. "The DEA. Wow. Hard to imagine those guys all the way out here, so far away from home." The two strolled along the deck.

"It's political. Trust me. By the U.S. government paying their way into our countries, they actually become advisors. Consultants. I had to go through additional training, in fact. And it was U.S. agents who taught the classes."

"I guess it's a living, huh?"

"That it is. That it is."

"Can I offer you a drink? Maybe orange juice?"

"I'd like that."

"Sarge!" a soldier called out from inside the yacht. Maldonado shared a look with Carlos and the two stepped inside. Carlos braced himself, ready to pull out his automatic weapon in an instant.

"What is it, Colon?"

"My dogs . . . they're going crazy downstairs."

They all stepped to the lower deck. The dogs were turning in place, panting excitedly and shaking. All of this was going on at the doorway to a guest suite—the one wherein Mario Nunez was hidden behind the mirrored wall.

"Would you mind opening the bedroom door, sir?"

"Sure, Sergeant. I don't see—" Carlos opened the door and the two bloodhounds jerked ahead, pulling away from their handlers. In the cabin, a table was set with candles and a dinner setting. The dogs attacked the table, pulling its contents, tablecloth and all, to the floor. The dinner plate had been covered with a silver dome to keep a T-bone steak and vegetables warm.

"Damn it! Grab those dogs!" Sergeant Maldonado shouted. The dogs were fighting over the steak, ripping it apart and trying to swallow what they'd managed for themselves.

"Sorry, sir!"

Carlos acted upset and said, "That was my late dinner."

"Sorry again, sir." The sergeant gestured to his men and they left the room with the dogs. Carlos looked down at the mess on the floor, and then at the mirrored wall, knowing that Mario was there, proud and protected.

Back on the outside deck, Carlos watched as the men climbed off of *The Pioneer* and back into their state-of-the-art vessels. Carlos was certain those boats had belonged to failed smugglers.

"I'll be sure to radio ahead, sir. You should have a clean bill of health all the way to your destination."

Those words were music to his ears. But just in case, Carlos had a second decoy at sail, more than a mile behind. If necessary, he'd make another call as a diversion . . . another lie about "a two hundred and fifty-kilo smuggler." It didn't matter that the operator would be caught, imprisoned, and made to spend life in prison. The only thing that mattered was getting the ton of coke safely to the States. People were waiting.

CHAPTER FORTY-SIX

There is the matter of Mike . . . our boy up at MDC. He's been questioned about everything by everybody. So far, he's kept his word. Not a peep. But you never know with these guys. Remember Sammy the Bull? It didn't matter who he killed, or how many. It only mattered that he turned on his oath."

"So what's that mean, Banks? We supposed to take care of him, too?"

"We might have to. Look at it this way, Chief. Charlucci's out of the way now. He's history. So the only link remaining between you and him is Mike. If anything ever got out in the open about MDC? About South Beach? About Nunez? You, me, and everybody on top of us will go down harder than any drug dealer in Lewisburg, any murderer in Colorado, or anybody on death row. The only link . . . the only one. You make the call."

"Let me think on it, Banks. Killing dealers. Killing killers of dealers . . . killers of killers . . . this not what I studied law for. It's not why I ran for office."

"Yeah, I agree. I remember those good ole days of campaigning . . . kissing babies, all that. I was right there with you, Van Dyke. But once we crossed the line, you knew up front that there'd be no turning back, that this could get grimy."

"Enough. Let's just finish counting this money and see

that everyone gets their share. We're winning now. That's all that matters."

While money was counted, packaged, and placed in satchels in the basement of Van Dyke's Belle Harbor estate, a Blackhawk chopper was hovering in the air above the estate. Pam Brown was pointing, matching the property below with the map she had in hand.

"That's the one, Briggs. Take her down. We're goin' in," Pam directed the pilot and the chopper carved its descent through the dim of evening, heading for the lawn in back of the home.

It was clear that Van Dyke was living large; larger than any dope dealer or kingpin Pam had ever taken down. There were tennis courts, basketball courts, and a miniature golf course on the plot, as well as an in-ground pool and waterfall that formed a sort of oasis. There was grass, and trees, and shrubs as far as the eye could see, and even a guest house that was large enough to be someone's dream home.

Still, Pam was not intimidated by the excess of it all. For years, she went by a rule that always stuck with her: the bigger they are, the harder they fall. She had six agents with her, and they were all too familiar with the burden they were about to bear. They had no warrant. They hadn't so much as contacted a judge on the matter. Even Chief Goldridge was in the dark about this activity. Bigger than that, the use of the chopper was unauthorized, as was the grouping of agents for the mission in store.

All of that didn't matter. Nothing did anymore. Nothing made sense. And since that was the case, this would qualify as one of those nonsensical actions—to pounce on the Chief United States Attorney for the District of Miami. Pam joked with her subordinates that there was a first time for everything.

"Full metal jacket, fellas. We're goin' hard." Pam spoke over the din of the chopper's propellers. "Even though I'm sure this guy's a soft ass, we should take nothing for granted. He's in there. That much we know. And so help me God, I'm goin' in to get him."

* * *

Moments later, the windows and doors of Van Dyke's home imploded under the force of Pam Brown's small army. The lights were on in the house, and yet the red-dot lasers of their assault rifles could still be seen skating across the lush interior of walls and furnishings.

"Up." Pam pointed to two agents and they took to the steps. "Down," she said to two other agents, pointing to the floor. And they went to search for a passage to the basement. Meanwhile, Pam led two remaining agents deeper into Van Dyke's world.

It was quite a week for Rose . . . to have to oversee the entire process of the funeral arrangements for Tucker. Misa and her friends were helpful, acting so ladylike as intermediaries between Rose and Tucker's immediate family. "We're Tucker's friends," Misa explained to a shocked Mr. and Mrs. Wilson. "And we've gathered our financial resources to help lay Tuck to rest in the most honorable way."

Tonya, Tucker's sister, was a little skeptical, but she couldn't deny the assistance at such an awkward time. Already, her mother and father had a distrustful attitude toward Tonya, especially since she had the altercation on the family's front lawn with the gunfire and all . . . and now the murder of Tucker. They were only left to imagine how all of this violence came into their lives so suddenly. To have this happen after so much planning and hard work to make life worth looking forward to for Tonya and Tucker.

Tucker's wake was a hallmark moment as well, how Tonya broke down in tears and pounded on her dead brother's chest, screaming, "How could you do this to us?" A couple of the girls, Trina and Charmaine, went to stop Toya . . . to console her. And later when Tonya faced Rose, she screamed at him, too, blaming him and then smacking him square across the face.

The pretty model, Dawn Struthers, was also at the wake along with her mother. Dawn's stomach had grown, and Rose knew that it was Tucker's doing. He fretted the outcome of the childbirth, with Dawn being a drug abuser and all. This was another consequence of Tucker's actions that would outlive him by generations.

All of this, not to mention how Tucker was murdered, took a toll on Rose's state of mind. He had to endure all of these images; he had to bear all of the burden; and still he couldn't forget what that man said out there that snowy morning on Strivers Row: "That means you, Tuck, women, children, whatever." This was how far Freeze was willing to take things—to the grave. It left Rose no choice.

Agent Joel Green had been tracking Freeze and his buddy Squirrel ever since Butch was shot down. He reported directly to Sal Goldridge in Washington and followed orders to continue surveillance, which included wiretaps and the assignment of two additional agents. As a team, the agents accumulated enough information about Freeze to imprison him on the moon. But a wiretap alerted the agents to an even bigger fish.

A man who called himself Poppo contacted Squirrel to set up a meeting at a 42nd Street hotel. Intel on the name "Poppo" didn't bring up anything except a possible link to Colombian drug lord Mario Nunez.

Agent Green thought that to be a far-fetched possibility, for Freeze or any of his street thugs to be involved with such an internationally notorious personality—one whom every agency lusted after. Green decided to let the meeting happen . . . to further investigate and to see who this Poppo was before the decision was made to move in on Freeze's operation.

Roberta took a deep breath before entering the Shamrock Bistro, a small restaurant off of Wall Street, just around the corner from the New York Stock Exchange. She'd been to a few of these places before, where the old fogies rub elbows with the new professionals of the financial district; where they talked about stock picks and shared hot details about mergers, et cetera; where they celebrated their blue chip stocks, their IPOs, and their quotas for the day.

Why Roberta expected anything different here, she couldn't say. There'd be mostly men who were snobbish or goal-oriented. And they'd recklessly eyeball her, as though they could see beyond her business suit down to her unmentionables. But this was a special occasion. Or else it'd be eventful—one or the other. Her American father, Brendan Novick, was here to meet Roberta for a father-daughter lunch date. And Roberta set this engagement up in order to have a little chat; to let him in on her relationship with Carl Paine.

Just inside the foyer to the Shamrock, Roberta found herself engulfed by the old-world elegance that massive wealth demands. From the subdued lighting, to the ritzy carpet, to the crushed velvet couches behind those shiny redwood tables. The smoke of Cuban cigars wafted in the atmosphere where colors were muted and where the wallpaper wasn't merely an interior decorator's wet dream; these were Renaissance-style paintings. The whole experience inhibited Roberta with the feeling that she'd stepped into a James Bond movie.

"Ms. Novick, I presume," guessed the man in the tuxedo.

Roberta was taken by surprise. There was no way this stranger had met her before. Roberta responded and followed the maitre d'. Brendan Novick was alone in a rear booth that sat adjacent to a large fishtank where small sharks lived. He was studying the Marketplace section of the *Wall Street Journal*.

"Dad."

"Roberta," Brendan answered over the paper and his horn-rimmed glasses. "Have a seat. Make yourself comfortable," he said as he folded up the *Journal* and nodded his approval to the maitre d'. "So, darling, what is it that you've wanted to tell me? I've been beating myself in the head with curiosity for the whole morning."

Roberta reached across the table to put a hand over his. "Relax, Dad. Let me unwind a little. I did just get here."

"Right. Sorry, darling. I didn't think. Here comes the menu."

Roberta ordered a turkey club. "Hold the bacon," she told the waiter.

After he left, Brendan said, "A turkey club without bacon is not a turkey club, Roberta."

"I didn't see a turkey sandwich, so I figured I'd have it my way. Ya know? What're you eating?"

"I ordered a roast beef melt. Told 'em to bring it out after you arrived."

"Okay then. I . . . I guess this is a good a time as any. Dad?"

"Yes," he said, stretching out the word.

"I think I'm in love."

"With a man, I hope."

"As opposed to a woman?"

"No, as opposed to a shark. Of course as opposed to a woman."

"Dad, I am in love with a man. Very much a man, in fact." One of my girlfriends from college calls him my Mandingo warrior."

"Oh?"

"Yes, I don't know how you'll take this, but . . . he's a black man."

"Really? What's his name?"

Roberta's face froze with confusion. "Uh . . . Carl. Carl Paine. But did you hear me, Dad? Carl is African American."

"I thought you said he was Mandingo."

Roberta wondered if he was missing the point. But Brendan Novick didn't budge from his poker face. Then he suddenly eased into a smile.

"Roberta . . . you have me mixed up with the Mrs. Really, I've been in the people business for years, and have dealt with all kinds, all colors, all nationalities. Nothing surprises me anymore. I'll admit that when I was your age I didn't know better. But we all mature, and we come to find out what's really important in life. It's a mystery to me how Mrs. Novick and I stayed together so long . . . her wanting to measure up to high society and all. That was never me. I'm more concerned with his hygiene, his character, and his intentions. Those of your love interest, of course." Brendan backed up in his seat to allow the waiter to set the food down.

Roberta was stunned by his response, trying not to stare at him as they prepared to dig in.

"So?" Brendan asked.

"So what?"

"So . . . how's his hygiene, his character, and his intentions? When will I get to meet this Carl?"

"Oh, Dad." Roberta dropped a tear. She never guessed that Brendan would be so understanding. And now that she saw he was, a mountain of burden was lifted from her shoulders. Roberta wiped her tears away, and Brendan reached over to hold her hand. It was all the compassion she needed to follow her dreams.

Ted Carson was already knee-deep in guilt. It was going on a month and a half since he'd seen Sheryl and the children. The last time he called home, he found out that his youngest daughter, Keisha, was sick in her stomach. Sheryl mentioned that it might have been something she ate in school. Ted would've argued with his wife; he would have asked her why the hell Keisha didn't take a bag lunch like she was supposed to. But Ted was in no position to argue. Not in the least. He was stuck between a rock and a hard place.

On one hand there was his family . . . his wife and gorgeous daughters. On the other hand, there was his job. However, it didn't feel like a job anymore. It felt like he'd dived off a high cliff into an ocean of his favorite chocolate pudding. He felt like a Romeo for hire. Roberta was in love. He was even . . . well, pretending to be in love. But the sex? That was no pretending. That was as real as it got. He was as involved as he'd ever fantasized. Ted felt like a scoundrel, too. How he faked out Roberta with the whole college student bit. With the whole serenading Lolita bit. Ted even went so far as to lie about receiving a cold shoulder from Latin women for this reason and that. He couldn't recall now what he'd said to get Roberta's sympathy, but it worked. It worked so well that he ended up in bed with her. Stroking that woman like his world was hers for the asking.

And now he was outside the Shamrock Bistro, sitting in the passenger's seat of Roberta's 4-Runner about to meet her father. Oh, brother!

Agent Carson's pager vibrated on his hip. It was a priority one, demanding his immediate response. He took out his cell phone.

"Agent Carson speaking."

"Carson, this is Pam Brown. I just got word from Washington that our boy might be in the States."

"Our boy?" Carson replied, looking toward the bistro's entrance.

"Mario Nunez. He may be there in New York."

"How legitimate is the intel?"

"Top shelf. That's the only reason I called you. You have to be careful, Carson. I'm putting two agents on you. And I should be in New York within two hours."

"How'd it go in Miami?"

"If I told you, you wouldn't believe it."

"Better question. Did you get him?"

"Oh, I got him all right . . ."

"Hey, she's back. I gotta go." Carson was abrupt. He flipped his cell phone closed and braced himself. He wondered how it went with Novick. Perhaps he wouldn't have to meet the guy after all.

"Honey, guess what?" Roberta said when Carson lowered the window. Carson tried to offer a compassionate grimace, in the event the answer was no. "He's ready and waiting. He can't wait to meet you."

Carson smiled and his eyes widened, but deep down he said it again: Oh, brother!

Junebug and K-oss had hightailed it back to North Carolina within an hour of the slaying of Freeze's boy, Butch. So Rose was left to stand on his own in the event Freeze wanted some get-back. He didn't mind though, because it was his experience that once violence came into the equation . . . once a dude's wig got flipped back into bloody oblivion, such as what happened to Butch, the beef died out.

Rose never got as much as a threat of revenge because he was never the instigator. He was never the bogeyman or the troublemaker. There were enough of them locked up with his father. Rose was cut and dried. He sold guns. He made money. He ate and he was boning Misa. There wasn't too much else.

But now, Freeze had attacked his weakest link. His cousin Tucker was gone; his family was wounded. Rose simply couldn't lay back and ignore this. He had to act.

"I gotta avenge this. I gotta."

"Baby, listen to me. Please, listen—please."

Misa was standing in Rose's way. He had already strapped up. He'd already made the phone call to some boys he knew . . . boys who he sold guns to, and who he knew were involved with jacking various drug dealers. He didn't want to have to slap the shit out of this woman standing in his way, but it was coming to that.

"Misa . . . I ain't gonna tell you again. Step the fuck out of my way." The way Rose said that was a force in itself, causing Misa to back up quick with her hands raised like she didn't want any trouble. In that instant, Rose swept past her, out of the loft where she stayed. He had to meet Roscoe.

You believe that shit, Trina? After all I done for that nigga, he gonna tell me to step the fuck off. Like I'm some chickenhead bitch on his jockstrap."

"Cool out, Meese. He's just hyped up . . . got his mind set, ya know? Ready for war. I'd understand."

Misa sucked her teeth. "Still."

"You know what I think, Misa?" Chanté was coming from the kitchenette, eating as usual. "I think we should watch his back."

"You right, Chanté," said Charmaine. "His beef is our beef. Plus, I was startin' to have feelings for Tuck. So this shit is really my beef. Like anotha nigga took somethin' that I coulda had."

The others were both surprised and amused by Charmaine's comment . . . a look inside their friend's thoughts.

"So that's it, then. Ride or die—like the song goes." Misa knew where the meeting was to take place since she'd overheard Rose on the phone with some dude named Roscoe. Plus, Rose took the beat-up with him, the type of car he wouldn't mind driving through a gun battle. And there was no way that Dodge was gonna get uptown before the Hot Girls' Suzukis could.

No matter how much you know about how that man operates and with who, you can't go and write just anything, Tina. You're not law enforcement."

"Look who's talking? Mister 'officials may be a part of the international drug trade' . . . Mister 'Mario Nunez is becoming the next Pablo Escobar.' Aren't those your opinions? Aren't those allegations?"

"But I've gathered evidence and witnesses to back my stories, Tina. You're just going on what you've seen, what a nosy neighbor suspects, and ultimately, what you suspect is fact. That's not good reporting."

"Don't tell me what good reporting is, Mister star reporter for the Albert Leonard *Purple Rose*." Tina dragged out her words.

"What is that supposed to insinuate?"

"Don't worry. I won't tell. Let's just say I also have my sources." Tina spoke as though she had the upper hand. And it was a riddle to Scott.

"Listen. Whatever. Tina, I want the same things you want. So, let's not bicker. I'm just saying there's a way to do this."

"How?"

"Okay. This A to Z story I'm doing is supposed to take the world by storm. At least that's what I want. So, since we've covered Nunez extensively, why don't you take charge of the back end . . . the street side of the drug war? Since you say you have information about the senator's wife involved in some suburban drug den and since you say you can tie two homicides in Harlem to an uptown drug kingpin, why don't we combine our resources? Do the story together since I'm already in with the DEA lady."

"You're on!" Tina interjected before Scott even had a chance to finish making his proposal. It was the opportunity she'd wanted to hear. All these weeks of interviewing neighbors in Harlem, in Westchester . . . the dozen or so people in rehab; the model-turned-dope fiend, Dawn Struthers; and the guy who had been ousted from that same Westchester home—the one where there was supposedly sex, drugs, and gambling—because of his coke habit and the stealing he'd done to support it. There was so much that Tina learned; so much that she wanted to tell the public in hopes that she might clean up the filth and scum that was hurting the quality of life in New York. Activities that were getting people killed.

"The first thing we should do is call Pam Brown. We should share some of these details with her. Take this to the next level. Plus, you never know, she may have stuff for us."

"Okay, Deputy Deville," Tina said with a conspirator's smirk.

Tonya Wilson took a last look in the mirror, staring straight into her own eyes and trying to find the devil that she knew was somewhere deep in her psyche. She searched for the worst of her; the worst thoughts backed by the ugliest intentions. Then she pulled her vanity to the side so that she could retrieve the gun that Rose gave her months back . . . the same gun that Squirrel emptied into the grass and threw at the house. Tonya told the police that she didn't know where the guy put the gun, but she had lied. And now that very gun was the answer. It was the answer to Tucker's murder. It was the answer to her own conscience unfolding, asking her what she was going to do . . . prompting her to respond. She knew where Freeze lived, so this wouldn't take a whole heap of mathematics. There was a time to be a lady and there was a time to thug it out. In Tonya's heart she was ready to do just that.

CHAPTER FORTY-SEVEN

The Golden Girl was one of the most popular titty bars in all of New York. It wasn't one of those that blazed the way; however, this club took the whole strip club experience to another level. It was a duplex set up with carpeting, mirrors, fantastic laser lighting, and a pumping sound system. On the first floor, there was a massive stage that could've been a runway for major league fashion shows. It stretched in one long strip through the center of the club. From the ceiling hung a dozen monitors that showed action movies, sports, or porn flicks. There were also four brass poles that ran from the stage to the ceiling, on which some of the dancers climbed, doing their fancy acrobatics, contorting their bodies for the most in-your-face views as they swiveled round and round toward the stage. Dancers also strutted along the bar, right where bartenders kept busy with the drink pouring, customer relations, and maintaining a constant exchange of singles for tipping. Meanwhile, the dancers bent over, knelt, or sat close enough to provoke their customers to toss their money or tuck it beneath the thong, as well as sneak a feel in the interim.

Roscoe told Rose to meet him on the second level of the club, the section where the more aggressive entertainment was featured, such as girl-girl sex shows, water sports in the peek-a-boo shower stalls, and where, for a twenty-dollar bill, the girls would also allow a certain amount of probing and touching.

Rose parked around back of the Golden Girl where cars lined the streets for blocks. This was an industrial zone with plenty of manufacturing plants, warehouses, and factories. Rose imagined that there was a sweatshop around there somewhere, waiting for daylight and a cattle call of immigrant workers. But for certain, he knew there were no parking lots.

He stashed his Uzi machine gun under the driver's seat, knowing that this was one of those gentlemen's clubs that did the shake-downs at the door. There would be suited bouncers at the front entrance and the requisite walk-through metal detector, typical of these types of New York nightclubs. As far as he could tell the security was tight. One of the patrons who entered before him was asked to step through the detector a second time since the sensor indicated some type of metal. When the sensor continued to sound off, a bouncer pulled out a handheld detector and waved it slowly about the patron's body. When it was decided that the belt buckle was the culprit, a request was made, the belt was removed, and the patron was eventually admitted inside. That simple measure of security was efficient enough that Rose felt sure about his safety. It was one thing to know guns; it was another to be caught without it when you needed it most. And, tonight at least, it didn't seem that so much as a nail clipper could slip past the Golden Girl's entrance without alert.

The passage inside was dark and called up a certain anticipation, with music funneling through, consuming Rose's senses with each step forward. He reached the interior of the club and was instantly overwhelmed with the dazzling laser lights and the thumping sound system. The cashier took his twenty dollar admission, ten for the first floor's entertainment and ten for the second floor, and Rose proceeded upstairs.

He'd known Roscoe for close to three years now and sold him guns on a few occasions. There was always a clean, cash-on-the-table exchange between them; a certain respect. The only other personal information Rose had about Roscoe was a pager number, and Roscoe had Rose's as well. The guy was a good customer. Nothing more, nothing less.

He spotted Roscoe as soon as he crossed the upstairs threshold. There was that signature Kangol cap he wore—it was lime green tonight—and he had some black silk shirt on that clung to his medium frame. When the two made eye contact, Roscoe waved. By the eyes around Roscoe and how they were directed, Rose could see he had at least two others in his company. One could've been a Trini, he guessed, with the big round cap and the medallion he wore. The other dude with Roscoe had a Yankees Windbreaker on and a matching baseball cap. Rose wondered if the guy was a fan or a walking advertisement.

Roscoe had been trying to figure out a way to hit Freeze for too long. And now he felt himself getting desperate. For one thing, he was waiting for short-ass Squirrel to contact him for, maybe, another job to secure a shipment. And secondly, Roscoe couldn't peg Freeze in any consistent routine. The man was here and there, and Squirrel did most of his running anyhow. Roscoe was about to say fuck it . . . he was about to hit Squirrel and see what he could get away with; whatever cash he could get. Then out of nowhere, Rose called. It was the opportunity Roscoe needed. Already Freeze could trust Roscoe and his boys to secure a transaction. But there had to be much more than trust to earn if he saved the man's life.

"Yo, Rose, whassup?" Roscoe gave Rose a pound and said, "These is my boys, Terhane and Tec." Rose nodded at the others, not one for too much handshaking. Roscoe offered Rose a drink, but Rose declined. This was about to be serious business. He had to have all of his wits about him.

There was little talk about how the Golden Girl came a long way, and how they had some of the flyest chicks in the city. But eventually, Roscoe popped the question.

"You sure about this? I mean, the way it sounds is like this is personal." Roscoe was digging, trying to find the motive as to why Rose wanted to have a surprise visit arranged for Freeze and company. Was this a heist, or something else?

"If I wasn't sure, I wouldn't be here," Rose said as his expression dared Roscoe to question him once more.

"Cool, dog. I'm just lookin' out for you. I mean, I heard that guy beat a man to death with a baseball bat. I wouldn't wanna see that happen to—"

"You definitely ain't gotta worry 'bout that. I can handle myself. Now, tell me where I can find this fool."

Roscoe tried to read the purpose of Rose's request, but couldn't. He's gonna jack him, Roscoe determined. And he's tryin' to do it without my help.

"I can take you to him."

"When? I ain't tryin' to wait."

"Now. I can take you to him now."

Rose looked the club over once with a quick scan, taking incidental looks at some nudity. Then, ready for whatever, he raised up from his seat without further ado. He followed Roscoe downstairs and through the rear exit of the club. Terhane was out in front of Roscoe and Tec was just behind Rose. The moment the four of them cleared the door, Rose could see another of Roscoe's boys coming from across the street to join up. Rose figured the guy was watching Roscoe's ride. Besides the cars that were parked bumper to bumper, there was the Bruckner Expressway towering above the dead end that ran the length of the club. Those images, the expressway and the cars, were the last objects Rose saw before the sudden blow to the back of his head . . . before the sharp pain, and before things went black.

T hey came in a pack, like deadly felines with sharp claws and malicious intent. Charmaine was out in front on her blazing yellow bike. Chanté and Misa were behind her on their black bikes. Trina had the candy apple red joint, and Liza and Iris doubled-up on the hot pink. All of the Suzukis were powerful and fast, with the sexiest ride-or-die bitches straddling them.

Charmaine led the Hot Girls down the ramp of the Bruckner expressway and into a tight U-turn so that they'd be on the block where the Golden Girl was located. There was a line of horny men out in front of the club, and every eyeball shifted in the direction of the bikers. The girls slowed up enough to look for Rose's car. When Misa didn't see it, she signaled the girls to circle the block so they could search around. The bikes traveled at a crawl while they investigated the block.

Chanté was the first to notice the beat-up. They stopped and Misa reached out to place her gloved hand on the hood of the hooptie. It was still a little warm. And Misa assumed that Rose couldn't have arrived more than thirty minutes earlier. The girls decided to park and dismount, pulling the bikes up on an adjacent sidewalk that was across and further down from the rear exit.

"Hey! Look!" Trina was still in her helmet when she noticed a few guys loading a limp body into the back of a Camry. And now that all of the girls came to attention, they were recognized. The motorcycles revved up and shot off to further look into the suspicious activity.

The Camry had already been started, and now that the men were all piled in, the car took off in the opposite direction. As it increased in speed, so too did the band of Suzukis. In time, this turned into a slow chase. Still unsure whether Rose was in the car, Misa directed her girls to cut to the far left and right of the car, vying for a peek in the window. By now, the vehicle could sweep any one of them off of their bikes. The vehicles accelerated to a more dangerous speed, and the Camry began to swerve side to side, actually trying to hit the girls.

Under her helmet, Misa cursed. She managed her bike with one hand, slowed a bit, and reached to her hip for the 9mm. She regained ground and began to focus. Then she aimed. Then she shot. She was aiming for the tires, but nothing dramatic happened.

Now the car was swinging a hard left onto the Bruckner Expressway. The motorcycles followed. One of the windows of the Camry lowered. Shots were fired back at the girls. All of this was happening so fast, and building at a deadly momentum. The girls buckled down to avoid being hit and swerved in crisscross maneuvers to throw off the shooter. A bullet danced off of Trina's helmet and she almost lost control of her bike.

The Camry abruptly cut to the left and wedged Charmaine, forcing her to scrape the wall of the fire lane. The bike shook and finally the front wheel twisted to the side, throwing Charmaine over top of the motorcycle. Her body somersaulted and hit the guardrail hard, while the motorcycle flipped up, cartwheeling end over end, until sparks and metal shot in all directions. Airborne now, the bike transformed into hot, twisted metal that collided with the front end of the Camry, causing the car to veer right.

At the same time, the yellow Suzuki was sent flying over the wall for that hundred-plus-foot fall. Iris and Liza stopped to see how bad Charmaine was hurt, while Chanté kept going, swinging her head back to check on her friends, then forward again toward the Camry. She accelerated and leaned forward in a more determined effort. Misa was closing in on the Camry from the left, and was able to pull out her pistol. She shot twice before the vehicle's front tire blew out and turned to scrambled rubber. The rim itself was now grinding against the pavement and sparks shot out from under the car. Head on into the shoulder of the expressway, the Camry was forced to stop dead in the road. Chanté made her bike skid as it completed a U-turn and finally came to a halt. She laid the bike down and marched toward the Camry with a loaded .45 in hand. Misa was just behind her.

"Get out! Get the fuck out!" shouted Chanté. She didn't wait for a response. She just started busting shots off at the front end of the car like a crazy woman. Misa was behind the car now, where both she and Trina covered the back.

"No, Chanté! Rose is in there!" Misa assumed right. When two men emerged from the partially wrecked vehicle with their arms raised in surrender, Misa hurried over to the car. Rose was laying on the backseat half conscious. The driver was bleeding from his head, but he'd be okay. A fourth man was begging for mercy, asking Chanté to let him live.

"I should blow your fuckin' head off!" Chanté said, and for an instant everyone, the girls and a number of strangers, believed Chanté was gonna take a life.

"Chanté," Misa said, realizing that there was a backup of vehicles accumulating in the wake of the collision. "There's people watching. Use your head, boo." Misa didn't give Chanté time to think. She just stepped out in front of her friend and gripped her wrist in an easy manner. "Let's go see about Charmaine. Come on," said Misa.

Chanté mumbled some unrecognizable threat before she snatched her arm out of Misa's grip.

"I should make you a new asshole!" Chanté growled.

Pop, pop, pop.

The shots that Chanté blasted didn't hit a soul; as long as you didn't count the Camry. Two more tires were flattened before Chanté joined Misa to help with the others.

Poppo was up on the mezzanine of the Trump Plaza at 42nd Street. From his perspective, he could see the entrance down there with all of the comings and goings through the revolving doors. He could see those who were eating at either of the two restaurants, the escalators that carried people from the hotel's street entry—with its waterfall and makeshift wishing well—up to a carpeted, furnished main lobby. Poppo had explained that Squirrel should meet him by the grand piano in the lobby, and that he shouldn't bother to look for anyone in particular. Squirrel should simply wait. Contact would be made.

Squirrel was recognizable the moment he entered the hotel. It was the clothes he wore; the black leather jacket, the skullcap and shades. Most everyone in the hotel, as far as Poppo could see, was in business attire or casual dress. Any dark colors were either blazers or pinstriped suits. Maybe even a trench coat. No thugged-out outfits here.

Poppo watched Squirrel for long enough to investigate the surroundings. Hotel security was obvious, wearing burgundy blazers to match the carpeting. One was busy escorting a beggar out of the lobby—this was no place to be homeless. Another was posted next to a bank of pay telephones, and a third was behind the reception desk. Poppo recognized the slender man in the hotel uniform who was emptying ashtrays and performing light cleaning duties with a dustpan and broom.

Meanwhile, Squirrel was game for anything. He didn't mind how the meeting was designed, as long as it happened. Freeze was out in a hired car on the Vanderbilt Avenue side of Grand Central Station. It was a location that permitted Squirrel to slide into the Trump Hotel undetected, because the good Lord knew who might be watching this guy. Sure, Nunez was the one the Feds wanted tied and nailed to a stake, but if they couldn't get to him, wouldn't they be hunting for the next best thing?

All Squirrel knew was that he was to meet Poppo, and that Poppo would make the deal on behalf of Nunez. The deal. Squirrel could only guess at what the deal would be. Freeze was open to anything right now, ever since the papers talked about the whole Operation Snowman thing down in Miami. It was time to change the game . . . to establish new connections. And if this Poppo really had any link to Nunez like he claimed to, this might be a pretty nice deal in the making.

From the taxi, through the brass doors of Grand Central Terminal, Squirrel sauntered down the ramp to the broad passageways that channel to various train tracks, gourmet shops, and ticket windows. If there weren't thousands of people mulling about on the concourse, then Squirrel figured there had to be damned close to it.

He negotiated his way through throngs of travelers to reach the opposite side of the terminal where a convenient side entrance to the Trump Hotel was situated. Once he saw the waterfall, he knew that this was a different environment; one suited for distinguished gentlemen and regal women. It seemed natural for him to instantly drop any cockiness and presume a business attitude . . . less of a street swagger and more of a sense of purpose.

He took the steps instead of the escalator, never appreciating the surrender to all-things-mechanical, and grabbed the early edition of the *Daily News* to keep busy while he waited near the piano.

"Psst," a voice came from nowhere, but then Squirrel realized it was the man in the uniform, the one with the broom and dustpan. "Make like you don't see me, amigo. Just keep reading the paper," the man said. Squirrel was able, at least, to sneak a peek at the guy. He had a cap on and it shaded his steel gaze, the scar under his eye, and the handlebar mustache.

"You Poppo?"

"Poppo is up there . . . on the mezzanine. You never know who's watching, so follow directions. There's a hallway to the left of the elevators . . . before the pay phones. See it?"

"Yup."

"Down the hall there's another set of pay phones . . . across from the restrooms. You'll see one of the phones off the hook. Look for the out of order sign I taped on it. Grab that phone for further instructions." The man didn't say another word. He continued sweeping at nothing, never looking up, until he drifted off to that very hallway.

Squirrel waited a few minutes to carry on with the pretending before he followed the scarred man's instructions. He folded up the newspaper, laid it down, and stepped off. He couldn't help wondering who might be watching other than Poppo up there on the mezzanine. Past the phones, the corridor was lined with boutique shops for gifts, stationery, and other tourist needs. Squirrel pretended to be a window shopper for a spell, just to get a look behind him. Nobody followed. At the turn, Squirrel immediately saw the eight or so phone booths. The furthest one was unhooked, marked OUT OF ORDER.

"Yo," Squirrel said into the phone, for the lack of an appropriate greeting.

"Is he with you?" a voice asked.

"Outside. In a cab."

"Okay, good. Go out to the lobby. Take an elevator alone to the mezzanine. Circle around until you see glass doors.

I'll be waiting for you in a black limousine." The voice had a deep Latin accent to it.

"Is this Poppo?"

"No, this is Mario Nunez."

Up on the mezzanine, Squirrel saw the man who was said to be Poppo. They made eye contact as Squirrel headed for the glass doors where the limousine was just beyond the exit.

Meanwhile Poppo gave a last look around, and when he was certain Squirrel wasn't being followed, hurried to open the rear door. Squirrel stepped in, and Poppo shut the door behind him, circling to the driver's seat. The vehicle remained still until Carlos, still in uniform, rushed from the hotel to the passenger's seat up front. Pulling away from the curb, the limo looped around onto a ramp and down to 40th Street.

Squirrel directed the Colombians across 39th Street, up Madison, and back across 44th Street until the limo double-parked aside of the taxi. Freeze got in and the limo merged back into traffic.

"Finally," Mario said, "I get to meet the man at the end of the chain."

"Yeah, and I guess you'd be the one at the head of the chain."

"Ahhh, my friend, not to belittle you, but I am no more important than you. In fact, without you and the network you have out here, my product would be worthless."

"Hmmm, I never looked at it that way."

"This is very true. And while our friend—our late friend—Charlucci served his purpose, he was merely a middleman."

Freeze didn't want to presume or read between lines. He wanted to cut to the chase. "He's dead?"

"Yesterday. The fool went running his mouth and his own people probably were the ones to shut it for him."

"Sounds like something I would've done."

"So now . . . I have this minor problem. The line of middlemen has been erased and I'm loaded . . . backed up with product. I was thinking that maybe you and I could come to some kind of business agreement."

"Could be. What're we talkin'?"

A gent Green was parked at the corner of Vanderbilt and 45th; close enough to see and far enough not to be seen. There was a hot dog stand a few feet away from the Chevy Caprice he manned, but he didn't want to blow his cover, so he'd have to eat later. There was round-the-clock surveillance on Freeze, and once an indictment was produced, the bust was expected to go down any day now. Green wanted to get on with it, especially since he heard that the big fish, Mario Nunez, might be in town. This was a takedown that every agent salivated over.

When the taxi pulled up to the westerly entrance to Grand Central, Green and his two subordinate agents didn't know what to make of it. The guess was that this was the meet with Poppo. But Freeze never got out of the taxi. Only Squirrel emerged. Green wanted to stay and watch the big man, while the other two scurried to keep up with Squirrel. They kept radio contact all the while.

"Hey, Jones . . . this is Green. You sure you still on your man?"

Green radioed his agents fifteen minutes later. "We don't have eye contact with him, but we're sure he hasn't left the hotel."

"Really? I've got a limo pulling up on our man now. And . . . he's switching vehicles—leaving the cab. I'm afraid I'm gonna follow. Over."

T he DEA agents had joked that the Bell Glades police and their lil' police station was a broken-down, backward simulation of Mayberry RFD. Pam Brown left an indelible impression on Sergeant Scott and his deputies Satch and Bo when she came through to commandeer the incident with Slim—the truck driver and his 500-kilo load of cocaine. She had threatened them with federal prosecution for how they beat up Slim after the illegal stop and search that late evening. They never forgot that, and it worked in Pam's favor when she returned, this time to make a deposit.

"Ain't the prisoner s'posed to be in some kinda separate cell? Some kinda protective custody? Since that's what the DEA-lady ordered."

"What is it now, Bo? Are you becomin' friendly with the prisoners again? I told you about that," said the sergeant.

"Ain't nothing, Boss. It's just he keeps snivelin', talkin' 'bout he's this and he's that . . . tellin' them other prisoners to keep away from him, or else. I'm sayin', if he ain't who he says he is, he puttin' on a damned good show back there."

Satch was coming in the entrance to the station now, carrying four coffees, two colas, and a bunch of tuna fish sandwiches in a cardboard caddy. "Feedin' time at the zoo," he announced.

"There you go, Bo; somethin' to keep yer ass busy and outta my ear with this prisoner bullshit."

Bo made a ho-hum gesture with his head and shoulders, and waddled away like his dream bubble had been busted.

When Bo and Satch got to the cells to pass out the food, one of the prisoners vied for attention. "Psst . . . hey, did you talk to the sergeant? Did you tell 'im?"

"I tried. Listen, this whole performance ain't gittin' you nowheres. You're a friggin' psycho . . . one who's locked up. That DEA lady was right, too, when she said you'd be claimin' all this stuff about bein' the U.S. Attorney."

"But I am the U.S. Attorney! Just call my goddamned office! They can confirm it."

"You really should eat yer food, buddy, 'fore it gets cold," Bo said with a sympathetic expression.

Peter Van Dyke felt that the deputy was joking, 'cause tuna fish sandwiches were supposed to be cold, or else he was seriously a lummox with no brain.

"If you could just be like yer friend over there, and keep quiet, things would be a lot easier around here." Bo was placing the tuna sandwiches and sodas on the crossbar of the jail cell for the prisoners to grab when and if they pleased.

Van Dyke was prompted to look back at Banks, wondering why in the hell he wouldn't speak up. But Banks had told Van Dyke earlier to keep his mouth shut about him being a cop.

The truth was that Banks wasn't a cop at all. He just knew how to play the role when it was convenient, like those private detectives, when there was dirty work to be done. He was furnished with a uniform, gun, a vehicle when necessary, and plenty of credentials, just to keep this trafficking program alive. Just to get the cash.

But now was not a time for charades. No pretending. To say that he was a cop would really make matters worse. Besides, this tall, husky homosexual who was locked up with Van Dyke and Banks might not take too kindly to someone being a cop.

"Come away from them, Bo. Just feed 'em and leave 'em," Bo's brother, Satch, commanded.

Van Dyke figured the other one would listen. "Officer, listen . . . I am an officer of the law, just like you. I ran for office—you must've seen my face in the press. We're only a few counties away from you. You must've—"

"Hey, buddy . . . I suggest you shut yer trap 'fore we have to shut it for you. You makin' a whole heap a noise back here and it's disturbin' the jail. Now, lemme have to tell you again and I'm fittin' ta put a new hole in ya."

Van Dyke made a flabbergasted sound with his lips. He took his sandwich and coffee from the bars and went to sit on the floor in the corner—as far away as possible from that freak, Lavender, the husky one they said was a homo. Surely, somebody would come to his rescue soon. In the meantime, Van Dyke nibbled at his sandwich, mumbled continuously about his rights to a phone call, and avoided eye contact if at all possible with Lavender.

CONCLUSION

CHAPTER FORTY-EIGHT

Here's my theory," Pam said to her Mobile Enforcement Team. "I believe Mario Nunez is here to do business with his sister. One of our agents is currently undercover . . ." A few snickers were audible, along with a comment about what undercover really meant. "He's in a very dangerous position, people—" Pam knew that her crew would realize she was speaking of Agent Carson.

"—no laughing matter here." Pam paused, hoping those words would set in. "We don't know exactly when contact will be made, or if it's been made already. What we do know for sure is that our man is in town. He's wanted all over the world, and yet, he's right here within our reach. There's only one objective here. We find him. We lock him up. Done deal. Questions?"

"Do you think he's operating here? Does he have an army here like in Colombia?" The agent had read the Drug War Report.

"That's a legit question, Evers. And I can tell you that based on our own intel, no. He's not set up here like that. As many informants as we have access to, we would've known about such things. For now, he can't be working with more than a handful, locals or Colombians, we don't know. We should be prepared for anything nonetheless. Question, Masters?"

"How do we treat resistance?"

"Another good question. And here's my answer—with deadly force."

Carson had been put up in an apartment that was in lower Manhattan, no more than six blocks from where he pretended to work at City Hall. There was a spectacular view of the East River and two bridges that stretched over into Brooklyn. This relationship that Carson was fabricating with the Nunez chick was now the talk of Pam's Mobile Enforcement Team; every agent wanted to know exactly how far and how much. Just a few agents had the privilege to listen in on the transmitters planted in the apartment. At times, the romance was common, like *When Harry Met Sally*. At others, it was raw dawg like a Heather Hunter flick. The word was that Carson had fallen too deep . . . that his devotion was to Roberta more than to the agency. He even forgot to check in with his supervisors now and again.

Baby?" Roberta was already up and dressed, ready to leave. "Honey?" She was nudging Carson—the man she knew only as Carl Paine—not really wanting to wake him. "I'm going by the parents' house, and then I have a little lunch date with Catherine."

Carson moaned, clutching his pillow as though it was Roberta. She stood over him for a moment, arms folded, staring down at his naked body, him curled up in a fetal position. She could only wag her head and smile, recalling how wild they had been through the night. She took a deep breath and sighed. She leaned in and planted a soft kiss on his forehead, provoking his unconscious smile, and then she left.

When Roberta got down to the parking garage, she was startled to find that her ventilation window had been broken. She eased in for a better look, thinking that her truck had been robbed.

Just then, a shadow came over her from behind and a firm hand gripped her mouth. Another arm was tight around her waist. "*Suavé . . . suavé . . .*" The grip finally loosened.

• • •

Roberto Nunez, aka Mario Nunez, turned his sister around to look in her eyes for the first time in almost two decades. He was hoping that she'd recognize an accent . . . maybe something familiar. He could see the shock in her eyes . . . the fear. And then she went limp and her eyes rolled back in her head. Mario caught Roberta well before she could fall and lifted her into his arms. He carried her to the van in the far corner of the garage where Carlos was hopping out of the passenger's seat. The rear doors were opened so that Mario could place his sister in the van, and he propped her up against numerous packages. Mario pushed and pulled between concern and marvel as he hastily fanned Roberta with a sheet of cardboard.

"My sister—my sister," he said in some dizzy effort to establish recognition. "God . . . my sister," Mario sighed.

Carlos and Poppo looked on in wonderment at Mario's humility . . . and at her striking beauty, as if she was a celebrity that had been teleported from the newspaper they first saw her in.

For Mario, this moment was a blitz, a fast rewind of images that reached back to Colombia, where their family was slaughtered, and they continued to fill his mental screen with the painful images of his finger being severed, the pressures he survived while in captivity, and the brainwashing that went on in light of the countless tortures that he witnessed and videotaped.

It was as if this was his reckoning, where he now came full circle, somehow coming to terms with the monster he had become . . . the bodies he maimed and the havoc he unleashed on his people in answer to his own voids, his own anguish and misery.

When Roberta opened her eyes, the van had long gone from the parking garage. They drove her uptown to the Holiday Hotel, a small enterprise that was near Co-op City, close to where Freeze had his ghetto fabulous penthouse.

Freeze would have offered to accommodate, but he ultimately decided against it. To stay nearby was convenient enough.

Once they arrived back in the hotel room, Poppo stood by the window, peeking out through the curtains, while Mario and Carlos sat by to see to Roberta's progress.

"Sorry to scare you, Roberta."

"Who? You're . . . oh, God." She was still working toward full consciousness.

"Roberta, I'm your brother. Our sisters were Maria and Elsa. Our mother and father . . ."

"Ro-berto?"

"It's okay to call me Mario. I'm sure you've heard about me in the news. I'm sure you think I'm a monster . . ." Indeed there was that, but Roberta just couldn't help the fix she had on Mario; akin to a mystery unraveled. "But I just had to see you. You're the only family I've got who's living . . . my blood."

Roberta's eyes watered as she considered that and the incredible confusion behind Mario's eyes. Was it really true what the newspapers said? Did he really do that . . . hack off other people's arms? Harm women and children? Roberta was afraid to ask. She rose from her resting position on the bed until she was propped up and supported on her elbows. It helped her to get a look at the man she now recognized, an aged rendition of what had been a distant memory.

Mario saw Roberta's concern. He sensed her fear. Then he sat beside her on the bed and began to live the past. He showed her his damaged hand. He explained about his anger and his hot temper. He told her about his becoming a slave to Batista and how he grew into a world of violence. Mario shared his own concept and philosophy behind leadership, power, and life and death. He equated his experiences and actions to that of past warriors, including the grave sacrifices that were necessary to survive . . . to achieve and to earn control.

The ideas that Mario shared—how his mind worked— were so different and far apart from the world she knew. It

was as though Mario was a master in the art of war, the state
of mind that Roberta would never come to realize.

"What about the children, Mario? I saw photos of children and women with their limbs cut off."

"I saw an article in the *Times* . . . about my rise to power.
I saw the pictures of the children. Roberta, you must know
that Colombia has been and still is a land busy with rebels
and unruly guerrillas, all of them scrambling to collect resources. Ninety-five percent of the crimes, the violence . . .
the murders go unpunished in our country. The cocoa leaf is
our export. It is what we farm. But it has also sucked us dry
of our ethics and morals. We are at war with one another.
Men who would be farmers, laborers, or even businessmen
are now gun-toting soldiers who will kill to protect, to grow,
and to make a point. They've done the same thing here in
America . . . slaughtered masses in order to take land and
call it their own."

Roberta studied Mario's passion for what he believed.
She knew the things that Mario said were true. She was at
least well-read on the subjects of Colombia being war torn
and divided, as well as she was knowledgeable about the
raping of America's true founders—native Indians.

"As far as the women and children go, I have not personally instigated or advocated such acts of brutality. Yes, we
have shot down government planes, we have killed soldiers
of the FARC and of the U.S. government, and we have killed
informants. But we have not just run into a village and
hacked off people's limbs. I do know drug lords, the ones
who operate rival cartels, those who have done such things.
But what they do is for their conscience to live with . . . to
bear. The paper was full of lies about me. Lies readers will
have no choice but to believe."

"But now the world wants you dead, Mario. They're
blaming you for all of it, calling you a criminal against humanity."

"Lies, Roberta. You must believe me. The papers . . .
somebody is making me the scapegoat for a war that started
long before I was born. They killed Escobar, and now they

want to kill me. Listen . . ." Mario looked to Carlos and gestured. Carlos picked up a Ziploc bag with miniature electronics—wires, as far as Roberta could tell. "Do you know what these are?"

Roberta wagged her head.

"We found these two transmitters in your 4-Runner, down in the parking garage."

That got Roberta to thinking. "How did you find me anyway?"

"Give your brother a little credit, Roberta. The *Times* article . . . your job at EAB . . . your parents' home in Long Island. We've been looking for you, sis . . . following you. I've even been to your friends' homes."

"Ooo-kay . . . so since I'm under investigation, what is this stuff? You been bugging me, too?"

"This isn't my doing, Roberta. My friends and I found these in your truck this morning," Mario repeated.

"Really?" Roberta replied as she held the Ziploc bag up in front of her.

"There was also a tracking device. But we obviously don't have that."

"Wow. Who would do all of this?"

"Somebody knows that you are my sister. Somebody, probably the federals, have been watching you. Maybe expecting that I'd meet you, or that we have already been meeting."

Roberta turned numb wondering who and how; she began to feel naked. She assumed someone had been peeking in her bedroom window, for how long she couldn't imagine.

"Who's closest to you, Roberta? What's your boyfriend's name?"

"Carl. But he's not a part of this. We're in love. We may even be married one day."

"Oh." Mario nodded and turned casually to Poppo at the window. It was as if to say they'd be checking on the boyfriend next. Mario didn't want to negate his sister's relationship without first checking further. He simply changed subjects. "Roberta, I can look into the surveillance, but I wonder if you and I can spend at least one day together. Find out more about each other . . . make up for lost years."

"I'd love that. When?"

Freeze and Squirrel painted the town together in a pre-celebration of their forthcoming wealth. Not only did they get to keep the drugs that Charlucci consigned to them, but they didn't have to pay him the money they owed. He was dead now. For the New York kingpins, that was a come-up.

And now, they'd get to deal directly with the Colombians. No middleman. It was the kind of windfall that made a man wanna drink himself to oblivion . . . or jump from a sky-scraper. The long night of celebrating ended during the one o'clock hour . . . while many were still club-hopping. Squirrel talked good sense, telling Freeze that he should get some rest. Sober up for the days ahead. There was work to do. Big business.

Agent Green had made the call to the DEA chief to let him in on what he'd observed: the limo, the individuals who later emerged from the limo, someone staying at the Holiday Hotel in the Bronx. The Chief approved a dozen agents to stake out the hotel, Freeze's building, and to tail certain vehicles in anticipation of a possible drug deal. The operation was labeled as Kingpin Takedown. Pam Brown and Chief Goldridge were en route, headed for the Holiday Hotel. It was the same day that Nunez met his sister in the parking garage.

After meeting up with Goldridge at JFK Airport, a mobile escort swept them across town. Along the way, Pam asked, "Who's heading up this operation, Chief?"

"Agent Green."

"So, if this turns out to be Nunez, it'll be his credit?"

"Not one hundred percent . . . when it comes down to it, you did spearhead this in the beginning."

Pam thought, In the beginning.

"But, Brown, this is big . . . a big team effort. There's no room here for heroes."

"I realize that, Chief. It's just natural I s'pose. The want to achieve . . . about making progress."

"What you've contributed to the agency in terms of man hours . . . in terms of energy and ideas, is priceless, Brown. We've progressed in leaps and bounds because of you."

Pam considered what the full extent of that might include. "So once we ID Nunez . . . if we ID Nunez—" Pam wasn't quite ready to give credit. "Do we rush him?"

"No. We wait twenty-four hours. Obtain warrants. Maybe we'll get lucky and catch him in a drug deal."

"And my theory about the sister?"

"We can apprehend her at her job . . . or even at the Long Island home. All the more property to confiscate."

Pam thought that to be a nefarious statement, but overlooked it as flippant. She also thought about Agent Carson.

"I should probably pull Carson then."

"If this is Nunez, maybe so. Or maybe we leave him, to find out how much the sister is involved . . . laundering and all that jazz." Pam nodded. Then Goldridge asked, "Have you by any chance heard from Van Dyke in Miami?"

"Me? Van Dyke? Why would I hear from him?"

"I dunno . . . I figured maybe since you had to deal with him on Snowfall . . . eh, never mind. I was just thinking about a follow-up—uh—whatever."

Pam never heard Goldridge stutter before. She stretched the topic. "I'm still wondering about his involvement in all of this. You think—"

"Don't be silly. I know the man personally. I can speak for his integrity."

"Hmmm . . . I guess . . . then that's all I needed to hear, Chief. How 'bout those Yankees?"

The Bronx was abuzz this morning. DEA agents galore. Local police from the 44th and 45th precincts were on alert. Air support was on standby; the choppers parked at the local Bay Plaza shopping mall, using its lot as a temporary heliport. All eyes were on the Holiday Hotel. All eyes were also on Building #4 of Co-op City's Section B.

It was early morning by anyone's standards. But for a Saturday morning in Co-op City, with its clusters of tall residential buildings, the atmosphere was rich with dew left from a chilly night . . . and early wasn't quite early enough for the women who would shop day long, who would see to their loads of laundry and run their weekend errands. These were the only residents who were leaving Building #4.

It was the same ole picture. Women and children. An elderly couple. The single folks who had nothing better to do but accumulate those weekend wages. All of these people were living their lives. Lives that one person in particular sat and watched pass by; lives that one person imagined living out to the fullest . . . imagined missing altogether. This was the other side of all things risky and violent and contentious. This was the other side of fast dreams, fast money, and the fast life. This was the fruit of hard work, consistence, and good faith. This was civility, liberty and choice.

But for one particular person—for Tonya—this was the beginning of the end of it all. She made her decision. Maybe she didn't use her rational mind to do so, but her rationale? It is what it is.

Freeze was struggling this morning. Struggling to fight the laziness that his nightlong partying had encouraged, struggling to maintain all of the thoughts in his head, struggling to assume a fresh slate for a new day. The cool air and the sun helped. But he couldn't help feeling that this was something like jet lag. He'd just cleared the vestibule of his building, wanting to kick the kid who was in his way with his bicycle. He had a hand in his pants pocket, feeling for his keys, hoping that he'd taken the right set for the Bentley— the car he wanted to sport today. It was something to show off to Nunez, a testament to his ghetto fabulousness.

As Freeze turned the corner to head for the parking garage, Tonya swung around from where she waited. The 9mm was in her hands tight. Her daring eyes squinted, concentrating on his. Freeze couldn't even focus. He wasn't even that alert yet. All he heard was, "This is for my brother, bitch-ass nigga." And then the blast.

• • •

Too many law enforcement agents were watching to just let this go. Otherwise, they might've turned their heads the other way, appreciative that Tonya Wilson had done them a favor—one less rodent in the city. But on instinct they moved in and arrested her. She was frozen there with the 9mm still in her hand, still smoking from the twelve shots that she'd squeezed off into Freeze's body.

Roberta never returned to Manhattan where Carson was staying. After that first encounter with her brother—the first in decades—she went back to Long Island, excited about the day ahead. She made all kinds of plans in her head about where they'd eat, the park they'd visit, and a lifetime's worth of conversation to be condensed into the brief time they'd be together. She knew that there would be special circumstances—something about a disguise, and Mario not wanting to be seen in public. However, Roberta didn't mind any of that. She merely wanted quality time . . . one on one with her brother.

Also in the back of her mind were the questions about Carl. Did he have something to do with the surveillance? Their relationship, their love . . . it was legit, wasn't it? Roberta expected to bring that up the first chance she got. It might've been this morning if Mario hadn't said to keep their day together a secret and that she should avoid calling her boyfriend for the time being. Of course she'd have to see him one way or another since her 4-Runner was still in his garage.

Mario, Poppo, and Carlos were suited to mean business. Sure, this was New York—nothing like the violent jungles of Colombia. However, there were the movies, the myths, and what people said . . . the idea that at any moment this city's worst side could show itself. So the weaponry was necessary. Poppo and Carlos expected to meet up with Squirrel this morning. And for that occasion they had on their jackets with ready submachine guns strapped and concealed underneath.

Mario was expecting to spend the majority of the day with Roberta. He had a baseball cap on and Ray-Ban sunglasses, and he taped a bandage to his cheek to help distort any idea that he might be the same man in the photo at any local post office. Mario also holstered an M-1 pistol under his brown flight jacket.

DEA and FBI agents were on the move all the while, going through the motions to acquire a warrant. They were certain that Nunez was holed up at the Holiday Hotel and they were ready to go in. But they needed to wake Judge Bernikow. Everything had to go by the book. Once the relevant evidence was shown, with photos, taped recordings, and such, the judge immediately signed off on the warrant.

The go-ahead was given to agents, who surrounded Room 106 at the Holiday. They knocked once. They announced their presence. And then the primaries simultaneously kicked in the door. Cautious and religious to their degrees of training, the narcotic agents were suited up in battle fatigues and helmets, and carrying automatic rifles. They stormed into the small dwelling, covering one another.

Empty.

Room 106 had a front and back door so that agents entered on both sides. Agent Green fumed.

"What happened?! Where are they?" Agents were puzzled and astonished while more than two dozen others converged on the hotel and Room 106.

"We had both entrance and exit covered all night," an agent said. "There's no way they could've left."

"Are you sure this is the room?" another agent asked.

"One-o-six."

"Excuse me . . . excuse me." Pam Brown had Agent Steve Masters lead the way through the growing body of law enforcement. Finally, Pam got into the room. "Did anyone bother to check with hotel registration?" Brown asked. Everybody stood with quizzical expressions.

"We saw them come in this room," Agent Green said.

"Yeah, but did you have the back entrance covered? No.

You couldn't very well have the back entrance covered when you first tailed them here, now could you?"

"But, a minute or two later . . ."

"A minute or two? Do you know how long it would take me to walk in this door"—Pam demonstrated as she spoke—"and out of that door? Do you, Green? Ten seconds, if that. Tell me you're not new to this. Please, tell me we didn't put one of the world's most wanted criminals in your hands."

"Easy. Easy now," Goldridge intervened as he entered the room. "We need to go check with hotel management. Maybe these guys are in another room. Either way, we don't have time to bicker."

Agents scrambled to leave the room. A few double-timed toward the front office. Pam shook her head, feeling duped and outwitted.

S hit! Shit! Shit!!!" Poppo exclaimed. "Feds! Across the way!" Poppo was looking out of the window in answer to the commotion out on the terrace. The in-ground pool and its patios were at the center of the courtyard separating the two sides of terraces and rear entrances to the various rooms. The three men scurried to gather the few things that mattered, and then they made for the front door to 206, on the opposite end of the hotel.

A gent Carson couldn't figure out why Roberta left him high and dry like she did. There was a note on the bathroom mirror that simply stated, "I love you . . . Later." Then, he was really surprised to find the 4-Runner still in the garage with a broken vent window. But ultimately, this was a first, for Roberta to be up and out like that, as if leaving the scene of a one-night stand. He called the Novicks' home, but the answering machine was on all day Friday. He left a message, then another. However, nobody called back. And Carson wanted to spend Friday night with Roberta, too. All in the name of duty, of course.

Instead, Carson spent the day having the 4-Runner's window fixed, he spiffed up the apartment, and he exercised to relieve tension. By five o'clock, he fixed a hamburger for himself and watched a Blockbuster video. When that was done, he became bored and stuck in another video . . . a porno flick this time. By 10 P.M., with no return call from Roberta, Carson sat alone on his couch and fondled himself, all exposed in his open living room. Moments later, he ran into the bathroom to finish up over the toilet.

It was only at that instant, after he was spent, that he thought about his family. Before the night's end, Carson called Sheryl and nearly testified against himself as he tearfully apologized for not being home. After the call home, Carson paged his supervisor. At the time, Pam Brown was working on getting the warrant. However, she returned the call, welcoming the agent back to reality. Carson asked how much longer this assignment would last. She updated him and further informed him of Saturday morning's mission—the bust at the Holiday.

The next morning, Carson expected that he'd make it in time to lend his support, but there was no siren or emergency light in the 4-Runner and traffic came to a standstill at a drawbridge on the Hutchinson River Parkway. By the time Carson arrived, agents had already kicked in the door. At a driveway on the southernmost end of the hotel, there was an unmanned vehicle blocking the way. The driver's side door was open, with the indicator *ding-ding-ding*ing away. The closer Carson got, the more red flags there were. And then he saw two agents duck walking along a terrace. By the looks of it there was a battle about to begin.

He immediately readied his weapon and jumped out of the truck.

Roberta arrived by taxi at the front of the Holiday Hotel, where visitors first stopped to rent a room. This was quite a way from the police activity. And since Roberta had been there just the day before, there was no need to stop at the front desk. Room 206 was simple enough to find. The Holiday was designed like one big horseshoe, with the 100-series rooms to the right and the 200-series rooms to the left. It was just after Roberta passed through the lobby that agents showed up at the front desk to find out where Nunez might be staying. Since the room wouldn't obviously be in Mario's name, agents would have to find out who registered the day before. They'd need descriptions. In the meantime, all entrances and exits would be closed off.

Poppo, Mario, and Carlos bolted down the hall, hoping that the front entrance was clear of agents. They figured, if anything, there might be one or two out there. Easy enough to overcome. In their hurry, they almost collided with Roberta. Mario couldn't believe she was here. He was supposed to pick her up in Long Island later!

As directed, the hulking Poppo swept Roberta off of her feet and carried her along as if she were a shouldered rocket launcher. They didn't want her to slow them, and they surely didn't want her caught up in the raid.

Although the three agents were armed and vested, they weren't expecting this—three Colombians (and one in tow) converging upon them rapidly, weapons at the ready.

As soon as the agent hollered "Gun!" Poppo unleashed a hail of automatic gunfire. The agents dived for cover. One grunted from a bullet wound to his thigh. Another pulled a kiosk of brochures in front of him. Carlos fired on an agent who turned up a cocktail table for cover. The agent was firing back as well. A bullet hit Poppo in the shoulder, forcing his Uzi to fall to the floor.

Roberta's harrowing scream caused Mario to make that effort to protect his sister. He pulled her from Poppo's hold and told her to stay put close to the reception desk where the receptionist had long run into hiding. Mario then aimed for the planter, where an agent was crouched. The agent cut around to return fire, his bullets aiming for nothing specific.

• • •

You hear that???" Brown asked of no one and everyone. She didn't wait for an answer. The sounds pulled her like a strong magnet would, and all others trailed her as she charged across the back terrace toward the front of the hotel.

Meanwhile, Agent Ted Carson had his back against the exterior of the hotel, just outside of the front lobby. He was giving himself a three-count. His gun was there in his grip, his arms stiff in a downward steeple. On three, Carson swung his arms and the Glock around and duck-walked through a foyer. An agent was down, lying less than ten feet from the entrance and moaning from a flesh wound. There was ongoing gunfire now, back and forth across the lobby. The window near the entrance shattered, and Carson sprang into a dive and roll to where another agent lay wounded. Still crouched, he dragged his coworker out of danger, close to where the cocktail table was turned up.

"How many?" he asked.

"There's four of them. The girl is an unarmed hostage. I think."

"What girl?" Carson asked.

"Over near the desk . . . I think," the agent corrected himself.

Carson was curious, unfamiliar with any females related to this operation. Except . . .

He almost stood up as he unconsciously attempted to get a better look. Part of him thought that Roberta being here was impossible. The other part was sure it was her.

"Roberta!" Carson called out when the gunfire ceased.

"Carl!" Roberta recognized his voice and almost stood herself. "No!" Roberta called out. Then she was all the way erect and rushing at Mario, whose pistol was concentrated on Carson. "No, Mario!"

The agent who had been behind the planter had a clear shot at Mario. Mario had a clear shot at Carson. The wounded agent wasn't about to let Mario hurt his partner. In the moments to follow, numerous shots were fired. All of them hit their intended targets.

*T*imes, Monday morning edition:

"BIZARRE IRONY ENDS A-Z DISTRIBUTION IN DRUG WAR"
by Scott Deville and Tina Worthy

Bronx, NY—This weekend a massive cocaine network that stretched from Colombia to the United States collapsed under intense violence. A bizarre Saturday morning coincidence found two major players of that network dead from gunshot wounds, while on Friday, a third player was pronounced dead by asphyxiation in Miami, Florida.

Charlie "Charlucci" Burns, 32, of Miami Beach, was apparently the first to succumb, found dead on Friday morning in his jail cell at Miami Detention Center in Florida. The officials at MDC reported a suicide. However, an autopsy found blunt-force trauma to the head as well as asphyxiation were to blame. An investigation is currently ongoing in light of alleged foul play.

On Saturday morning, Brian "Freeze" Carter, 29, a Bronx, New York, dealer to whom Charlucci apparently distributed drugs, died instantly when Tonya Wilson, 19, of Riverdale, shot him repeatedly at point-blank range in front of his Co-op City residence. Ms. Wilson is now in custody.

Mario Nunez, 22, of Colombia, one of law enforcement's most wanted and said to be the manufacturer of the cocaine that feeds the entire East Coast, was slain during a raid by federal agents. Also injured during the raid were Agents Brad Singleton, 42, of Pelham Manor; Jordan Schwartz, 28, of Long Island, NY; and Ted Carson, 30, of Spring Valley. Both Singleton and Carson are currently in stable condition at Montefiore Medical Center, while Schwartz succumbed to his wounds early this morning. Also caught in the cross-fire was Roberta Nunez, 22, sister to the slain drug lord, who is in intensive care at Montefiore.

For years, federal agents had been investigating a cocaine trail that began with the infamous Mario Nunez (the Colombian drug lord), grew with the help of Charlucci (the South Beach drug smuggler), and ended with Freeze (the New York drug kingpin). Authorities finally closed in on two of the principals during a rare get-together here in the Bronx. The network, which the Drug Enforcement Administration estimates to be responsible for smuggling more than 10 tons of cocaine a month into the United States from Bogotá, was the largest most aggressive operation since Pablo Escobar's billion-dollar empire, officials said.

The drugs entered the States initially by cargo planes and yachts, and by individuals (mules) who carried balloon-wrapped cocaine deposits in their stomachs. Once the drugs hit Florida, they were usually transported by truck or car to other parts of the country, such as New York City.

In New York, the drugs were then distributed through a network that included a chain of bodegas, a circuit of popular nightclubs, executives on and about Wall Street, and associates within casinos in nearby Atlantic City, New Jersey. There was also a small collective of dealers in North Carolina and parts west of New York, investigators said.

"So far there have been more than 125 arrests relating to this vast network, with many more indictments to follow," affirmed Drug Enforcement Administration Chief Sal Goldridge. "The streets will be a little safer . . . a little cleaner, thanks to the heroic work of our agents."

Pam huffed after reading the *Times* article, knowing that there was so much more to the story. She stopped by the Chief's office just down the corridor from hers.

"So that's it. I guess the whole Nunez network is shut down. Put to bed for good."

"Oh, I'm certain there are a few who fell through the cracks, Brown. They're out there like mosquitoes, these street-corner drug dealers . . . these two-bit smugglers who tote the stuff from other countries. We still have Mexico and Los Angeles to address . . . the inlet seems to rotate every so often. Just like the high of choice."

Pam nodded and looked at the floor. She wanted to kick herself for what she was about to say. "I somehow get the idea that it's more than the drugs."

"What do you mean? Speak up, Brown."

"I . . . I kinda think that the drugs are merely an object—a means to an end."

"To what end?"

"To the point that we use the substance to attack people."

"Brown . . ."

"No, hear me out, Chief. The drugs are already attacking people. Physically, it takes a toll on their capacity to think. Mentally, it destroys people's brains . . . their right thinking. It makes 'em brain-dead. But what bothers me is how drugs test and tease those who are undisciplined . . . those who are already at the end of their mind's rope.

"If a person lost a job, or if they're homeless or just want to earn a piece of the American pie, they should have other options. They should have other means of getting by . . . of competing for the resources in life. But for a certain population, people who in many cases don't know any better, the choice they have is drugs—using, selling, et cetera.

"What I'm saying is that this choice buys them just the opposite of what they're looking for. They're looking for wealth, but it bankrupts them morally and ethically. If not the individual, then their family or friends are looking for a high . . . a getaway. But instead, they're getting addicted to a death wish. The substance keeps pulling a person in deeper until they've reached a point of no return . . . depleted of their own beliefs and mental balance . . . depleted of their dreams. And somehow, drugs promise them a better life, a fascination of some kind—heaven. But instead, it brings the opposite. It brings death of the worst kind. Hell. The loss of liberty.

"Not to mention that the hundreds of thousands of people

we've managed to catch have families and loved ones who are not a part of this game. They're law-abiding folks who *do* have discipline and guidance. They're hardworking contributors to society.

"The bottom line is that this war we're fighting is with ourselves. We're fighting good and bad people. Some of the bad people would always be bad, drugs or no drugs. But the good people . . . we're attacking them relentlessly with guns and money and manpower. We don't even step in to stop a crime that we're investigating. We just let it commence, just so that we can have a body. Why don't we stop them, tell them it's wrong, and offer guidance? And maybe then . . . then if they persist . . . we can tell them they're coming with us. But we just sit and watch, like predators."

Pam was teary-eyed and choked up, and her boss was turning red in light of the truths she spoke.

"So this is your opinion?"

"My opinion? No, Chief, I'm tired of the Nunezes, the Freezes, and the Charluccis. I'm tired of wounded or dead agents. I'm so tired of deciding a man's fate like some puppeteer. I'm tired." Pam took the badge that was draped around her neck and reached in her back pocket for the ID within the confines of her leather billfold. "Go ahead and do your confiscations of money, property, and people. That's what this is all about. Go on and do that without me." Pam threw her credentials on the Chief's desk. "Oh, by the way, you'll want this."

"A key? What's this for?"

"Your attorney-friend. I know you guys are close. I don't know how close. But . . ."

"Van Dyke?"

"Van Dyke. Huh. I locked him up for the weekend. He's down in the Bell Glades. He should be nice and scared about now. Scared straight, that is." Pam turned on her heel while the Chief bobbled the phone trying to make a call. The last he saw of Pam was her taking off the DEA Windbreaker and tossing it to the office couch as she left.

◆ ◆ ◆

O n Sunday, it was the same ole' routine in Bell Glades with Satch and Bo serving the inmates. They already entertained the inmates with a full gamut of jokes about never leaving their cells "until Hell freezes over," and about "checking in and never leaving."

Banks was quiet as a mouse, knowing damned well the jokes were just that . . . jokes. He was content to simply be able to eat in peace, what little there was, and to let the judicial system work its magic. So far, things were in his favor. No criminal charges or illegal search and seizure. They didn't read him his rights. Everything spelled hoax. Banks was willing to have that DEA lady play her hand. He knew in his heart that she had it all backward.

Peter Van Dyke, on the other hand, was irritated about the most frivolous things: the food being cold; some guy named Leroy and his bad breath; Lavender, the six-foot-plus homosexual who kept looking at him. What kind of name is Lavender? And of course, he was growing razor stubble and in need of a clean change of clothes. Some people in the world were glad to have access to drinking water, yet Van Dyke was sniveling about petty shit. He was beginning to piss off some inmates, but not Lavender.

Lights in the cellblock went out at 11 P.M. Van Dyke used the blanket he was issued to mummify his body, a way to isolate himself from everything and everybody. Late in the night, he felt something tickle his leg and he fidgeted, thinking the fly would go away. But the tickle was reoccurring. Then Van Dyke felt a caress. It made him jolt. He jumped up and out of his blanket. It was Lavender. Van Dyke screamed. Bo was on duty alone and moseyed to the back. The disturbance woke most of the inmates.

"Lemme out! Lemme outta here! Now! Lemme away from this big freak!" And Van Dyke let out a grief-stricken holler.

"Hey you! Keep it down!" Bo said as he approached the bars.

Van Dyke was shaking like crazy and perspiring now. He

grabbed hold of the bars and pressed his head against them as if to squeeze through. He tried to rattle them.

"What's wrong with you, man? I was sleepin'," said Bo.

"I swear to you on my grave. I'm gonna sue every last person in this town if you don't let me outta here *now!*"

"I ain't scared 'a you, Mister wanna-be-an-attorney."

"That's U.S. Attorney."

"Well . . . Mister U.S. Attorney . . . word is on the street that everybody and their momma is tellin'—tellin' on you. So . . . you need to get real comfortable in here. Make a lot of friends."

Van Dyke thought about Lavender as his friend. He panicked. "Uh-unh . . . I'm not gonna do another day in here." Bo made a face. "You know why? Lemme tell you a secret." Van Dyke's statement got Bo curious, actually enticing him closer. In that split second, Van Dyke's arm fell and his hand snatched Bo's revolver from its holster.

"Hey!" Bo went to reach through the bars to get it back. But Van Dyke backed up. The inmates, all three of them, choked back an expression.

"You! Ya big freak . . . you think you can go around touchin' people? Huh?" Van Dyke had the gun pointed at Lavender. It was easy for anyone to see that this guy never used a gun before. "Ya goddamned freak."

"Pete, put that gun down," Banks said.

"You! You are the last person I want to hear from. You're supposed to be my friend."

"Supposed is a big word, especially now you got that gun pointed at me."

Van Dyke realized this and pointed the gun back at Lavender. By this time, Lavender was already lunging at Van Dyke. The gun went off. Lavender went down.

"Shit, Pete!" Banks said. Bo ran from the cellblock for help. Van Dyke was engrossed with awe. "No!" Banks shouted again. But it didn't stop the U.S. Attorney. The barrel of the revolver was still in his mouth as his body gave way. When Van Dyke fell over, Banks could see his blood and guts all over the cell bars. He winced and turned his head away.

◆ ◆ ◆

I'm sorry, Roberta," said Carson. He was there in the wheelchair just days after the raid, posted by her bedside as she clung to life. "It was a job. But it turned out to be more than that. I really did feel something."

Carson couldn't be sure if Roberta could comprehend anything, but it was just as well. This was the type of moment when he'd rather not hear her response. Carson, the coward.

She had her eyes closed. Intravenous tubes ran in both arms, and an oxygen mask was affixed to her nose and mouth. It appeared that Roberta was unconscious, but a tear still escaped her eye. After all she'd done to progress, it seemed the cards were against her all along, building her up for the great fall, unwilling to let her go from the very realities that were haunting her since birth.

And so it was for the dope boys, the runners, the gun-toting derelicts, and, alas, the last kingpins. Born to survive, built to progress, they were men and women who were trapped by their own choices or lack thereof. The game was either pleasure or pain or tragedy. It was never a winning choice for anyone, whether at the top or the bottom—just a big trap of excess, material gains, and false acquaintances.

And yet circumstances being what they were, whether it was Freeze, or Pops, or Ms. Sharon . . . whether it was Junebug, Preacher, or Charlucci . . . even the grimy law enforcement officers, the Robertos, and the Big Slims of the world were either tempted, enticed, or pushed; they either created the game, got caught up in the game, or they lost the game altogether. Still, they are human beings. We *all* are human beings with the very same basic needs, wants, and desires; all of us cast into a world to scramble for available resources like crabs in a barrel, experiencing the universe with all of its glories and with all of its blues.